ILYANA

ILYANA

John Orford

ORFORD
BOORAGOON   AUSTRALIA

British Library Cataloguing-in-Publication Data.
A catalogue record for this book is available
from the British Library.

In the interest of historical accuracy John Orford has
referred to a large number of authorities. References may
be found in the bibliography at the end of each chapter.

Dedicated to the doctors, surgeons, nurses, men and women
at Royal Perth Hospital Heart Failure Clinic, Coronory Care
Unit (Ward 4F) and Intensive Care Unit, Western Australia,
for their loving care and commitment.

ISBN 978-0-646-55552-2
Printed in Great Britain by
Arthur H. Stockwell Ltd
Torrs Park   Ilfracombe
Devon

CONTENTS

INTRODUCTION

In this book, the names of senior staff for Waffen-SS unit Leibstandarte, other Waffen-SS units and regular German Army units are factual. For example, Sepp Dietrich, Kurt Meyer ('Panzermeyer'), Max Wunsche, Hugo Kraas, Paul ('Papa') Hausser and Erich von Manstein are all actual characters. On the other hand, Max Rieker, his sister Greta, Paul ('The Baron') von Wittenburg, platoon sergeants Fritz Kohler and Hans Muller and the heroes and villains that interact in their lives are fictitious; however, the ordeals they endure, adventures they experience and opinions they express could be considered a fair cross-section of what took place during this period.

The story is wrapped around actual events that occurred in Germany and German-occupied territories during the period from the end of the Great War in 1918 through to the end of the first half of Second World War in 1943.

Factual narratives cover Weimar Berlin, the German Revolution, the Brownshirts, the Night of the Long Knives, the Blackshirts-SS and several other significant organisations and events leading up to the Second World War. Second World War campaigns involving the Leibstandarte-SS Adolf Hitler unit include the Polish Campaign (1939), the Western Campaign (1940), the Balkan Campaign (1941) and the Russian campaigns from the initial invasion in mid-1941 to the Battles of Kharkov in early 1943.

This story is groundbreaking insofar as it is an English-written novel focusing on the German side – both its angels and devils. It also corrects misconceptions about members of the Waffen-SS.

Additionally, insights written into the storyline should appeal to other readers apart from readers of war fiction and enthusiasts of modern history. With a humanitarian flavour it draws attention to the innumerable choices individuals are presented with during their way forward in life and how these choices might steer them in certain directions. Albeit the story is set in Nazi Germany, such a tale could be set in any period of time, in any nation. It matters little.

The reader is invited to settle back, imagine and feel the heights of ecstasy and depths of despair, the loves, hates and enlightenment of the characters brought to life in these pages; ponder their journeys for what they were, then let them go to dissolve into the hoary past of forgotten memories, for all is in its right place.

John Orford.

PROLOGUE

This historical drama is set in the years from 1918 through 1943, during Germany's Weimar and Nazi periods. Its spotlight focuses on a variety of characters: salt-of-the-earth, larger-than-life, honest, witty and brave, vain, brutal and cruel, those with a conscience, and those without.

In everyday life, the union between our thoughts and feelings is crystallised, brought into the world as reality, by word of mouth, action or inaction; and, depending on quality, can be sincere and compassionate at best, vicious and brutal at worst.

A whole plethora of binding attachments between individuals, groups and nations are created as a result of these emotionally charged physical exchanges. Such attachments vary, ranging from loving and everlasting friendships to petty disagreements, open hostility and, in some instances, world war.

Life is indeed a divine stage, as Shakespeare appropriately penned in his comedy *As You Like It*, for we all act our roles shaped by the colour of our emotions and quality of our thoughts. Any action or inaction demonstrated outwardly is merely a reflection of the overtures made by our thoughts and feelings from within.

What we do in any given moment creates the path we will tread in later life. Consequences are merely those effects – the results of causative actions set up earlier. Such outcomes close the circle, so to speak; what goes around comes around.

Causative actions steer one in certain directions – destiny if you wish – but destiny can be altered. It depends upon the individual and whether he or she is ready and willing to confront those consequences created by earlier actions.

For some, life's pathway will become rocky and fraught with hazard if discrimination or recognising the need to be accountable for one's actions has been overlooked during the journey forward. It's at this point he might contemplate whether his predicament was caused by him in the first place; but then, this is life and the world stage turns out to be simply a universal school of learning.

Like individuals, nations too are exposed to the same causative principles. Take Germany for instance; consider the earth-shaking series of events from the end of the Great War in 1918: unthinkable defeat and its aftermath, where millions were left limbless, poverty-stricken, malnourished, frozen, orphaned or cut down by the deadly Spanish flu pandemic; the Western Allies' enforcement of the crippling terms of the Treaty of Versailles, with its humiliating 'War Guilt' clause and the onerous task of making war reparations; the turmoil of the German Revolutionary years; and the Weimar government's desperate tussles with persistent Marxist takeover bids. Social decline ran parallel with political upheaval during this period; hyperinflation left the Reichsmark virtually valueless. Tens of thousands of woman were widowed, and, with no practical means of support, many resorted to soliciting for sex. Berlin became aptly labelled 'The sex capital of Europe'. All this culminated in 1929 with the Great Depression. In its wake, unemployment rocketed beyond 6 million. Ineffective and impotent, the Weimar government could no longer deliver as it had in earlier years. Its end was assured when National Socialism, under the leadership of Adolf Hitler, took up the challenge and provided fresh alternatives.

A series of events per se that crystallised to form the front end of an even greater chain of events would eventually steer the nation to virtual destruction in the Second World War.

So it was that the Rieker orphans – baby Max and toddler

sister Greta – eagerly awaited their turn to leap on to the nation's merry-go-round of causative actions along with millions of other youths. Here they were to learn powerful and priceless lessons in life.

By far the biggest influencing factor of their times came in the form of an intriguing gift-wrapped ideological package that appealed to their young and susceptible egos; it was the theory of the 'master race'.

Used as a national character-building incentive after the catastrophic disaster of the Great War, the teaching of a 'pure race' could have proved to be a great stimulus for a nation weighed down with guilt and by continuous attempts to destroy its national heritage. But the positive benefits of such an ideal were short-lived and, instead of acting as a motivating tool for a nation seeking redemption, it spiralled menacingly out of control to finish up as a weapon for its leadership to wield to gain their own political ends.

But embracing and committing to the original ideals only helped shoulder a chilling energy that cascaded from the top down through to the common folk. Accordingly, an entire nation would be compelled to pay the 'butcher's bill' for a path chosen for it by a line management that held the power.

Alas! collectively it would be impossible to reverse the situation once caught in the causative wave of international events. But, in the divine way of things, we are all here for a reason, and it is at individual level, not collectively, that a man may discover his true purpose in life.

Ironically, one learns most by negation, through the knocks of life. Thus, in times of great savagery a courageous few will venture outside their mental and emotional encumbrances to attain personal freedom and, just as the ancient phoenix rose reborn from the ashes, awaken their true spiritual natures to discover loftier virtues lying deep within.

PART ONE

BRUTAL HIERACHY

Unawareness is a state of mind when an individual is oblivious to the moral consequences caused by his remarks, actions or failures to act.

Ignorance, on the other hand, is a state of awareness when the individual consciously chooses not to recognise or assume accountability for the moral consequences caused by his words, deeds or failures to act.

Acts of ignorance may be linked with bitterness and deep-rooted anger and, if continued for a substantial period of time, these emotions may overwhelm and desensitise the natural conscience, rendering a man insensitive, uncaring and brutal.

1

OUR LITTLE HEAP OF MEN

Flash Forward to Eastern Front, Army Group South, 1630 hours: 28 January 1943.

He pulled the window down an inch or two and felt an exhilarating icy blast whip across his face as the troop carrier sped east.

For several hours all Master Sergeant Max Rieker had seen was the vast flatness of the snow-filled Russian steppes passing by his peripheral vision. Riding shotgun beside the driver, he settled back into his seat and listened to the sound of air whistling through the cabin.

He liked to ride up front; it relaxed him and helped get him through the lengthy journeys.

Other than an occasional chat with Driemel, the driver, he sat quietly suspended in a world inside his head. Demons from the previous year's campaign occasionally claimed his attention, but more often than not he remained cocooned in his inner realm, far removed from the stark reality that would soon explode into mayhem and unparalleled violence in the material world.

The red sun behind the convoy of carriers was about to dip below a range of low-lying hills in the distance.

This was Rieker's second mission to the merciless Eastern Front. His first had ended in personal disaster, but, as loyal soldiers do, he prepared to confront the challenges he'd met during the Barbarossa operations of 1941.

He popped two cigarettes, lit one and offered it to the driver, then lit his own.

Leaning back into the seat, dragging on the cigarette, he spoke: "Your first time on the Eastern Front, eh, Driemel?"

"Yes, Sturmscharführer, I've heard it's tough this side."

"Certainly is. Gone are the days of glorious victories. Yes, Ivan is a tough enemy – you wouldn't want to be taken prisoner by him, for sure. Trouble is they're like weeds. For every hundred we cut down, a thousand take their place. It's a gloves-off contest this side of the Vistula."

His boxing analogy sparked another question from Driemel: "I heard you were a good boxer, Sturmscharführer?"

"Yes, Hitler Youth champ for 1936, and I reached the semis of the Olympic eliminations in the light-heavyweight category. I lost to the Olympic silver medallist, Richard Vogt. You have a sport, Driemel?"

"Fencing – sabre."

"You should have applied for the 15th SS Cossack Cavalry Corps," Rieker joked.

"I opted for the best, Sturmscharführer."

"Yes, the best is right here, Driemel – the best of the best."

Rieker stubbed out his cigarette, leant back and reassumed his quiet state.

The human payload being transported east with all haste was the Reconnaissance Battalion of SS-Panzergrenadier Division Leibstandarte Adolf Hitler. It was the Führer's personal division and it was bound for the southern sector of the Eastern Front, close to the city of Kharkov.

Leading the battalion was Kurt Meyer, known to his men affectionately as Panzermeyer. Rieker's immediate commanding officer was Hauptsturmführer Paul von Wittenburg, nicknamed the Baron. They had served together since 1938, when Leibstandarte was only regiment-sized.

The journey from France to the Russian Ukraine took six days. The first leg was by rail, through to German-allied territory, and then to Bucharest in Romania following a half-day of reshuffling; the remainder of the journey was by road, crossing the border into the Ukraine south of the Carpathian Mountains.

They reached the outskirts of Kharkov in the early hours of the evening but did not stop there. Instead they continued eastwards to the River Oskel, a tributary of the River Donets, the scene of intense fighting the year before. The men of Leibstandarte knew this area well: they had fought here in the first crippling Winter Campaign of 1941/2.

The rest of the evening and the entire next day they spent recuperating from the journey. The intense cold brought back bad memories from the previous year, when they were ill-equipped, with minimal winter clothing and only 150 grams of rations per day per man. Leibstandarte had fought desperate defensive actions along the River Muis and River Donets in temperatures down to -30°C against persistent Red Army efforts to annihilate them.

The current Winter War was proving disastrous for Germany. It had begun in November 1942 with the Soviets successfully breaking through on the River Don on both sides of Stalingrad, eliminating two Romanian armies and the German 6th Army.

The Red Army's advance towards Rostov and the River Donets caused the Italian 8th and the Hungarian 2nd Armies to vacate their strong positions in fear of being outflanked and surrounded. By the end of January 1943 the offensive had swept on to reach the Lower Donets and the Oskel.

Despite serious numerical inferiority, the German objective was to engage and bring about a decisive result against the Soviet armies streaming towards them.

Leibstandarte's commanding officer was Sepp Dietrich. On 30 January he called a meeting at Divisional HQ to brief his senior officers on their first undertakings to defend a ninety-kilometre front. When the briefing was over, Meyer returned to Battalion HQ to cascade the instructions down through his own chain of command.

Referring to an operations map spread across a table, he addressed his officers and master sergeants.

"Grenadiers, Leibstandarte has its first job. Our orders are to advance to the town of Chegavayev and set up a bridgehead there. The army's 320th Infantry will extend the line of defence on our southern flank. Our battalion will be holding a front of ten kilometres."

He pointed to Chegavayev and ran his finger along the ninety-kilometre front line Leibstandarte would be defending and the ten-kilometre strip where his reconnaissance battalion would be positioned.

"Additionally, we must establish contact with the 298th Infantry and shuttle them back to safety. They are currently fighting rearguard, falling back towards Kupjansk, south-east of Chegavayev. The 2nd and 3rd Companies will meet up with them and assist with their disengagement then return to our line at Chegavayev. Remaining Italian and isolated army units are coming from further afield. We'll meet and greet them, allowing their safe passage westwards for rest and recoup to take up the fight again later. Our main task is to repulse and destroy the pursuing enemy. Gentlemen, we are equipped with the very latest armour, artillery and automatic weaponry. In this freezing godforsaken land we will indeed give the Red Army a much warmer reception than we did last year. We'll move up to our new positions at first light tomorrow. Good luck, comrades. God be with you."

Rieker and the Baron walked outside into the cold evening air, back to where 4th Company was bivouacked. A full moon peeked through a clear patch in an otherwise overcast night. The temperature was -18°C – mild compared to some of the sub-zero temperatures encountered during the campaign the previous year. They walked without speaking, their attention drawn to the big snowflakes dropping out of the blackness of the night and their breath flowering into puffs of silvery mist before them.

The gentle fall of snow created an uncanny silence. Time seemed to stand still. Unease about past deeds and fears of retribution seemed a universe away. It was as though they had been whisked out of a world of insanity and set down in a place of sweet tranquillity. They drifted slowly along, absorbed in their dreamlike surroundings.

Max broke the silence: "Truly a magical night, Paul. And what will tomorrow bring?"

"One thing is for certain: whatever it brings will quickly bring us back to reality. I haven't savoured a night like this in a year or two," replied the Baron.

"No love lost between us and Ivan, eh? Here we are again, back in the thick of the slaughter and bloodshed. Can't say our Waffen motto, 'My Honour Is Loyalty', has any meaning this side of Berlin. I could understand if we were freeing these people from Bolshevik suppression, but it appears our Einsatzkommandos are working a different agenda with their senseless killings of civilians. Surely honour suggests a virtue, and so does loyalty? But if loyalty means bearing witness to butchering old men, women and children, then how can this be an honourable quality?"

"It isn't supposed to be, Max. Linking loyalty to honour emotionally obliges one to carry out the dictates of the party regardless of the inhumanity of some orders; the concept is a fallacy. Regarding the party's agenda, it appears it's taken a page from Ivan's book. The Soviets launched their own pogroms in the thirties. Imagine if they'd taken hold of Western Europe and what they would have done to dissenters! Make no mistake, National Socialism has played its part in checking the Marxist scourge, but by adopting Soviet methods it's certainly destroyed any ideas of an honourable master race."

"Master race – goddam master race! Look what it's brought us. The whole world is against us now. The only loyalty worthy of honour is the loyalty we owe to our men and the officers who lead us. It's a question of survival, and ultimate victory over Ivan. Dying for the Führer has lost its gloss in the wake of the party's sickening agenda."

They lapsed into silence again. Huge snowflakes settled softly on a pure-white blanket that covered all. For Max, there was something about winter that suggested closure; he wondered if this winter would be his final one.

The Baron too was lost in thought. The moon reappeared through a patch of broken cloud then disappeared behind dense cloud. He sensed it would be its last appearance that night, and silently bade it farewell.

Reluctantly, the pair left the wooded area to pick up the track back to where they were bivouacked. Within seconds, the familiar noises of people being busy suddenly came into earshot.

"Max, brief the company tonight, can you? We'll get together in the morning before we move out."

"*Jawohl*, see you then."

The Baron strode off in another direction to settle down for the night.

Max caught sight of one of his NCOs and shouted over to him: "Kortmann, go and get platoon sergeants Kohler and Muller, will you? I need to brief them on our forthcoming task in the morning."

Kortmann acknowledged the order and rushed off at the double.

Max, Fritz Kohler and Hans Muller had been buddies for many years. They'd met in the Hitler Youth. Along with the Baron, the three NCOs were classified as the 'old boys' or 'old guard' of the company. They had seen it all: the pre-war years and the growth of their unit from regiment to full Panzergrenadier division size. As combatants for the Waffen-SS, they had experienced the initial discord with the German Army and the outstanding successes of the early war years. Now victory was in the balance, but, all things considered, they still loved their jobs and, in particular, treasured their comradeship.

As well as acting as 4th Company's master sergeant, Max also led his own platoon. His final job that evening, after briefing Fritz and Muller, was to inform the men of his own platoon.

Early next morning, following breakfast, the unit prepared to move out. They pulled on their winter combat gear, which included the new warm and cosy white reversible smocks – a luxury they never had the previous year. The sounds of whistles and horns signalled for all units to muster and move up to the front line.

By mid-afternoon Meyer's battalion had reached Chegavayev and moved into the old Russian positions from the winter fighting of 1941/2. The following days would be spent improving these defensive positions to receive the Red Army.

The 2nd and 3rd Companies continued along the main Chegavayev–Kupjansk highway to meet up with and support the 298th Infantry, which was currently fighting a desperate rearguard action against overwhelming Soviet forces converging on Kupjansk.

On 3 February the first stragglers from isolated German units began to appear over the horizon. Reconnaissance greeted them with smiles and hot drinks. Soon after this, battered Italian units began to appear up ahead. The retreating men hauled themselves over the bridge. Heavy of heart, they had come from far afield and were no longer fit to fight, but they were relieved that they had not been trapped by an unforgiving enemy.

The following day 2nd and 3rd Companies rejoined the battalion. The 298th had successfully disengaged from the Soviets without serious loss of manpower.

In the afternoon Panzermeyer took Max's platoon up the Kupjansk highway to gather stragglers. On the way back they could make out in the distance silhouettes of Russian tanks slowly working their way westwards on both sides of the road. It was obvious they were preparing to take the German bridgehead at Chegavayev from both sides. As a result, Max was ordered to arrange for deploying anti-tank guns on either side of the road.

Reconnaissance was positioned under cover of a wooded bank in wait for the Soviet attack. Max had perched himself in the branches of a huge tree. Acting as one of several observers, he trained his binoculars back up the main Chegavayev–Kupjansk highway and across the terrain on the near side – the enemy's right flank. He could see the Soviet armour positioned in the deep furrows. They were stationary, waiting for the order to strike. The snow-covered ground sloped uphill in front of him for about 1,500 metres, culminating at a ridge.

Suddenly his back straightened. He refocused to confirm what he'd seen.

"Here they come!" he bellowed.

The Russian vanguard appeared up ahead on the highway, at the ridge. They stopped as if to size up what lay ahead of them, then started up again. Armoured trucks and infantry began filtering down both sides of the highway towards the German positions. The off-road armour had also sprung into action; they would spearhead the attack on the German bridgehead.

Max climbed away from his perch and slid down the tree trunk like a fireman to rejoin his platoon. All was tense; the adrenalin flowed freely.

"This is it, lads – time to pay back Ivan. Don't open up until Sturmbannführer [Meyer] gives the order."

Fritz and Muller barked similar orders to their own platoons. Their hearts pounded as the Red Army column came closer.

Tension grew as the range count reached 200 metres. The Soviets passed the 150-metre mark, but still Meyer remained silent. At 100 metres everybody grew wide-eyed and anxious.

Then, at seventy-five metres, Meyer yelled the order to fire. German firepower was ferocious and lethally accurate. The ground opened up as huge explosions threw great chunks of earth and limbs into the air. Deadly shrapnel ripped through human flesh, killing and maiming. The wretched men never had a chance. Within moments burnt-out wreckages of transport and equipment littered the main road. Russian armour fared no better – the leading elements were destroyed within minutes. The first wave had been dispassionately eliminated.

Just then a dogfight in the sky caught Max's attention; the Luftwaffe had pre-empted a Soviet air strike on Chegavayev and beyond. The distraction was only momentary – Panzermeyer suddenly barked out another order for his men to receive a second wave.

The Soviet transporters following up suddenly unloaded their human contents. The soldiers poured out of the trucks and gallantly charged towards the German defences. They ran into hails of automatic machine-gun fire and exploding rockets and mortar shells. Hordes of Russians continued attacking relentlessly, without falter, but all were doomed to the same fate.

The top section of the tree which Max had made his observation post earlier received a direct hit from an advancing Russian Stalin-II tank which was taking up the lead.

When it was time for German anti-tank fire to open up it quickly rendered the second wave of armour into burning hunks of iron, transforming them into ovens, incinerating the men trapped inside.

Not an hour had passed before even the rear elements of the Soviet attack force ceased to exist. As the order to stop firing filtered down the line, Max gazed across the ghastly scene in front of him. The eerie silence was broken from time to time by the cries of the wounded. Some units were sent out to silence their death throes.

It appeared the Soviets were under the impression that continuous battering would eventually break the line of German defence, but this never happened in the opening clashes. After several days, the Soviets changed strategy, disengaged and waited for the main force to catch up. Upon regrouping they resumed their overall push towards Kharkov by implementing a pincer movement. Their aim was to encircle the city and annihilate anything that was trapped inside the circle.

By 8 February a crisis was developing on both flanks of the German defences east of Kharkov. The intensity and sheer momentum of the southern pincer's thrust breached and separated the right flank of Leibstandarte from the 320th Infantry, forcing Leibstandarte to withdraw west back across the Donets. To the north, the Russians pounded the German units there relentlessly.

In some instances, Soviet forces outnumbered the Germans by six to one.

Despite the setbacks, the Germans realised the salient created by the Soviet advance in the south lacked protection on its flanks. At this point, Sepp Dietrich's Leibstandarte was given its second job.

In the evening of 9 February, Sepp Dietrich addressed his senior staff.

He pointed to a huge operations map pinned to the wall and told them, "Gentlemen, as you know the enemy has forced a breach between us and the 320th Infantry. Our instructions are to disengage from the Donets and prepare to attack south of Kharkov through Merefa. Our objective is to cut through the enemy salient and link up with the 320th Infantry to eliminate the threat to our right flank and prevent the encirclement of Kharkov. Our attack will be three-pronged, made up of three battlegroups. On the right, Kurt's Reconnaissance Battalion will move south to Merefa, here. In the centre, the Der Führer Regiment from SS-Panzergrenadier Division Das Reich, together with our own panzer regiment will extend across to secure Borki, here. On the left, our 1st SS-Panzergrenadier Regiment will take Rogan, here. Gentlemen, brief your men and prepare to move out at 0700 hours tomorrow. Do your duty with honour, men – we owe it to the title on our sleeve – and good luck."

The following morning, in the middle of a blizzard, the whistles blew and Meyer's battalion assembled for its withdrawal. They pushed west then turned south towards the edge of the Russian salient and reached the area of Merefa around midnight.

In the early hours of the following day everything was ready to go. Panzermeyer informed his battalion of its almost impossible objective of cutting through the Red Army's main thrust. During his address, he couldn't help noticing the expressions on his men's faces. Not one appeared anxious, and no one seemed daunted by the mission; they all listened intently.

Undoubtedly, the battalion's strongest weapon and most binding force at this time was the absolute loyalty shown to him and the comradeship the men offered one another. Their faces glowed red in the freezing cold, eyes ablaze. They were all eager to get on with it. The Firefighters, as they were known, were indeed a group of elite combatants.

Panzermeyer wished them luck and they returned his blessing with a hearty roar of appreciation, then they mustered into position for the attack. The blizzard reduced visibility to almost zero.

"Holy Moses, look at this!" said Max, peering up ahead through the white-out. "Where's the road?"

"It's the main road over there." The Baron pointed to a small, undefined point in the lily-white landscape through the raging snowstorm.

"Hardly a surprise attack fronting up on the main road!" said Muller sarcastically.

"Listen, Muller, anyone crazy enough to make their move in these conditions is going to surprise anybody – including Ivan," said Fritz.

The high snowdrifts had rendered off-road advances impossible, so they were compelled to keep to the main roads.

The 4th Company bundled into their half-track personnel carriers and set off with the rest of the battalion. Fritz's earlier comments prevailed: fears of adhering to roads that might expose their position quickly proved to be unfounded. The severe blizzard conditions provided a prime source of cover, and the advance towards the village of Merefa, their first objective, went undetected.

Panzermeyer led his battalion straight into the village. Enemy troops were everywhere. The surprise and shock of the attack caught Red Army forces completely off guard. As the enemy was ejected, Panzermeyer bellowed for his men to assume a 'hedgehog' defence strategy in preparation for an inevitable Soviet counterattack.

The Baron's company was assigned to defend the eastern perimeter of the village.

As soon as they mustered, he yelled his own orders: "Max,

take your platoon to the right; Muller, centre; Fritz, you take the left flank. At the double, lads, and prepare for an immediate counter."

The company burst into action and deployed within minutes.

It wasn't long before the Soviets regrouped and launched a fierce counterattack.

"Tank, tank!" shouted Max as the silhouette of a KV-II loomed in the foreground followed by a mass of infantry. Two *Panzerfausts* were quick to fire their deadly payloads. Boom, boom – the tank burst into flame, wheeled away out of control then blew up completely.

"Here they come!" bellowed Max. "Rapid fire!"

The Russians attacked the entire length of 4th Company's perimeter defences. It was mayhem. The rattle of machine guns and explosions from mortar fire and hand grenades ripped into the ranks of the marauding Soviets. Those that got through came through doors, windows, breaches in walls and alleyways between buildings. Deadly hand-to-hand exchanges followed.

Bitter fighting went on through the following day, and, in the hectic confusion, survival for the battalion became uncertain. All through the vicious encounters the three platoon sergeants spurred on their men, keeping them focused; it was no place for the faint-hearted.

In spite of the extent of the Soviet units ranged against them, Reconnaissance was ordered to advance on the village of Bereka, further south.

As they prepared to leave Merefa soon after driving off yet another attempt to overrun their position, Max raised the question: "What are the chances of being spotted between here and Bereka, then?"

"Highly probable," replied the Baron as they clambered into their half-track carriers.

Amazingly, considering the confusion raging at the time, their move on to Bereka went almost without mishap. The only incident occurred when they came upon a unit of dead soldiers from the

Das Reich battlegroup. They had been captured and horribly tortured by the Soviets. Some had their eyes gouged out and others had their genitals cut off. It was a grotesque scene. Atrocities by both sides were common in the Eastern Front campaign, but the Soviets had a knack of refining their torturous activities.

Reconnaissance passed by in silence, knowing that capture would mean a similar fate for them.

Fritz broke the silence: "Better to fight to the last than to be captured by Ivan, eh?"

"Bastards!" added Muller. "I heard of a story where 300 of our wounded were bedded up in a makeshift military hospital in the Crimea last winter. The Russians attacked and took the hospital. They flung all the wounded out of the windows, naked, threw water over them and watched them freeze to death."

Reconnaissance stormed Bereka in the same fashion as they had Merefa, but with less impact; this time Ivan proved harder to eject. The column announced its arrival by unleashing a deadly barrage from its leading armoured trucks. Grenadiers housed in the half-tracks following up raked the Soviets with machine-gun fire. Max and the members of his squad leapt out of their half-track before it stopped.

The battalion quickly cleared the areas closest to where the column of trucks and carriers had come to a halt. Max led his squad toward a group of Russian soldiers amassed further away. Some fled in panic, but others decided to stand their ground.

"Gotz, take your unit over there behind the PaK guns. We'll soften up that strongpoint further along." Max turned and bellowed for a mortar squad to follow his lead.

Gotz and his unit settled in and exchanged fire with the stubborn Russians dug in to receive them. Max sought cover for his own men and the mortar squad that had joined them. Several salvos fired from the mortars threw the Russians into disarray. It was time to storm their positions.

They deployed smoke grenades and began the assault. Max

dashed through the smoke and ran straight into a big Russian. The impact of the collision knocked both of them over. The Russian grabbed his bayoneted rifle before Max could gain full consciousness. Just as he was about to make his fatal lunge another German appeared through the smoke and picked him off with a burst from his automatic. A second Russian close behind Max fired a shot into the German that had just saved his life. Max swung the back of his automatic into the Russian's groin. He doubled over but managed to clout Max's helmeted head with the butt of his rifle. Max rolled away disorientated. Before the Russian could use his bayonet, another German stuck him from behind. A third Russian emerged from the dugout making a frenzied beeline for the soldier who'd just saved Max's life; it was Gotz. In an instant Max returned the favour by firing a burst into the crazed Russian. Suddenly, two more Russians rushed from the dugout heading for Gotz. Max took aim but his gun jammed. He threw it at the second Russian, quickly unsheathed his dagger and threw himself at him. The leading Russian slammed into Gotz and both fell to the ground in a deadly tussle.

Meanwhile Max had lunged at his adversary, but the Russian managed to grab hold of his wrist and avoid being stabbed. He was clearly stronger than Max, and in sheer desperation Max frantically headbutted the helmetless Russian several times. After some anxious moments, the Russian's grip loosened as he drifted into unconsciousness. For one reason or another Max never followed up with the kill; instead he made sure Gotz had survived the encounter with the other Russian.

As the smoke cleared, remaining Russians gave themselves up. They were taken prisoner, but, under the circumstances, their fate was in the balance.

The Germans eventually cleared the village, but only to face another ferocious series of Soviet counterattacks.

Despite steadily mounting casualties, further orders were received for Reconnaissance to help defend Alexeyevka, a town at the most easterly point of Kharkov that was still in German hands.

The Baron passed on the new instructions to his platoon sergeants: "OK, boys, we're on the move again. This time it's Alexeyevka, east of Kharkov."

They all looked at one another, gasping.

"What the hell's happening, Hauptsturmführer?" said Muller.

"Looks like we have to tackle each crisis one at a time, Muller. I guess that's why they call us the Firefighters, eh? Let's go, men. Get your boys ready to move out!"

The Battle of Alexeyevka Village, noon: 13 February 1943.

A drone in the sky prompted Max to glance up. A reconnaissance plane circled and dropped a message attached to a smoke canister. Soon after, Meyer gathered his men.

"Grenadiers, we have received mixed news. The bad news is that we are completely surrounded by the Red Army. We've little armour and artillery and no combat trains and we are also low on fuel and ammunition.

"Men, I know we've lost many comrades, and those of us that remain are tired and hungry, but we're here now and, God willing, we will hold out until relief arrives. And that's the good news! Max Wunsche is leading a relief column our way, but just when he will get here is the key question.

"Company commanders, deploy your men. We'll defend the village in the usual manner."

Fighting began shortly after Meyer's address; it was non-stop. It continued through the night and reached its climax when the remains of the unit were pushed back to the middle of the village. The scene suddenly turned into a desperate last stand. Meyer bellowed orders for his men to form a human square making up the four sides of the 'hedgehog' strongpoint. It was reinforced with its remaining armoured cars, *Panzerfausts*, mortars and heavy machine guns.

The Baron's company, now at half strength, assembled and

crouched to form one side of the perimeter.

"Never thought we'd adopt a British square," remarked Muller.

"Not quite your Waterloo, eh, Muller?" added the Baron.

"Give them hell, boys," shouted Max as flares lit up the sky, turning the blackness into a floodlit battle arena.

The Soviets launched their assault, but they were surprised when confronted with the German square. Amazingly the strongpoint held. Meyer, sensing that his strategy had actually broken the momentum of the Soviet attack, ordered an immediate counterattack, throwing the enemy right out of Alexeyevka and returning the Germans to their old positions.

It had been a staggering night.

As dawn broke to herald a new day, Max focused his binoculars and saw new Red Army preparations taking place all around them.

"Doesn't look good, Hauptsturmführer. We'll be hard-pressed to repulse another attack if they decide to attack from all sides simultaneously."

Panzermeyer had come to the same conclusion. He mustered his men and addressed them.

"Grenadiers, we are facing a grave situation. The Soviets are preparing for another assault. We are desperate for ammunition and we still don't know when Wunsche will get here. We cannot withdraw. Our strongpoint is here, but if the enemy decides to attack on all fronts we will be pushed to repel such an attack. Our only option is to launch a pre-emptive attack one side and hold out until Wunsche comes."

He looked across for reaction at the unkempt, battle-weary, beleaguered few standing in front of him. The expressions on their faces were astonishing. They shone like beacons in the early grey dawn. There wasn't a sign of defeat to be seen or felt. He was clearly awestruck by the extraordinary raw courage shown by the loyal dogs of war standing in front of him.

"Grenadiers, this may be our last attack together. I am so proud to have led you. It will be a privilege to die in your company."

He saluted and they returned his salute in silence.

"Prepare to move out in five minutes."

As they prepared for the attack reality became apparent, and, once more, gallows humour set in.

"Yes, but I thought we were waiting for Ivan to attack us?" said Muller, breaking the silence.

"You know the old man," said the Baron, referring to Meyer. "Assemble your platoons. Let's get stuck into them." The Baron's enthusiasm was irreproachable.

Meyer's unit moved up on two sides to within striking distance of where the Soviets were bivouacked on the east side. The enemy were apparently totally unaware of what was about to happen.

The noise of whistles filled the air, signalling for the attack to commence. The Germans fanned out and came in from two sides, meeting up in the middle, then swept through the encampment to the far end like a wave. Their task was simply to kill and eject the enemy. It was chaos as they moved methodically through the Soviet positions, picking off individuals and blowing up surprised and unprepared enclaves of Soviets.

Panzermeyer's pre-emptive strike was an unpredictable move that paid off. It caused the enemy to flee in panic and disarray.

After the slaughter, the Baron holstered his Luger and surveyed the gory scene before him.

"Max, take your platoon and go salvage those guns and ammunition stored over there. We'll set up along the northern perimeter. Ivan will attack us shortly."

"How on earth we pulled that off I'll never know. I thought we were history last night, let alone this morning. The old man must have a guardian angel sitting on his shoulder," gasped a blood-spattered Max.

"Let's hope there's an angel sitting on all of our shoulders, eh? We'll need it if we are to survive the rest of the day."

Captured enemy guns, equipment and ammunition were distributed among the men, who anxiously dug in and waited for the inevitable Soviet onslaught. It wasn't long before movements were perceived over to the west.

"Fritz, there's some movement up ahead. It must be Ivan moving up," said Max as he moved across to fetch his binoculars.

"Prepare to meet thy Maker, Maxy boy," joked Fritz as he strained to make out the situation. "I'll get back across to my platoon."

The sound of gunfire up ahead came into earshot. Max focused the binoculars towards the source of the noise, trying to make out what was going on. Suddenly, a wide grin lit up his face.

He spoke out loud: "It's Wunsche, boys, it's Wunsche." He raised his voice: "God bless Max Wunsche. They've made it through."

He climbed out of his dugout to get a better view. He stared up ahead in disbelief. Others held their firearms, waving and roaring their appreciation for the eleventh-hour snatch from almost certain annihilation.

It was as if their passionate cries of joy could be heard echoing over the bitter cold snow-filled landscape, across the desolate steppes, into the mountains, over the forests, along the rivers, and across the fields, all the way back to their beloved homeland.

As the cheering subsided, every grenadier came over to Panzermeyer, thanked and saluted him. Meyer returned each salute with a beaming smile.

BIBLIOGRAPHY

Gordon Williamson: *The Blood-Soaked Soil: The Battles of the Waffen-SS,* 'The Battles for Kharkov'. (Osceola Press, 1995.)

Kurt Meyer: *Grenadiers: The Story of Waffen SS General Kurt "Panzer" Meyer*, pp. 160–74. (Stackpole Books, 2005.)

Charles Messenger: *Hitler's Gladiator: The Life and Times of Panzer Army Commander Sepp Dietrich*, pp. 111–12. (Conway, 2005.)

2

PYRRHIC VICTORY

1918: a generation earlier in November of this year, the once mighty Imperial Army of the German Empire staggered in disbelief. It had just lost the greatest, fiercest, toughest, most violent war the world had ever seen.

Bismarck's Second Reich, forged in blood and steel less than fifty years earlier, reeled in shock, pounded by the ferocity of the final Allied offensive and totally bewildered by the fact it had actually lost the fight. The German High Command signed the unconditional treaty of surrender, the armistice, in a small railcar in the French town of Compiègne, not far from Paris.

It had taken the combined effort of two great empires: France and Great Britain supported by the youth, wealth and power of the United States of America to bring the Central Powers of Germany, Austro-Hungary, Bulgaria and Turkey to their knees.

A belated American arrival proved decisive at the eleventh hour. Unlike its European cousins, it had been spared from the horrors of countless casualties and the savage attrition of its younger gentry. After enduring more than four years of bloodbath and slaughter, the unlikely union of Britain and France stood the victors, arms stretched widely over each other's shoulders, joyous but completely worn out, mouths agape in awe at the price of it all.

Great European nations that had once been proud, noble and shining lights would never again glow with the lustre they'd had merely a decade before the colossal carnage.

The victory had been a pyrrhic one. Both sides had paid a

price nobody would have dared imagine at the start of the conflict back in the summer of 1914. The doctrine of attrition had won the day for the Allies: "Kill three to every four of our boys and we will prevail," stated the generals, revealing a terrible truth about war.

It is said that truth lies at the bottom of all things. Clear away the scales of glory and illusion melts away to reveal its horrific reality.

Back in the midsummer of 1918, minutes before the French barrage signalled the start of the Allied counteroffensive in reply to Germany's spring offensive masterminded by General Ludendorff earlier that year, Master Sergeant Hans Rieker and First Lieutenant Otto Katzmann led a reconnaissance unit of storm troopers along the western side of the River Marne.

Under cover of thick hedgerows they cautiously made their way along both sides of a narrow lane. The early summer's morning promised another hot day. The melody of sweet birdsong was the only sound to pierce the silence as the soldiers moved stealthily behind enemy lines. The sun had risen to shine on all, friend and foe.

Set in this picturesque countryside, it began: the awesome French barrage opened up, taking the small unit of men completely by surprise. They all crouched in instinctive reaction to the sound of the heavy guns firing from up ahead.

"What the hell!" exclaimed Rieker, in response to the shells whistling overhead.

He looked across at Katzmann to await instruction. Katzmann knelt and peered down the lane, pondering what to do.

"No sense continuing, Sergeant. Sounds to me as if it's the prelude to the big one," he replied, referring to an Allied counteroffensive. "We'll abort this mission and return to the main force immediately."

The artillery fire came from a battery set up on a ridge a kilometre or so up ahead. It was one of many big gun emplacements deployed through the entire length of the Allied front line.

Scuttling back under the relentless shelling, the platoon stopped short of its base to wait for the barrage to cease. Once the nightmare was over, they rejoined the main force, which was in a state of panic. It was blatantly obvious that Allied resistance had not been broken; moreover, it appeared they were in no mood for further retreat.

The bombardment had chopped up the front-liners badly. Having hardly regrouped from their previous exhaustive efforts, the Germans had little time to set up a decent defence to repulse an imminent enemy counterattack.

As a result, general withdrawals to stronger defensive positions were ordered for all units making up the cutting edge of the German salient. Katzmann's Berlin regiment was among the first to fall back.

For the first time in the four-year conflict, the stench of defeat hung in the air like a thick pall. Ludendorff's trump card had been overtrumped and for the German Empire the Great War was tragically nearing its end.

The armistice was signed at 11 a.m. on the eleventh day of the eleventh month of 1918 – a fitting farewell to such a bitter and epic struggle.

1919 welcomed the defeated Germans like a rattlesnake. For Berliners existence was an exceptional hardship; they were paying dearly for their country's tragic defeat. The original Allied blockade remained in place, resulting in a serious shortage of food and fuel, and in the wintery conditions city folk froze and starved. Physically weakened, thousands would soon die in the Spanish-flu pandemic that had already begun to ravage Europe and other parts of the world.

Politically, the country was turned upside down. A brief account of political events in Germany during this period is necessary:

Liberal Party leader Prince Max von Baden was appointed Chancellor of Germany in October 1918 in order to negotiate peace with the Allies. His initial task was to form a new coalition government that included the Social Democratic Party (SDP) led by Friedrich Ebert and Philipp Scheidemann.

Late in October 1918, 40,000 sailors and marines seized the port of Kiel after bitterly objecting to German Naval Command's order to engage the British Royal Navy in a last-ditch effort to retrieve some national pride.

The uprising signalled the start of what became known as the German Revolution. It quickly spread throughout the country, and by early November workers' and soldiers' councils had taken control of most German cities. To exacerbate the situation, in Berlin the Marxist Spartacus Union (the Bolsheviks) had declared the city a socialist republic.

On 9 November, in an overreaction to the Bolshevik 'socialist republic' announcement, without conferring with his colleagues, the SDP leader Philipp Scheidemann proclaimed, from a balcony of the old Reichstag building, a new German republic. Although nominal Chancellor, Ebert was initially furious, the action proved to be a good move, painting the new coalition government as more fundamental than they were.

On the same day, in an attempt to avert a revolution, von Baden announced the Kaiser's abdication then immediately resigned office himself. The task of negotiating peace with the Allies was given to Ebert. In a telephone conversation with Wilhelm Groener, second in command (after von Hindenburg) of the German Army, Ebert was offered a proposition: Groener had settled terms for the armistice and would agree to sign on condition that the army could return home and crush both the rebellion and the Bolshevik-led revolution. Ebert accepted and agreed to retain the German Army's role as an integral part of the new German state.

The first soldiers appeared in Berlin on 11 December and were greeted by a thankful and exuberant Ebert.

It wasn't long before government troops set out to put down the rebellious sailors and marines. However, Berliners were called to action by the Bolsheviks and government troops pulled back, unwilling to fire on a crowd that included women and children. This indecisive operation did achieve partial success by substantially diminishing the power of the mutinous council.

The Bolsheviks, however, had interpreted the government's indecisive action as a weakness, and they stepped up their own campaign. On 1 January 1919 the Spartacus Union created the German Communist Party. The following day 200,000 supporters marched on Alexanderplatz, situated in the centre of Berlin.

The following days were mayhem; revolution appeared to be at hand, but this time government response was swift and decisive. The result was resounding defeat for the Bolsheviks. No quarter was given; enclaves of resistance were ruthlessly dealt with. Many demonstrators were summarily executed; others were taken prisoner.

The Marxist bid for Berlin had been quashed by the alliance between Ebert and what remained of the German Army. Additional support for Ebert had come in the form of the newly formed Freikorps. Freikorps was the term used for paramilitary organisations – groups of civilians trained and organised in a military fashion – that sprang up around Germany as soldiers returned home in defeat from the Great War.

In spite of its success in quelling uprisings, the new coalition government's popularity suddenly took a dive on 28 June 1919 with its agreement to sign the Treaty of Versailles. The treaty officially ended the war between the Allies and the Central Powers.

The terms of the treaty were severe and humiliating: Germany was stripped of all its overseas colonies, thirteen per cent of its home territory, and ten per cent of its population. The province of East Prussia was to be separated from the rest of Germany by the Polish Corridor. Germany's westernmost territory, the Rhineland, was to be occupied by Allied forces for fifteen years and kept demilitarised indefinitely after that. The German Army (Reichswehr) was to be limited to 100,000 men and its general staff was to be disbanded.

By far the harshest provision of the treaty was the infamous 'War Guilt Clause'. It required Germany to accept full responsibility for causing the war and pay large amounts of compensation (war reparations) to the Allies.

The situation for Ebert and his new coalition government was hopeless. Germany was virtually forced to sign the treaty under the threat of invasion. Despite this overwhelming pressure, and the fact that a counter-proposal was submitted but rejected outright, in the eyes of Berliners and other Germans the new government was branded as spineless.

While the nation struggled to find some balance during this period, at a personal level the fight for survival was just as harrowing.

In December 1918, Hans Rieker and his commanding officer, Otto Katzmann, returned to Berlin, but not in civilian clothing; their service in the army hadn't finished with the signing of the armistice. Their regiment was involved in putting down the sailors and marines uprising and the Bolshevik bid to take over Berlin.

During the Bolshevik revolt the battalion was shuttled into the city on trains. The men mustered in the station yard at Lehrter and began the lengthy march towards where the demonstrators were amassing at Alexanderplatz.

Their route took them around Karl Ufer; it skirted a section of the River Spree. Rieker relaxed his focus from the tension of the moment to savour the sight of his hometown river. They veered off at Karl-Strasse, turned into Friedrich-Strasse, then crossed the Weidendamm Bridge to the cheers of a few Berliners gathered there. After several minutes they turned into the wide boulevards of Unter den Linden.

The scene along the famous tree-lined avenue wasn't welcoming. Poverty-stricken and malnourished people were everywhere, huddled around wood-burning fires; all were homeless and freezing.

The troopers crossed the Spree Canal at Schloss Bridge, then recrossed the Spree at Kurfürsten Bridge on to Königstrasse, which led straight into Alexanderplatz. In the distance they could see masses of Bolshevik supporters gathered, together. Frenzied shouts and jeers filled the air in reaction to their leader's rabble-rousing addresses.

As they came within striking distance, the soldiers fanned out to form a wall of men, raised their rifles, aimed and fired into the angry, emotive mob. The action caused widespread panic and the Bolsheviks scattered in all directions.

Some pistol fire was returned, and several troops fell to the ground dead or wounded. Rieker's platoon, led by Katzmann, chased a group of Bolsheviks into the backstreets.

They caught up with them when the hapless party ran straight into an alleyway with a dead end. Several raised their hands in surrender while some opted to fight to the death.

The skirmish was over in just a few minutes. What remained of the group was marched off to a confinement area.

As they walked back through the streets, the prisoners in front with hands clasped behind their heads, Rieker spoke: "To think we lost this wretched war and now find ourselves fighting our own countrymen in our own backyard! Doesn't make sense, does it?"

"The world's gone mad," replied Katzmann. "Bloody Bolsheviks – they're everywhere!"

Rieker responded, "How on earth did we end up like this? The devil has taken us for sure. What are the chances of this lot taking charge?"

This question referred to the chances of the Bolsheviks pulling off a successful revolution in Germany, similar to the Russian Revolution of 1917.

"No chance whatsoever. Sure there are a lot of people dissatisfied with the current situation and their lot in life, but not enough to overturn our national heritage and Germanic way of life. Russian life differed. It was medieval in comparison. Tsarist rule kept the peasant class in virtual bondage – the old English feudal system. Germans haven't suffered like this. Let's face it: before the war we'd never been so strong; taking on half the world didn't help, but at least we have avoided invasion and occupation."

"F*****g Allies!" Rieker cursed. "It's history repeating itself. We were in a similar position during our fights with that horrible Frenchman Bonaparte before German unification. The Treaty of Tilsit raped us. We were forced to pay huge war reparations. Back then, Prussia had a strong leader in King Friedrich Wilhelm III. He immediately began to reconstruct his military forces and rebuild to get back at the little dictator. We are basically in the same position as Prussia was back then. We need to adopt the same principle. Germany should recuperate, rebuild and have another crack at the bastards."

"I agree this is what we should do," replied Katzmann, "but we should keep it a European affair next time. The fresh-faced Americans made all the difference in those last months of the war."

Rieker, apparently still seething over the Allies, continued: "Our mutinous sailors should have sailed straight out of Kiel and taken their chances against the British Navy. After all, we gave them as good as we got at Jutland," he said, referring to the naval battle fought in 1916 which ended up indecisive in terms of vessels sunk by each side.

Their conversation drew to a close as they approached the confinement area where hundreds of Bolshevik supporters were being rounded up in similar fashion.

The New Year takeover bid was quelled quickly. Rieker's Berlin regiment was demobbed and the men finally returned home to their families.

Big Hans rejoiced in the reunion with his wife, Regina, four-year-old daughter, Greta, and baby son, Max, who'd been born in September 1918, conceived when Hans was granted some leave following Germany's withdrawal from the Russian Front.

Now the Riekers faced each day knowing it would be another kind of battle. The unexpected defeat of his country had frustrated Hans; he became cynical, continuing to curse the Allies for the life his family was now forced to lead.

But, hardened from his experiences in the field, he endured the constraints brought on by the continuing Allied blockade and the wintery conditions and managed to hold his family together.

The first quarter of 1919 brought about several changes. Rieker, Katzmann and several other men from their old platoon had joined a local faction of Freikorps in response to the Bolshevik threat. Unfortunately, Bolshevik takeover bids for Berlin would continue for some time to come. Each time Freikorps would be called upon to provide their specialist services and retaliation would be swift and savage. As the pandemonium continued so did the seeds of discontent grow for the Bolshevik mobs and the Soviet Union, which backed them.

Freikorps' involvement was a crude version of army participation. Confrontations ended in brutal street battles where individuals wielded all sorts of weaponry – anything that could seriously maim or kill an opponent. Gunfights were commonplace. Sometimes Rieker would return home nursing minor wounds. Regina would lovingly take charge and tend to him.

Despite the dangers on the streets, being back with his family was exceedingly comforting for Hans.

Also during this period, Rieker and Katzmann found some employment working as coopers at a large brewery near home. Pittance as it was, the remuneration got both families through this most challenging time.

Despite his cynicism, Rieker was a big, kind, honest, salt-of-the-earth type of individual. He worshipped his family, so when the Spanish flu killed his wife several months after his homecoming, he fell to pieces.

Several weeks after Regina's death, Hans too succumbed to the deadly virus, leaving his children abandoned and alone, exposing them to a world fraught with turmoil and discontent.

The Rieker children managed to survive the days that followed their parents' untimely death supported by neighbours and old war buddy Katzmann, and his family. The orphans had no known relatives, and there was no one else to take care of them.

BIBLIOGRAPHY

David Clay Large: *Berlin,* pp. 153–64. (Basic Books.)

3

BOND OF LOVE

The effects of the Spanish flu were horrific: victims literally drowned in their own body fluids. Symptoms were similar to, but worse than, a combination of cholera and pneumonia.

Regina drifted in and out of consciousness before passing away. In her lucid moments she'd be able to talk. Just days before her death she managed to speak to her friend.

"Hilda, I'm going to die from this dreadful disease. If my husband dies too, there won't be anyone to look after my children. Their grandparents are dead, I have no sisters and my two brothers were killed in the war. My husband's family is pretty much in the same state. The wretched war devastated both our families.

"Look, Hilda – there's an orphanage not far from here in Pankow. It's the one on the way to the city centre. It's called Schonhaus Orphanage. If the worst happens, could you arrange for the children to be admitted there?"

"I'll try for you, darling. Isn't it a Jewish-run facility, though?" She implied that the children would not qualify as they weren't Jewish.

"Yes, it's run by Jews, but I heard they accept German children too. At least there the children can get an organised upbringing, shelter and food. We have a few valuables that you can take to the pawnbroker and exchange for cash if an admission fee is required."

That was to be her final conversation with Hilda before she

died. As predicted, Hans followed several weeks later. Hilda kept to her promise and arranged with the Schonhaus Board of Governors for Greta and baby Max to be admitted. It was a girls' orphanage, but the board agreed that the children could stay together until Max's fourth birthday, when he would transfer to an orphanage for boys in another part of the city. The other condition was that they were to be brought up in the Jewish faith.

Regina had also grabbed a chance to talk to young Greta. She was to set her an undertaking.

"Greta, come here, darling. Pull up your stool and sit by me."

Fighting for breath, she turned her head to face Greta and relayed her message in broken sentences.

"You know if God calls for Mama to go away . . . you will need to look after baby Max for Mama. . . . God will want you to protect him . . . and give him lots of love . . . just like Mama does. When he's sad . . . you must make him laugh . . . and when he's angry you must bring him peace."

Greta listened, paying close attention.

"Now you'll promise Mama . . . that you will do this for me?"

"Yes, of course, Mama. Max will always be by my side."

As young as she was, Greta listened intently and nodded her understanding. She pledged herself to the duty of rearing young Max in the manner her mother had just described. Regina managed a smile and rested her head on the pillow and sank back into a semi-comatose state.

When Hans died, Hilda explained to Greta the arrangements being made with Schonhaus Orphanage.

On a hot July morning, Greta prepared herself and wrapped Max neatly in a cosy cotton shawl. Accompanied by Hilda they left the house for the last time.

A tram stop was nearby. Max was sound asleep in Hilda's arms. The tram arrived and they stepped up into the carriage and found some seats. The conductor came over, peered lovingly at Max then gave Hilda her ticket for the Schonhaus stop.

Berlin's tramway service was one of the largest and best in

the world. Defeat in the Great War had not caused any dramatic breakdown. It had operated since 1865, and before 1919 it had been made up of many independent tramways. However, political unrest during this period compelled independents to merge into a single municipal undertaking. By May 1919 the merge had resulted in a single adult fare of only 15 pfennigs for travelling anywhere in the Berlin metropolitan area.

They sat in their seats in silence. Hilda motioned when it was time to get off and they shuffled along to the rear exit of the tram. The tram stop was just metres from the orphanage gates. Hilda negotiated the iron steps then balanced Max in one arm and held out her free hand to assist Greta as she gingerly stepped down on to the pavement.

Greta recollected how she'd passed the orphanage many times before with her mother on her way to the Ackerstraat Market Hall. Her mother had described it as the place where children who hadn't any parents stayed. Little did she know at the time that this would be her home for the next decade of her life.

The orphanage was about thirty years old. It was a solid-looking structure built in dark-grey masonry. Ornamental brickwork set off the sills, arches and quoins. The roof was covered with dark-grey slates with grey lead flashings to match. A mansard roof structure accommodated the live-in attic area. Huge brick decorated chimneys formed a prominent but bleak-looking skyline. Black steel grilles bolted to all ground-level windows rounded off its uninviting image.

The facility accommodated about forty orphans. The basement incorporated the galley, mess hall and some storage areas. The ground floor included the reception area, assembly hall and some classrooms. More classrooms made up part of the first floor, and cold and colourless dormitories filled the remainder of the first floor and entire second floor. The third and attic floors were devoted to the director and his family. Some of the rooms were set aside for the teaching staff.

The grounds were surrounded by a two-metre-high perimeter

wall built in the same material as the superstructure of the main house. The wall was reinforced with brick buttresses. All visitors and passers-by were greeted by a pair of three-metre-high gates. A wicket gate was built into one side, and it was this gate that most visitors, new arrivals and those discharged walked through. The landscaping was a mix of grassed and cultivated areas fastidiously maintained by the orphans. At the rear was a quadrangle enclosed by a number of workshops and a synagogue for prayer.

The tram trundled away leaving both gaping across at the ominous-looking building. They moved slowly toward the big black iron entrance gates. As Greta approached the open wicket gate, she gave a shudder and hung back as if a huge barking dog was waiting on the other side.

"Come, Greta – these people will take care of you and Max. You won't go starving and you'll have plenty of friends to play with once you settle in, darling."

Hilda tugged Greta's arm to arouse her from her brief waking nightmare.

A wide briquetted pathway branched off from the gravel entrance roadway. It cut through a lush green lawn and led up to the entrance porch.

"Let's go and knock on the front door," said Hilda.

Greta followed her as they walked up to the front door. Max was still fast asleep as Hilda rapped the heavy brass knocker twice. Moments later the door swung open and a tall, matronly dame greeted them.

"Ah, you must be the Riekers. Welcome to Schonhaus."

Hilda confirmed her opening comment.

"Come in, come in," the woman said, pointing the way for them to go inside.

Greta walked into the dimly lit foyer. She cringed as visions of unfamiliarity greeted her.

The old dame introduced herself as Mrs Brenner. She beckoned for Hilda to lay young Max down in a comfortable leather armchair. They spent several minutes chatting until Hilda said she had to arrange for the children's belongings to be delivered later that day. She kissed Greta farewell and promised she'd visit her regularly until she settled in and made some friends.

Mrs Brenner focused on Greta as soon as Hilda left. Sensing her anxiety, she took her hand, led her over to the couch, sat down so their eyes could be level and spoke softly: "Don't be frightened, child. You'll be happy here."

Greta smiled. As dour as the old dame appeared initially, she turned out to be quite friendly.

"Would you like a cup of tea?" she asked.

"Yes, please, Mrs Brenner."

Mrs Brenner brought out an old tin full of biscuits.

"Help yourself, darling – but not too many. Lunch will be ready at noon. You'll get a chance to meet some of the other children then."

After tea they climbed the wide timber stairway to the first floor and walked down a lengthy corridor, stopping at a room at the end of the building.

"This is a special room for you and Max."

It was a small room with a window overlooking the quadrangle at the rear. There was a chest of drawers, a small table, a mirror, two chairs, a bed and a cot for Max. Communal toilets and washrooms were situated midway down the corridor.

"I'll go get young Max, and you can settle in together. I'll come and get you for lunch."

She closed the door behind her.

Greta stood there perplexed for a moment, then pulled one of the wooden chairs towards the window and sat down. She gazed out of the window across the quadrangle, looking for any signs of movement or familiarity.

The orphanage was no substitute for family life, and in the beginning it was hard for Greta to adapt to the new way of life. The tie with her mother had been strong, particularly during the time Hans had been away at war. His homecoming had been the most joyous part of her young life so far, but losing both parents in such a short space of time had caused her great distress.

But looking after young Max proved to be a lifesaver for her. It helped carry her through the initial challenging period at the orphanage.

Older girls were given the responsibility of looking after the younger ones, and the senior assigned to Greta was Heidi. Heidi was a friendly, responsible type who made her feel at home.

For Max, settling in wasn't so bad; he was still too young to take in the recent family tragedy and the radical change of environment and lifestyle.

Although the Rieker children were not Jewish, the board of governors had ruled that all those admitted should practise the Jewish faith during their stay.

A routine day began with a visit to the synagogue and chanting holy recitals. Breakfast followed. For those under the age of six years, there was the kindergarten; for those older, there was elementary schooling; and for those aged eleven years and older there was secondary education. Lessons commenced at eight o'clock and broke for lunch and leisure time at noon. The afternoon session started at two and finished at four.

Children were treated well; punishment was given in a fairly strict authoritarian manner, no different to other schools during those times. If children became sick, there was a medical room. A nurse was available to tend to their needs.

Katzmann kept in touch with the children. Greta had got to know Katzmann well in the short time after Hans's return home from the war.

"Many a night Daddy and 'Uncle' Otto would return home from work and drink beer straight from the bottle, free-issued by the brewery, discussing the ills of the world, sometimes laughing, sometimes serious," Greta recollected.

At least one weekend in the month, sometimes two, the children would spend time with the Katzmann family. Katzmann's contribution to the care and welfare of the Rieker children was priceless. He'd felt obliged to keep an eye on the children – after all, it was the least he could do for his old friend. His family became Greta and Max's only contact with the outside world.

Years passed and baby Max grew into a toddler. According to the board of governors' ruling, he was to be discharged from Schonhaus on his fourth birthday and transferred to a boys' orphanage in another part of Berlin.

Separation was traumatic for the siblings. For Max, it was his turn to feel the effects of leaving a place of familiarity and security – a mirror reflection of what his sister had experienced three years earlier. At the boys' orphanage, he missed the caring attention she had given him. In turn, Greta missed his playful, boisterous nature. She felt that his transfer had cut short her promise to raise him in the way their mother desired. She wondered whether, now that they were apart, their very special bond of love would be broken; only time would tell.

BIBLIOGRAPHY

Peter J. Walker: *One Hundred Years of the Berlin Tramways.* (Brockwede, 1965.)

Inge Lammel: *Jewish Orphanage in Pankow.* (H. & P. Druck, 2001.)

John M. Barry: *The Great Influenza: The Epic Story of the Deadliest Plague in History. (Penguin, 2004.)*

E. W. Goodall: *A Short History of Epidemic Infectious Diseases.* (London, 1934.)

4

WEIMAR

The new German republic formally came into being six weeks after the Treaty of Versailles. On 11 August 1919, Reich President Ebert and his delegates gathered in the city of Weimar and declared the new republic named after the city. Weimar was chosen to announce the new constitution because Berlin was still considered a dangerous place.

The republic lasted from 1919 to 1933. The German Revolution filled the early years, with takeover bids continuing in Berlin and other parts of Germany until October 1923 – a date considered marking the end of this period.

Not all attempts were Bolshevik-led. An unexpected attack from the right took place in March 1920. Soon after the signing of the Treaty of Versailles the Allies decided to enforce the requirement of reducing Germany's armed forces down to 100,000 men and to disband the 250,000-strong Freikorps completely. This action infuriated the German military, which saw the new government as being responsible for the nation's hardships because of its signing of the treaty.

The takeover bid was known as the Kapp Putsch. Wolfgang Kapp (a civil servant) and Walther von Lüttwitz (the leader of a group calling itself the National Association and commandant of the Berlin Freikorps) wanted to establish a military dictatorship. They seized Berlin and proclaimed that a new Nationalist government was being established with Kapp as Chancellor.

The confrontation turned out to be a chilling challenge for Ebert and his leadership. He found himself isolated, unable to call upon the support of the army or Freikorps.

Backing the National Association was General Ludendorff. His involvement, however, didn't influence the army. Instead, they chose to stand back, refraining from offering support to any side.

For Freikorps, its decision on whether or not to support the Kapp Putsch hung in the balance. During the tense few days, they convened meetings to vote on whether or not to support Kapp.

Katzmann's unit, made up from old cronies that had fought alongside him in the war days, belonged to a faction of the Berlin Freikorps. At the meeting he opened up the debate: "Well, how should we vote, men? Let's have your views."

Kolzig said, "I heard Ehrhardt's Marinebrigade will be supporting Kapp."

"Yes, but they're a belligerent mob that would revolt at the drop of a hat. They're made up of naval personnel and have been pissed off ever since they were ordered to leave Kiel and take their chances with the British Navy; volatile and unreliable, if you ask me. Further, they should have done what they were ordered to do in the first place and had a crack at the Royal Navy."

"Who else is in with Kapp," asked Saalbach.

"Nobody of any importance, save Ludendorff. Look – I think if these guys take over and form a military dictatorship, our country will be invaded by the Allies. We don't want this; we're not strong enough to fight another war and partisan action won't be enough. OK, we all want to get back at the bastards, but now is not the time. I say we stand aside and wait for the outcome. After all, Ebert still wants the army to be an integral part of the new republic, despite the army's lack of active support in this instance."

Degen agreed. "OK, let's vote not to interfere, then."

"Is the vote unanimous, *Kameraden*?" Katzmann asked.

"*Jawohl!*" was the overall response.

All other factions of Freikorps voted the same: to take no active part in the putsch.

Ebert's response to the crisis was nothing short of a miracle. In order to paralyse the movements of Kapp and Lüttwitz's supporters, he called upon the people of Berlin to participate in a general strike. The outcome was a resounding victory, forcing Kapp and Lüttwitz to leave Berlin. Success had been a result of the working class's willingness to support Ebert's government.

For Katzmann, his fighting days with Freikorps came to a sudden and sad end when he and his men got caught up in a street skirmish in mid-1922. His Freikorps unit chased a mob of Bolsheviks through the streets – a repeat of the action back in January 1919 when he, Hans and the platoon participated in the quelling of the Bolshevik New Year revolution. But this time the outcome was different. Previously, as soldiers they had all been well armed, but this time Katzmann and his men only had a couple of pistols between them. Most of his group wielding an assortment of timber and metal weapons were totally unprepared for their more heavily armed opponents, who carried more than a few firearms between them.

As before, the Bolsheviks found themselves cornered in a dead-end alleyway. As Katzmann and his men moved in, preparing to fight, the Bolsheviks opened up in panic. Katzmann was one of the first to fall. His men scuttled back out of the alleyway, diving for cover. The Bolsheviks ran back out of the alleyway and off down the road. The men were incensed. As Katzmann lay there mortally wounded, gasping for breath, some remained to look over his dying body and others took up the chase again. The Bolsheviks ran into another group of Freikorps at the end of the street and a fierce gunfight ensued. There was to be no pity, and the Bolsheviks were slaughtered to a man.

Katzmann's family was now without its provider. For Greta and Max, there would be no more weekend excursions; and for his family, the struggle to survive was just about to begin.

It was during the German Revolution that National Socialism first made its presence felt through the formation of Freikorps. Ehrhardt's Marinebrigade, one of Lüttwitz's main fighting forces, put a sign on their helmets to identify who they were: it was the swastika.

Not considered part of the German Revolution was Adolf Hitler's famous Beer Hall Putsch, which took place on 8 and 9 November 1923. This was when Hitler, together with General Ludendorff and other party leaders, tried to gain power in Munich, Bavaria and Germany.

After the attempted putsch, Hitler and some of his leaders were arrested and tried for high treason. At the trial Hitler gave a remarkable display of oratory, acting for his own defence, but despite his appeal to sympathetic ears he was sentenced to five years' imprisonment. However, owing to an amnesty, he did not serve out the full term and was released in December 1924. He refounded the NSDAP in February the following year.

Disease and political unrest weren't the only challenges the Weimar Republic faced in its early years. There was a rapid decline socially too, mainly as a result of the devaluation of the German mark. The mark lost virtually all its value between February 1920 and November 1923. In February 1920 the mark stood at ninety-nine Reichsmarks (RM) to the US dollar. In June 1922 it stood at RM 331 then dropped to RM 670 at the end of July.

In January 1923 French and Belgian troops marched into the Ruhr. The Germans had reneged on coal and coke deliveries required by the Versailles reparations agreement. The Allied incursion sparked an outbreak of patriotic protest across

Germany. Passive resistance by German workers paralysed the Ruhr's economy, causing the total collapse of the German currency.

In early February 1923 the mark stood at RM 42,000 to the dollar; in July RM 160,000 and in August RM 3,000,000. In late November 1923, one US dollar was worth a staggering RM 4,210,500,000,000.

When the madness had finally run its course in 1923, millions of Germans were left destitute. The mark's collapse had affected the whole way of life of the German people.

Despite the struggle of the early years, the mid-1920s gave rise to the term the Roaring Twenties. It was a time when Berlin shared some vibrancy with the rest of the world. There were variety shows, vaudeville acts and revue bars modelled on the *Ziegfeld Follies*. Packed houses staged extravaganzas of sexy, high-heeled, sheer-stockinged, bare-breasted girls, providing an exquisite opportunity for onlookers to soak up the raunchy atmosphere.

Cabaret was also a favourite, typically consisting of short revues, which were sharply political in nature, interlaced with songs.

'Resi' nightclubs catered for the wild and not so normal Berlin public and drew in foreign visitors of the same ilk. They were dens of vice. In Resi clubs, every table was equipped with a telephone, making it possible for clubgoers to call anyone else in the place and get acquainted. In these places, men and women cross-dressed. Those who dressed normally were usually perverts.

Private clubs catered for homosexuals, transvestites and sadomasochists. Berlin became a 'Klondike' – a wild and bizarre playground for the rest of the world. It became the sex capital of Europe. Reasons for this were twofold: Germany's defeat in the Great War left thousands of war widows, many of whom had no realistic means of supporting themselves other than by prostitution; and the economic collapse and hyperinflation period had led to moral anarchy in the desperate struggle to survive.

The Roaring Twenties was short-lived. In 1929 the Great Depression brought the razzamatazz to an abrupt end and heralded the swift decline of the Weimar Republic. In 1932 unemployment catapulted to beyond 6 million. Germans became frustrated at the republic's inability to find answers, and they looked to another party, the National Socialists, under Adolf Hitler's leadership, to make things right.

While all this was happening, the Rieker children had been growing up in formal establishments. But the protection offered by stone walls and the stability of a regular routine wouldn't be enough to shield them from the impact of the metamorphosis taking place outside.

The question arose, just what roles would they play in the new and exciting world awaiting them?

BIBLIOGRAPHY

David Clay Large: *Berlin*, pp. 164–75, 179–81, 184–5. (Basic Books.)

Wolf von Eckhardt and Sander L. Gilman: *Bertolt Brecht's Berlin: A Scrapbook of the Twenties*, pp. 22–3.

Barbara Ulrich: The Hot Girls of Weimar Berlin.

Mel Gordon: *Voluptuous Panic: The Erotic World of Weimar Berlin.*

Christopher Isherwood: *The Berlin Stories.*

5

THE LAW OF REVERSED EFFORT

Unlike at Schonhaus, the Jewish community did not run the boys' orphanage; the famous German industrial giant Krupp provided the primary support. It was linked to an institution for apprentices, where Max would be transferred once he became of age.

He never lost touch with Greta, who was permitted to visit him twice weekly on a regular basis. This reset the fracture that had developed when they were parted, and it would go on to cement their strong loving bond.

As the years passed, Max grew into a healthy young lad and Greta into a pretty, bubbly young teenager.

Max grew ahead of his years. His strength of character was already reflected in his young face.

In early 1930, during his eleventh year, he was given an important lesson in life when three older boys suddenly made up their minds to bully him and some of the other boys. The bullying started when a new boy set out to assert himself at the expense of some of the younger boys. Max found himself in the victimised group.

Max was big-hearted and didn't like to offend people too much. He preferred to joke around and play the clown, and he won plenty of friendship and attention that way. The bullying took him by surprise and threw him out of his comfort zone. Confrontation wasn't part of his nature then, so he tried to keep clear of the bullies – the ringleader, Heinz Reus, and his two henchmen, Esser and Kolb. They interpreted his behaviour as fear, which encouraged them to pick on him even more.

Max eventually grew angry at the continuous intimidation, and it wasn't long before thoughts of ways to get even filled his mind. As he boiled over, one evening he made up his mind that the following day he'd confront all three, one after the other, starting with the weakest, Kolb, and finishing with the strongest, Heinz Reus. He scheduled 'payback' for after breakfast – when the boys were split up, attending to their chores.

Having decided when, he sized up his opposition. Kolb was about the same age as himself, Esser a little older and Reus, by far the toughest of the three, had almost two years on him. Realising he might not be able to come out on top in all three confrontations, his minimum aim was to gain some respect and a reprieve from further humiliation.

He awoke early next morning and worked hard to finish his chores before breakfast. During breakfast Reus and his buddies sat at a table close by, taunting and throwing insults at Max and the other youngsters.

Max had had enough; it was time to give the bullies a surprise. He glared across to the other table, fixing his eyes squarely on Reus.

Reus was surprised by Max's reaction and, in defence, jibed, "Little Maxy boy looks angry – ahhhh!"

His offsiders chuckled sarcastically, unaware of the surprise they would soon be receiving.

"I'll teach those bastards," said Max.

His friends looked at one another quizzically.

Max finished up and left the canteen in a hurry, but as he passed Reus's table he received yet another barrage of abuse. He set off to prepare himself mentally, and after a few minutes he left his dorm to seek out Kolb – his first target.

Max spotted him busily sweeping the quadrangle. Looking up, Kolb immediately grew wide-eyed, realising Max was coming for him to settle a score. The eye contact and aggressive body language said it all. Max wasted no time. He waded in with several haymaker punches followed by a strong kick. Kolb fell to the ground and rolled up into a ball, pleading for his assailant to stop hitting him.

Max walked off, shouting a warning: "Any more bullying, Kolb, and I'll give you an even bigger beating. Understood?"

To gain an edge on Esser would involve the element of surprise. Esser was confident, strong and Reus's right-hand man.

Max made his way towards where Esser was working in the canteen. He sighted him through the small observation panel in the door and waited for him outside. Esser was busy packing up his cleaning utensils, and it wasn't long before he would be leaving. As he came through the door, Max made his move. He planted a swift punch on to Esser's chin, following through with a savage kick. Esser reeled away in surprise. Wasting no time, Max secured a neck grip and wrestled him to the ground, thumping his head on the floor. He pinned him down and began to slap and punch in between the flailing arms of Esser, who was trying to block the blows and get up. Esser's nose streamed blood.

They exchanged heated words, but Esser was in no position to achieve a reversal.

"If you persist in bullying me or the other boys," Max said, "I'll give you another beating just like this one."

He climbed off and stood up, glaring at Esser.

Esser pulled himself off the ground and returned the glare; it was obvious he wasn't ready to concede. They clashed for a second time, exchanging blows in a furious flurry of punches. Max came off best and Esser finally fell to his knees in tears.

Max stood over him and pushed his head with his hand in an aggressive gesture. Then, without comment, he wheeled around with thoughts on his final target – Reus.

Unfortunately a situation had arisen that Max had not considered. In the clash with Esser he had sprained a thumb.

55

The injury left him deep in thought: his stand would come to nothing unless he achieved a result against Reus, so he was left without a choice. He would have to endure the pain and continue with his strategy.

His passion faltered as he made his way towards where he knew Reus would be. To worsen the situation, the fight with Esser had eaten up some emotional energy and depleted him of some physical strength. Now, at a serious disadvantage, he decided to regain his composure and recoup for a few minutes. Returning to the washroom, he splashed his face and ran his sprained thumb under the cold-water tap, tugging it hard in an attempt to make it more flexible.

Thoughts filled his head: to end the bullying he would have to make his mark on big Reus – that much he knew – but apprehension had crept in and a battle with his mind took place in the few minutes he stood there recovering. He realised that focusing on the job at hand and adopting a positive attitude should be his foremost concern, and not what damage Reus might be capable of doing to him. This was 'the law of reversed effort', and, as young as he was, he knew it would mean the difference between winning and losing.

Picture yourself balancing on a four-inch-wide kerb eight inches from the ground. Easy! Now picture yourself balancing on the same kerb ten feet above the ground. Different. What's the difference? The difference is in the way you think about it. With the ten-foot kerb you think more about falling than walking. This is the law of reversed effort.

Max held his task foremost in his mind, closing the door to any thoughts that might adversely affect his performance; he was truly living in the moment.

This done, he was ready to take the final step. He left the washroom in a positive frame of mind. Unfortunately, by the time he caught up with Reus the worst had happened: all three boys were together.

Max maintained his aggressive body language and assumed a fighting stance, keeping his eyes squarely on Reus. He was relying on the fact that if he confronted Reus directly, the other two boys would not interfere.

"Let's be having you, then, Reus." He beckoned with his right hand.

Reus smiled, and punched his open palm to indicate he was ready to give Max a fierce hiding.

Reus was lean, tall and strong. Max would be hard-pressed to get any sort of gain from this encounter, but his heart was in the right place.

Reus opened up with a verbal threat and then rushed in to deliver a series of punches. He drove Max back across the quadrangle, pushing forward to secure a wrestling grip. Max backed away quickly, managing to avoid initial attempts to grapple him to the ground. Unfortunately, he was unable to maintain an effective defence, and soon Reus was connecting with several strong punches. Inevitably, despite dogged resistance, the stronger boy got the upper hand and Max was overwhelmed.

He fell to his knees with a bloodied nose, silent tears trickled down his cheeks, and his head was bowed in despair.

"How do you like that, Maxy boy?" snarled Reus as he moved in to finish him off.

In panic, Max snatched a handful of grit from the ground and threw it up into Reus's face. Reus jerked his head back quickly to avoid the flying dirt, but in that instant Max sprang to his feet and threw out a kick into Reus's groin. Reus gasped in surprise and stooped forward, trying to catch his breath. Max came in with two quick hammer-like punches into Reus's exposed head, and then he even managed to apply his own head grip. He continued to hammer at Reus's head with his free fist.

It was the need to recover from the shock of the kick that forced Reus to accept the punches to his head. But the two-year advantage proved him to be supreme in all departments. Once recovered, he simply threw Max off and launched his own barrage of punches and kicks. He finally got a neck lock on Max, wrestled him to the ground, found his balance and prepared to beat the daylights out of him.

Just then, as Reus was about to administer the final decisive blows, Klinsman, the maths master appeared from behind the building.

"Stop that fighting at once," he shouted.

Reus was startled. He stopped immediately, saving young Max from a serious drubbing.

Reus leapt up from the floor and stood to attention with a guilty look on his face; it was obvious he had been in a similar situation before. Unlike Reus, and not in full appreciation of Klinsman's timely intervention, from the floor Max drove his foot into Reus's ankle, knocking him to the ground. The impact winded him, and in that moment Max rolled over on to him and threw as many punches as he could in the few seconds he had available.

Klinsman couldn't believe his eyes. He scurried across to where the boys were fighting.

Max's advantage was short-lived. Once again Reus recovered and wildly threw him away.

"If you boys don't stop fighting this instant, you'll be expelled from this orphanage today," shouted Klinsman.

Max got to his feet, exhausted and battered. He knew that Klinsman's timely assistance had helped him achieve his objective. Reus stood there with a bloody nose glaring at Max, astounded by the battering he'd just received from someone so much his junior.

Klinsman marched them off to the director's office – but not before stopping off at the nurse's medical room, where their wounds were examined and treated. Max had a black eye, a bloody nose (remarkably not broken), two sprained thumbs and a multitude of scuffs, grazes and bruises. But the fight had won him Reus's respect and, therefore, Esser and Kolb's too.

It was a good thing the boys formed a friendship, because their altercation had been pencilled in as an issue for the board of governors to deal with at its next monthly meeting.

The incident marked the end of the bullying and the beginning of new friendships. From then on, all four played sports and studied together. Above all, Reus, who had previously been a member of a boxing club, taught Max his boxing skills.

It was then Max knew instinctively that boxing would form a major part of his future.

BIBLIOGRAPHY

Wohlfahrtseinrichtungen der fried: *Kruppschen Gussstahlfabrik zu Essen zum Besten ihrer Arbeiter und Beamten.* (Brussels, 1876.)

6

THE BROWNSHIRTS

1929: several weeks before being discharged from Schonhaus, Greta had a chance encounter that would have a significant bearing on the rest of her life.

It was a hot Saturday afternoon in August and she was diligently weeding a flower patch. A straw hat protected her head from the sun. The face beneath it was that of a remarkably pretty fifteen-year-old. Classes finished at eleven o'clock on Saturdays and she always looked forward to enjoying her time off from study.

It was good to get out of her standard-issue weekday clothing: a cotton dress, a pinafore overgarment and brown cotton stockings. She'd replaced them with well-worn blue jeans, a white cotton shirt and a pair of old brown sandals. Despite the tomboyish attire, it was obvious she was transforming into an attractive young woman.

In the distance the unfamiliar sound of a band parading down the street pierced the air. She ran across to the entrance to find out what was going on. She looked on excitedly as the parade passed by. The musicians were a group of uniformed male youths. She followed the band with interest as it continued on its way. Just as she was about to go back inside, a flaxen-haired youth strolled up to her.

"Good morning, Fräulein. Did you like the procession?"

His bold approach startled her at first, but the warm greeting told her something about him.

"Yes. I've never seen a musical parade made up entirely of youths before."

He smiled and nodded. "My name is Dieter Stang and I am pleased to meet you." He gave a slight bow. "The procession is made up of members of the local faction of the NSDAP's youth organisation, known as the Hitler Youth.

"Are girls allowed to join this youth organisation?" she asked.

"At the moment there is no official girls' youth organisation, but there are some informal groups that have got together as a result of introduction through their brothers, or people like me, promoting the movement and getting the word out. These groups are referred to as the Hitlerjugend Sororities."

Greta hadn't really been interested in a movement for girls. She wanted to prolong the conversation with Stang as she felt immediately attracted to him. He was a tall, slim, handsome young fellow, and he wore a uniform that matched that of the boys marching down the street.

"I have a younger brother that would be interested in your youth organisation. Have you any promotional literature?"

"Sure I have." He opened the brown leather satchel hung over his shoulder, fished out two sets of pamphlets and passed them to her. He explained: "The first gives details of the youth movement and the benefits of joining up and the second is a condensed manifesto of the NSDAP."

Greta thanked him for the literature and focused back on Stang, judging him to be about her age – fifteen.

"I'll read it in my dormitory later." She gestured with her eyes toward the official-looking building behind her.

Looking up at the sign, 'Schonhaus German-Jewish Orphanage for Girls', Stang said, "Oh, you're an orphan, then. You are Jewish!" He sounded disappointed.

"No, I'm German. It's run by the Jewish community primarily for Jewish girls, but I'm one of several German girls. I've been here for ten years now, and I'm due to be discharged in a few weeks' time."

Her response brought the smile back to his face. "Have you a job to go to?" he asked.

"No, not yet, but I'm hoping the orphanage committee will fix me up with one shortly."

"I work in a publishing workshop in the eastern part of the city. From time to time there is a vacancy. I can let you know if you wish."

"That would be excellent," Greta replied with enthusiasm.

The conversation paused as they gazed at each other for a few moments. Alas! the brief romantic intermission was interrupted by frantic yelling. An elderly woman, Frau Marquette, the deputy director, was bearing down on them like a runaway train. She snatched the pamphlets from Greta's hand, crumpled them and threw them to the ground. Then she yelled at young Stang, making disparaging remarks about the party he represented and criticising the Sturmabteilung (SA), commonly known as the Brownshirts.

At that time, the Hitler Youth came under the control of the SA. The SA functioned as a paramilitary wing for the NSDAP and played a key role in Hitler's rise to power. It was notorious for its numerous acts of violence against the communists and other socialist groups throughout the 1920s, typically in minor street fights. In the early years members had been recruited from the ranks of the former Freikorps, and these men had considerable experience in the use of violence against their rivals.

Their famous khaki shirts, originally intended for soldiers in Africa, were bulk-purchased from the German Army. The uniform was finished off with swastika armbands, ski caps, knee breeches, thick woollen socks and combat boots.

"Brown-shirted thugs!" Frau Marquette bellowed. "You young boys are even dressed up like the adults. You should be ashamed of yourselves."

Greta and Stang were shocked at the indignant remarks coming from the orphanage's deputy director; this kind of aggression was usually reserved for the SA. Stang backed off nervously, silently cursing her untimely intrusion.

Frau Marquette's attention then turned to Greta: "Pick up that rubbish, Greta, and throw it in the garbage bin on your way over to detention. You'll sit there for two hours and forfeit your lunch – and think about who you talk to next time. These people are terrible; they're thugs and troublemakers, the lot of them. This poor boy will get himself into a lot of strife."

Greta stuttered her apologies, picked up the crumpled paper, then scampered back toward the main house.

Seemingly satisfied with her outburst, Frau Marquette suddenly settled into a softer tone: "Now hurry along, young man."

Stang stood there completely perplexed as she turned and walked off.

As Greta reached the porch, she looked back over to the front gates, where she could see Stang still hovering outside. He'd hung around just to get another glimpse of her. Having recovered from the shock of the scathing verbal attack, he smiled and gave a little wave before walking away; then he quickly refocused on his task as if nothing had happened.

Greta ignored the order to discard the NSDAP handouts; instead she smoothed out the pamphlets, folded them neatly and tucked them into her back pocket, intending to read them later that day.

For most of that sunny afternoon, thoughts of young Stang occupied her mind. She replayed in her head every aspect of their chance meeting. His appearance had made her day; in fact, it had made her year.

Lost in pleasant thoughts, and reflecting on the words they'd exchanged, her two hours of detention passed quickly. Having forfeited the hot meal served in the canteen, she picked up a standard 'take-out pack', which included a sandwich, a piece of fruit and a candy bar. She returned to her dormitory to review the NSDAP literature. She liked what she read. The party manifesto would become the influencing force behind her forthcoming desire to study political science.

Regarding the literature covering the Hitler Youth, 'This would be ideal for Max,' she thought. She decided to pass it on to him at their next meeting.

Discharge for orphans who had not been fostered or adopted was for the Schonhaus Board of Governors to determine. Their ages ranged between fourteen and sixteen, and what happened to them next depended on the standard of education the orphans achieved during their time at the orphanage.

After the Great War the republic established a free, universal four-year elementary school (*Grundschule* or *Volksschule*). At Grade 5, eleven-year-olds commenced their secondary school education. There were several types of secondary school: first, the *Hauptschule* was for the less academic pupils, who usually finished at fourteen years and found work outside; second, the *Realschule* was for pupils with a technical or business ability, who usually went on to complete another two years' higher education; and third, the *Gymnasium* was for academic students, and here an extended programme led to a diploma – a prerequisite for university.

Greta's orphanage catered for elementary and secondary schooling, covering curriculums for *Hauptschule* and *Realschule* students, depending upon their abilities. Greta was a top-grade student, and she was looking to go on to the *Gymnasium* when she left Schonhaus – then, perhaps, university.

Her curriculum at Schonhaus in her senior years included grammar, literature, biology and domestic science. For the fifteen-year-olds, the board thought it apt to include a course on housekeeping. By August 1929 Greta had completed this course, most of which was practical: daily chores for the upkeep of the orphanage.

Despite having to work hard for their food and shelter, they were treated fairly by the director in other ways. He was progressive insofar as he wanted his girls to be freethinkers, responsible and accountable for their actions, well prepared to face the world when it was time to leave.

In setting out to achieve his aim, he'd made the older girls look after the younger ones. His attempts to break the isolation of orphanage life and city-dwelling included arranging regular outings for the girls. They were allowed to go for walks in groups to discover the city and go shopping. Newspapers were freely available and all senior girls were instructed to read them on a regular basis. Weekly discussion groups were formed, and these gave the girls a chance to air their views on current affairs and world events. Greta was aware of the NSDAP but did not know to what extent they were a serious opposition to the current Weimar government.

All this helped mould her into a competent and confident teenager, preparing her for the next step in life – a step that was shortly to take place.

The reason she'd been overlooked for fostering or adoption in her younger years was not apparent. Moreover, at this late stage she hadn't yet been shortlisted from any job interview. In recent months this might have been because jealous wives precluded her because of her good looks, or maybe it was just plain providence – the invisible force that determines life's timing.

It was just a few days after her chance meeting with Dieter that she was finally chosen for a job as live-in home help. The interview had gone well with her prospective employers and the board was pleased to inform her that she had been selected for the job. She would be working for a wealthy Berlin couple, Friedrich and Emma Holtz. Emma was a rich career woman and Friedrich an ambitious executive working for Krupp Industries. Their residence was in the salubrious Berlin district of Charlottenburg, west of the city centre. She was to carry out cleaning services together with a multitude of other domestic duties. The Holtzes would provide her with her own room and a portion of the weekly wage. The balance of her wage would be given to Schonhaus Orphanage as it was the service provider.

The home-help position didn't fit in with Greta's ambitions, but she was mature enough to realise that the new assignment would provide a platform from which she could step up to bigger things and greater challenges. Besides, she would be living in a luxurious apartment in uptown Berlin, and that was a comforting thought.

Her employers had chosen her for different reasons. For Friedrich, her attractive looks made the choice much easier; Emma intended to take full advantage of the cheap labour the orphanage was offering, and she planned to keep Greta very busy.

Surprisingly, leaving the orphanage wasn't easy for Greta. She'd made many friends there and the thought of letting go of old familiar surroundings and attachments didn't pass without a few tears. Those years that had shaped her into what she had become were stored away as memories that now would form part of her spiritual history file.

Everything moved so quickly in those last few days that she didn't get the chance to break the news to Max about her change of fortune.

Instead of being happy for her he was upset, and he grew envious at her new-found freedom outside the confines of what he now considered to be virtually a prison. Frustrated and angry, all he wanted to do was to get away from his orphanage.

Greta sympathised but could do nothing to help as he was still under age for formal discharge. Besides, being there meant he was in line for a trade apprenticeship, which would provide him with a way to make a living when he became of age.

His attachment to Greta was strong. He feared he would lose contact once she was away from the orphanage, catching the fresh breeze of Berlin's city life. It took persistent assurance from her to convince him that this would never be the case.

"Max, how could we ever be apart? I'll be here until it's time for you to leave; then we can be together as a family again. Now you must keep your chin up."

He brooded for a while, looked up and said despondently, "You promise, Greta?"

"Yes, of course, Max."

In the same conversation, she mentioned her meeting with Stang, the young herald for Hitler Youth and passed Max the promotion pamphlet. But when Greta left, Max lapsed back into a mood and returned to his dormitory, mulling over his situation. Preoccupied, he tossed the pamphlet into a drawer without reading it.

On her last day at Schonhaus, she bid her farewells to friends and the staff who had taken care of her over the years. The Holtzes had arranged for a taxicab to drive her to the four-storey town house in Charlottenburg, just a short journey across a section of the city.

As the taxi drove off, she stood on the pavement for a moment, looking up at the large, impressive town house in front of her. There were several stone steps leading up to the front door and on either side were fancy handrails. She rapped once and stood there nervously. As she waited, visions of a similar experience crossed the screen of her mind, taking her back to when she was a five-year-old standing under the porch in front of the big black front door of Schonhaus.

As Emma opened the door it struck Greta that she was a younger version of the old matron at Schonhaus who'd greeted her, Hilda and baby Max back in 1919. Just to underline the similarities, Emma welcomed her and asked if she would like a cup of tea and biscuits.

'Déjà vu!' thought Greta.

Over tea, Emma put Greta in the picture about her background: "My parents are both in the medical profession. Mother is a GP and Daddy, a surgeon working out of the Krankenhaus Rudolf Virchow, at Augustenburger Platz 1, just north of here. My preference was law. I am a lawyer and work for a solicitor named Fischer, F. (Charlottenburg) at Sophie-Charlotte-Strasse 23a nearby. I specialise in medical malpractice lawsuits. I guess my parents' professions rubbed off on me in this way. Friedrich, my husband, works for Krupp Industries. He often goes overseas, so we'll share the place alone when he's away. Friedrich's younger than me. He followed his father into Krupp and has established himself well in its corporate structure. He has always been well connected, with friends in the right places. He'd met them during his time at university in the early twenties. Our marriage was arranged by our parents – a professional union, you might say."

All the while Greta sat there nodding, impressed by Emma's candidness.

Once they'd finished drinking tea, Emma took her on a tour of the house. The place dripped with opulence. Most of the furniture was German Biedermeier, a blend of elegant simplicity: exquisite secretaires, armoires, bergères, récamiers, display pieces, sofas, armchairs and tables filled every room in splendid walnut or mahogany veneers. Even the lighting and mirrors were from the same period. Drapes and furnishings were lavish arrangements, and the colour coordination was impeccable. One room was filled with the soft resonance of Mozart.

After taking in the flood of information, Greta was grateful to be shown to her room.

Emma opened the door and it was all too much for her. The room was such a vast difference from the dormitory at Schonhaus. Her face lit up with sheer delight. She thanked Emma and set about unpacking her meagre belongings from a red holdall she'd been supplied with by the orphanage.

She quickly settled in, and after a few days began enjoying the new taste of freedom the job offered her. Previous experience and good training at the orphanage had taught her to plan her schedule thoroughly. It gave her time to soak up the excitement of the city on a daily basis.

She learnt that Emma was extremely competent at her work and represented her firm admirably, supporting barristers and defending clients of medical practices and hospitals brought to task through litigation. She also learnt more about Friedrich. He had a good nature, a quick wit and a sharp intellect. His incisive mind helped him make profitable decisions and he was regarded as a stellar performer in the business world. By the time he'd reached his thirtieth year he had risen into line management and established himself as a high flyer within the Krupp Group.

Friedrich worked hard, and he also played hard on his frequent trips abroad, revealing a cavalier attitude to his private life. In contrast, Emma stood on a moral high ground. She considered Friedrich a little immature and used her mental prowess to control him intellectually. This ensured a degree of domestic harmony. Otherwise, his zeal and drive were unstoppable.

Greta found it difficult to understand the relationship between them; love seemed lacking. They tolerated each other's company, and appearances were upheld in front of the many guests constantly invited to regular dinner parties at the town house.

The contrast between Emma's seriousness and Friedrich's light-heartedness was interesting. Friedrich always had a glint in his eye and he would sometimes focus it on Greta when Emma was out of the house.

Emma, staid as she was, knew her husband well and kept a vigilant eye on him. Greta was sensible enough not to risk losing her new job through flirting with him.

When he tried it on, she adopted the guise of sweet innocence, deftly fending off his covert approaches. Unfortunately, her responses only made him even more wanting, knowing that she, 'in her innocence', knew exactly what he was up to. Seducing Greta and getting her between the sheets became one of Friedrich's top priorities. He considered this to be a challenge equal to any he'd faced so far as a dynamic executive at Krupp Industries.

Greta defended her virginity well. She successfully fought off his many covert sexual propositions without upsetting him too much. She was a natural in personal survival skills, extremely diplomatic in her reproaches, and managed to maintain both job and dignity.

1930: the first half of that year saw huge changes for Greta and Max.

Max had weathered the bullying incident during the earlier part of 1930 and was now fully committed to his new friends, Reus, Esser and Kolb. It was during this period that he took up boxing and his best friend, Reus, was teaching him well.

With the passing of time came physical growth, and six months saw him shoot up almost five centimetres in height. This, together with some extra pounds in the right places, brought Max to within a hair's breadth of the size of Reus, almost two years his senior.

He eventually read the Hitler Youth pamphlet Greta had left with him. She had been accurate in her appraisal of the leaflet. It contained exciting information, and the thought of matching his boxing skills against others in the Hitler Youth seemed just the right challenge – a great way forward.

For Greta, academia at the Charlottenburg home was rubbing off on her. She was blossoming into a bright and mature young girl – sweet sixteen and the apple of Friedrich's eye.

Providence, however, was about to change the direction of her life. Several months into her sixteenth year, an errand took her to the east side of Berlin. Instead of taking the tram she decided to walk a part of the way back. Her route took her through the city's central east by way of a busy commercial area.

Nailed to a board outside a print workshop, a sign advertising a part-time job vacancy caught her attention: 'Part Time Work, Apply Within'.

She stepped into the workshop and walked over to what looked like a small reception desk. She scrutinised the workshop floor; there were several people busy at work. A woman stopped what she was doing and stepped over to Greta.

"Can I help you?" she asked.

"I'm enquiring about the part-time job vacancy."

"Oh, you'd like to apply?"

"Yes," said Greta.

"Hi, my name is Marlene. I'll go see if Georg is available now. Wait a second."

She disappeared into an office, then reappeared some moments later.

"Georg can see you now. Go straight in." Marlene pointed the way into the room, where Georg Jackel was beavering away at his desk.

"Please sit. You want to apply for this job, then?"

"Yes," replied Greta.

He leant back in his chair.

"Let me tell you a little bit about us. We are members of a political party, the NSDAP, and our job involves printing various information bulletins and promotion leaflets. We've leased these premises."

Suddenly, the penny dropped: she had accidentally fallen upon the very same print workshop that young Stang had mentioned in their conversation outside the orphanage a year before.

"Oh," she said, looking surprised.

Georg picked up on her surprised reaction: "Do you have a problem with that?" he asked.

"No, not at all; it's just that I met one of your members this time last year and he told me about this workshop. I just happened across it today."

"Can you remember his name?"

"Oh, yes. It was Dieter Stang."

"Yes, Dieter's still with us, but he was transferred to another print room across town."

"We lost touch after the chat, but I never forgot him," said Greta.

"He'll love to hear that," said Georg, appreciating Greta's good looks. "Well, as far as I'm concerned you've got the job. Your work schedule is two afternoons a week for three hours each afternoon." After a short pause he asked her a question: "By the way, you're not Jewish, are you?"

"No, I was brought up in a Jewish-run orphanage, but I'm German – an Aryan, as your party manifesto sets forth."

Georg gave a small sigh of relief. She observed his reaction quizzically, but, at that time, she couldn't have guessed how important the race issue would turn out to be later when the party took control of the country.

"Have you any questions?" he asked.

"None," she said.

He led her on a brief tour around the workshop and introduced the staff, which included several older girls who appeared to be very friendly. After the short tour, Georg offered her a cup of coffee and chatted some more before bidding her goodbye.

Greta left feeling excited. She couldn't wait to embark on her new venture the following week. It had been one of those perfect days. She stepped out into the main street and strolled off towards the city centre. A few minutes down the road saw the buildings change from offices to department stores and other shops. The change brought a new excitement for her, for now she could participate in one of her favourite pastimes: window shopping. Ambling along, she soaked up the warmth of the day and looked at the many choices the various retail outlets had to offer.

She glanced up into a stunning cloudless sky. Suddenly a lone Junkers G38 droned its way across the blue strip between the buildings above. Greta could make out the hum of its four engines; it had just taken off from Berlin's Tempelhof Airport.

Tempelhof was first officially designated as an airport in October 1923 and Lufthansa, the famous German airline, was founded in Tempelhof in January 1926 following a merger between Deutsche Aero-Lloyd (DAL) and Junkers Luftverkehr. The Junkers airplane flying overhead was painted with Lufthansa's motif and it was one of the very first to be put into commercial service for both scheduled and chartered flights.

It wasn't long before a display in another department-store

window grabbed her attention. She moved through the shopping precinct at a snail's pace, but as soon as the last classy retailer had been scrutinised she decided to catch a tram for the remainder of the journey home.

Convincing Emma she could carry out both jobs without neglecting her domestic duties was a little difficult, but Emma admired the teenager's enterprising attitude and granted her the time off.

Emma had grown fond of Greta, and several weeks earlier had asked whether she would be interested in furthering her education. She confirmed that she would provide financial support and Greta had eagerly taken up the offer; however, Emma was taken aback when Greta talked of her passion for political science. Somewhat surprised at the choice, Emma nevertheless enrolled Greta for her first year.

Greta never revealed the name of her new employer. She recalled how Frau Marquette had ranted at young Stang outside the orphanage the previous year, and she didn't want to trigger a similar reaction in Emma. Over the following weeks, she forged new friendships with the other girls working at the printing house, and she eventually caught up with Dieter. Life for her blossomed, but it suddenly turned upside down a couple of days before Max's twelfth birthday.

Emma had inadvertently come across some party literature that Greta had carelessly left on top of her bed. When confronted with the discovery, Greta admitted her part-time involvement with the NSDAP. Emma was shocked, and she felt betrayed because Greta had not been open with her. Shock quickly turned to anger and Greta was given just a day to leave the household. Emma was strongly against National Socialism because she was Jewish, but what she saw as Greta's deceit maddened her even more.

Greta panicked. Emma advised her to report back to the orphanage, but, of course, she was too old to stay there now. She begged Emma to change her mind, but without success.

Distrust had broken their bond and Greta found herself suddenly alone.

Friedrich was disappointed when Emma announced Greta's dismissal. He had no political leanings, but Emma did for obvious reasons. He would miss Greta's happy and fresh-faced presence. Worse, his failure to claim her maidenhead was a blow to his ego.

The hunter in him wouldn't let that challenge go; so, managing to pull her aside before she left, he spoke to her: "Greta, if there is anything I can do for you, or if there is anything you need, please feel free to contact me on my business telephone number. I'll miss you lots." He offered her one of his business cards.

Upset as she was, she managed a smile.

"Thank you for your kindness, Friedrich. I'll miss you too."

Greta's mind whirled and she grew anxious. The thought of being alone on the streets of Berlin at just sixteen years of age was frightening. A crossroad in life had come earlier than expected. With her small bundle of belongings, she made her way across to the print workshop and distraughtly told her friends what had happened. Sympathetic to her dilemma, two workmates, Marlene and Traudl, suggested she stay with them at an apartment they'd recently rented in East Berlin. She wouldn't have to contribute towards the monthly payments until she'd secured a full-time job.

Georg soon got to know about Greta's situation. He realised she was a great asset to the party because of her education and full-time availability and suggested that she should continue her political-science education, adding editing to her curriculum. There would be a full-time position for her in the party should she upgrade her skills accordingly. She smiled; her topsy-turvy life had righted itself in such a short space of time.

While Greta's life took new turns, back at the boys' orphanage, Max's best friend, Reus, had reached his fourteenth year. He would soon transfer to the Krupp-supported apprentice school for boilermakers. There he would serve out his apprenticeship for a large Berlin-based company. He was excited when he broke the news to Max; he was looking forward to working in the busy metropolis, a 'free man'.

Once again, Max didn't take the news well. First his sister, now his best buddy was about to leave him 'imprisoned' in the orphanage. He aired his resentment, using Greta as his sounding board during her next visit.

She took the story back to her flatmates. To her surprise her flatmates came up with a suggestion: should Max decide to 'discharge' himself from the orphanage, he would be welcome to stay with them.

Greta conveyed the welcome news during her next visit. It meant that he would have to forfeit the orphanage's arrangement with Krupp's apprenticeship scheme.

"You look older than your years, so you could stretch the truth about your age and get some sort of job to help pay for some of your keep," Greta advised.

Max was overjoyed and made plans for breaking out of the orphanage; it was a step in the right direction.

Making his escape wasn't difficult; he packed a small bundle of clothing and a couple of books and stealthily made his way to the most secluded sector of the perimeter after nightfall. He scaled the wall easily, without disturbing the occupants inside the orphanage or startling any Berliners the other side of it. Greta met him a few blocks down the road at a predetermined place and time. They hugged and kissed when they met up, and then they made their way happily towards the apartment in the eastern part of the city.

For the next few months, Max stayed at the apartment and joined a local faction of the Hitler Youth. He lied about his age, because at that time formal membership started at fourteen years of age. He was big enough to get away with it. He looked older than he was. He was quick to join the boxing section as this would help enhance and improve his skills. Best of all, he was finally back with his beloved sister.

Living with Greta's friends, Marlene and Traudl, was new and exciting for him. They teased him in more ways than one. Despite his physical maturity, he was bashful with girls, although puberty was apparent and brought with it some strong sexual feelings.

One morning he caught Greta unawares. She was kneeling on a comfortable sofa, resting on her forearms, deep in thought, soaking up the heat of the sunbeams lancing through the window across her shoulders. His sudden presence startled her and she coiled around, revealing her bare torso. He stood there dumbstruck as his eyes locked on to her naked body. He quickly looked away in embarrassment, but he hadn't failed to notice her firm and pleasantly rounded breasts. He backed out of the room, stuttering an apology.

Greta gave a giggle, and then nonchalantly resumed her previous position, pondering in which direction the next crossroads in her life would lead.

7

VOGEL

*Offer a man an ideal. Garnish and imbue that ideal with
passion, then stand back and observe how the union between
thought and feeling gives birth to action and behaviour in
the material world.*

*In those days such forms were represented by prejudice,
anger, vanity and a revitalised lust for avenging old
grievances.*

1931: it was a fresh spring morning when Greta, her flatmates
and Max attended a large SA rally. The rally took place in
Lustgarten, close to the Berliner Dom (cathedral). The main
speaker was Ernst Röhm, the chief of the SA. After an emotional
delivery to the large gathering of supporters, several boys from
the Hitler Youth were handpicked to meet him. Young Max was
one of the boys chosen.

Röhm's aggressive performance for the crowd depicted him
as a formidable, arrogant individual, but the following experience
would reveal another side of the big man's character. The boys
stood to attention as Röhm moved through the line-up. He stopped
for a brief chat with each youth. As he came closer to Max,
scars on his face became apparent, making him look even more
daunting. Max learnt later that he had received them during the
Great War.

"And who do we have here?" Röhm asked as he focused on
Max and held out his hand.

Max took his hand and noticed how fat Röhm's fingers were. Röhm shook his hand vigorously.

"Max Rieker, sir. I am pleased to meet you."

Röhm smiled. "How old are you, son?" he asked.

The simple question put Max on the spot; he couldn't find it in his heart to lie to Röhm.

"I'm thirteen years old, sir."

"You're a big lad for your age; you have wide shoulders, eh?"

"Yes, sir, I box for the Hitlerjugend."

"Ah, yes," he replied. "And what would you like to be when you grow up, boy?"

"I'd like to become a professional boxer, sir."

It was the right answer. Röhm's face lit up, and in his delight delivered several fierce pats to Max's shoulders with his fat hands. It was hard enough to pile the youngster into the ground beneath him. Max winced at the pounding, but responded with a proud grin.

There had been a purpose to the line-up. All the youths handpicked to meet Röhm that day had been orphaned, and they were all to be given a chance to become personal aides to prominent members of the SA. As aides, they would have to serve and assist their leaders both at home and away at the various rallies and gatherings organised by the party throughout Germany. It would be a great opportunity for Max to travel and see his own country. He volunteered with enthusiasm.

Max was appointed to Michael Vogel, a Prussian who had served his time in the military. During the Great War Vogel had achieved the rank of major. Max had drawn a most fortunate straw. Vogel became the father he never had at a time in his life when a youth is most impressionable.

Such was Vogel's character that he brought a sense of balance and calm wherever he went. The turmoil the SA carried with it mellowed in Vogel's lofty presence. He was a most unlikely SA member. He was a wealthy aristocrat, exceptionally well educated, and he carried an air of nobility around with him. In contrast, the majority of the SA line management were drawn from uneducated backgrounds and lower ranks in the army; few had class and intellect, albeit there were some notable officers who had been seconded from Reichswehr who didn't fall into this category.

Röhm reflected the side of the movement that was powerful and zealous – the perfect vehicle to drive a new party forward. Vogel added depth to a young political group lusting for identity and power. He headed up the legal section of the organisation. As a result, he was often in the company of and liaised with the luminaries of the party, taking him beyond his role in the SA.

He saw that any actions made by the party should be done in accordance with the legislation of the day. Hitler learnt his lesson well when he was sentenced back in 1924 after the Munich Beer Hall Putsch. On his release, he made sure that all actions were scrutinised and verified for legality before being implemented. Vogel was the advisor who made sure that all the actions of the party were above board.

Max too had noted the differences between Vogel and most other SA leaders. Vogel was a good listener; he wanted to hear what others had to say. He was also a philosopher and a champion of ancient dialectics – lines of argument practised by some of the famous Greek philosophers of classical times. During debates he had an incredible ability to twist an adversary's words around for his own benefit, using them to belittle or contradict the unwitting fellow's original argument. He was truly a dialectical wizard: nobody seemed able to get the better of him in the long-drawn-out discussions that were common in the top echelon of SA members vying for favourable opinion.

Röhm and others of his ilk never wanted to listen. Their responses were shallow, self-centred and ignorant. Anybody they considered represented a threat to the party would be ignored or humiliated, beaten up or even worse, depending on the seriousness of the threat.

As impressionable as he was, thuggery wasn't part of Max's

ambitions; neither was it Vogel's. Having said this, it would be unfair to label the Brownshirts as the only group that used violence against political adversaries. Violence was common during this period. It had been the norm since the end of the Great War, through the period known as the German Revolution and beyond. The Communist Party (KDP) was still very active. It was one of the major parties alongside the SDP and NSDAP. In fact, the communist movement in Germany was the largest in Europe, and it was seen as the 'leading party' of communism outside the Soviet Union. Needless to say, the communists were well backed by Moscow and very capable when it came to protecting their own or disrupting an NSDAP or SDP gathering. The SDP, too, had its belligerent wing, which was equally capable of cooking up a storm when necessary. It would be fair to say that the Brownshirts were better at it, having been born out of the early Freikorps organisations.

The only naivety evident in Vogel's beliefs concerning the party was the fact he had totally convinced himself that a fledgling NSDAP would eventually blossom into an organisation fit to govern and carry Germany through to meet the demands of the new world. It was this belief that labelled Vogel a dreamer in the eyes of other SA members.

But being jealous of his lofty connections didn't stop his adversaries granting him the respect and space he needed to accomplish his work. Vogel wasn't soft, though, and he had a balanced character. Behind his calm, focused and seemingly mild exterior, he was firm and could be a strict disciplinarian when necessary.

In his private life, he was an aged playboy. He had a huge appetite for sex and enjoyed regular capers with very young girls. Any debutante ambitious for social recognition would do anything to get her photograph in one of the trend-setting magazines of the time, and Vogel was a perfect vehicle for fulfilling her dreams – at a price, of course. *Die Dame* ('The Lady') was a magazine which any socialite seeking recognition would love to appear in. It prospered on the reputation it had built in the 1920s through its coverage of sophisticated entertainment, and many of its articles were written by famous writers of that era.

Vogel's sexual preferences were reassuring for Max, for he'd heard rumours that many SA senior staff used young boys to satisfy their sexual perversions.

Weimar Berlin of the early 1930s had mellowed somewhat in the wake of the Roaring Twenties. The Great Depression and high unemployment figures had been the main cause for its decline, but it still maintained its status as a Mecca for sex and excitement. Most of the previous exotic choices could still be found, albeit no longer in the abundance of former years. Glittering cabaret shows still thrived, and one or two of the most notable were favourite haunts for Vogel during his times of relaxation. On other occasions he would visit his favourite Resi telephone nightclub – where there were real women at the end of the telephone line, not men dressed up as women.

Age never appeared to be a constraint for him. For example, he had the eyes of a hawk. Even in the darkest of clubrooms he could immediately deduce from a single table light the body language of the occupant or occupants seated there – whether she was fun-loving or seductively mysterious. His choice depended on his mood at the time. He would start off by sending over an expensive cocktail or bottle of champagne, and this would be followed up with a phone call. His silver tongue would wrap up the introductions. This was Vogel's forte, as he soaked up the ambience and challenges of the seedy nightlife.

He took great delight in providing Max with explicit details about his sexual adventures.

Knowing Max was still a virgin, Vogel decided to find him his first sexual partner. The date for this unforgettable event was Max's fourteenth birthday in September 1932. Vogel arranged it by way of an incidental introduction to a lady associate, Sylvia Genest. Sylvia lived in a plush apartment in downtown Berlin. She was connected with Vogel through business interests, and they enjoyed a platonic relationship. Vogel considered Frau Genest too old for himself. Sylvia regarded Vogel as similarly unsuitable; her fancy was drawn to younger men. In their lighter moments she had often spoken to Vogel of her desire for young boys. Assuming that providing her with a vigorous teenage lover would benefit his future business dealings with her, he offered to set up young Max while her husband was overseas on business. Sylvia accepted his offer with lurid enthusiasm.

Vogel's plan was for Max to deliver a package to her home on the evening of his birthday. It would be up to Sylvia to carry out the seduction there. Previously he'd whetted her appetite with his descriptions of young Max's looks and character, describing him as several years beyond his age with a fine athletic physique. She was eager to meet him.

The day arrived, and in the afternoon Vogel sat down with Max for a chit-chat over coffee.

"I've an errand for you to run a bit later, Max. It's an antique I need you to deliver. I've boxed it up, so please be careful. The address is written on the box; it's downtown, 42 Klosterstrasse. The nearest U-Bahn station is Alexanderplatz. Take the rear exit out to Neue Friedrichstrasse and turn right. Turn left at Kaiser Wilhelm, then left again into Kloster. The road forms part of a square surrounding the old Catholic church. Frau Genest is an important business associate of mine, so I would appreciate you respecting and fulfilling all her wishes – particularly if she requires your personal services. Just take your time there – no need to hurry back."

Just before Max left the apartment, Vogel reiterated his earlier statement: "Don't forget, Max: make sure you see to all Frau Genest's wishes."

"Of course, Herr Vogel," replied Max, looking quizzically at him, wondering what he was getting at.

He followed Vogel's directions and located the town house without mishap.

'These are nice places,' he thought as he checked the address and rapped on the fancy scrolled-pewter knocker.

Sylvia opened the door, and her piercing blue eyes sparkled as she greeted him. Max was a little surprised at the warmth of her welcome.

Instead of taking the package and bidding him farewell, she invited him inside: "Please come in and make yourself comfortable for a while."

The friendly invitation surprised Max for a second time. Recalling Vogel's explicit instructions, he obliged.

"Let's go into the lounge," she added, pointing the way forward. "My name is Sylvia. Yours is Max, eh?"

"Yes," he said.

He melted down into a huge comfortable sofa and took in the surroundings.

"Nice place," he said.

She thanked him for the compliment. "Yes, we own the premises but the depression almost destroyed my husband financially. As a result, we had to convert the building into two units. We have the ground and first level, and Dr Drax, a GP, has leased the second and third floors. He operates his practice from here. The entrance next door opens up to a long staircase leading to his surgery. My husband eventually recovered, but his new job takes him overseas for long periods of time, leaving me here by myself."

She raised her eyebrows mischievously and touched Max tenderly on his shoulder. As young as he was, her innuendo didn't go unnoticed.

The lavishness of the decor was beyond anything he'd seen before. The room was filled with art-deco furniture and bronze and silver sculptures of sensuous nude women and men, setting the perfect scene for seduction.

Sylvia busied herself and offered Max a choice of drinks. He was comfortable with a red wine because Vogel had often poured him a glass during their regular dialogues.

83

"Michael thinks so much of you, Max, and I understand it's your birthday today," she said, handing him the glass.

"Yes, I'm fourteen today," said Max.

"My, my, you look so much older," said Sylvia, looking at him as if she were stripping him naked there and then.

"Yes, I keep fit and like to box," he said nervously.

"Oh, that's a dangerous sport," replied Sylvia.

"It's OK," he said in a nonchalant way.

Sylvia hadn't been the only person in the room checking the other out. Max hadn't failed to notice his voluptuous hostess. She was a very well-endowed woman, and she wore a flimsy blouse unbuttoned to display an outstanding cleavage. Her hips and thighs were perfectly rounded and her firm and shapely calves completed a symmetry that flowed through the entire length of her body. She was a natural blonde, fair-skinned with freckles sprinkled across her attractive face.

She sat next to him and looked into his eyes. Her perfume had a heady fragrance.

"You've got nice eyes."

"So have you," Max replied sheepishly.

They clinked glasses and sipped on the wine. Sylvia flirted unashamedly. Her behaviour was a first for Max, but he lapped up the attention. All of a sudden he realised the meaning of Vogel's comments earlier that day.

Eventually the small talk stopped and the scene lapsed into a period of stillness. Their eyes met several times silently, and both knew what was about to happen.

"Come."

She took his hand and led him out of the lounge towards the bedroom.

"Have you had sex with a woman before, Max?"

"No," he replied.

"Don't worry about it – I've had plenty of sex with men," snapped Sylvia.

Max smiled nervously.

She led him into the en suite.

"Here, take a shower," she said, hanging a huge white towel over his arm, "then make yourself comfortable in the bedroom. I'm going to change. I won't be long."

He showered quickly and slipped into the bed, eagerly awaiting her return. It wasn't long before she reappeared. There she was, draped in a full-length, black, filmy negligee. Her long blond hair hung loosely down her back, making her appearance wild and foxy. Inside the negligee was a stunning sculptured body clad in a sensuous satin underwear ensemble: camisole, French knickers and an exquisitely thin suspender belt supporting a pair of black, pencil-seamed stockings. The whole vibrant package was finished off in strappy black high heels that fastened an inch or two above the ankle.

"What do you think?" She struck a model's pose for Max, awaiting his approval.

He sat up. "You look wonderful," he gasped, with mouth wide open.

She pulled the sheets back, admiring his muscular youthful body and healthy erect penis that had been nowhere but in his own hand. She drew down on the lace bow of her negligee and let it drop to the floor, then deftly slipped the camisole over her shoulders revealing a large pair of breasts set off to perfection with pert light-brown nipples. Play-acting, she crouched, climbed on to the bed and straddled him like a wide-eyed mountain cat; then she lowered her body to allow her bosom to brush up against his chest. As their faces met she kissed him on the lips and looked into his eyes.

"Nervous?" she asked.

"No. I'm OK," he replied in a soft, cosy voice.

He felt his own nipples react as her warm breasts pressed down on to his chest; it was a first and felt wonderful.

They kissed again. Her alluring perfume filled the air and, for Max, the heady fragrance became intoxicating. She invited him to fondle her breasts. He squeezed them gently, then glided his hands around the curves and over her ripe nipples. She felt a rush of excitement as he clasped a breast with both hands and tenderly kissed her nipple. She shuffled up towards his chest, raised her hips and leant back resting on her hands. Then she motioned for Max to unbutton the flap at the crotch of her panties.

The flap fell away to reveal a moistened inviting crotch.

"Straighten your hand, Max, like this."

She demonstrated, guiding him to the appropriate spot.

"Just here . . . ahhhh! Wait a second."

She stretched across to the bedside table for a small bottle of oil, and applied it generously.

"OK, I'm ready," she said, prompting Max to continue. "That's wonderful."

She arched her body, tensing her thighs and buttocks. It wasn't long before she was breathing deeply.

"Don't stop, Max," she said as her breathing became more erratic.

Her moans became more intense as she came nearer to climax. Max became anxious that her wild cries of ecstasy might be heard by the doctor upstairs. Indeed, they were becoming loud enough to wake up the entire neighbourhood, he thought.

Suddenly she gasped, "I'm going to come. Don't stop. Don't stop." Then she burst into orgasm.

Her body quivered in the aftermath for several seconds. She settled back on the bed. Her eyes remained closed, her mouth agape, as she soaked up the most pleasurable experience. For Max, his first sexual experience with a woman had been wonderful. Sylvia quickly recovered.

"Now, my young Max, are you ready?"

He grew wide-eyed.

She sat up, straddled him and clasped his penis, guiding it to a place it had never been before. Warm, moist flesh enveloped his engorged member; it felt wonderful as she moved in a mechanical rhythmical motion.

"Do you like that?" she asked.

Max nodded but never spoke.

Because of inexperience, Max's pleasurable moments were short-lived. He reached orgasm early, but Sylvia wasn't disappointed. In fact she was thrilled about her new conquest. The thought of taking his virginity gave her a pleasant rush.

In the weeks that followed, she taught Max everything she knew. In that time they grew extremely comfortable with each other. He learnt how to control his orgasms and let go like her. They were both insatiable for sex. Max was tireless and as eager as a butcher's dog, and Sylvia took full advantage of his youthful virility.

His episode with Sylvia represented another major crossroad in his life. 'Sex in the bush, not in his hand' opened up his world to new awakenings.

After several bliss-filled months, their trysts came to an abrupt end when her husband returned from overseas. The sudden ending left Max feeling downcast and abandoned. On a visit to Greta, she asked him what was going on. When he confided in her about his secret 'affair' with Sylvia she was intrigued, and she couldn't help but relay what she'd been told in confidence to Marlene and Traudl.

They were impressed, and they looked at Max in a new light now that his virginity had been taken. Knowing he'd become sensually aware made flirting with him even more fun.

While learning about sex and sensuality from Sylvia, he never lost his enthusiasm for boxing. As part of his training programme he fought boys older than himself. This gave him a vast edge when it came to competitive bouts with boys of his own age in local tournaments.

Vogel supported and encouraged him towards gaining excellence in the sport. The relationship between the youth and mentor was truly one of friendship and it resulted in continuous growth for both of them.

Vogel's tutelage included imparting his experiences from the military. He taught Max about battle strategy, duty and loyalty. It was Vogel who first suggested that Max should join the army as an NCO. He judged Max to be perfect material for the job.

His vast knowledge of Eastern metaphysics and Western philosophy established him as a sage in its truest sense. He could find something lofty in almost any topic of discussion. On one hand, he could talk about love, and on the other, the art of war, power and control; and always his words had a meaningful spiritual connotation.

In one such discourse Vogel talked about 'spiritual physiology' and how clever orators are able to influence a collective mass of people. Vogel sat back in his leather armchair sipping a glass of cognac and opened up the conversation: "Stand yourself in front of the mirror, lad, and behold the mortal staring back."

Max looked at him quizzically.

"Go on – take a look at yourself," he urged.

Max stood up, walked across to the mirror and stared at his reflection.

"What do you see? A fleshy body? Yes, but look closer and use your spiritual eyes. I'll help you see more."

Vogel believed man to be comprised of several distinct sheaths or bodies.

"The first sheath is the one you see in the mirror – your physical body. The five senses – smell, touch, taste, sight and hearing – are the tools for its survival in this material world. The fleshy body is used as the vehicle for action, by deed or word. The five senses interact with the inner sheaths – those you cannot see with your material eyes.

"The second sheath serves as the vehicle for imagination, feeling and emotion. It is known as the astral body. Emotions are expressed through the physical body in a series of chemical reactions. Such chemical action determines what emotion will finally be acted out in the material world – love, hate, sadness, joy, guilt, fear, ecstasy or rage, to name a few. To demonstrate:

you've heard of the clichés 'good chemistry' or 'bad chemistry', to describe what happens when two people meet? Well, there's a lot of truth in this. Meeting people triggers a chain of chemical reactions within. Emotions are not part of the mind, as such. The two systems are separate, but they interact with each other, as I'll explain to you soon.

"The third sheath is literally a store for memories. It is often called the causal body. One engages this body when recalling a memory from the past. It is considered the lowest section of the mind.

"The mental body or conscious mind is the next sheath. It is a transmitter of thoughts and operates through the physical body by electrical impulses. It also reacts with the body's emotional relay system in the same manner. The outcome in the material world is simply an emotion that matches the quality of thought being transmitted. The cerebrospinal system is the organ of the conscious mind and is considered the middle section of the mind. The mental body is the channel through which we receive conscious perception from the five senses of the fleshy body, mentioned before. But the mind isn't capable of creating original thought; it needs the services of the soul to perform this function. If the mind becomes aberrant or perverted in one way or another, the condition will prevent the soul from creating original thought. The mind, by default, will draw upon its own reactive counterpart stored in its subconscious section, the fifth sheath – the storage place for the seed of all actions within man. We'll discuss the fifth sheath next, but not before I give you a couple of working examples of what I have just described.

"Take a fearful situation: if you react to whatever is generating the fear, the source for your action will not be from the soul but from the reactive part of the subconscious. On the other hand, if the fear is confronted and overcome, the original thoughts used in overcoming or controlling that fear would have been sourced from the soul (the sixth sheath).

"The same process applies to a habit. Repeating the habit is a default action drawn from the reactive subconscious. Overcoming that habit comes by way of fresh soul-generated thoughts.

"Hence an individual has a choice of adopting one of two mindsets: creative or reactive. I call the creative choice the mature mindset, where people exercise discrimination and are accountable for their actions. On the other hand, falling back on the reactive choice is immature and is typically seen in individuals who ignore discrimination and accountability; they become slaves to the alluring whispers of the subconscious mind.

"Creative or reactive, once the conscious mind has satisfied itself that the thought is true it is sent to the subjective mind – another part of the subconscious – to be brought into the world as reality. The conscious mind is merely a transmitter of what it receives.

"The subconscious mind is the fifth sheath, often called the etheric body. It is this part of the nature of man that orators, politicians and other influential speakers are interested in.

"Take another look in the mirror. The figure you see in front of you is the embodiment of every experience you have ever encountered – personal, incarnate or genetic, pending your religious or non-religious preference.

"The calibre and substance of your make-up – the way you view life – is absolutely unique, and it corresponds with the countless array of experiences amassed in the brain of the subjective mind, commonly known as the subconscious self.

"The subconscious is the source of all man's nightmares, fears, habits, all mental and emotional attachments gathered from previous experiences and instinctive forces. Whatever is contained in the subconscious self – good, bad or indifferent – paints your perspective of, and determines how you react to, everyday situations if you ignore choosing the purity of the soul for the basis of your discrimination."

Vogel viewed the mind as an obedient slave but a bad master when left to its own devices.

"That", he claimed, "is the difference between a mature mind (one steered by the soul) and an immature mind (one driven by the reactive whims of the subconscious).

"Now, let's get down to the art of controlling others. The reactive mind is the negativeness of the subconscious mind. It is also the source of primitive thought and the pleasure principle. A speaker will appeal directly to both these aspects. The greater the number of people amassed together, the more effective it is. With carefully chosen words, physical mannerisms and body language, the skilful politician can appeal to those forces hidden away in the subconscious, creating a wave of collective emotion that will overrule their intellects. Individuals will be hard-pressed to retain their individuality when a mass is acting as one; they abandon their free will and submit to the collective will. This is how it's done.

"To round off, the soul is the final sheath for man and it is the true spiritual part of the individual. It is a vehicle for love and utilises the mind as the instrument for making contact with the material world. The soul's job, when it is accessed at mind level, is to create original thought. Original thought replaces the default mode of the phantoms and demons, fears and guilts locked away in the reactive mind of the subconscious.

"Therefore, an individual operating from the soul is likely to handle any situation brought before him with love and maintain a degree of control. Individuals of this ilk are not what the politician seeks. But then, they are few and far between, and those who do achieve this lofty height usually choose not to interfere or participate in political or religious ventures anyway."

The dicourse ended just as old Vogel finished the last drop of his cognac. Max was mesmerised. He could have listened to Vogel all evening.

There were many such interludes. Vogel's other discourses took him on tours through Greek and Roman philosophy and Teutonic history, including the party doctrine of Aryan superiority.

The thought of a supreme, just race appealed to young Max,

and nobody could explain it quite like Vogel could. He was slow, exacting and precise in his deliberations and Max would always come away buzzing from tutorial sessions with his mentor.

BIBLIOGRAPHY

Kirstin Wilhelms: *Women's Journals in the Weimar Republic.*

Paul Twitchell: *Dialogues with the Master.* (1983.)

Paul Twitchell: *The Tiger's Fang.* (Illuminated Way Publishing 1988.)

Paul Twitchell: *Eckankar: The Key to Secret Worlds.* (1988.)

Paul Roland: *The Nazis and the Occult.* (Chartwell Books, 2007.)

8

BRAUN

1933: in December, life for Max took a dive when the ageing Vogel unexpectedly died. It was a heart attack, evidently triggered during a passionate night of sex with one of his teenage 'off-the-shelf' girlfriends.

An SA officer who obviously hadn't cared much for Vogel broke the news to Max at Vogel's apartment: "Rieker, your boss is dead. He keeled over having sex with one of his floozies at the Resi club last night. You'll have to pack your belongings and get out of here immediately." He had a smirk on his face.

Max stood in the doorway, unable to respond. They stood looking at each other for several seconds before the young officer broke the silence.

He barked impatiently, "Hear what I said, Rieker? You'll need to go now. We'll let you know if another opening comes up."

Max snapped out of his trance, and, under the watchful eye of the officer, he gathered his few belongings, stuffed them into a holdall and left Vogel's apartment for the last time. He made his way across the city back to Greta's place to inform her of Vogel's untimely death.

She could see he was still very upset and immediately reorganised the apartment to accommodate her distressed brother.

Vogel's funeral was a sad affair for Max. It was first time he had experienced the death of a close friend. His sending-off was carried out in military style and the salute was a single shot, denoting a fallen warrior. The funeral took place at the Alter Garnisonsfriedhof cemetery in Central Berlin, and Vogel was buried alongside other former Prussian officers. Max stood alone under a huge oak tree behind the group of prominenti gathered there. Joseph Goebbels attended for the party, and Ernst Röhm represented the SA. Most of the others were Vogel's old Great War associates.

The dreary day had reached a sub-zero temperature; it matched the mood of Max's young heart. His old friend was dead and he had no one to take his place. Vogel had been a father, teacher and comrade to him; he had treated Max as an equal, and Max had loved him for it. It proved difficult letting the old man go. When the ceremony finished he made his way out along a narrow gravel path that weaved back to the access road and entrance.

As usual Greta was there to steer him through his days of melancholy. Her support and Max's love for boxing helped overcome the grief for his old comrade.

During a boxing tournament not long after the funeral Max received instructions to present himself at the East Berlin faction of the Sturmabteilung, which was located in Holzmarkt close by Jannowitz U-Bahn. He checked in and an administrative officer informed him of an opening as aide to another senior SA official, Berti Braun.

Max was unaware that Braun had dumped his former aide when he learnt of his availability. Unlike Vogel, the avid womaniser, it was rumoured that Braun liked young boys more than he did women. He'd admired Max from afar.

Max recollected having seen Braun several times before and knew him as one of the SA's top leaders. The idea of acting as aide to a lesser man than Vogel depressed him for they'd shared a perfect relationship; nevertheless, he realised he had little choice in the matter if he wanted to remain in the limelight of the fast-growing NSDAP. The party had already been voted in to govern the country and it was soon to celebrate its first year of power – on 30 January.

The administrator emphasised that the offer would greatly enhance Max's chances of promotion once he became of age. Max accepted. The administrator appeared pleased and told Max he would get the opportunity to meet Braun before formally commencing duties.

Despite Braun's reputation, the meeting went relatively well. Braun appeared to listen to what Max had to say, but he cut the conversation short. Max, sensitive as he was, picked up on the man's ignorance, but swallowed his pride.

'Oh, what the hell, let's give it a try.'

Living with Braun was routine and mediocre compared with sharing life with Vogel. Braun snapped out orders in military style and Max responded in the same manner.

There were very clear differences between Vogel and Braun. Braun had no class, no finesse. He was ill-mannered and uncouth. Vogel had listened; Braun didn't. Vogel had given; Braun took.

Vogel's skill in dialectics wasn't a subtlety Braun possessed. He didn't have the skills to manipulate an adversary's words and logic in order to sway an argument back in his favour. But he did apply his own form of rationale, albeit in an immature way.

To get his way, Braun's strategy was to promote a different point in the hope that if he gained that, it would lead him to his real goal. He didn't wish his adversary to know about his real agenda until his objective had been achieved. Then, of course, it was too late. Had his adversary taken the time to dig a little deeper, he would have discovered Braun's real intentions. Vogel had taught Max about this immature behaviour, which he'd labelled 'emotional dishonesty', stating that it was harmful to the perpetrator.

Braun rarely thought ahead in order to support his statements; so if he saw he was losing an argument, he would fly into a rage and get what he wanted that way, assuming he outranked the person he had been arguing with.

He lacked humour. All he could offer was a form of sick mockery; it was not funny, but it made him chuckle with delight.

Vogel had been a connoisseur of the finest German and French wines, and he knew when to stop drinking; Braun didn't. He was a heavy drinker. He'd start with beer and move to schnapps when the evening wore on. When sober, Braun was an ignorant disciplinarian and came close to being tolerable; when he drank, he made Max nervous and edgy with his sexual innuendos.

He barked out orders and expected total loyalty without giving anything in return – not that Max wanted anything, apart from some recognition now and then. He became increasingly anxious during his first few weeks with Braun, but quickly began to pre-empt Braun's mood swings, managing to stay just a step or two in front of him. Braun caught on, and he decided Max was trying to outsmart him. The relationship then turned into a battle of wills, with Braun flying off the handle, shouting Max down and making demands that were plain stupid and vindictive – pettiness at its worst. It was abhorrent, as were Braun's lack of character and coarse mannerisms, all of which instilled in Max a deep and lasting revulsion for Braun and anyone else who behaved as he did.

Vogel had been tall and slim; Braun was big-boned and fat. He had the notion he would be able to use his aggression and size to force Max into offering sexual favours. Max, for his fifteen years, was slim but well built, muscular and athletic. It was his physique that had attracted Braun to him in the first place.

Several weeks into the arrangement, Braun made his first demand for sex. He'd returned to the apartment from a night out with colleagues. He had been drinking heavily. To Max's surprise, he opened up a pleasant conversation.

"How did the fight go, Max?" he asked, referring to a bout Max had fought recently.

"It went well. The fight was stopped halfway through the last round. My opponent's eye was cut – technical KO."

"Good, good. You fancy some schnapps?" Braun asked, offering the bottle and a shot glass.

Max declined: "No, thanks. If you haven't got anything for me to do, I'll get to sleep now."

"Yes, let's sleep together tonight. You must be sick of that sleeping bag," said Braun.

He went to take hold of Max's hand. Max recoiled sharply. He instantly felt sick and angry.

"Hey, I'm here to serve you and carry out your requests, Herr Braun, but loyalty to you does not extend to providing my body for sex. You can dismiss me and find someone else for this purpose if you wish, sir."

All the while his eyes bore into Braun's; he hoped his anger would compel Braun to finish with him and find a replacement. Braun was initially taken aback by Max's response, but in defence he roared out laughing.

"My, my! The boy can get angry. Do you want to fight me, eh?"

Braun lifted his fists and, in a mocking, skylarking way, shaped up in front of Max. He lunged with a punch, but Max simply avoided it. Braun laughed and made light of the matter, but he was seething inside.

At the end of his masquerade he smirked and muttered coldly, "Make no mistake, it's just a matter of time before your arse is mine, boy."

The challenge gave Braun a weird, sick rush. Unable to have Max, he fulfilled his sexual needs with other, 'cooperative', young boys who were too frightened to put up any resistance. He believed he could wear Max down and eventually have his way with him. In the meantime, other boys would do.

The following months saw Max fending off Braun's continuous hinting and manoeuvring for sex. Life became tedious. He leant on Greta, who provided him with balance and humour. She listened to him and became his relief valve. His only other escape was the Hitler Youth; even Braun fully endorsed his boxing programme. It was in the Hitler Youth that he became entirely focused, consumed in a world of boyhood, comradeship, dreams and ambition.

1934: on 30 June in this year, acting on Chancellor Hitler's orders, Ernst Röhm, the leader of the SA, convened a conference of its leadership at the Hanselbauer Hotel near Munich in the resort town of Bad Wiessee.

Most of those attending arrived the night before the conference and met up for food and some serious drinking. As the banquet was drawing to a close, Braun barked out an order for Max to return to the room and wait for him there.

On his way back, Max grabbed the opportunity to take in his surroundings. It was a sultry summer evening, and the grounds outside the hotel were tranquil. In an almost trance-like state he let the serenity pour over him as he pondered where his next experience in life might take him.

The answer to his thoughts just put out into the ether would come sooner than he expected. He returned to the room, after taking a roundabout route, in time to watch the sunset from the window. All felt pleasant and calm in the midsummer atmosphere of Wiessee.

Braun and other SA leaders drank into the early hours of the morning.

Just after dawn Braun barged into the room like an uncontrollable bull, startling Max, who had been sound asleep in his sleeping bag on the floor. Max became alarmed at the sight of three men. The two men accompanying Braun were Wolf Kugler and Bruno Burger. He sensed immediate danger as all three were raving drunk and the two men with Braun were leering at him. Max realised they must be perverts like Braun.

Kugler shouted, "Get out of that sleeping bag, lad!"

Max froze with fear. He did as ordered and stood in front of them in only his underpants.

Burger spoke: "That's a fine body you have there, boy."

Horrified, Max knew what they were there for. Braun was smirking. He knew Max stood no chance of defending himself against all three of them. His associates were also big men. He felt he had Max trapped.

"I told you I'd get my way, boy. Now, drop your pants and lie across the bed."

Max just stared at the mean-looking men.

He was fighting down his terror when Kugler, the biggest of the three, bellowed the command for a second time: "You heard Berti – do as you're told and take your pants off!"

Max bowed his head and shook it in defiance.

Kugler became enraged and barked, "Last chance, lad: take off your pants or prepare for the beating of your life. One way or the other, we'll get our satisfaction – the choice is yours."

Max stood there terrified but continued to shake his head.

"Let's see if this will change your mind."

Burger stepped forward and, with his huge hand, slapped Max hard across the face. The impact threw Max across the bed. Burger jerked him back up on to his feet and lifted his hand, preparing to throw a second slap. This time Max was prepared. He clasped his hands and, as Burger swung, blocked most of the impact with his arms. His eyes grilled into Burger's defiantly. Surprised by the effective block and insulted by Max's insolence, Burger stepped back and came in with a fierce kick to the shin. Max fell to the floor in agony, holding his leg.

Unperturbed by his cries of pain, demands were spat out for a third time. Max couldn't acknowledge them but just rolled on the floor in agony. Kugler came over, rolled his hand into a fist and punched him hard in the face. Max lay on the floor with blood seeping from his mouth. Braun, taking advantage of the numbers, pulled Max back on to his feet, then, while pretending to help him, suddenly headbutted him squarely across the top of the nose.

"Nice one, Berti!" said Kugler.

Max fell back on the bed, only semi-conscious, as his nose burst with blood.

"Let's work him over a bit more and I'll get rid of him tomorrow," said Braun.

Just as they were about to beat Max half to death, the door crashed open. The three men simultaneously looked up in surprise and stepped away from Max, diverting their attention to the intruders.

Standing in front of them were two huge helmeted men in black uniforms holding Lugers ready to shoot. They ordered the SA men to raise their hands and back up against the wall.

"What are you doing to this boy?" one of the gunmen asked.

"He's been insubordinate," replied Braun.

"Stand up, clean yourself up and get dressed, boy!" commanded the other gunman.

Max, hardly comprehending, staggered into the bathroom. A crimson trail ran down his face on to his chest.

With their attention refocused on the SA drunks, they demanded to know their names. Once identified, they took aim and shot the three down in cold blood, calling them homos and traitors to the Fatherland.

Max heard the shots and the sound of the three men slumping to the floor. He emerged from the bathroom. All three were twitching in their final death throes. He stood there in disbelief and looked down at Braun. A thin dribble of blood was seeping from his mouth.

"Why? Why?" mouthed Braun as he gasped his final breath.

It was an execution – Max's first experience of violent death. The shock ran through him like a chemical chain reaction. In disbelief he struggled to make sense of the macabre scene before him.

His attention was suddenly diverted when one of the gunmen stepped across the room to check the bodies. Burger was still gasping for breath, so the gunman fired another bullet into his head.

Looking up at the other gunman, he said, "They were resisting arrest, weren't they? Look, this one drew his weapon."

To cover up the murderous act, he took out the Luger from the dead man's holster and wrapped it in his hand.

Max's nightmare resumed as the gunmen switched their attention to him. He thought his life was about to end. Blood was still dripping from his nose on to his chest.

"Finish cleaning up, boy, and get dressed at the double!" ordered one of the gunmen. "Let's get out of here."

Relieved they hadn't shot him on the spot, Max's mind was still racing, fearing what might become of him. He dressed and eventually managed to stop the blood flowing from his nose. As they left the hotel room, one of the black-shirted assassins cursed their victims again. They holstered their Lugers and began talking as if nothing had happened.

Max discovered they both held the rank of sergeant.

One spoke to him: "Why were they beating you, boy?"

"I was Braun's aide. I was at his beck and call, but my loyalties didn't extend to gratifying him or his associates with sexual privileges. They were in the middle of giving me a serious beating just before you came into the room. Braun said he would throw me out on the street once they'd finished. I appreciate your timely interruption."

They smiled. He realised that their mission had been to kill the senior SA officers, not any accompanying youngsters.

Outside in the street black-shirted gunmen were everywhere. The scene was wild and noisy – whistles were blowing – but there were no sounds of concentrated gunfire, just the odd shot now and again. At one point, a group of SA officers were scrambled out of the building and bundled into an awaiting troop carrier. Once aboard, the luckless band was taken away to a nearby establishment for interrogation and possible summary execution.

Max was directed to a carrier where other young aides had been rounded up and were already seated inside. They spoke softly together in a huddled group, unsure what their fate might be at the hands of the Blackshirts.

That morning all SA leaders staying at the hotel, including their boss, Ernst Röhm, were either arrested or killed. Those known to be homosexual had been shot on the spot. They were just a few of the victims of a purge that became known as the Night of the Long Knives.

The Night of the Long Knives took place from 30 June to 2 July 1934. It was the elimination of the SA leadership together with some of Hitler's other political opponents.

Hitler had come under pressure to control Röhm and reduce his influence. But Röhm had secured army funds during the early days of the Nazi movement and Hitler was fond of him. To break the bond, Himmler manufactured evidence against Röhm, presented it to Hitler and convinced him that Röhm intended to use the SA to overthrow him. Röhm was invited to take his own life. He refused and was shot in his prison cell.

The Night of the Long Knives resulted in the de-escalation of SA power. It became expendable. A new leader, Victor Lutze, was elected as Ernst Röhm's replacement, but, unlike Röhm, he was weak. His leadership accelerated the decline of the SA and brought the Brownshirt era to an end.

On 26 July 1934 the SS, previously linked to the SA structure, was separated from the SA with Himmler as its Reichsführer, answerable only to Hitler.

9

BLACKSHIRT-SS

As the truck sped away from Wiessee towards an unknown destination, two thoughts ran through Max's mind: 'What will become of me?' and 'Who are the soldiers in the black shirts?' These men differed from the Brownshirts; they appeared to be highly disciplined as well as physically fearsome to look at.

Two massive armed guards were positioned either side at the tailgate end of the truck. They sat bolt upright. Before the truck set off, they'd ordered the boys to assume similar positions and not to talk. Max remained uneasy despite having formed a connection with one of the gunmen back in the hotel room.

He turned his head to look around, but one of the guards shouted across, "Keep your eyes to the front, boy!"

Max quickly did what he was told and settled for losing himself in his racing thoughts, reflecting on what had just happened at the hotel.

Several kilometres into the journey one of the guards broke the silence. As if in telepathic response to one of Max's earlier thoughts, he introduced his unit: "I suppose you're all wondering who we are, eh? We are members of the Armed-SS. SS is short for Schutzstaffel. The name of our regiment is Leibstandarte and our commanding officer is Josef 'Sepp' Dietrich. We are the bodyguard regiment for the Chancellor, Adolf Hitler. Our job is to protect our beloved Chancellor from anybody who would threaten his welfare, just like the treacherous scum we have just gathered up."

The boys listened in awe.

After that short introduction the guard stopped talking and assumed his original position.

Max felt a little more positive about the likely outcome of the morning until one of the boys nervously cried out, "Will you shoot us?"

The other guard reacted swiftly: he leapt up, leant over and slapped the boy across the face, bellowing, "Be silent, and keep your eyes to the front!"

Despite his chequered experiences, Max convinced himself that he and the other boys were not destined for grisly ends. Thinking back, he blessed the beating he'd received from the SA men just before the gunmen had kicked in the hotel door. Giving in to their demands would have placed him in a compromising position, and he might have shared their fate.

It was a long journey all day, into the night and through to the early hours of the following morning. The summer heat picked up early to penetrate the canvas-covered roof, causing all inside to sweat freely. The truck, it was revealed, was bound for Berlin, and it entered its southern suburbs around nine o'clock. Its destination was just short of the city centre.

They arrived at Lichterfelde Kaserne, the headquarters of Hitler's personal bodyguard: Leibstandarte. Its previous function had been that of a Prussian cadet training school. The massive entrance gates opened on to a vast parade ground, where several squads of black-shirted soldiers were practising parade-ground drill.

The truck ground to a halt outside the main headquarters building. The tailgate swung down and the two guards leapt out.

"Right, all out!" a guard shouted. "Line up and stand to attention over there!" He pointed to a spot on the footpath.

Max jumped down from the rear of the truck, stretched and looked across the vast parade ground in wonderment. A huge stone eagle adorned the parapet of the roof of the main building. Three flagpoles were housed behind the eagle, each flying the national flag with the party's swastika emblem. The flags gently flapped in a warm morning breeze. It was one of those moments that Max never forgot for the rest of his life.

Max's brief spiritual excursion was rudely interrupted when a guard pointed to him, and snapped the order: "You, line up at the end of the row!"

Earlier, in 1933, shortly after Hitler came to power as Chancellor of the Reich, Sepp Dietrich formed the first headquarters guard of loyal SS men titled SS-Stabswache Berlin. It acted as a 'praetorian guard' responsible for protecting Adolf Hitler. The unit comprised 120 of the most capable and trustworthy men, all personally picked by Sepp. By the end of May, this first bodyguard unit was renamed SS-Sonderkommando Zossen. A few months later, a second unit of 120 men, SS-Sonderkommando Jüterbog, was formed.

In September 1933, the two Sonderkommando special detachment units merged to become SS-Sonderkommando Berlin. This single unit soon grew and by November was 800-strong. It was given its first colours and a new name: Leibstandarte Adolf Hitler (LAH). All members swore personal allegiance to Hitler, which set the unit apart from other Armed-SS units.

In early 1934, Himmler ordered that Leibstandarte be renamed Leibstandarte-SS Adolf Hitler (LSSAH).

Max had witnessed Leibstandarte's very first action: the Night of the Long Knives.

A second lieutenant came out from the building to collect the boys standing to attention. Most of them were Hitler Youth members and were well trained.

He addressed them: "Welcome to Lichterfelde Kaserne, the home of Leibstandarte-SS Adolf Hitler, named after our glorious Chancellor. Count off, stating your names and ages."

There were twelve of them, ranging in age from twelve to fifteen years. Max was one of the eldest and biggest, so he was picked out to lead them around the perimeter of the parade ground to a building where the mess hall was located. The officer accompanying them scrutinised each of the boys as they marched along.

On his way around, Max observed several squads of soldiers conscientiously and meticulously practising their parade-ground drill. The precision and quality of the soldiering made an indelible impression on his mind.

The column stopped outside the mess hall.

"At ease. Follow me!" barked the officer.

They followed him into the building.

After a hot meal they were led to an administrative area to undergo questioning. The youths were split into three groups of four. Max was in the eldest group. He struck up a conversation with the boy seated next to him, who introduced himself as Fritz Kohler.

Each youth was called out separately for questioning. Max patiently waited his turn, wondering what form the interrogation would take. At last a guard appeared and called out his name. Max jumped to his feet.

"Follow me!" barked the guard.

He was led around the corridor to a large, glossy black door. The guard knocked and a voice from inside shouted, "Enter!" He opened the door, motioning Max to enter, then closed it and remained outside.

Inside, three stern-faced officers wearing smart black uniforms were seated behind a long mahogany table. Max walked in and stood to attention about three metres from the table, anxiously awaiting their questions.

There in front of the officers stood a youth who showed signs of a recent battering. He had a huge swelling at the bridge of his nose. His lip was thickened and his face was bruised and disfigured from the beating. He also had a slight limp from the kick he'd received.

"Where did you get those injuries, Rieker? Did you resist arrest?"

"No, sir, I didn't resist arrest. Three SA men were beating me because I refused their demands for sex. They were all homosexuals and very drunk, sir." He explained his story much as he had to the gunmen at the hotel the previous morning.

The three officers looked at one another knowingly and one commended him for showing defiance under pressure. Max shifted his body slightly and squared his shoulders in response. The approval of his actions coming from the panel was encouraging.

"You're a big, fit-looking lad for your age. Do you take part in any sport, Rieker?" asked another officer.

"Yes, sir. I'm a member of the Hitler Youth. My sport is boxing and I'm good at it, sir."

They smiled at one another, pleased with the enthusiasm of the naive youth.

"Very commendable, Rieker," one of the officers replied.

With introductions over, more serious questions were levelled at him. Max explained that he had been orphaned when he was a baby. His only kin was a sister, Greta, who was an active member of the party. He told them how he became involved with SA as an aide for Michael Vogel, then Berti Braun. In his description of Vogel, he emphasised that Vogel had recommended he join the army and train to be an NCO.

The final remark was connected with the Vogel comment and surprised Max when the leading officer asked, "Would you like to be a member of Leibstandarte, Rieker?"

Max broke out into a wide smile. "I would love to be a member of our Chancellor's personal unit, sir."

"OK, Rieker, you can leave now. Go and sit down and we'll call you back later."

He left the room and returned to his seat, very happy. Fritz Kohler was up next.

An hour later, Max was called back. The walk to the glossy black door was an anxious one: he knew that, beyond it, his destiny was about to be decided for him. The air became electric as he stood to attention, awaiting the result of the officers' deliberations.

"Well, Rieker, your record is praiseworthy for a lad of such a young age. You're well connected; your sister, Greta, works for the party; Vogel and Braun were prominent figures of the SA; your health, sporting record, physique and height – all these things make you a prime candidate for the Armed-SS."

"We'll sign you up as a nominee for Leibstandarte. You'll continue your time with the Hitler Youth until you are eighteen. There you will participate in the major programmes and activities. Short term, you will remain here at the barracks helping out. We'll think about a posting for you for the interim period, until you become of age."

"Now, go back to your seat. Someone will come to collect you and get the paperwork done."

"Yes, sir," Max replied excitedly.

He went back to his seat elated, gasping in wonder at his good fortune. Realising he'd reached a major crossroad in his life, he savoured the accomplishment in his mind over and over again.

Several minutes later an officer directed him to another office, where an administrative NCO filled in the paperwork that established him as a nominee.

Of the twelve detained youths, ten were regular Hitler Youth, and two were homeless, picked up off the streets by the SA perverts. Only Max and his newly found friend, Fritz Kohler, were retained at Lichterfelde.

The under-age issue – Max and Fritz were a little over two years short – had posed a problem for the seniors who'd seen the boys' potential. After several days, a plan was agreed to cover the first year: the boys were to be seconded to the women's detention centre in the town of Moringen. There they could work and learn to take orders during the weekdays and continue their sporting and indoctrination activities with the local faction of the Hitler Youth in the evenings and at weekends. Meantime, they remained at Lichterfelde until their transfer.

At the barracks the boys adapted to army life quickly. Despite most of the jobs being just mundane chores, they never complained and carried them out with verve and enthusiasm. It was all new and exciting – they had discovered themselves. They'd arrived at the barracks with only the clothes they stood in, but once they were in uniform, as junior as they were, it felt as if they had been accepted into the finest unit in the nation.

Following an induction programme, the boys were issued a long-weekend pass to visit family or friends, to catch up and inform them of what was happening. Max was looking forward to seeing Greta. She was an attractive twenty-year-old confident career woman. Despite her elevation in status, she was still the same loving sister and she still doted on her younger brother.

He updated her on his adventures: how he'd witnessed the action at the Wiessee resort and had been grabbed by the SS and taken to Lichterfelde.

Recent events had also affected Greta, but she was pleased to hear the SA had been brought under control. In her opinion, "The purge represented a new way forward for the party."

The long weekend went well. They had cemented their ties and Greta realised Max was quickly growing up.

In recognition for its actions during the Night of the Long Knives, Leibstandarte was expanded to regimental size and upgraded to a motorised unit. Sepp Dietrich was promoted to SS Obergruppenführer, equivalent to a German Army general.

On 2 August that year, the ageing President Hindenburg died. Hitler assumed his vacant role and combined the offices of Chancellor with President, and he declared himself Führer.

In September 1934, the boys were transferred to Moringen Detention Centre. Moringen is a small town in the southern part of the federal state of Lower Saxony, about 100 kilometres south of Hanover. The detention centre was located in the middle of the town and was first used in October 1933. It held approximately 1,350 women from all over Germany. Their offences ranged from being members of labour movements to being social democrats, communists or prostitutes. They were detained for 'defamation of the state'.

Detention-centre life was hard. The senior SS guards dished out punishments and scolded the detainees on a daily basis. Roll-calls were repetitive and acted as an additional form of punishment. The boys did not take an active role in the punishment crews; instead they were placed under the keen eye of the deputy detention-centre commander, Max Gebhard, who was a friendly sort, considering the position he held. Gebhard wanted the boys to attend interrogations and get a feel of what types of character the party considered enemies of the state. Their job was to observe detainees while they were under interrogation, and then provide an appraisal.

Max excelled at this particular task. He discovered that he could instinctively detect when a person was holding back or lying. Gebhard noticed his talents and before long had him compiling formal assessments.

Extreme torture techniques weren't practised at Moringen, but some overzealous seniors were capable of frightening women into disclosing information, if they had information to disclose.

Max was surprised to discover that the most callous guards appeared to be the females. He soon worked out that cruelty ran parallel with a lack of humour. The cruel ones exuded a seriousness that often culminated in intense fits of rage. The ability to control others using fear and punishment as tools gave them a heightened sense of power and satisfaction. Max's insight into human character was growing by the day.

Fritz, on the other hand, was more practical. He eventually diversified, assisting maintenance and repair crews.

During the time spent at Moringen their friendship strengthened. They were often together. Red-blooded lads, they always found ways to bring excitement and adventure into their lives. Many of the women held in custody were attractive and in some cases their attractiveness was irresistible.

"Did you see the new batch of detainees that arrived this afternoon, Fritz?"

"Yes, most of them were attractive, weren't they? Which block have they been assigned to?"

"B Block, I think."

"That's my block tonight," said Fritz.

"Lucky bastard!" said Max.

"You'll get your turn tomorrow," replied Fritz.

The boys had devised a challenge; it was a competition between the two – a way of getting a cheap thrill. Under cover of darkness, they would slip over to the women's quarters to go 'peeping Tom', hoping to catch a view of the women in their underwear or undressed.

They adapted the Olympic Games medal system: a woman spotted in her underwear scored a bronze; bare breasts scored silver; and a naked crotch scored gold. At the end of the night they would meet up and compare medal tallies.

One evening, Max's game went off beam when one of the women caught him peering through the gauzy curtaining pulled across the window. She screamed and jumped away in fright. Then, realising that he was just one of the youths, she stepped forward and swore at him, calling him a little pervert. Max scuttled off into the darkness, totally embarrassed about the whole thing.

Later he met up with Fritz and told him how he'd been caught out. Fritz rocked with laughter. But Max, still smarting from the humiliation of it all, announced his immediate retirement from the voyeur business. He was afraid that if the incident were to get back to Gebhard, it might jeopardise his nomination for Leibstandarte. Fritz, recovering from his bout of hilarity, agreed with Max and reminded him that he'd won the contest that evening.

However, the decision to clean up their nightly antics was to be eclipsed by a new adventure created by the adults. It was rumoured that members of male and female staff were having sex with some of the female inmates. This seemed to be the height of hypocrisy, considering some inmates had been detained for prostituting themselves outside.

Both boys were handsome, beyond their years and likeable. The women detainees saw them as the bright-faced youths who did not pose a threat – unlike most of the adult staff.

Shortly after the peeping-Tom incident, one detainee kicked off a caper that would keep Max and Fritz busy after nightfall. She was wealthy, with an eye for young boys. It wasn't hard to bribe a guard to arrange for meeting up with the boys: he got his compensation, she got her satisfaction; and the boys had the time of their lives. News quickly spread, and several other guards discovered they could make money selling the boys' services to the richer female detainees. Their services didn't stop with detainees: they soon extended to some of the female staff running the centre – those that weren't lesbian, that is.

For all involved, the brief interlude offered much needed relief from the severity of discipline. Max had relinquished himself of his peeping-Tom reputation, and, to his delight, had become known as one of the 'young studs of Moringen', as was Fritz.

The plight of those detained went over their heads. Detained women were forbidden to converse with their overseers, except when compelled to answer questions. Indeed, they weren't allowed to talk to one another except during rest periods, meals and at the end of the day before lights-out. Despite the silence ruling, the boys would sometimes acknowledge those they'd 'serviced', if there was no one around to report them. The women were usually too frightened to break the ruling, but they sometimes acknowledged the boys by the subtle use of body language. The boys' youthfulness protected them, allowing them to get away with what would not be tolerated once they reached the age of eighteen years.

1935: in August, their days at Moringen Detention Centre came to an abrupt end. Regular reports about their progress had been sent back to Leibstandarte at the Berlin Lichterfelde HQ. The boys were to be transferred to the Dachau concentration camp. They would remain there until their eighteenth birthdays, when they would rejoin the unit in Berlin. They were soon to find out that the strict disciplinary practices carried out in Moringen were nothing compared to what went on in Dachau.

However, before we turn to Dachau another episode is worthy of mention – a caper Max and Fritz were involved in during their senior years in the Hitler Youth, while they still saw the world through the rose-coloured glasses of youth.

BIBLIOGRAPHY

Rupert Butler: *SS-Leibstandarte: The History of the First SS Division, 1933–1945,* pp. 9–21. (MBI Publishing Company, 2001.)

Heinz Hohne: *The Order of the Death's Head.* (Penguin Books.)

Robert Lewis Koehl: *The Black Corps: The Structure and Power Struggles of the Nazi SS.* (Madison, 1983.)

10

HITLER YOUTH

Youth organisations always played an important part in German society. Formed from various bodies, such as church organisations, political parties and non-sectarian groups, comradeship and healthy exercise were always part of their appeal. The largest and the most successful by far was the Hitler Youth.

Max loved his time in the Hitler Youth. His senior years in the movement covered 1935 and 1936, the year Berlin hosted the Olympic Games. They were the happiest times of his life. Here he developed a strong sense of comradeship with the other boys while taking part in the activities he most enjoyed, such as boxing and athletics, war games, marching and singing.

Competition was encouraged in the Hitler Youth. Every year a contest was held to find the best sportsmen in the Reich at boxing and other athletic events. In 1936 Max took part in the boxing competition.

The war games were also competitive, and they were arranged and monitored by army officers. Hitler Youth units competed against one another, and – the ultimate challenge – against regular soldiers.

Marching was used as a means of endurance training. There were short marches lasting thirty-six hours, and long marches lasting at least a month. The long marches took in sites of historic significance; they served as rehearsals for entry into enemy-occupied territories.

The concept of Aryans as 'the pure race' was promoted as

114

an essential subject for study. The party's aim was twofold: to introduce the Hitler Youth to the concept of a master race and Aryan superiority and to inculcate the view that communists, social democrats, Jews, gypsies, and other 'undesirable' groups were destructive forces. Max loved the history behind the theory and the classical references that supported it; the idea of the gods descending into the physical world and the concept of a master race appealed to his youthful ego.

The highlight for the Hitler Youth each year involved a march to Nuremberg to attend the rally there. The first Nuremberg Rally was held in 1928, when only 600 boys participated. By 1936 the number attending the rally had increased to 50,000. Hitler would address them directly, inviting the eighteen-year-olds to join the party and enrol in the SS, Gestapo or any other section they might be eligible for.

Max's leadership skills developed during the time he spent in the Hitler Youth. By his seventeenth birthday he had become powerfully built. His boxing skills had won him the respect of his subordinates, while his ability to think on his feet and interpret orders intelligently had earned him the respect of his peers and seniors. His steadfast loyalty to all marked him as good NCO material.

Signs of forthcoming maturity, however, hadn't dampened his zeal for life. It was never as abundant as when he and several of his comrades took part in an event jointly organised by the army and the movement during his first senior year in late 1935. The event promised several weeks of adventure and challenge, beginning in Berlin and finishing up in Bavaria, Southern Germany, where it was to culminate in war games. The winning team would be given a chance to have a crack at the regular army boys.

The Berlin legion totalled some 400 boys. It was split into four company-strength groups. For competitive purposes each group was designated a company colour: red, blue, green and white.

Each company left Berlin from a different starting point. The leaders were supplied with route maps and coordinates, and it was their job to get their company to the Bavarian military camp in the shortest time. An added challenge came in the form of picking up various pieces of hardware on the way. Coordinates and clues were laid out, and the pieces of hardware represented military objectives. Points for each company were accrued in accordance with the number of objectives achieved and the overall time taken to reach the military camp.

Max and Fritz were among seven youths to lead Company Blue down to the Bavarian military camp. Competition on the way down was demanding, and it brought out the best in the youths. All four teams arrived within several hours of one another.

The following morning the entire legion was made to assemble in the yard for reveille and an induction briefing. The legion then separated into its companies to undergo further training. Each company was split into two units and instructions were given to each: Red Unit 1, for instance, was instructed on 'How not to be seen' (the art of concealment) and 'How to assault' (the art of movement and mobility), while Red Unit 2 was instructed on 'How to observe and defend a position'. On the first day, regular army instructors walked the boys through the tough routines.

Over the next three days companies were put to task testing their skills in competition with one another. The winning company was informed it would get a chance to challenge the army regulars. Their objective would be to infiltrate defences and gain access to a mock 'Army HQ' without being observed by its defenders.

Army HQ was the ruins of an old medieval churchyard located on a steep mount overlooking a small village several kilometres from the camp. A bell tower was the only structure that remained intact. The churchyard was surrounded by a low stone wall. A graveyard outside the wall flanked half the churchyard's perimeter. Gaining access into the churchyard undetected would be considered a victory over the army, but the attackers' ultimate goal was to lower the national flag flying atop the bell tower.

The winning team had twenty-four hours to plan its attack,

then a further twenty-four hours to achieve its objective.

There were three ways of infiltration: first, up an escarpment at the rear (the most risky but the least defended); secondly, by way of a forested area (the trees came down to one edge of the cemetery); and thirdly, by a frontal approach across fields, using the cover of a crop of wheat, not yet harvested, or along a narrow road leading up from the village.

The army's job was to stop the boys from penetrating their defences. Elimination was simply by observation – by calling out the number pinned to the back and chest of a youth's overgarment. Nightfall would make it difficult for the defenders, when identification would have to be effected by torchlight. Those totally undetectable could remain in the game, but they needed to achieve the objective within the twenty-four-hour window.

Being more experienced, the army defenders held the upper hand. They knew they could use the inexperience of the boys to their advantage. Moreover, those deployed outside the churchyard would be camouflaged, which would make it difficult for the boys to evade them.

The winners of the original competition were Company Blue, and two of its leaders, Max and Fritz, were as keen as mustard to get one over on the army regulars.

Planning day had arrived and was utilised for working on strategies. In the early morning a group of boys had gathered to talk tactics.

Max surprised everyone there by suggesting a deviation from the rules: "We could catch the army boys off guard if we sent a small detachment ahead of time, before they set up position at the churchyard Army HQ."

"Deployment before the scheduled start time is forbidden. It will be considered as cheating," said Franz Huttner, one of the other leaders.

"Yes, but the thought of it," added Fritz – "getting one over on the army! Wouldn't it make you feel good? Besides, they wouldn't know we cheated, if we can pull it off."

"I'm all for it," added Hans Muller.

"Me too – a great idea," chimed in Gunter Schnell.

"Sounds good to me, then. Let's have some fun. What do you say, Franz?" Max said, looking across to Huttner.

"That's OK, but we'll all need to be present after reveille in the morning – thought about that?" Huttner added.

"Four from 100 or so wouldn't be missed; besides, the entire legion will be lined up. Company Blue will line up behind Company Red and we'll all take to the trucks straight after. The only difference from any other day will be that our company will be dressed up for the competition. It shouldn't present a problem. So who's in? Fritz?"

"Yes, I'm in."

Muller and Gunter volunteered to make up the foursome.

"So, what's your plan, *Kameraden*? How would you make a break from here – leave through the front gate?" said Huttner sarcastically.

"We'll leave tonight from the rear of the camp, under cover of darkness. Lights-out and curfew might present a problem, so we may need to set up a diversion to ensure our breakout goes smoothly, without being discovered."

"Diversion?" Huttner quizzed.

"Our sleeper block is of simple construction, built from timber studding with weatherboards on the outside and timber panelling on the inside. It should be possible to free up the panels on the inside and loosen the weatherboards on the outside during the day without being noticed. We can replace the weatherboards loosely, ready for the break tonight. This will ensure the swift exit we need in order to leave the camp without being spotted. The perimeter wall surrounding the camp won't present a problem – it's not as if it's electrified," said Fritz.

"But the diversion – what will it be? This won't be easy to pull off. The sleeping blocks are under surveillance by camp guards all through the night. It's like a concentration camp here."

Schnell offered a solution: "Well, curfew begins with lights-out. Our other block can assist by breaking the curfew in one way or another. Diverting attention on to the other block should provide us with the short time we need to make an exit unnoticed."

"Sounds good!" agreed Muller.

"Is that good enough for you, Franz?" said Max. "Assuming the break goes well, once outside we can move on to the churchyard under cover of darkness and gain access to the bell tower before the regulars arrive. We'll hide up in the bell tower all through the day into the following night and lower the flag when it's still dark, before dawn breaks."

"If we could slip back out without being discovered, and bring the flag back with us, that would really rub it in, eh?" said an excited Fritz.

Muller spoke, "Schnelly, you've lots of money. Get over to the quartermaster's store and 'buy' four sets of regular army uniforms; we may need them if we encounter any army defenders in the churchyard on our way out."

Gunter agreed.

Taking a bribe from a wealthy youth wasn't hard, and the quartermaster's assistant handed over the uniforms without hesitation.

The boys were aware that no Hitler Youth company had previously been successful in the competition; achievement would mean an entry into the record books. Previous success in defending had made the army smugly confident, but they would remain as vigilant as ever. They were about to find themselves totally unprepared for the caper about to be launched, however, as were the four youths taking part in the deception.

All the preparatory work went well during the day, including consolidating the plan for the diversion.

That evening, just before lights-out, Max, Fritz, Gunter and Muller dressed in full kit, packed their rations and army uniforms, then quietly began displacing the loose panels. They exposed the timber weatherboards and waited. Two hours after dusk, one youth from the other sleeping block broke the curfew.

The diversion worked well. A youth was caught smoking outside. A duty guard and his dog discovered him, and the dog's fierce barking raised the alarm. Most of the duty guards rushed to the source of the commotion.

Within seconds Max and the other three youths were on the outside of their block. Max, the last to leave, replaced the loose weatherboards, then he disappeared over the wall to join the others. Silently, they slapped each other's backs, congratulating themselves for the smooth breakout; then they slipped away into the night towards their objective.

Army HQ was about six kilometres away. Initially they would need to circumvent the village close by the camp to avoid bumping into any of the staff. Their route would take them up the road for several kilometres before they branched off into the forested area to come up through the cemetery, into the churchyard then into the bell tower. There they would wait throughout the day; and they would lower the flag before dawn the following morning, under the cloak of darkness.

They circled the village and trotted up the road at a steady pace. Only one vehicle disturbed them: it was a speeding limousine. As it approached, its headlights lit up the sky and all four boys dived for cover into the shallow ditch running parallel with the road. Once it had passed, they dusted themselves off and continued on their way.

They needed some good orienteering skills to find their way through the forest in pitch darkness with only finger torches to assist them, but they had been well trained and they made their way slowly through the trees towards the cemetery.

When the cemetery came into view they stopped short and settled down in the darkness to regroup and consider whether any changes of plan would be needed. All that remained was the apparently simple manoeuvre of crossing the cemetery, slipping over the wall and hiding up in the bell tower before the army arrived to prepare their defences.

Suddenly the sound of a convoy of trucks filled the night air. To their astonishment, it was the army: they were moving up into the churchyard earlier than expected. The boys grew wide-eyed at the scene unfolding before them. The following hour was taken up with frantic preparatory work by the army; searchlights were installed, and a small base camp was being erected.

'These boys are serious,' thought Max.

They all looked on in surprise, feeling uneasy as the soldiers busied themselves.

"Change of plan, eh, *Kameraden*? We'll have to settle back here and pick our time when to make our move," Muller said.

"They'll be deploying some men into this area at daybreak to prepare to eliminate boys from the attacking force choosing this approach," added Schnell.

"We'll have to find spots that are well hidden; otherwise they'll catch us before we've even got off the ground," Fritz quipped.

"Damn!" cursed Max. "First glitch, eh!"

A heavy downpour greeted the camp the next morning. It proved advantageous in the line-ups and reveille went without mishap; the boys appeared to have got away with it.

Alas! as Company Blue made their way out to load up the troop carriers, one of the officers, Heinz Krehl, decided to perform a mental check of the men filing past him. Although he wasn't endowed with a photographic memory, Krehl felt a tug of suspicion when they'd finished loading up. Something didn't add up; he searched his memory for a face or two that he thought belonged to Company Blue. But was he confusing this with the other companies?

Krehl hurried along to the leading truck, slapped on the door and ordered the driver to turn off his engine.

"I need these boys to get out and line up in two rows, along here."

The driver looked at him quizzically. Outside the trucks they mustered in two neat lines.

"All leaders step forward," barked Krehl.

It was about this time that Franz Huttner's heart dropped.

'Good God!' he thought. 'The lid is off our caper.'

Only five of seven leaders stepped forward (at the time, Muller and Schnell weren't part of Company Blue's leadership).

"Not quite the number we're looking for, is it?" Krehl remarked, eyeing the remaining sheepish-looking leaders.

"You – what's your name?" he barked, pointing to Huttner.

"Franz Huttner, sir."

"Huttner, where is the rest of your leadership?"

Franz froze at the question and stuttered an almost inaudible, "Not sure, sir."

"What was that, Huttner? You're not sure?" Krehl bellowed. "Do you think this is funny, Huttner?"

Huttner winced. "No, sir, I don't think it's funny, sir."

Krehl turned to the NCO standing nearby: "Staff Sergeant, sound the alarm and get these boys back inside and lined up in the yard for questioning."

Refocusing his anger on the forlorn leadership standing to attention, he growled, "You boys, come with me!"

They were marched into the administrative building for detailed questioning, which quickly turned into an interrogation. They were threatened with severe disciplinary action if they did not reveal all. As the sense of adventure drained from their faces, the boys quickly folded and revealed the entire plan.

The unit garrisoned at the churchyard were informed of the deception by radio. In minutes, the place was a hive of activity; the sounds of whistles and sirens filled the air. The churchyard and bell tower was teeming with soldiers looking for the missing boys.

The boys heard the commotion from their forest hideouts and deduced, by the sudden change in tempo, that the caper must have been uncovered back at camp.

"Now we're for it," Schnell muttered.

"What's Maxy boy going to do now?" remarked Muller, a little disconcerted.

Max stayed silent.

Meanwhile, the army was momentarily perplexed. The boys weren't hiding up in the bell tower. Could they have had a change of heart? Were they waiting for the main force to catch up? The consensus of opinion was that the army's early arrival had dashed any hope the youths had of accessing the bell tower before they had a chance to set up.

The garrison used loudspeakers, naming the boys and threatening severe disciplinary action should they not turn themselves in immediately.

'Things must have gone horribly wrong back at camp,' thought Max.

They remained in their covert positions, but they were wavering. As the competition had been called off, they wondered if their stubbornness was just a waste of time. They knew they could expect disciplinary action, which could affect their Leibstandarte nominee status – something they had not considered in their zeal to get one over on the army.

Several hours passed, and the senior staff were spitting nails, surprised that the boys had not given up or been captured. They held a meeting and agreed that if the boys had not given up by noon, the search would be called off and a second bulletin would be issued announcing reinstatement of the original challenge. The decision was based upon their belief that the boys wouldn't stand a chance of achieving their objective anyway.

The boys were well hidden in the forest about thirty metres from the edge of the cemetery. They'd all managed to avoid detection, despite a vigorous search carried out by a unit from the churchyard garrison before the challenge was re-established. At one point, live ammunition was fired over their heads, and a number of hand grenades were detonated near the edge of the forest in an attempt to scare the boys into giving themselves up.

They waited until nightfall then regrouped at a prearranged location to plan a new strategy. Eight hours remained to access the churchyard undetected. They remained adamant in their resolve to reach the bell tower and lower the flag.

Muller and Gunter remained in their field gear, but Max and Fritz stripped theirs off and changed into their regular army uniforms.

The new plan required the group to separate into pairs. Max and Fritz would access the churchyard by way of the cemetery, and Muller and Gunter from the other side. This meant Muller and Gunter had to set off fifteen minutes earlier in order to synchronise their arrivals.

It was time. The four spread their arms over one another's shoulders forming a tight circle.

"OK, lads, this is it, then," said Max. "Good luck, Gunter, Muller."

They all shook hands and exchanged good wishes.

"Let's go!" snapped Muller.

The pair disappeared into the blackness toward the back of the churchyard.

Just before kicking off their attempt, the boys spent time scrutinising the two searchlights sweeping the cemetery and across into the edge of the forest. They saw that the pattern was as regular as clockwork.

"We should be able to get through to the perimeter wall without being spotted, Fritz. Let's keep within thirty metres of each other on the way there. You start from here and I'll start from over there," Max whispered, pointing to the right. "Good luck, Fritz."

"You too, Max,"

Using the wider headstones as cover in between sweeps of the searchlights, they gained ground at a steady pace, hopping from one headstone to another. From their dark vantage point, just twenty metres from the perimeter wall, they were able to make out silhouettes of regulars deployed in the churchyard. A sentry was posted at the entrance to the bell tower.

They both reached the perimeter wall about twenty metres apart. The toughest part of the operation would soon unfold. All they had to do was wait!

Suddenly, the sound of whistles and furore filled the air. This was the signal. Muller and Schnell had been discovered attempting an entry on the other side. The diversion had been deliberately planned as the boys' final trump card. Max and Fritz's hearts were pumping madly – would the strategy work? The few guards overlooking the cemetery wheeled around, attracted by the disturbance on the other side. Most of them left their posts to investigate what was happening. This was the boys' one and only chance. Both scrambled over the wall unnoticed. They composed themselves and quickly assumed the role of army regulars.

The word was passed around that two had been captured. In the darkness the guards that returned to their original posts didn't notice the two new additions. They had blended in well. According to the original ruling Max and Fritz had already won the challenge; however, for the boys it was all-important to access the bell tower and lower the flag.

They kept each other in sight, and then focused their attention on the sentry positioned outside the bell tower. Several troopers were still shuffling around, and loud voices could be heard coming from where Muller and Schnell had been discovered across the yard. Angry shouts unsettled the two youngsters.

Despite the intense pressure, they kept their minds centred. Max feigned a yawn and stretched as he walked close by a soldier. He felt himself being scrutinised. This unnerved him, but the soldier did not follow up his suspicion. As the confusion subsided, all soldiers resumed their previous positions.

Max motioned for Fritz to hold his ground, and he carried on walking towards the bell tower, intending to circumvent it and come around the other side behind the guard. As Max came back into Fritz's vision again, Fritz approached the guard, asking him for a light for his cigarette. The sentry begrudgingly acknowledged his request and stepped forward a couple of paces. Max stealthily slipped behind him into the bell tower and raced up the steps.

Fritz offered the sentry a cigarette. The sentry thanked him and fumbled for his lighter. He flicked it several times before the spark eventually made a flame.

Fritz and Max were tall and well built for their ages; but still, at seventeen they couldn't hide their fresh-faced looks. As the sentry lit up the cigarette, they both looked into each other's eyes and, for the sentry, the penny dropped. But Max was already lowering the flag. Fritz beckoned the guard to step back from the bell tower and pointed upwards. They both watched the silhouette of the flag being lowered in the moonlight. Turning to the guard, Fritz gave a wry smile and comically raised his arms into the air in surrender. The sentry gasped and blew his whistle to sound the alarm, but it was in vain: the objective had been well and truly achieved.

Max had cut off a corner of the flag with his knife and tucked it in his sock. When he came down from the bell tower he walked into a group of furious and frustrated regulars. Congratulations were not offered; instead both youths were frogmarched to a truck and bundled into it along with Muller and Schnell.

Back at camp rumours of their capture were already in the air, but nobody knew whether they had beaten the army. All the boys were desperate for more news.

The truck arrived at camp and the four youths were unceremoniously shuffled through the camp towards the administration block. As Max neared his company, he stooped down and took out the flag cutting he'd tucked into his sock; then he flicked it into their midst. As it dropped to the ground, the boys recognised it for what it was and let out a howl of delight.

"They did it, they did it!"

Huttner stood there with a wry smile on his face, and all 400 boys erupted in a frenzy of delight, applauding and cheering.

Then they broke out into a Hitler Youth song.

The regulars were not amused; gloomy officers ordered the guards to fire into the air to silence the jubilance. The four boys were ushered away to await the deliberations of the army officers.

The inquiry was a serious affair. Senior officers weren't in agreement and their judgements were mixed. Finally, it was decided that a victory could not be recorded because Max and Fritz were not dressed in their prescribed combat uniforms; nor did they achieve it in the allotted time period, having absconded the night previous.

The senior officer presiding passed the final judgement: all four boys were to spend a week in an army internment camp to learn a little more about discipline. However, much to the chagrin of a number of his subordinates, in his final statement he commended the youths on their initiative, teamwork and stealth.

Despite Max's bitter disappointment over the decision, the incident was never serious enough to dampen his voracious appetite for life and the Hitler Youth, but it marked the beginning of his transition to the seriousness of adulthood.

The attitude in the Bavarian camp was a clear marker for far uglier events to come, and Max's forthcoming experience at Dachau would constitute the first harsh lesson.

11

DACHAU

1935: Max and Fritz transferred to Dachau concentration camp in August of this year.

Dachau, located some fifteen kilometres north-west of Munich, was opened in March 1933 and was one of many prison compounds that sprang up around Germany. It was built to house thousands of political enemies of the new regime, after Hitler became Chancellor in January 1933.

Dachau was initially run by Ernst Röhm's Brownshirts, but within the year Himmler and the SS had taken over. Himmler appointed an ambitious and ruthless SS man, Theodor Eicke. It was rumoured that Eicke, together with another SS man, murdered Ernst Röhm in his prison cell. The reward for his loyalty during the Night of the Long Knives was his appointment to the position of first inspector of the Reich's entire concentration-camp system.

Eicke immediately set about making reforms and establishing new guarding provisions. Those who joined Eicke's units were required to act in blind obedience and carry out without question the orders of their superiors, no matter how harsh or malevolent they were.

His policy of inflexible harshness set the tone for the way all concentration camps would be run. The barbed-wire fences and harsh rules became models for other camps.

Eicke would go on to mould his guard detachments into a nucleus of an armed force strong enough to rival existing Armed-

SS units. They later came to be known as SS-Totenkopf, otherwise known as SS-T.

He earned himself a fearsome reputation. Even within the SS he was described as brutal, evil, distrustful, cruel, exuberantly ambitious and full of hatred for anybody who did not agree with party doctrine.

His appointment as inspector of the Reich concentration-camp system would come to an end in November 1939 when he was given the command of his Totenkopf units. They would eventually be trained to combatant standards and become a full division of the Waffen-SS.

Eicke wasn't the camp's commandant when Max and Fritz arrived there, but in his capacity as first inspector he spent time there, setting up and supervising various training programmes. One of these visits coincided with the boys' transfer.

The camp commandant, SS-Oberführer Deiwel received the boys and, after a brief introduction, informed them they were to meet the big chief himself – Eicke – to be given his 'blessing'.

Deiwal's adjutant showed them the way to Eicke's office. The guard posted outside opened the door and gestured for the boys to enter. Once inside, they walked up to Eicke and snapped out simultaneously a party-style salute, clicking their heels and shouting, "*Sieg Heil!*"

Eicke was seated. He didn't seem impressed by their snappy synchronised entry; he remained silent, apparently preoccupied with a form in front of him. They waited patiently for his deliberations. He finally looked up at the boys, his eyebrows raised as he scrutinised them.

"Two young lions for Leibstandarte; two of Sepp's boys," he mouthed softly, with his chin resting in the crutch of his hand. There was no sign of emotion. His eyes flashed from one youth to the other. They felt uncomfortable, as though they were suspects being held for performing some dark deed against the Reich. They felt guilty without even having done anything.

Surprisingly, Max was first to break the chilling silence: "Yes, we've both got just over a year to serve before we can apply for full membership of the unit, sir."

Eicke did not acknowledge or respond to his statement. He told them, "Your time spent at Moringen was a waste. Don't think for one minute it will be the same here. Dachau is not a place for jests or boyish pranks, or running sloppy time schedules."

"Yes, sir," they both replied simultaneously.

Eicke continued: "Now we have a good understanding. We'll see if we can shape you up into good SS men. Get out and serve your year. Good luck!" His attention immediately refocused back on to the form on the desk in front of him.

The boys snapped out another crisp, synchronised "*Sieg Heil!*" and left.

"Some welcome from our illustrious boss of the concentration-camp system!" said Fritz as they walked off to eat.

Although he didn't show it, Eicke had read their records and was satisfied with their enthusiasm, ambitions and loyalty. Fritz's raw toughness and practical skills impressed him, and, much as Röhm had, he respected Max's boxing abilities and the competence he had shown in assisting with the interrogation process at Moringen.

Max had now met both Röhm and Eicke. Ironically, it was Eicke that had been honoured for the execution of Röhm. Max's first impressions were similar for both men: awesome to behold. Arrogant Röhm had at least been friendly to youngsters. Eicke was clearly not the friendly type – not even to youngsters. A heavy sense of evil hung about him. If he was upset, he would brood and he made sure that everyone around him received a piece of his foul mood.

As far as Max was concerned, it was a good thing that Eicke would not be permanently based at Dachau. The camp's current commandant, SS-Oberführer Deiwel, had been trained by Eicke, but, as insensitive as he was, he could never match the unbridled barbarism and inhumanity of his instructor.

Deiwel encouraged Max's specialist skills in assessing political prisoners. He set him to work with Standartenführer Vanselor, who was in charge of legal matters and prisoner interrogation.

At Moringen, Max had only attended cross-examinations as an observer and provided an opinion after the session had concluded. Now his duties were upgraded to include, in some cases, personal interrogation.

Despite the upgrade, Deiwel kept him away from the torturous side of interrogation methods. Unlike Moringen, in Dachau there were specialists who carried out harsher treatments, which varied according to the severity of the crime and the character of the prisoner.

Fritz assisted with overseeing the various ongoing construction works inside the camp. He was a practical lad and excelled at the job.

In addition to their specialised tasks, the boys were set to work with the guards who ran the camp to help carry out the many mundane day-to-day duties.

Being excluded from implementing the cruel punishments that the camp guards handed out on a daily basis didn't stop them from actually witnessing the treatments, but they never developed the cold harshness of their superiors and other camp guards.

Dachau was a hell on earth. "Forget your wives and children. Here you will die like dogs" was the chilling greeting prisoners were given upon arrival at the camp. There were many ways to die in Dachau. Malnourished inmates were forced to work a minimum of eleven hours per day, six days per week. Inadequate amounts of food and very poor sanitation didn't improve the chances of survival.

The slightest misdemeanours brought about harsh penalties. For example, stealing a cigarette brought twenty-five lashes and being late for roll-call would result in solitary confinement in complete darkness. Under these conditions, some prisoners broke down and went insane.

Inmates were forever being intimidated. It was here the boys witnessed numerous humiliations, annoyances, insults and ill-treatments. Inmates would be forced to make their beds again and again on the smallest of pretexts. If any fingerprint marks showed on their cupboards, they would be ordered to rub them off immediately. While washing dishes they were not allowed to spill water. In winter they were ordered to assemble outside for roll-call without overcoats or scarves. If a prisoner laughed or smirked, his entire unit would have to undergo punishment duty.

Political agitators were executed, and the same fate awaited those who merely voiced opinions that were construed as running counter to party policies.

Guards were ordered to shoot any prisoner attempting to escape, refusing to obey an order, or simply suspected of being mutinous. This amounted to an invitation to murder any prisoner who was disliked.

Dachau inmates provided the labour for camp alterations and new extensions. Camp workshops provided barbed-wire fencing, and a tailoring workshop provided the prisoners' uniforms. Outside, teams of prisoners would work in the fields, as it was a requirement for all camps to provide their own food, which was always in short supply.

As their first days at the camp passed, Max and Fritz realised that, compared to Moringen, their new workplace was a quantum leap in evil. One morning they discussed the differences.

Fritz opened the conversation: "This place isn't nice, is it?"

"Yeah, you can feel it, can't you? There's such a heavy atmosphere here – suppression, fear, pain and anger. Brutality hangs over the camp like a guillotine."

"The guards are plain animals – not a glimmer of a sense of humour."

The boys could see that the guards trained under Eicke were far more serious about their duties than were their counterparts at the Moringen camp. Bright-eyed youthfulness didn't merit any leniency at Dachau. Being young and inexperienced suddenly turned into a liability. Along with a hundred other sneering jibes from the camp guards they got to be called the 'Leibstandarte boys' when they were together, or just 'Leibstandarte' when they worked alone. The guards never recognised their individual names and used 'Leibstandarte' only in a disparaging manner.

Eicke's code of conduct was 'Any pity whatsoever for enemies of the state is unworthy of an SS man. Max soon realised that each and every guard lived up to this diabolical code.

It was in Dachau that Max first discovered the huge dissimilarities between the soldiers of the Armed-SS units and the camp guards of the Allgemeine-SS. He considered such coldness and heartlessness to be a strange state of being, but he never openly expressed his opinion or allowed his disgust to show. He didn't want to be accused of having a conscience and showing pity in this place, so he kept his head down and never uttered a word. To overcome discomfort when witnessing harsh treatment of inmates, he simply lost himself in his day-to-day duties. Fritz assumed a similar stand but was somewhat less attached overall; he never let what he saw remain inside his head as Max did.

The pair shared the same opinion of the guards: ignorant, malicious, petty, angry and vain. Both were counting the days, looking forward to returning to Berlin, Lichterfelde and their own unit.

Soon after the NSDAP gained power, Britain and America began to dispatch spies into Germany under cover of the business world.

Britain's main concern was with Germany's increase in militarism while the Americans were mostly looking for evidence to support claims of violations of civil rights. Of special interest was the persecution of Jews who had strong ties with America and American affairs. America used many different tactics to extract information from Germany.

Early in 1936, the year of the Olympics, when all international interest was focused on Berlin, the host city of the games, three visiting American journalists gained permission to talk to party representatives covering women's matters in Germany under the new regime. One topic they wanted to cover concerned the many detention and concentration camps that had sprung up there since the party had taken control.

Being at the centre of the world stage, the party realised it would have to open its doors a little to shed some light on its internal policies. It decided to allow the journalists to visit the women's detention centre at Moringen. Max was called back to Moringen for a brief four-day excursion to prepare for and receive the foreign journalists. The first couple of days were filled with an extensive briefing. in the form of lessons in modern political history. He was to learn the real reasons behind the party's stand against Bolshevikism and its vehement dislike of Jews and freemasons.

The journalists arrived the following day. Max waited for them at the entrance. They introduced themselves as Shirley McDonald, Peggy West and Jean Simpson. At the small security post, Max asked them to register in as visitors. As they registered, he scrutinised each woman carefully and he suspected that at least one of them was Jewish. Moreover, he assumed they were spies using the cover of their magazine to glean information on concentration-camp activities in Germany and the suppression of Jews. All could speak the German language well.

Following registration, the security guard motioned his permission for the party to enter.

Max noticed how the journalists scrutinised their surroundings during the short walk across to the administration building, but Moringen was only a detention camp. It wasn't modelled on Eicke's concentration camps, all of which were run on the same lines as Dachau. Inviting the women to Moringen had been designed to provide a misleading picture. Nevertheless, the visitors weren't stupid – they had, no doubt, been fully informed of the differences between detention centres and concentration camps before they'd left the USA.

It was a cold day and a couple of paraffin heaters had been provided to heat the small meeting room. The women settled in, introduced themselves as writers for the new *Women's Life* magazine and waited for Max to speak. With a disarming smile, he opened the meeting by introducing himself.

"*Guten Morgen*, ladies. My name is Max Rieker. Please call me Max. Before we start, I have a question for you: why does it take three journalists to attend this interview?"

Peggy West obliged: "Each of us has a different assignment concerning women's issues in the lead up to the Olympic Games here in Germany. It's our first visit to your beautiful country, and we've decided to travel and complete our assignments together – to keep each other company, so to speak, and get to see the country from a tourist's perspective too. I'm covering detention centres and concentration camps. Shirley is covering the League of German Girls [the female counterpart of the Hitler Youth] and Jean is covering the woman's role in your party's master-race theory."

As she spoke, Max's attention focused on Jean – the woman he thought of as Jewish. He'd also noticed she had a slight nervous mannerism. While the others seemed relaxed, Jean remained serious and, for Max, this seemed to be a sign that her interest had an emotional basis. He refocused and nodded his acknowledgement of Peggy's response.

Jean sprang into life and opened up with the first question: "Why are there so many women locked away in your camps, and what are the main reasons for their detention?"

Her question was fired from the hip and very direct. Max was quick to realise there would be no punches pulled at this interview.

To lessen the impact, Max responded with another question: "What makes you think there are so many women in our camps? There are not so many. What was your source of information? Moringen is a detention camp for women, sure, but that doesn't mean the number of women locked up in German prisons is any higher than, say, woman held in French prisons."

"I'm not sure I agree with that statement," replied Jean. "There can't possibly be an equal number of women held in French prisons just for their political beliefs."

Max was momentarily put on the spot – it was obvious Jean

was talking sense – but he was centred and responded quickly: "That might be, but a considerable number are granted freedom after only a short stay. Our policy ensures that an individual does not represent a threat to national security. It's a sort of a screening process."

Peggy quoted some statistics recorded in American news journals. "It is what the media is telling us back home in America," she said.

Max explained that the statistics were an overestimate, and he said that they must have included many women who had now been released.

"Many of our women internees are political dissidents – those with strong views that the NSDAP considers are a threat to our values. One has to remember that Germany is host to the largest communist party outside the Soviet Union. It was only twelve years ago that the period known as the German Revolution finally came to an end. Our leaders don't want such disruption to happen again. The whole world should thank Germany for its fight against the red menace. Prostitutes and common criminals form the balance of women held in custody. As in any other country, lawbreakers must pay the price for breaking laws set up under the constitution."

"Seems a little drastic to imprison prostitutes – a far cry from the Roaring Twenties and the Berlin scene of Weimar," said Shirley.

"Legislation is legislation. Our Führer has cleaned up the streets somewhat since taking over from the corrupt and decadent Weimar government."

Jean came back at him: "There are rumours that Jewish women have been imprisoned just for being Jews, and, moreover, they have been exposed to inhumane treatment – beaten and abused and even sexually assaulted."

"If there are any Jewish women interned at Moringen it's only because they fall into one of the categories I have already stated. Women are treated most humanely. They have their own bunks, clean toilet blocks, washrooms and canteen facilities. I'll take you on a short tour once this interview is over. Ladies, may I remind you that the British Empire was the first power to use a concentration-camp system – and not so long ago either. In 1902, during the Second Boer War [1899–1902], the British introduced these camps to intern many Dutch South African women and children in order to prevent the Boers from resupplying themselves from their homes. Many tented camps were built: forty-five for Boer internees and sixty-four for black Africans. These were prisons."

"I am aware of this," stated Jean. "The system was not successful. Many women and children died of starvation and contagious diseases. Our fear is that the same will happen here in Germany."

"No deaths have been recorded here among detainees due to disease. Hygiene is good here at Moringen."

"Yes, but what about other camps?" remarked Jean. "I've heard that your concentration camps are a little different to this place, for example."

Max didn't respond to Jean's question, but he continued: "Deaths have occurred, but only through natural means or, on the odd occasion, by accident."

The journalists shuffled their bodies, appearing frustrated with Max's stock answers. They felt they weren't gleaning any information that wasn't already known to them. Max knew he was stretching the truth, but he strictly adhered to the guidelines given him at his briefing the day before.

Peggy offered up the next question. Referring to the exclusion of Jewish athletes at the forthcoming Olympics, she wanted to know why only Aryans were allowed to represent Germany.

Max thought about it and responded: "The Great War in Europe didn't happen overnight; it took years to ignite. The Sarajevo assassination was the straw to break the camel's back, so to speak; it was the result of colonial rivalry at its worst. Defeat in the war gave the Allies the opportunity to blame Germany for starting it. The Treaty of Versailles formally endorsed this and saddled Germany with a huge bill for war reparations. It was utterly humiliating and compelled our proud nation to stand in the corner like a naughty child for years after. Further, since the armistice in 1918, political factions and groups hostile to our German heritage have sought to overthrow or destroy our Germanic way of life. Our leader has simply picked us off the floor and restored our national dignity, which had been taken away by the merciless Versailles treaty.

"Let me take this a step further. Our stand against the Jews for example, has its roots in sound cause; two in fact. I'll elaborate.

"I am sure you are all aware that Judea declared war on Germany on the 24th March 1933. The American Jewish Congress proclaimed a massive protest at Madison Square Garden and called for an American boycott of German goods. As a result protests and rallies were launched in other major cities throughout the world around the same time. In London, front page headlines in the 'Daily Express' called for 'Jews of the world to unite in action to boycott all German goods.' Our, then Chancellor's speech of 28th March ordering a boycott against Jewish stores was simply in direct response to the Jewish declaration of war.

"For the second fact, let us focus on Bolshevism and the role Jewish involvement has played in its organisation. Leadership in the fledgling 1917 regime was predominantly Jewish; Trotsky, real name Lev Bronstein headed the Red Army. Yakov Sverdlov (Solomon) was executive secretary and – as chairman of the Central Executive Committee – head of the Soviet government. Grigori Zinoviev (Radomyslsky) headed the Comintern, the central agency for spreading revolution in foreign countries. Other prominent Jews included press commissar Karl Radek (Sobelsohn), foreign affairs commissar Maxim Litvinov (Wallach), Lev Kamenev (Rosenfeld) and Moisei Uritsky. Lenin himself was one-quarter Jewish.

"Remember also the rebellion of the 1st of January 1919 when the Bolshevik 'Spartacists' movement led by Karl Liebknecht and Rosa Luxemburg, both Jewish, declared Germany a socialist Republic.

"Let's not stop here. Whom did Lenin and Trotsky get their inspiration from? As you know, it was the Jewish radical Karl Marx. Karl Marx's theories were set out in his 'Communist Manifesto'. Careful scrutiny of Marx's manifesto reveals that it wasn't a new theory and based upon an earlier doctrine connected to freemasonry, hence we must take yet another step back. In 1776 another Jew named Adam Weishaupt formed his own organisation at the clear behest of the newly formed 'House of Rothschild' – a European dynasty of German-Jewish origin that established European banking and finance houses. Weishaupt believed that only a chosen few could qualify to guide and control the world. He and his associates set out to gain followers from various lodges and secret societies of the day. Upon obtaining control of certain Masonic lodges Weishaupt eventually drew up its aspirations in the form of six major points that promoted the abolishment of:

1 Ordered or nationalistic governments in the form of monarchies or similar
2 Private Property
3 Inheritance Rights
4 Patriotism to nationalist causes.
5 Social orders in families, sexual prohibition laws and all moral codes.
6 All religious discipline based on faith in a living God, as opposed to faith in nature, man and reason.

"Marx's main precepts in his 'Communist Manifesto' virtually mirrored Weishaupt's six points. Rumours had it Marx was a freemason and the startling similarities between his and Weishaupt's earlier principles for a new world order went a long way in confirming this fact.

"Our Fuhrer had recognised the Judeo-Masonic-Bolshevik link and naturally, through past experience, treats the connection seriously and suspiciously because of their threat to nation states like Germany. Let's face it, had the 1919 Sparticist rebellion in Germany been successful, the whole of Europe would have been at the mercy of Bolshevism.

"Interestingly, none of these groups have actual physical borders, albeit the Balfour Declaration bequeathed Palestine an area for the

Jews to settle in and share with the Palestinians and gentiles there. No borders to call their own yet they represent serious threats to all nation-states because of the way they could infiltrate and influence governments by way of manipulative politicians, very rich businessmen and bankers.

"Weishaupt's original theories of world order carried through into the 20th Century by the Bolsheviks diametrically opposed, undermined and threatened the very precepts of German national life. Marxism viewed the family as the primary obstacle to dismantling nation-states. He stated 'The social and political health of a nation-state is inversely proportional to the degree of racial, lingual, and religious diversity within it.' In other words, the greater the 'diversity' in a nation-state the less stable and enduring it is – a principle well understood by Bolsheviks everywhere.

"Hardly a surprise these circumstances have compelled our Fuhrer to act in the way he has. For me, it is blatantly obvious why he created his concept of 'Master Race'? Purely to counter the threat the three non-nationalistic groups I just mentioned, present. Besides promoting the Aryan race in itself isn't such a bad thing. Let's face it, all nations think they are the best anyway; our party has simply applied the idea literally as a means of countering the forces that wish to destroy Germany's national heritage. You Americans would agree?"

The women looked at one another but didn't comment.

Then he answered the original question. He was aware that almost all Jewish athletes had been barred from participating in the Olympics, but he quoted an exception: the half-Jewish fencer, Helene Mayer, who would later claim a silver medal in women's individual foil. The only deviation from his briefing happened during this particular conversation when he genuinely sympathised with the journalists, understanding their position. He considered the spirit of the Olympics was for all to participate.

The women picked up on the sincerity in his last few sentences. They felt they had come from the heart, not the head. They had touched on the real man behind the uniform.

Just then, Jean seized the moment to bring back the topic of concentration camps. Referring again to the Boer War, she said, "The British were cruel, food was scarce and hygiene did not exist. Are you certain that the same will not happen here in Germany?"

Max noted the anger in her voice. He'd already concluded that she had a personal interest in the subject that went beyond producing a story for a magazine.

Jean hesitated for a couple of seconds before venturing into dangerous territory. She wanted to make a point.

"Many Jews are being expelled from Germany and stripped of all their assets and personal belongings," she said calmly.

Max came back with an unlikely and unrehearsed response: "Jews have been expelled from many parts of Europe in past years, Fräulein. Statistics indicate that European countries have expelled Jews for one reason or another over forty times in the last thousand years. It appears it is happening once again here in Germany, for reasons I have already explained. But, historically there is a third factor and if you want, I can also elaborate on this."

The women all nodded their agreement.

"Back in the year 1215 the English King John signed the Magna Carta. One of its 'guarantees' concerned the law of Usury whereby no Christian could lend money and demand an interest on its return. Breach of this law was punishable by death. Back then, the Canon Law did not apply to Jews and Judaism permitted loans with interest between Jews and non-Jews. As a consequence Jews grew rich off of other people. They acquired a reputation as extortionate moneylenders that made them extremely unpopular with both the church and the general public. Finally, in 1290 the English King Edward I issued the edict of expulsion.

"Usury is commonplace now, adopted by many rich businessmen and bankers, an unsavoury part of life that has its roots many centuries before King John and the Magna Carta but propagated by the Jews throughout history. No Jews are detained just for being Jews. As I said earlier, all prisoners are political dissidents or enemies of the state."

He'd taken a flyer on his last response, but he had never checked Moringen's records so he couldn't know whether his answer was correct. Certainly in Dachau he'd known of a number of individuals imprisoned for being Jewish. But, then it occurred to him that many Jews had been politically active against Germany for years; many were members of the German Communist party (KDP). Even the Social Democrats (SPD) had its links with the KDP insofar as the former Spartacist League – who declared themselves the German Communist Party in January 1919 – had originally been the 'far left' wing of the SPD. And, the SPD itself had contributed the majority of its membership to Germany's former Weimar government that had comprised of many Jews. It was little wonder NSDAP leadership had viewed these aspects warily.

A degree of tension had arisen between Max and Jean. To defuse it, Shirley McDonald fired off another question about the forthcoming Olympics.

Max was pleased to be presented with an opportunity to discuss his personal involvement as one of eight boxers in his weight category to participate in the eliminations for the Olympic boxing team.

Jean remained unimpressed by his comments. She was still seething from the previous verbal exchange. Her silent annoyance showed on her face.

Unexpectedly, Max felt obliged to ask the question: "It appears our conversation is focusing on Jews. Are any of you Jewish, then?"

A chorused answer came back from all three women: "No!" – but this was followed by a period of pregnant silence that dampened the atmosphere of the interview. Despite this, the women continued to ask Max questions. His responses to the politically charged questions were obviously scripted and revealed little. He was satisfied that he hadn't provided additional material to fuel a steadily growing fire.

The disappointing interview drew to a close within the hour.

Jean regained some of her composure, even managing to give

Max a smile as he motioned for them to leave the room for a short tour of the detention centre. They were escorted over to inspect the canteen, several workshops and some other areas, including a makeshift library which had been installed to create the right impression. Some sections had been designated 'off-limits', and Max explained that they were administrative areas and therefore not relevant.

During the short tour, a discomfiting incident Max hadn't planned for occurred when he was showing the journalists around the workshops. He recognised several women detainees and a member of the female staff whom he'd 'serviced' before his transfer to Dachau. The detainees didn't react too much – fortunately their subjugation kept them from acknowledging him – but the female staff member wasn't so impassive.

As she walked by, she remarked, "Wow, if it's not my young lover boy! Where have you been all this time, Max?"

Max acknowledged the greeting with great embarrassment, stammering an uncomfortable "Hi!"

The journalists looked at one another quizzically and then smiled.

Peggy commented: "You've been here before, then, Max?"

"Yes," he stuttered.

Concluding the short tour, he took them back to the interview room and ordered coffee and biscuits. After some thought, he decided to follow up his original gut feeling that they were all spies. They continued small talk for a few minutes, and then Max announced that he'd like them to meet a senior officer.

On this pretext, he left them momentarily to make a brief telephone call. This gave him the chance to call his Gestapo contact and relay his suspicions. He returned apologetic, stating the officer was unavailable. When they finished coffee, the journalists offered their thanks for his time and prepared to leave.

Max escorted them back across the yard to the entrance gate and wished them good luck, adding that he trusted the rest of their stay in Germany would be a memorable and eventful one. They bade their farewells and walked across the road to a waiting car.

On his way back across to the administration building, Max glanced back over his shoulder. He was focusing on the journalists' car, which was just about to leave, when suddenly two limousines appeared. The first pulled up in front of them, making it impossible for them to move forward, and the second parked up close behind them.

One plain-clothed, fedora-hatted Gestapo officer accompanied by two uniformed policemen alighted from each limousine and walked over to the stationary car. After a brief conversation, the journalists got out of the car. They were split up, hustled along to the Gestapo limousines and taken away for questioning.

A few weeks later, Max received news that Gestapo interrogation had uncovered the fact that all three women were indeed spies. Their mission had been to glean information for American Intelligence about female Jewish internees in German concentration camps.

As part of the 'good-faith protocol' leading up to the Olympic Games, Shirley McDonald and Peggy West were sent back to America.

Jean, however, suffered a far different fate. Under interrogation she revealed that she'd joined the team in an effort to locate her sister, whom she suspected of being detained at one of the camps for no apparent reason. Jean, it turned out, was Jewish and an Austrian citizen from the city of Linz. Lofty connections in America had sanctioned her involvement and arranged for the false ID and paperwork. She was charged with espionage and considered an enemy of the Reich. It was also discovered she was separated from her husband but had an eight-year-old son, Heinrich.

Max could only reflect on the woman's bravery. The risk she'd run had been extraordinary. Her sympathy and affection for her sister had betrayed her and she would now experience first-hand what life in a concentration camp was really like.

Max was congratulated for his prowess, and he acknowledged the credit for uncovering the spies, but he felt uncomfortable that Jean and her son had been left to the mercy of the Gestapo –

particularly as she was only trying to track down one of her close family members. Her elaborate deceit hadn't worked and now she had to pay the price of the times.

For Max and Fritz, Dachau represented the final days of their youth. Within its confines they were catapulted into the serious world of the adult. A world of suspicion, prejudice, violence and malice replaced youthful fun, spontaneity and adventure.

They hated the way the Dachau camp guards treated them; it cut deep. One evening Fritz pulled Max aside and sat down, totally exasperated.

"Can't say I'm forming a bond with the camp guards here, Max. Most of them are outright wankers. Their sick sense of humour is pissing me off."

Max agreed. "They don't give up, do they? Miserable and petty, eh? The inmates are handled so inhumanely in this place. I'd hate to be on the receiving end of some of the punishments that are dealt out to them."

"Poor bastards! As cantankerous as some of them can be, they don't deserve that. Primitive, if you ask me!"

"I guess it takes a certain type to work in a place like this, Fritz."

"Glad I'm not one of them! I swear the next bastard that addresses me as Leibstandarte, I'll thicken his lips."

"Trouble is that we have an obligation to Leibstandarte. If we complain, they might consider we are incapable of following orders," said Max.

"Yeah, you're right. How can we get back at the bastards without endangering our nominations?"

"I suppose we could be derisive like them and address them as 'Totenkopf' – as long as it isn't an NCO or someone who could pull rank and accuse us of being insubordinate."

"Difficult, isn't it? I guess we can eyeball the bastards?"

Fritz had always been close to retaliating several times. His fuse was shorter than Max's. It was a good thing Max had been close by to constrain him.

They agreed that the only way they could get some sort of satisfaction was by eyeballing their peers. Even then the action had to be carried out with careful judgement: just enough for an adversary to know where they were coming from, but not so excessively as to be considered insubordinate.

Other than that, both settled for tolerating their predicament, and, as much as they loathed the spiteful remarks, they pushed them aside and just got on with it. Besides, interacting with the officers proved a little more rewarding. Officers didn't get involved with actually dealing out sadistic punishments, albeit they were the ones who issued the orders, in strict adherence to the precepts laid down by Eicke.

At Dachau, the boys' early brushes with elements of the Allgemeine-SS sowed the seeds for future discontent. There would come a time when their hatred for those consciousless and barbaric types would boil over and explode into an ugly, warped, uncontrolled desire for revenge.

BIBLIOGRAPHY

Thomas Dodd Research Centre: 'The Nuremberg Trial Files of Senator Thomas J. Dodd', 'Dachau'. (Thomas Dodd Research Centre.)

The Third Reich: The SS. (Time Life Books, 1989.)

12

BOXER

In September 1935, just after his seventeenth birthday, Max received notification from the German Amateur Boxing Committee that he had been shortlisted for the elimination rounds to determine who would represent Germany at the summer Olympic Games in the light-heavyweight category. Eight contestants were to battle it out head-to-head during the first quarter of 1936.

Deiwel, the camp commandant, was aware of Max's boxing skills and impressive record on the amateur boxing circuit – all at only seventeen years of age. Not yet a full member of the Armed-SS, the rules were relaxed and Max was permitted to train at a boxing club in a nearby suburb of Munich. Here he would undergo an intense training programme in the months that followed.

Kurt Wedemeyer ran the boxing club; he trained youths and adults from both amateur and professional circuits. Wedemeyer had been a sergeant in the Great War. He was a tough, stocky forty-four-year-old now. His amateur boxing career had begun soon after he returned home from the war. In the early 1920s he'd joined the paramilitary Freikorps and, when he wasn't boxing, spent most of his time quelling Bolshevik takeover bids. Later he turned pro and fought as a middleweight, slugging out the final years of his career with lower-ranked professionals. By the time he retired from the ring there was hardly a trick he didn't know. He went on to become an exceptional trainer, so when he first scrutinised Max in action, he saw great potential. He became Max's formal trainer, manager and boxing mentor.

After the tough training sessions, they'd find time to discuss their love for the sport. Wedemeyer was an avid talker and his tales about past fights fascinated Max. Wedemeyer reminded Max of his old mentor, Michael Vogel.

Unlike Vogel, Wedemeyer wasn't a philosopher, but when he talked boxing it was as though the subject was a philosophy in itself. His fight stories filled the air with the same magic as Vogel's discourses. Max shared in Wedemeyer's enthusiasm and hung on every one of his words. He appreciated deeply the tactical information Wedemeyer so readily imparted to him. Like a sponge, Max soaked up everything he had to offer.

Max had the unusual ability to box using two stances: orthodox and southpaw. Although he primarily led with his left hand in the regular orthodox stance, he could switch to southpaw if he felt it would be advantageous. Wedemeyer had recognised his aptitude for switching stances, so he set out to enhance an ability that could confuse an opponent in a critical moment.

Wedemeyer's assessment of Max's boxing skills was summed up under the following qualities: his speed and agility were second to none; his footwork ranked with the finest Wedemeyer had seen. Opponents always found it hard to get a firm fix on him. Working-out and adhering to a rigid training regime was a priority; it gave Max an edge on opponents who cut their training programmes short and relied purely on strength and punch power. His disciplined efforts in the gym were rewarded by improvements in his muscular physique and stamina.

Boxing was second nature to him; he could read an opponent like a newspaper, so he was able to avoid punches and find his target with well-placed counterstrokes. Counterpunches administered immediately after an opponent throws a punch exploit the opening in the opponent's position.

Max's jabs were crisp and fast, and his combination punches were strong. Combination-punching involves a series of punches, ending with the most damaging – for example, two quick left jabs ending with a right cross. Max's most effective punches were the left hook (driving up or around, exploding at the jaw or to the side of the head) and the right cross. In orthodox stance, where the left foot is leading, the right cross is delivered by throwing the punch with the right hand across the body to the opponent's head or jaw.

Wedemeyer saw weaknesses too. Occasionally Max appeared slow to build aggression. It didn't appear to be caution; on the contrary, Max was fearless in the ring. At the time, Wedemeyer was unaware that the level of Max's aggression depended on the behaviour of his opposition. He hadn't yet learnt that the young boxer abhorred loutish and ignorant types – a result of his time with Berti Braun and the SA. Squared up against an opponent who fitted one or other of these stereotypes, Max didn't need to build aggression. Moreover, he assumed his challengers, too, didn't need to build aggression: they were already naturally ignorant and angry bastards.

Secondly, Max needed to work at his close-quarter entanglements. Possibly because of inexperience, he was vulnerable to being caught on the ropes. Wedemeyer would need to teach him some tricks for escaping from a boxer who was skilful at driving an opponent into the ropes.

Finally, Max hadn't the brawn or experience of a fully grown adult. There were tricks he still hadn't learnt, and many of his opponents were likely to be tougher and more experienced.

The former sergeant had only five months to transform his boy into an adult. Without wasting a moment, he set out to do it.

Wedemeyer was well connected on both amateur and professional circuits. He also had military links with the Dachau training academy. His first job involved talking to his Dachau contacts. They came up with a plan to accelerate his maturation. It was to be a twofold affair. Firstly, Max and Fritz were to be enrolled, on a part-time basis, into a training programme being conducted at the nearby NCO training academy. Secondly, a number of bouts with several experienced adult fighters were to be arranged. Wedemeyer figured that pitching Max against adult boxers would be the best means of testing the young man's heart and calibre. They believed a combination of the two programmes would achieve the result Wedemeyer was seeking.

At the training academy there were no special privileges for youth. Max and Fritz were made to train under the same disciplined conditions as the adults. At first, the programme was a nightmare for them. They were picked on, just as they were at Dachau. Army regulars constantly hurled verbal abuse at them, and this intensified when it was revealed the young aspirants were earmarked for the Leibstandarte unit. Despite their fitness, the boys found the rigorous endurance training alongside hardened, experienced adults extremely challenging.

Max accepted the challenge; it was his chance to get some of his own back on those who mocked him.

With some intense training behind him, the weekend of the fights against the adults soon came around. The venue would be the Munich sports hall where they trained. Wedemeyer briefed Max on the schedule. There was to be a total of three bouts: two on Saturday afternoon and the third on Sunday morning. Each bout would consist of two three-minute rounds. Wedemeyer chose to deviate from the regular three-round bouts; he considered two rounds would be enough for the time being. Whether or not thoughts of protecting his boy came into his decision, he never let on.

Wedemeyer and Fritz covered Max's corner. Max had no idea what experience his opponents had.

Soon after Wedemeyer finished his brief pep talk the first challenger appeared from the dressing room. He was a fat Berliner named Karl Brandt. As they were called to the centre of the ring Brandt leered mockingly at Max.

"He's just a kid. This'll be a pushover," he said to the lieutenant who was acting as the referee.

The comment brought an instant reaction from Max. All through the mandatory Queensberry Rules recital, he glared into Brandt's eyes with a desire for vengeance that was clearly visible; it signalled an aggressive start for the challenge. The fat man showed a degree of surprise as he picked up on Max's aggression.

To cover his surprise he mouthed out loud, "Won't last the two rounds, boy!"

"We'll see," said Max as he walked back to his corner for the start of the fight.

The bell rang. Max bit down on his gumshield and came out of his corner, buzzing around Brandt like a wasp, jabbing continuously. Brandt was quick despite his bulk, and although he tended to swing his punches, they were powerful. Max simply avoided them, but he remained vigilant, aware of the danger they represented should one connect. Max bounced in and out continuously, intending to frustrate Brandt into making rash mistakes and dropping his guard.

The shorter Brandt had a technique where he literally jumped at his opponent. Midway through the first round, the technique paid off when an overhead lunge caught Max in the head, disorientating him momentarily.

Noticing Max had been hurt, Brandt threw some verbal abuse: "Not so cocky now, eh, lad? Your clever punches aren't making it, sonny boy!"

Max was aware that although his jabs were accruing points they were having little physical effect on the thick-necked scrapper.

"It's not over yet, fat man!" he retorted.

Brandt continued his ridicule, and it was beginning to upset Max. To make matters worse, he caught him with a swinging haymaker. Mockingly Brandt bellowed, "Give up, boy. You just can't fight!"

At this remark, Max lost it. Egged on by Fritz, who was yelling his own abuse at Brandt, he picked up his pace and came in with a fierce combination of punches. Successfully avoiding Brandt's counters, he repeated his three-punch combination, quickly followed by another. The bout suddenly changed into a street fight.

In an effort to cover up the fact that he'd been hurt, Brandt continued to goad Max: "You're a lousy boxer, son. I'd change my sport if I were you."

The bell sounded for the end of the first round.

Max returned to his corner, seething. His adrenalin was flowing freely, and before the bell sounded he was up off his bench like a dog straining at the leash. He glided around Brandt, levelling sharp jabs at him and swift one-twos. He quickly got the hang of Brandt's style and used Brandt's aggressive advances to his benefit. As Brandt lunged forward, he sidestepped and picked him off with crisp right-cross counterpunches. They were sharp, very fast and, after catching Brandt several times, began to punish the fat lout.

Halfway through the round, Brandt started to breath heavily. He wasn't so abusive now. Max's combination punches were continuous, and they were administered with fearsome accuracy. After several attacks of a similar nature, he added a shuddering left-hook to his repertoire for a finale. The hook was well delivered and visibly shook Brandt. By this time, Brandt's verbal abuse had ceased altogether; his breathing was irregular as he struggled to take in air. He was clearly slowing down.

Before Max could deal out another damaging set of punches the referee called the fight to an end.

Brandt reopened the abuse as he was led off to his corner: "Lucky punch, junior. Wait till the next guy gets in the ring. He'll kill you!"

Max followed him over to his corner: "Next time I'll finish it, fatty!"

The referee pulled Max away from the potentially explosive situation.

"You'll need to rest up for the next sixty minutes or so. Save your energy, boy," he advised.

Wedemeyer made sure he was kept warm and fired up.

The second opponent was a former associate of Wedemeyer's, Hans Schmidt. Schmidt was a retired pro who had been called back into the ring just for Max's benefit. Wedemeyer gave Max an edge and briefed him on Schmidt's style during the interval.

"Without a doubt, Schmidt will have quite a few tricks up his sleeve."

The sixty-minute rest proved adequate. The final five minutes was taken up with warm-up exercises. The contest started better than the last had. Unlike Brandt, Schmidt showed Max a degree of respect when they met in the middle for the Queensberry Rules recital.

Although Schmidt was that much fresher, Max was fired up from the previous bout so they probably clashed at around the same degree of preparedness. Max moved quicker, but he felt the ex-pro's punches when they connected. The first round went even, but a few hard punches thrown by Schmidt caused Max some pain and gave him a bloody nose. Despite this, he noticed that Schmidt, the older boxer, was breathing heavily as he walked back to his corner; he obviously hadn't been working a regular training programme since his retirement.

The rest between rounds gave Schmidt an edge in the first minute of the round, but Max's fitness began to tell from then on. His jabs and one-twos began to take effect, as they had against Brandt. Schmidt came forward often, but his advances gave Max the chance to counterpunch with some well-placed right crosses, just as he'd done against Brandt. Credit is due to Schmidt: he fought back with equal ferocity. Towards the end of the bout, Max began to stretch himself to full capacity. He threw in combinations at every opportunity, and at one point he picked off Schmidt with a vicious right cross, forcing him down to one knee. At the count of six, Schmidt stood up, acknowledged the punch, then defiantly came back to resume the offensive.

Max boxed out the remainder of the round with jabs and good footwork.

When the contest came to a close, the boxers hugged and Max walked back to his corner feeling more comfortable about this performance than the previous one. Wedemeyer congratulated Max for his sound performance against Schmidt.

Max's second performance had impressed onlookers, but he sensed that the last fight, to take place the following morning, would be the real test. His thoughts were confirmed when one of the officers walked across to him.

"Well done, young Rieker, let's see what you can do with a fitter and heavier opponent, then." The officer spoke with a derisive smirk, as if he knew Max was going to be demolished the following morning.

The organisers had saved the big one for last.

"I trust I can oblige, Herr Lieutenant," said Max in response.

He was up early the following morning, mentally preparing himself. He met up with Fritz and they ate a light breakfast. Wedemeyer met them at the sports centre. They walked and chatted for a while then returned to the gym for Max to commence his warm-up exercises. Wedemeyer had arranged for a brief sparring session to ensure that when Max met his final opponent he would be warmed up and ready.

Max climbed up into the ring and sat on his bench waiting for his third opponent – a Prussian named Franz Bachmann – to emerge from the dressing room.

The silence in the hall was suddenly broken by the sounds of the dressing-room doors swinging open. Out strode the fit-looking Prussian, obviously currently boxing for the army. Bachmann was heavier than Max; his muscular body suggested at least a three-kilo bodyweight advantage.

Max sat on his bench, sizing up Bachmann as he strode confidently towards the ring. Bachmann was stony-faced and had a clinical air about him.

'This'll be a tough one,' Max thought, but he knew that once his gloves were back on he'd feel no fear.

Wedemeyer pulled the gloves over Max's bandaged fists and barked out his instructions: "Use your speed; plenty of footwork. Don't let this guy drive you into the ropes. Avoid close encounters. Just chip away at him. He'll come forward. Use your right cross-counters – they're as good as I've seen. Remember to breathe properly. Let that air out through your lips when you punch." With a pat on the shoulder he motioned Max to meet his opponent in the middle of the ring.

As the referee recited the Queensberry Rules, the contestants stared at each other. Max matched Bachmann's stony glare. This would be a good opportunity to get some satisfaction for the jibes the youngsters had been taking from the army boys back at the Dachau training academy. They touched gloves and Max walked back to his corner, mentally going over everything Wedemeyer had instructed.

The bell rang and they clashed in the middle of the ring, jabbing simultaneously. Bachmann took his task seriously. Max's footwork was outstanding. He knew his jabs would accrue points, but in order to hurt Bachmann he would need to deliver some solid combinations and big punches. The first round was truly one of the hardest he'd experienced in his entire boxing career so far. It was an outstanding performance. Breathing heavily, but still sharp, he retired to his corner. He'd stretched himself to produce his best boxing skills in order to avoid the clinical finishing of Bachmann.

"Well done," said Wedemeyer as Max slumped down on to his stool.

Wedemeyer continued giving encouragement while working on abrasions from blows Max had taken on his cheekbone and eyebrow.

The bell announced the second round. Bachmann had his own schedule. In his own mind he had allowed Max to survive the first in order not to destroy his confidence. This wouldn't be the case in the second round, for he would be out to teach the youngster a lesson in boxing. An experienced boxer, he'd managed to avoid many of Max's jabs and countered swiftly with his own. His weight advantage was sapping Max's strength. The jabs were crisp and jarring when they connected. Max knew he would need to keep vigilant and react quickly to his opponent. He knew Bachmann was moving into another gear and setting him up for a knockout.

A short way through the round, Bachmann's first attempt at knocking Max out came. A sharp, crisp, three-punch combination put Max on the floor. Dazed by the barrage, he took a count of eight. The referee checked his condition before allowing him to box on. Bachmann, in no mood to let Max off the hook, came in with some fierce jabs, preparatory punches, signalling that another lethal combination was imminent. Max was aware that being caught with a second volley might finish him. His instincts were superb; despite still being disorientated he anticipated Bachmann's strategy well and wheeled away at the vital moment to avoid the deadly knockout blow.

Bachmann came forward relentlessly; Max was beginning to slow up. His mind raced as he struggled to maintain mobility on his feet. In an effort to confuse Bachmann, he suddenly switched to southpaw and came in with a ferocious combination. The tactical change did surprise his opponent, but only for a moment; it wasn't enough to achieve any kind of reversal. Bachmann came back quickly with his own combination and floored Max for the second time.

Max took a count of seven. The referee checked him over.

Looking into his eyes, he smirked and winked. "Not good enough for this guy, eh, young Rieker?"

He placed his hand on Max's shoulder to escort him back to his corner and call the fight over.

"It's not over yet."

Max pushed him aside and wheeled around, signalling to Bachmann that he was ready to continue.

The referee yelled, "Stop boxing, lad!"

Max spun around, glared at the referee and punched his own gloves together in a gesture to show he was ready to go again.

The referee shrugged his shoulders and barked, "Box on at your own peril, then!"

Throwing all caution to the wind, Max turned, took up his stance and launched into Bachmann. He hung on close to Bachmann's body to stop him from countering or throwing a deadly uppercut.

In a last-ditch effort to make his mark, as they separated he jumped forward and unleashed a left hook that caught Bachmann clean on the jaw. Bachmann reeled back against the ropes and fell to one knee.

He was up at the count of six.

Max came in with several combinations in an effort to finish him off, but Bachmann counterpunched his way out of danger.

Bachmann was clearly staggered by the spirited effort of the youngster. He was unable to launch an effective response and spent the remaining seconds slugging out the final round. Onlookers were spellbound, and they applauded when the bell signified the end of the bout and the end of Max's test.

Max looked over to the referee: "Not bad, eh!" he said scornfully.

The referee was no longer smirking. As he led Max back to his corner he told him he had just fought two rounds with the current army light-heavyweight boxing champion. The two boxers took off their gloves, hugged and slapped each other's shoulders.

Max had fared well. The fat Berliner, Brandt, had stayed over to watch the last bout and came over to congratulate him. His face now wore a beaming smile, and Max realised his behaviour the day before had been an act.

The results got back to the Dachau camp and the NCO academy. Although they received no better treatment at the concentration camp, the NCOs at the academy looked at the boys in a more favourable light. The act of bringing the army boxing champion down to one knee had opened the door of acceptance for both of them. Max's boyhood had been well and truly knocked out of him; the transition to adulthood was complete. Wedemeyer had achieved his objective and Max was ready to take on anybody.

13

THE OLYMPIC YEAR

1936: it was the Olympic year, and the prestigious event was to take place in Max's hometown, Berlin. It had been selected as host city in May 1931 by the International Olympic Committee. The choice had signalled Germany's return to the world community after its defeat in the Great War.

Unfortunately, the welcome hadn't deterred Hitler from breaking the terms of the 1919 Treaty of Versailles by ordering the reoccupation of the Rhineland – the demilitarised zone along the River Rhine's western border. On 7 March, more than 32,000 soldiers and armed policemen crossed into the Rhineland. The terms allowed Germany political control of the area, but forbade them to put any troops into it.

Hitler had gambled that Germany's former Continental enemies, France and Belgium, would not react. As a fallback, he had ordered his generals to withdraw if the French and Belgians showed the slightest hint of making a military stand against them. This didn't happen, and Hitler's gamble paid off.

The quarter-finals for the boxing eliminations took place in the famous Munich Boxhalle. On the eve of the event, Max found time to reflect on what he'd learnt from Wedemeyer, and what practical experience he'd picked up since being notified of his selection.

As well as gaining further experience on the amateur circuit, the bouts arranged at Wedemeyer's Boxing Club had been priceless. Brandt, the rotund Berliner, had taught him never to underestimate an opponent, no matter how sloppy and overweight he appeared. Extra weight, used properly, can have a devastating effect on a lighter man. The fight with Schmidt had taught him to look out for tricks not yet learnt through inexperience. The clash with army champion Bachmann had brought him down to earth: there were better opponents out there, stronger and equally stubborn.

In every situation, no matter how tough the opposition, Max resolved to give his best, keep focused on his own ability, and never get sidetracked by the law of reversed effort (where one focuses on the opponent's capabilities), which is caused by a fear of failure. Max knew that, while Bachmann had been superior in most respects, his own heart and courage had not let him down. His efforts and belief in himself had paid off.

'God does help those that help themselves,' thought Max.

He'd since learnt that Bachmann had been one of those shortlisted, but he had opted to move up a weight category and participate as a heavyweight.

Now the real challenge was at hand. Weighing in at eighty kilos, he was a good three kilos heavier than he had been during his earlier encounters at the sports centre. His opponent was a twenty-one-year-old from Munich: Hermann Gruber. Gruber also weighed in at eighty kilos.

The contest was an evening affair. Max was naturally excited about the forthcoming challenge and, on the day, Wedemeyer had to keep him relaxed and centred until it was time to psyche him up in the changing room, ready for the clash in the ring.

The two boxers came out to a split stadium, who roared their appreciation. It was by far the biggest crowd Max had experienced in his boxing career. He was dumbstruck by the energy and excitement in the air.

Wedemeyer and Fritz were acting as his seconds. Wedemeyer repeated a warning not to take chances in the opening minutes.

The bell sounded the start of the bout. They met in the middle of the ring, circling around, sizing each other up. Both boxers were cautious, and during the first half of the round their repertoire of punches was limited to jabs and one-twos. Gruber was the more aggressive, forcing Max to demonstrate some exceptional footwork to avoid being caught on the ropes. The impasse broke halfway through the round when both boxers opened up. Max was quick to get on top of his opponent's technique, managing to avoid or cover up, thereby reducing the effectiveness of Gruber's punches. Gruber was better in the clinches, and by the end of the round he was clearly ahead on points.

The second round went much like the first until the final thirty seconds, when Max took the initiative and went on the offensive. The round ended even.

Max knew he would need to maximise his efforts in the last round in order to stay in the selection. His corner never stopped encouraging him.

"Give it all you've got, boy. Your strength and fitness will prevail. If you're tired, he is too. Go out there and do what you've been trained to do and win!" remarked an excited Wedemeyer.

"OK, Kurt," Max replied as he got off his bench and moved to the centre of the ring.

They touched gloves and Max proceeded to take the fight to Gruber. Midway through the round he saw a half-chance and let loose a vicious left hook. It connected well and Gruber fell to the canvas. Gruber was up by the count of six, but still a little groggy. Max sensed the kill and came in with everything he had. The arena was filled with roars of approval from his supporters. Gruber kept on his feet despite all Max's efforts to topple him for a second time. The bell sounded for the end of the bout and Max returned to his corner feeling elated with the knock-down. He believed this might swing the result his way. He hoped the judges would agree.

They did. Max's arm was raised in victory; the knock-down had proven to be the decider. He sprang around the ring in jubilation. Wedemeyer and Fritz clambered through the ropes and all three linked arms, jumping for joy, knowing Max had won his place in the semi-finals.

Four weeks later Max and Wedemeyer were shuttled up to Berlin for the semis. Berlin's new Olympic annexe was the venue.

Max was aware he'd be facing a formidable opponent, a mature fighter, Richard Vogt, with many knockouts under his belt. Vogt was from Hamburg and was popular throughout the northern part of Germany. It was rumoured that he would turn professional after the Olympics. In this contest Max was clearly the underdog, but he was acutely aware that winning it would give him a real chance of making the Olympic team.

Max hadn't had the opportunity to study Vogt in any depth, so he fell back on Wedemeyer's report and his advice on what to expect.

The Berlin stadium was full to capacity and, as before, Max was awestruck. He ducked under the ropes and stepped into the ring to a round of applause. This time, however, allegiances were not even. Despite the fact that the fight was taking place in the city of Max's birth, the spectators were overwhelmingly in favour of Vogt.

Wedemeyer knew that a cautious start was out of the question for this fight.

"Max, what is needed here is continuous harassment and hustle. You've got to keep Vogt unsettled. As you are the underdog, he will assume you will be cautious. You have to surprise him. Use your footwork; you have three rounds in which to keep on your feet. Now, give it your best."

Max knew that to climb back out of the ring with anything left would signify a shortfall in his efforts – a situation he might regret for the rest of his life.

They both opened up aggressively, as if it were the third and final round. Max maximised his footwork to avoid Vogt's punches and keep out of harm's way. Vogt was hard-hitting, but when they clashed Max was swift to absorb Vogt's attacks and counter with his own punches, maintaining his objective of keeping him unsettled. From the onset, the spectators picked up on the pace of the fight and roared their appreciation of the entertainment it provided.

The first round had brought out the very best in both boxers. Max had suffered more damage, particularly from a face punch that opened up his nose. The injury gave his corner plenty of work, stemming the flow of blood. Sitting there, Max realised Vogt was a cut above anybody he had fought previously.

The opening moments of the second round witnessed a brief moment of inactivity. The boxers circled around, sizing each other up; it had become a battle of wills and strategy. Despite Vogt having the strength advantage, he clearly respected Max's skills. He recognised that although he had a higher gear he could shift into at the right moment, this could also be true of his opponent.

The brief period of inactivity didn't last. The boxers were at each other's throats and the spectacle turned into a street fight.

Vogt was fit and more experienced than Max. Any relaxation in focus on Max's part might mean disaster. Making an impact on a classy, stronger puncher was challenging his stamina. Vogt's continuous aggression gave him a clear points advantage. Max needed to grab an opportunity to throw his devastating left hook; however, lining Vogt up wasn't going to be easy.

Late in the round Vogt decided to switch into overdrive. He came in with a punishing combination, the last blow of which knocked Max down. The crowd roared, but the sound of the bell to end the round saved Max from immediate defeat.

Wedemeyer worked furiously in his corner to bring him back to full consciousness. As Max sat on the bench, his dream of being an Olympian seemed remote. He asked himself how he could get to Vogt. He hadn't had a clear opportunity of delivering his mighty left hook yet.

The bell rang for the start of the third and final round. The boxers touched gloves in the middle of the ring and immediately launched into each other again. Vogt was coming in for the kill, but Max had recovered sufficiently to pick up from where he'd left off before the knock-down.

A series of short skirmishes finished in a head-to-head slugging match. Max had never experienced swapping so many punches in a single clash. He reeled away, dazed and unable to focus himself. The volley of punches aimed at his head should have knocked him down, but, miraculously, he managed to stay on his feet. To his surprise, Vogt never followed up to deliver the decisive blows.

The entire stadium was in uproar. Both boxers were gasping for breath. Vogt had taken some precious seconds to regain his composure. They recovered about the same time, and Max reverted to jabs to accrue points, despite knowing that only a knockout would win the fight now.

He didn't want to leave the ring knowing that he hadn't thrown his best shot, but picking the right moment to deliver it was still proving difficult. A half-chance came midway through the round, when he managed to unleash his left hook with full ferocity, throwing Vogt across the ring. Disappointingly, Vogt took most of the impact on his glove.

Time was running away and Max needed, at least, a knock-down. Vogt came in with a series of crisp combination punches, but Max's right-cross counters were solid too. Anticipating that Vogt would come back with a similar combination, Max pre-empted with another thunderous left hook. Both boxers connected at the same time, they staggered away and both fell to one knee, dazed.

They both made it to their feet by the count of eight to the deafening roar of the spectators. Hardly conscious, Max realised that Vogt was hurt too. He prepared himself and came forward with some desperate one-twos, but his equally tireless opponent countered with similar combinations, pushing Max back into the ropes. Max desperately slugged his way off the ropes, fearing the prospect of being caught in a clinch. Vogt simply reeled around and came forward again, but his approach was sloppy and he momentarily dropped his guard. This provided Max with the opportunity to throw yet another left hook. The punch connected well, but Vogt managed to stay on his feet. Max was surprised that Vogt hadn't gone down. Vogt came back and caught him with a hard right cross.

Max lurched away, knowing he was almost incapable of defending himself; but instead of finishing off the job, Vogt used the time to recover from the enormous left hook he had just received. For a few seconds they stood and looked at each other. Max had difficulty focusing. His head was spinning and blood was running freely from his nose and a small cut over his left eye.

As Vogt came at him, Max delivered a wild right cross that connected well. Once again, Vogt remained on his feet.

The two fighters looked at each other, each thinking much the same thought: 'When is this guy going to lie down?'

Raising his last reserves of strength, Vogt came in with a hard combination that drove Max back into the ropes. At that moment, much to Max's relief, the bell rang to end the contest. They immediately stopped boxing, hugged each other, then staggered back to their corners.

The spectators were on their feet, applauding the epic contest between the two men. Max had clawed something from his heart that he never knew existed. But was his fearless effort good enough to win the competition?

They stood on either side of the referee, drooping and gasping for breath, exhausted from their punishing efforts. Awaiting the judges' scores was one of the tensest moments in Max's life so far.

The scores were announced and the result went to the favourite, Vogt. Max bowed his head in despair as the bitterness of defeat sunk in. Vogt stretched over to put a hand on his head. They hugged each other like two old friends would. Max wished him the best in the forthcoming Olympics and left the ring to the applause of the spectators, including Vogt's supporters.

Back at the concentration camp several of the guards managed to raise a look of approval, but, for the majority of them, sports and the Olympic Games were far from their focus and area of interest.

The daily routines at Dachau quickly pitched Max down to earth with a thud. He pushed his sporting disappointment to the back of his mind, knowing that expressing too much distress would be frowned upon.

Later that year a significant consolation came along when, following two further bouts, he became the Hitler Youth boxing champion for 1936. With that, his amateur boxing career came to a close. What mattered now was his career as a soldier. For Max, life was all about loyalty and his duty to Leibstandarte.

Berlin had undergone a huge facelift since being selected to host the Olympics, but when Hitler became Chancellor in 1933 he decided to put even more effort into the event. A mighty stadium, designed to accommodate 110,000 spectators, was constructed. It was an inspirational development with a superb supporting infrastructure, incorporating swimming pools, a polo field, enormous sports halls and several smaller stadia that included the building where Max had recently boxed. It was by far the most ambitious project yet to stage the Olympics.

Hitler's enthusiasm for the games was for a purpose: it provided the party with an opportunity to promote its doctrine of Aryan superiority. Poster boards depicted Aryan-faced athletes with chiselled muscles and heroic strength. Its statement to the rest of the world was that Germans were descendants of an original super-race. The images also reflected the importance the party placed on physical fitness – a prerequisite for military service. Max was an archetypal Aryan, aligning perfectly with the policy of the day.

He celebrated his eighteenth birthday in September. Fritz's eighteenth had been a little earlier, in August. Much to their relief, their secondment to the Dachau concentration camp had finally come to an end and they were ready to join the Armed-SS proper.

Unlike some other aspirants, Max and Fritz had already shown many prerequisites for entry during their time served at Moringen and Dachau. The senior staff at Dachau reported them as good, loyal workers and they were both commended for their zeal and enthusiasm.

Inauguration into the SS began immediately upon their return to Lichterfelde. The first task was to pass the hurdle of the racial commission. Fortunately the orphanages that had housed and cared for them throughout their orphaned years had kept records of their parentage. Both were found to be of good Aryan stock. A panel queried Max about his first years at the Jewish-run orphanage at Schonhaus, and he confirmed that he couldn't remember much about his experiences there as he'd left on his fourth birthday.

Following racial clearance they would need to pass ideological instruction courses where the 'basic constitutional laws' and 'Laws of Honour' were taught. Achievement of this rendered them eligible for entry to the SS. The whole process would take about two years. In the final ceremony they would be assigned the rights to wear the SS dagger and to fight for their honour according to the commandments of the Schwarze Korps (Black Corps).

So far 1936 was proving a momentous year for Max, and it wasn't over yet. The climax would come late in the year when he was informed he had been selected as one of eight youths to meet Adolf Hitler and Heinrich Himmler, the chief of the SS, in person. All eight youths had excelled in one way or another. Max was chosen because of his archetypal Aryan looks, his physique, his boxing achievements, his records at Moringen and Dachau and his imminent entry into Leibstandarte, Hitler's personal unit. Hitler and Himmler had been briefed on all the boys' backgrounds so they could use the information as points of discussion. The thought of meeting the Führer in the flesh was overwhelming for Max; it would be the icing on the cake to wrap up 1936 as a year he would never forget.

The meeting took place in the old Reichstag building in Berlin. Much of the building had been destroyed by fire in February 1933, but the library and archives had been saved. Hitler apparently hated the building because it reminded him of the Weimar Republic. But he admired its architecture so he used its remaining structures as a place from which to make his propaganda speeches, hold exhibitions and screen films promoting his policies. It ceased to serve as a parliament building. Instead, the Kroll Theater was used for Hitler's speeches and party gatherings.

A Leibstandarte truck picked up the eight youths on the big day. Himmler's interest in them revolved around the satisfactory fulfilment of a number of procedures and final tests they would have to pass to become full SS members. Once they were full members they would be eligible for a choice of positions in the Allgemeine-SS (General-SS) or the Armed-SS. However, Max and Fritz were already aspirants for Leibstandarte. It was clear that membership of the Armed-SS would suit their characters, as normal hot-blooded soldiers, whereas the Allgemeine-SS appeared to be reserved for those with political leanings.

The truck came to a halt outside the old Reichstag building. The tailgate swung down and the boys jumped down from the truck and stood to attention in single file, waiting for their escort to lead them inside. They all felt nervous as they marched along the cold corridors, listening to the echo of their own footsteps.

At the end of the corridor was a large hall, and by the time they'd entered it Max's heart was in his mouth.

The officer leading the small unit snapped out an order for them to halt and stand to attention in one neat line in the centre of the hall. A hush fell over the hall as they waited for the big moment. Suddenly, the silence was broken as the sound of double doors swinging open echoed through the hall. This was the moment they'd all been waiting for.

Hitler and Himmler entered. The sound of their footsteps on the parquet floor seemed to bounce off the walls. The air became electrified as the Führer and Reichsführer approached the line of youths standing bolt upright. Max could feel their presence as they came closer. The boys snapped out the traditional Nazi salute.

"*Heil Hitler!*" they bellowed simultaneously.

The illustrious pair stopped short of the line. Hitler puffed up his chest and eyed them with pride, and Himmler nodded in satisfaction. There, in front of them, stood the fresh-faced epitomes of the Aryan race.

They made their way slowly down the line, shaking hands and having polite conversations concerning each young man's achievements. Hitler appeared genuinely happy to meet them. Max was last in line, and the Führer greeted him with a vigorous two-handed handshake.

A brief conversation followed, during which Max felt as if he was in a dream. Somewhere in the brief exchange Hitler mentioned that he hadn't been feeling too well that day and had a headache. Max naively came up with a suggestion, recommending a herbal remedy for quick relief.

Hitler, somewhat taken aback by the comment, smiled and turned to Himmler, saying, "Here is a man after your own heart, Heinrich." He glanced back at Max and waved his hand as if the problem was irrelevant.

They backed off a little and the Führer spoke: "Behold, Heinrich, my young lions," he said, extending his right arm towards the boys in a venerable way, nodding his head with pride and admiration.

He had prepared a short speech: "My fellow Aryans, you represent the first wave of young men entrusted with the task of building a new future for the Fatherland. You have been chosen to lay the foundation stones. Your names will be among the first to be embroidered into the tapestry recording our Reich's glorious history. Our future is destined to last for 1,000 years. As bearers of the sword of destiny, your strength and courage against our enemies will be paramount in the forthcoming struggle. You will engage in great battles and subdue the scourges bent on destroying our magnificent nation. Our race will reign supreme, and your children's children will remember you for your incredible feats against the foe. All I ask of you is your loyalty, for your honour is loyalty and to die for the Fatherland is the greatest honour one could ever seek. I love you all."

The boys responded with a mighty cheer and snapped out a second *"Heil Hitler!"*

With that, Hitler and Himmler turned away and walked out of the hall.

Over the next few days Max lived in a dreamworld. His mind kept replaying the meeting. He reflected obsessively on what he should have said to make the perfect impression and berated himself for advising the Führer about a remedy for his headache. Despite this, he doubted whether any future experience could match up to the one he'd just had.

It was during this period that control of Germany looked complete for Hitler and the party. Hitler had brandished a two-edged sword. One edge cut for the people; the other didn't. So far his master-race doctrine had worked well for motivating the nation. He and his line management were telling the people what they wanted to hear. They were re-establishing Germany as a major European power and overcoming the shameful legacy inherited through defeat in the Great War. Support for the NSDAP during these times was forthcoming and natural; a bigger picture was shared by all. The other edge of the sword appeared to serve the party only.

Whereas the bigger picture formed the backdrop and absorbed the attention of the majority, the few at the top, albeit those who held power and their extremist followers, deemed it necessary to focus on their prejudices against Bolsheviks, Jews and other minorities. It was this sinister deviation that propelled the doctrine of the master race into infamy.

The war years offered the perfect opportunity for the leadership to step up its long-held grievances against what it considered to be serious threats to its national heritage. As the entire country was embroiled in the horrors of the most devastating conflict the world had ever seen, it was hardly in a position to achieve any reversal on party policies. Regrettably, the legacy of prejudice adopted by the few compelled an entire nation to travel the causative path to its bitter end.

Nobody could have envisaged what would happen in the years to come. In 1936 the nation was on a wave: the Führer had remilitarised the Rhineland without international incident and the country had hosted the best Olympics the world had seen. For the party, 'getting ahead even more' was the only way to go.

BIBLIOGRAPHY

David Clay Large: *Nazi Games: The Olympics of 1936*. (Norton & Company.)

14

GATHERING STORM

The geopolitical concept of Lebensraum ('living space') had been discussed by German leaders long before Hitler came to power. In 1871, 'Lebensraum' was a popular political slogan. At this time, Britain and France were busy empire-building, accruing overseas colonies from the continents of Africa and Asia. Germany simply wanted to follow suit.

Hitler, on the other hand, rather than obtaining overseas colonies from other continents, wanted to make Germany larger within Europe. In November 1937, at a secret meeting at the Reich Chancellery, he announced his plans for expansion and acquiring 'living space' for the German people. Hence, the party's modified theory of Lebensraum became Germany's foreign policy during this period.

In 1938 Germany took its first steps towards acquiring Lebensraum with the annexation of Austria and the occupation of the Czech Sudetenland.

In March, owing to constant pressure from Hitler to accommodate the Nazi movement in the country, the Austrian Chancellor, Kurt von Schuschnigg, proclaimed a plebiscite: the Austrian people were to vote to decide whether or not they wished to remain independent from Germany. This action infuriated Hitler and he threatened to invade if the plebiscite wasn't called off and Schuschnigg did not resign. Both these demands were met, but Hitler had made up his mind to invade anyway.

On the morning of 12 March, a regular-army panzer corps,

under the command of General Heinz Guderian, crossed the German–Austrian border.

A day later, in the Austrian city of Linz, Hitler announced the legislation on the 'annexation' of Austria into the German Reich.

Later that year Hitler focused attention on the Czech-owned Sudetenland. The Sudetenland had formerly been part of Germany, but after the Treaty of Versailles it had become part of Czechoslovakia.

When Hitler came to power, Sudetenland Germans began to complain that the Czech-dominated government discriminated against them. Germans who had lost their jobs in the depression were arguing that they would be better off under Hitler.

Hitler wanted to take the Sudetenland by force, but on the advice of his generals he chose diplomacy instead.

In September 1938, Hitler attended two meetings. The first was at his retreat in Berchtesgaden with the British Prime Minister, Neville Chamberlain, but Hitler's terms were declared to be unacceptable after Chamberlain had discussed the issue with France and Czechoslovakia. The second meeting was held in Munich, and delegates came from Great Britain, France, Italy and Germany. Neither Czechoslovakia nor the Soviet Union, which had offered it aid under the terms of a 1935 pact, was invited.

Desperate to avoid war, the British and French leaders agreed that Germany could annex Sudetenland without the need for a plebiscite. In return, Hitler promised not to make any further demands in Europe.

The resultant Munich Pact permitted immediate occupation by Germany of the Sudetenland. When Chamberlain arrived back in London he gave the infamous announcement that he had secured 'peace in our time'.

On 1 October, Guderian's XVI Panzer Corps moved in and peacefully occupied the Sudetenland without meeting resistance from the Czechoslovakian armed forces.

As the Sudetenland contained nearly all of Czechoslovakia's

mountain fortifications, the country could no longer put up an effective defence against further aggression from Germany, and six months later, with total disregard for what had been agreed at Munich, Germany crossed over into the remaining provinces of Moravia and Bohemia, marking the final dismemberment of Czechoslovakia.

The year 1938 saw Hitler acquiring 'living space' and building an empire at home without losing a single man in battle.

BIBLIOGRAPHY

Charles Messenger: *Hitler's Gladiator: The Life and Times of Panzer Army Commander Sepp Dietrich*, pp. 68–70. (Conway, 2005.)

Louis L. Snyder: *Encyclopedia of the Third Reich*. (The Promotional Reprint Company Ltd, 1995.)

Andreas Hillgruber: *Germany and the Two World Wars*, pp. 41–7. (Harvard University Press, 1981.)

15

NCO

When asked to explain the lack of great statesmen in the world, Napoleon once said, "To get power you need to display absolute pettiness; to exercise power, you need to show true greatness."

For military leadership, the same applies, but only a few ever cross the abyss between selfishness and selflessness. The crossing involves the ability to, in a word, surrender. Those who are prepared to surrender their vanities and self-indulgences should never look back, for the road will be strewn with their blunders, echoed by past acts of pettiness and ignorance.

The immature mind is selfish, vain and egoistic. Siren whispers of sweet aggrandisement appeal to the little self, and discrimination and accountability are cast aside in the clamour to obtain power and glory.

The mature mind is selfless – one that has learnt to master the insidious sirens within and that operates from the greater self, leading for the good of the whole.

While Germany was playing political chess with other European powers, Max and Fritz were about to embark on their military careers with the regiment.

On 9 November 1936, the anniversary of the Munich Beer Hall Putsch, they were accepted as applicants for the Armed-SS and allowed to wear an SS uniform without collar patches.

On 30 January 1937, the anniversary of the day the party had come to power, they became cadets and were therefore entitled to a provisional SS pass.

They spent all of 1937 at the Berlin barracks as SS cadets, undergoing basic training and being drilled in the most demanding of parade-ground skills. Here they came to understand why the other Armed-SS units called Leibstandarte men the 'Asphalt Soldiers'.

On 20 April 1938, the Führer's birthday, Max and Fritz received their collar patches and permanent SS passes. Swearing the oath of loyalty to the Führer, a privilege reserved for members of Leibstandarte only, took place that day. The oath-taking ceremony was intended to give the newcomer a taste of that mystic bond uniting the charismatic Führer with his black-uniformed acolytes.

On 1 October 1938, soon after their twentieth birthdays, Max and Fritz formally entered Leibstandarte. They were now required to undergo the final part of the initiation process, which was a question-and-answer ceremony.

Passing the questions and answers successfully ended with celebrations and an unforgettable night on the town.

In the period between swearing the oath and official entry into Leibstandarte, Max and Fritz were sent back to Dachau, but not to the concentration camp; they had been enrolled into the SS non-commissioned officer (NCO) training programme at the nearby academy.

They received the news with mixed feelings: on one hand they would miss Berlin and their comrades at Lichterfelde; on the other a successful graduation would further their careers, moving them closer to an ultimate goal both so sorely sought.

Dachau brought back bad memories for them; the thought of Eicke's concentration-camp guard units rekindled old animosities. But there were happier memories too, including their training with the army regulars at the academy to which they were now being transferred. This time they would be training for the full period under exacting SS standards, hopefully graduating to a non-commissioned rank.

Their first day back at Dachau held a surprise for them: among the others assigned to the academy that year were two of their old Hitler Youth buddies, Hans Muller and Gunter Schnell. The reunion was joyful – the four were happy to be drawn together in one place again.

Experience in the years since their separation had moulded them all into confident and strong characters, although their personalities and habits differed extensively.

Muller was tall and big-boned and spoke with a slight stutter. He was the secretive, sombre type who always appeared to be hiding some dark secret from the past. His insistence on being addressed as Muller, not Hans, was beyond comprehension, but Max and the others respected his wishes.

In the war years, he would lead his platoon with an iron fist, demanding utmost loyalty. He was extremely stubborn and downright vindictive in some circumstances, ideal for SS, commanding by the book.

Forever controversial, Muller always put forward the other side of the coin. For this reason, in the war years, whenever Max, as company master sergeant, needed a second opinion, he'd call upon Muller to provide a judgement, knowing that it would differ from his own. He would weigh up the two opinions, and this would often lead to a compromise that was a better solution.

Of the four, Muller was the most ambitious, and he took his job somewhat more competitively than the others. This sparked some rivalry between himself and others, particularly when he was attempting to prove he was better officer material than they were.

Unlike the others, Muller never volunteered. This indicated a quality that would make him more cautious in combat – a tendency that had its advantages. He was no shirker, though, and would dive into the sharp end of an encounter if the situation called for it. Hence he would become a reliable and trusted individual for performing vital supportive roles.

Muller never ventured to form a serious relationship with a woman. He loved sex and used his women solely to satisfy his huge sexual appetite.

Fritz Kohler was a freckle-faced street fighter, naturally strong and brave-hearted – a salt-of-the-earth type of guy. His boisterous and positive nature would win him the respect of the platoon assigned to him during the war years. He would not hesitate to volunteer in any combat situation and was always first in line to wade into his army counterparts when the rivalry got hot. Fritz was perfect NCO material. He had a natural ability to lead. Although he was a hardened individual, and steady under pressure, his soft spot was for his men and he looked after them like they were his own offspring. He was driven by a passion for battle and challenges in the field. He was the loyal type, but also a tough realist – unlike Max, who, although similar, remained a dreamer.

Fritz was of average height with a muscular body and powerful legs, ginger hair and ears that stuck out slightly. Although he was not conventionally handsome, he appealed to most women. His silver tongue and sense of humour could sweep any young damsel off her feet. His relationships with women, however, took second place to his greater love: Leibstandarte, and the rush of fighting in the field.

He would jump in where angels feared to tread, and in combat situations he led by example, nearly always suffering a minor wound or two for his efforts. He had no personal ambitions other than war and love. Max had long ago decided that, in the absence of war at home, Fritz would probably have become a mercenary fighting in some remote part of the planet.

Gunter rounded off the quorum. The shortest of the four, he brought some balance to the team. Like Muller he was serious, but without the dark secretiveness. He worked at his job and was the proficient type, which made a good NCO. Also like Muller, he led by the book.

At first glance, Gunter seemed to be good officer material. However, he had a stubborn independence – a trait that sent a clear message to his superiors to keep him at NCO level. Like Max, he abhorred orders that were unreasonable, poorly considered or immature. Soft-spoken for an NCO, Gunter treated those under his command like family and won their respect. Despite being short and quiet in manner, he radiated a presence that made him seem as big as any of his comrades.

Dachau Academy had originally opened for army training several years earlier. A little later Himmler focused his attention on the school and set apart a section of it for SS NCOs. He appointed Major Anthony Riessman to run it – the ideal man for the job. Riessman was a tough individual who insisted on hand-picking exceptionally hard-nosed army sergeants to train his boys.

He stood just over six feet in height. At the age of fifty-two, he still sported a fit and athletic physique. His family had a fine military background dating back to old Prussia and the Napoleonic Wars.

Riessman's red mop of hair stood out in any crowd. The cadets nicknamed him the Red Baron, after Baron von Richthofen, the ace fighter pilot of the Great War.

Riessman had fought as a first lieutenant in that war and continued with the army after the armistice. During the Weimar period, he was promoted to the rank of captain. Soon after joining the SS in 1934, he was promoted to Sturmbannführer, and his specialised skills were put to use for training purposes.

Riessman was totally dedicated to his job – conscientious, intelligent, ambitious and exceptionally thorough in his training methods. He was a soldier's soldier who had won the respect of his fellow officers and the cadets who had passed through his training programme. He interviewed every cadet personally before they embarked on their rigorous training programme.

He monitored the progress of each cadet by utilising feedback from his team of disciplinarians, the trainers, and he often dropped by personally to question cadets. Their comments were meticulously recorded for use in future classes.

His job at the training academy was to create a dedicated and elite line of middle management that would bridge the gap between the ranks and the commissioned officers, moulding them into one cohesive force.

His team of toughened trainers would steer the cadets through a programme of simulated front-line hardships. He was aware that all cadets had latent survival skills. The harsh simulated conditions were designed to bring these strengths to the surface. All challenges were made more exacting insofar as they had to be accomplished against the clock. The aim was to teach the cadets how to endure, remain loyal and confront their fears in what appeared to be hopeless or critical situations.

Their attitude during the programme, innovativeness, fitness and staying power determined whether they failed or passed. They were his 'boys', but those who couldn't perform under the pressures were ruthlessly eliminated. Any SS participant who failed was immediately transferred to a regular army unit and advised upon which posting they would most aptly fill. His cadets admired and feared him both at the same time.

Riessman abhorred slovenliness and slackness. He was often heard stating, "Stay alert and stay sharp at all times; this could be the difference between life and death."

For Riessman, NCOs were the lynchpins in a battle situation, making sure orders were carried out. They nurtured and inspired the men under their command, particularly the new recruits and replacements. He figured that one had only to talk to several NCOs to establish a clear picture of the state of morale in the field. They were men who rarely minced their words – practical and honest.

There were clear differences between non-commissioned and commissioned officers. The commissioned boys had a ladder to climb, and the journey to the top, more often than not, involved rivalry and competition. Most NCOs were content to be where they were.

One evening, lying back in his bunk, Max brought up the topic of commissioned-officership.

"Officers!" he said aloud, inviting his peers to share in a discussion. "There are some I have a problem with and others I don't. As I see it, there are two kinds of officer: the 'warrior' type and the 'political' type. I get on well with the warriors, but I have a hard time understanding the politicians."

"They're all politicians," grunted Gunter.

"Pedantic and vain," added Fritz.

Muller didn't comment.

"Yes, but warrior types appear to be team players, whereas the political types seem to harbour hidden agendas for their own gain," remarked Max.

"That hidden agenda is ambition and continuous focus on how one can get one over on one's peers," quipped Muller.

"Remember Eicke," said Fritz. "He was one of your worst political types – ignorant, no conscience, angry and ruthless."

"There's another political type," said Gunter, "not as harsh as your version, Fritz; men of this type aren't cruel and do have a conscience, but they're still ambitious and competitive."

Max agreed. "It's the pettiness I abhor – so immature, isn't it? Warrior types don't seem to have this pettiness, do they?"

"By *warrior type*, I assume you mean the born-leader type? These guys adopt a more mature approach to leadership, but they are still ambitious disciplinarians who expect supreme loyalty from their subordinates at any cost."

"Where do you think Riessman fits into this hierarchy?" asked Gunter. He answered his own question. "I think he drifts between warrior and politician. Dedication to his boys tempers some of his worst qualities, which are apparent in his political tendencies."

"He does have a degree of ruthlessness about him. He wants

the SS faction at Dachau to be the best in Germany, and he eliminates the dross quickly."

"It's this streak in him that the cadets are fearful of," remarked Fritz.

"Wonder what he'd be like in the field under real combat conditions?" asked Max.

"I heard he won an Iron Cross, first class, in World War One," replied Muller.

"Looks like he can practise what he preaches, then," said Gunter.

Max stretched back and got lost in his thoughts. So far, his exchanges with the political types hadn't been successful. He could see right through them. Their behaviour infringed his personal code of honour, colouring his opinion of this kind. His innate optimism was nurtured, however, through knowing that all officers in Leibstandarte were dynamic, positive individuals with all the qualities demanded by warrior types.

The opening interviews with Riessman went well and he sensed the class of '38 would be one of the best he'd trained. As for the four cadets, it appeared they had all met Riessman during their senior years in the Hitler Youth. He'd been on the panel that had judged the caper they were involved in at the Bavarian training camp. He'd stuck with the rules, voting 'no result'. But Max then recollected that he was one of the few officers who had congratulated the boys on their innovation and courage under pressure.

Any idea that they might gain some favouritism because of the Hitler Youth incident was soon quashed: Riessman was stricter with them than with anybody else. He wanted to push them extra-hard to ensure they would graduate as four of his finest cadets.

Part-time participation in the NCO training programme with army regulars in late 1935 provided Max and Fritz with an edge over all the other boys. As a result they settled into the training programme well. Riessman began to savour 1938. He knew that war in Europe was looming, so he was grateful that such excellence should appear just at the right time.

His hard-nosed staff gave no quarter during the gruelling training sessions. Weaknesses were exploited and the trainers played on them exactingly. There was no middle path – the cadet either failed or endured. As ruthless as they were, they acted in the cadets' best interest. They knew that whichever battleground they ended up on would be swarming with a hostile enemy who wanted to maim and kill as many of Riessman's boys as they could. For this reason they needed to know just how far each individual could be pushed physically, and what their mental and emotional thresholds were.

All cadets took their share of goading and humiliation. Max's clowning trait would be tempered by the intensity of the character-building disciplines levelled on him by the trainers. Levity on duty was considered a weakness in the SS, and even the slightest weakness would not be tolerated as the programme progressed. If a cadet could not overcome a weakness, he was transferred.

The four young cohorts took to their tasks enthusiastically and endured the challenges handed out by Riessman's tough army sergeants. The programme was transforming them into professionals capable of thinking on their feet in the toughest of situations.

For Max, the final test would be the one which determined whether or not he would become an NCO in the elite ranks of Leibstandarte.

The final test came in the form of a dog-handling course. A German shepherd was assigned to each cadet for six weeks. The dog-handling programme created many unforgettable experiences for Max and his dog, Winston. Winston was an exceptionally intelligent and obedient dog, and by the end of the training man and dog had forged a warm, reciprocal relationship. Winston had derived his name from the English politician, Winston Churchill.

The dog-training course commenced with general obedience

then advanced to military-specific exercises, which involved a number of tasks.

Sentry dogs were the most commonly needed of the 'dogs of defence'. They worked as guard dogs at military installations, providing warning of intruders. Scout dogs were trained to operate silently, to sniff out snipers and other dangers. Scout dogs were also used for tracking fugitives on the run. Messenger dogs were taught to act as couriers, carrying equipment or documents in both combat and non-combat conditions.

Winston was to be trained in all aspects and allocated to the task he performed best – so Max was led to believe.

The day before the end of the programme, Max and five other NCOs that had participated in the training were ordered to assemble on the parade ground. After several minutes, an officer, Karl Gotze, arrived. He stopped at one end, then, walking slowly along the row of cadets, inspected each with a keen eye.

'Strange!' thought Max. 'What's happening here?'

Following the inspection Gotze stood in front of the group, pumping the balls of his feet, hands clasped behind his back.

Cutting an arrogant pose, Gotze made an announcement that stunned his captive audience: "Your dog-handling course finishes tomorrow and you will be parting company with your faithful dogs in the morning," he said with a smirk. After a short pause, Gotze continued: "As a final initiation for SS NCO graduation you have been chosen from your remaining class of twenty-four cadets to execute your dog."

The air turned icy. All cadets maintained the attention stance, frozen in their surprise.

Gotze went on: "Ugly news for some of you, no doubt! You will garrotte them in this yard at 0530 hours tomorrow morning before breakfast."

It was indeed ugly news. They'd worked so closely with their dogs and now they had to kill them.

'Why us?' thought Max.

What he didn't know was that the six had been selected

because they had shown the most affection to their dogs during the training period.

The officer looked down the line with a sardonic smile on his face. He was aware that each of them had created a special relationship with his dog. It would be a difficult time the following morning, but this was the SS. Max remained at attention as a wave of disappointment surged through his body.

Gotze finished up: "Any cadet unable to carry out his duty or showing signs of compassion during or after the execution shall be expelled from the academy and transferred to a regular army unit. Is this understood?"

The line-up stood in silence.

"Good, good. You are dismissed!" Gotze bellowed.

Max's mind raced as he walked across into the building. The thought of garrotting loyal Winston made him feel sick.

Back at his billet, his anger overflowed. "Why me!" he exclaimed, venting his frustration, using Fritz as a sounding board.

"Max, this is an extra test for you, my friend, and to pass you will need to handle it appropriately. If you don't carry out this instruction with the gusto expected of you, then all will be lost. You will find yourself kicked out of Leibstandarte and relegated to the regular army. That's not want you want, is it?"

Reluctantly Max nodded his agreement.

"Fritz, I understand membership of the Armed-SS isn't for the timid, but to kill a loyal, fully trained animal that is unable to defend itself seems senseless to me."

Fritz's response was brief: "Do your job, Max."

At 5.30 a.m. the following day, Riessman's trainers lined up to witness the senseless slaughter of six fully trained German shepherds. The garrotte used for the execution was a mechanically driven device.

Max, heeding Fritz's words, led Winston into the tank yard, stopped at his designated position and secured the dog to a steel post. He looped the wire garrotte over its head and tightened it. Gripping the handle on the wheel he cranked it around swiftly. His heart raced as the dog started to choke and attempt to pull back from the wire noose. Winston's yelps echoed through the yard as Max turned the wheel like a maniac to give his dog the swiftest possible death. It was all over within a few seconds.

Max had ensured that the wire had been secured around the most vulnerable part of the dog's neck. At the end of the ordeal, he stood to attention, gave a formal party salute and walked back towards the canteen block for breakfast.

In the canteen, an officer who had witnessed the execution caught Max's attention and beckoned him over for a chat.

"Nice kill, Rieker – swiftest kill I've ever seen. Loved the dog, did you?" The remark implied that Max had shown signs of sympathy.

"Killing a defenceless dog isn't one of my fortes Obersturmführer – a little different to killing an enemy of the Reich. I happen to love dogs, but orders are orders." Then, quoting Theodor Eicke's comments at Dachau, he assured the officer he would show no pity in front of the enemy, that his loyalty would be unfailing on the battlefield.

The officer acknowledged his rather surprising response: "I see, Rieker, but I don't care for your reference to 'defenceless dog'. We are not looking for the compassionate types in the SS, you know – particularly among you non-commissioned ranks. You should keep such remarks to yourself."

Max fixed his eyes on the officer: "Yes, Obersturmführer, I fully understand."

He gave a very snappy salute and awaited his dismissal. The officer dismissed him, but Max sensed that steely eyes were following him as he walked back to his table.

The incident with the officer caused Max some anxiety all that day. Would his comments cost him expulsion from Leibstandarte? It wasn't long before Riessman got to hear of the incident and called Max across to his office. He gave Max a severe admonishment for his 'defenceless dog' remark. Time stood still for Max as he stood to attention, watching Riessman pacing the floor in front of him and mulling the incident over and over in his mind. It was obvious Riessman was in a quandary: whether to pass or fail Max.

The decision lay in the balance; the situation challenged mandatory requirements for entry into the Armed-SS – that is, showing signs of compassion meant expulsion. Riessman thought hard. He was angry with Max because he had been the perfect cadet in every other way.

Suddenly he came to a decision: for once he was prepared to overlook the incident. First, there had been no official complaint or objection – just hearsay. To let him go would be a disservice to the Armed-SS. Riessman had made up his mind, and he immediately dismissed the incident as irrelevant. He proceeded to congratulate Max for graduating in a most memorable class.

Fritz, Muller and Gunter were notified of their graduation through official channels later that day.

They all left the Dachau training academy with the rank of Oberscharführer (senior squad leader in army terms). Riessman and his tough trainers had taught his boys basic and advanced military survival skills, rigid discipline and loyalty to their commanding officers. They also were now fully proficient in the use of almost every weapon in the German Army as well as being able to identify and use some Russian and British weapons. Additionally, the academy's driving section had ensured they came away with driving licences for motorbikes, light and heavy personnel carriers and other vehicles.

Three of the four new NCOs returned to Berlin to Sepp Dietrich's Leibstandarte, while Gunter was assigned to an equally formidable Armed-SS regiment, Das Reich.

The new NCOs had been disappointed that they had missed Leibstandarte's participation in the advance into Austria earlier that year. However, they were elated when they heard they would take part in the second action concerning the move into the Sudetenland. Here they would try out their new skills as sergeants, leading their own squads.

For Riessman, his training days at the NCO academy were numbered. In August 1939 he was recalled to the Reichssicherheitshauptamt (RSHA) building at 9 Prinz-Albrecht-Strasse, Berlin, to undertake a new administrative role. His job would be to monitor and control the internment programme for political prisoners and other non-combatant offenders, including Jews, Gypsies, homosexuals and those who were members of extremist groups, such as Freemasons and Jehovah's Witnesses.

As usual, he applied his expertise to the job, and within months of his appointment he had created a matrix and reporting system that was second to none for all labour/concentration camps throughout the Reich. His expertise was later extended to the six major concentration camps built in Poland after 1941.

Despite the new assignment, Riessman never lost touch with the NCOs that graduated from his academy. He used his administrative system to monitor the whereabouts, welfare and progress of every one of his former cadets. He knew where they were, when they were promoted, and if they were wounded or had fallen in battle.

Max wasn't to know, but a time would come when Riessman's excellent monitoring network would help him get through the most challenging time of his life.

BIBLIOGRAPHY

Robert Lewis Koehl: *The Black Corps: The Structure and Power Struggles of the Nazi SS*, pp. 132–41. (Madison, 1983.)

Richard Schulze-Kossens: *Die Junkerschulen: Militärischer Führernachwuchs der Waffen-SS*, pp. 37–40, 139, 151. (Osnabruch, 1982.)

16

SPYING FOR THE FATHERLAND

While Max was being finely honed into an elite soldier, life for Greta was also moving forward. In March 1935 she celebrated her twenty-first birthday. She'd blossomed into an attractive woman with sparkling hazel eyes. Her wavy hair bounced off her shoulders when she walked. She took care of her health and kept fit, and as a result she had developed a firm, symmetrical body with all the curves in the right places. There was every reason for the air of independence she radiated, for she'd come a long way with the party since her dismissal from the Holtzes' Charlottenburg household.

At seventeen she lost her virginity to Friedrich Holtz. He'd always been the friendly sort, chatty and funny, and before she'd left the house he let her know she could call him at any time.

Soon after moving in with Marlene and Traudl, Greta took up his offer. It wasn't out of need that she called him; it was more just to listen to his voice. She missed his company and sense of humour.

Not long after the telephone call she actually bumped into him in a Berlin department store, Kaufhaus des Westens. As their eyes met she found his warm smile irresistible. Unconstrained by Emma's presence she felt at ease with him as they struck up a conversation and arranged to meet again. She was so excited at the thought of it.

With make-up well applied and wearing expensive clothing, her aim was to look a bit older and more appealing for him, but she needn't have bothered; she looked stunning.

After several lavish lunches at swish downtown restaurants, Friedrich had virtually swept her off her feet. But the same applied to Friedrich; touching base again enabled him to resume his mission of getting to bed her.

It wasn't long before he was making reservations for a luxury hotel suite. Here they indulged in a passionate love affair, and at last Friedrich had achieved his desire.

The affair was hot and exciting, until Friedrich showed himself to be a butterfly. After several months, his eyes turned to other flowers and he dropped Greta like a hot potato. The sudden rejection devastated her. She spent months getting over him, and vowed she'd never become so emotionally absorbed in a man again. Any future lover would be chosen according to how much he could help her in her quest for advancement within the party. Greta toughened up.

Toughening up didn't mean retracting her love for Max. The bond of love was solid. Blood was thick, and neither kept any secrets from the other. When the opportunity arose they'd spend long evenings talking politics, relationships, ambitions, their fears and day-to-day experiences. Good or bad, they never held anything back. They shared information they could never share with anybody else – the penalty for betraying secrets was execution. The relationship was truly one of love, trust and care.

Despite the genetic connection, their characters had little in common. Greta was a sharp-witted intellectual, while Max was athletic, a bit of a clown with a sensitive and somewhat emotional nature. Greta viewed life from a psychological perspective; she studied people and their behaviours. Max was sensitive to people, but in a different way; he was more intuitive. He took a philosophical view of life. Greta was a realist; Max was a dreamer. They saw life through different-coloured glasses. Similarities were in their drive and healthy sense of humour – a quality they were able to fall back on when life became complicated and tough. They were survivors in tumultuous times.

She'd joined the print workshop as a sixteen-year-old, and worked at the part-time job while studying for a degree in political science.

Her enthusiasm and loyalty was soon recognised and earned her a permanent job in the publishing offices, firstly editing, and then going on to write various articles of her own.

In 1932 she applied to join the party just after her eighteenth birthday. Formal entry included racial screening. The screening process delved back into her past. The party's main concern was her time spent at the Jewish-run orphanage, Schonhaus.

Party interviewers knew that the orphanage board's ruling was that all children chosen for admission should practise the Jewish faith as part of their daily routine.

Her comment on having to attend the synagogue daily was that, like most of the other German children there, she never committed herself to the Jewish faith; to her it was like any other orthodox religious teaching, and she compared it to German children attending Bible classes at Sunday school.

Greta's answers were generally honest and to the point, but they were diplomatic when necessary. She emphasised that the religious teachings had not influenced her in any way that would compromise party doctrine.

Her responses appeared to satisfy the interviewing panel, and thereafter nothing else about her upbringing at Schonhaus was discussed.

In March 1935, the first edition of the *Black Corps* (*Das Schwarze Korps*) was published. This was the official newspaper of the SS, published in close cooperation with the SS secret service.

The *Black Corps* was a free weekly newspaper, and it appeared each Wednesday. All SS members were required to read it and inspire others to read it. Circulation rose swiftly, and in November of that year its distribution reached 200,000.

Writing articles meant Greta had to liaise with secret-service members to obtain their approval of her articles. During this period, several men from the secret service had tried to seduce her, but her earlier experience with Friedrich Holtz had made her wary and she always managed to avoid that trap by using her work and obedience to the party as an excuse for refusal. She'd become far too absorbed in her career to allow meaningless affairs to interfere with her ambitions. She skilfully maintained her personal freedom without overly upsetting the men who spent their time chasing her.

On the other hand, if the need arose she'd use her femininity to her own advantage. Greta's forte lay in her body language and her understanding of a man's mindset. She knew exactly how to manipulate the right man at the right time.

By the time she had achieved her political-science degree eyes were watching her, and a major career change was about to take place that would elevate her closer to the upper echelons of the party.

It was in March 1936, following a *Black Corps* weekly approval meeting that a particularly suave secret-service officer, Ernst Jager invited her to dinner. She accepted with her typical cool poise while inwardly bubbling with excitement. The dinner went well, but she was surprised to discover that Jager wasn't angling for a night of passion. Instead, he asked if she'd like to work as his personal assistant at the Sicherheitsdienst. Known as the SD, it was the intelligence service for the SS and the NSDAP.

It was an offer she couldn't refuse, and it represented a quantum leap in her career. Within weeks she had settled comfortably into the new workplace, performing a job that seemed to have been made for her.

During her time at the SD she took twelve weeks' leave to give birth to a baby boy. She'd volunteered to become pregnant in response to Heinrich Himmler's announcement that it was the patriotic duty of every man in the SS to sire at least four children for the Reich.

The programme had been launched in December 1935. It evolved to become one of the most bizarre of the SS agencies: the Lebensborn, or Fountain of Life.

In 1936 the first Lebensborn home was opened near Munich to accommodate and look after 'racially and genetically valuable expectant mothers'. These, of course, were the wives and girlfriends of SS men or, as in Greta's case, volunteers for the cause. Scores more Lebensborn homes were then established throughout Germany. Mothers could either keep the children born at the homes or place them for adoption with SS-approved families.

Being a volunteer, Greta was given the opportunity to choose the father, but it wasn't until her third date that an appropriate suitor emerged. She chose a tall, strong and handsome senior officer attached to the Armed-SS unit Verfügungstruppe. Her decision had been swayed by his keen sense of humour and their agreement that there would be no strings attached to the relationship after she had given birth.

Several weeks after giving birth, Greta transferred her infant son to the care of an approved family. This enabled her to continue with her position for the party at the SD, which was about to enter another phase.

During her pregnancy she'd enrolled in an advanced French class. Her command of the French language was very good, but she wanted to achieve the highest level of proficiency. The intense programme gave her the ability to speak and write the French language fluently.

There was a reason for her choice: all successful participants were placed on a shortlist of applicants to become agents in espionage activities.

On her very first day back from maternity leave Greta was offered the opportunity to work on an assignment. Her first job wouldn't be a foreign assignment, though. Before she could work as an international agent she would need to undergo further training.

Her first assignment was a minor role in a set-up that involved rounding up members of a suspected communist spy enclave in Berlin.

She was seconded to the Gestapo, and after several days of basic training she took to the field and played her part well. The activists were arrested and whisked away for interrogation. Greta was well aware of Gestapo methods and techniques of interrogation, but, like Max, she didn't care too much for it. She turned a blind eye to the darker side of the job. On the other hand, embarking on a job in the spy business brought a completely new level of excitement into her life.

Her appointment with Jager ended when the working relationship suddenly developed into a whirlwind of passion. It was a mistake, and the romance almost wrecked her career. She had to endure a day of relentless interrogation. Only her immaculate work record, loyalty and good connections enabled her to avoid dismissal.

Jager, a married man, was ordered to end the relationship because the department didn't want complications concerning employees' private lives.

Jager's line manager, Franz Paulus, was a close colleague of his. After the near-disastrous incident, Jager confided in him, asking if he would consider Greta for a position that was about to be advertised in the department.

Paulus made an informal visit to Greta to check her out for the position. He concocted an excuse to get to meet her and struck up a brief conversation. The verbal exchange was enough for him to form an assessment which supported Jager's recommendation, and Greta was duly asked if she would like to work directly for Counter-Intelligence. She was stunned when she realised she'd been made personal assistant to Jager's line-manager, Hauptsturmführer Paulus, who answered directly to Walther Schellenberg.

Germany supported two counter-intelligence organisations during this time: the SS and the Abwehr, which acted as the Ministry of Defence.

The Abwehr wasn't a party-created agency. Its chain of command was such that the chief of the Abwehr reported directly to the German High Command. It ran from 1921 to 1944 and dealt exclusively with human intelligence. Raw intelligence reports were gathered from field agents and 'other sources', implying involvement in counter-espionage.

The operations branch of the German High Command, known as the Oberkommando der Wehrmacht (OKW), compiled the intelligence summaries and disseminated them through to the intelligence-evaluation sections of the army, navy and air force.

The Abwehr's headquarters was at 76/78 Tirpitzufer, Berlin, adjacent to the offices of the OKW.

It was while holding this position that Greta received her clearance for participation in international espionage activity. International agents would need to undergo an extensive training programme.

The first part of her training involved familiarising herself with the various departments. It was necessary for all agents to get acquainted with the complex organisations, numerous departments and services. Security was extremely strict. In every office was posted the following admonition:

You must only know what is essential for **Your Work**; whatever you learn, you must keep it to yourself.

Officials and collaborators had been shot for breaking this rule. One story told of the execution of an official for merely telling a colleague from another section about the work in which he'd been involved.

Such strict security had its downside. The 'patriotic duty of silence', as it was sometimes called, hindered the effectiveness of the security and intelligence sections of the organisation. It meant that quite often subordinates could not be provided with sufficient background information to act speedily and independently.

Excessive compartmentalisation was another closely related problem. Nobody knew what any other section was working on, and this led to inefficiencies, interference in one another's operations, and lost opportunities. To make matters worse, information gathered at the lowest level had to be passed to another section – the executive one – and then on to the end user. Unfortunately, reports were not just passed on but rewritten at several levels. The outcome was that the final product bore little resemblance to the original report.

All-powerful officers sat at the top of this organisation, and their many subordinates were petty-minded bureaucrats who were keen to guard and maintain their personal domains and privileges. The result was a slack, shoddy product, seriously weakened by dangerous inaccuracies.

Greta soon became aware of the shortfalls in the system, but she was too junior to make waves. Besides, if she upset the wrong person, life would turn sour. So she just got on with it.

The second part of her training called for her to spend time at the Kripo, where she learnt the fundamentals of police work and the basic notions of police science. Then she spent a further three months back at the SD with Paulus, followed by another three with the Gestapo. Final training involved the art of surveillance and other field techniques of the spying business. By the time she had finished, she was more eager than ever to participate on an international mission.

The department in which she worked was equivalent to the British MI6. It focused on gathering material, statistics and information on Germany's enemies, which included Britain, France and the Soviet Union. The information was classified in one of four different security classes: secret, top secret, secret information exclusively for the headquarters command, and secret information of the Reich. Greta held a high-priority pass, which made her privy to top-secret information.

Added security came in the form of a quarterly interview, when a committee of senior staff would question all department employees. The questions covered their personal activities, including relationships begun and ended over the period. If answers proved satisfactory, a fresh security pass would be issued for another three months.

Despite the previous incident with Jager, the new position with Paulus wouldn't be without its romance. Like Jager, Paulus grew fond of her. After her training the many hours they spent working closely together led to a familiarity with each other's habits, likes and dislikes. Soon a sexual tension developed between them, but initially Greta resisted it. She'd come close to dismissal when her affair with Jager was discovered, and she doubted she'd be given a second chance. Although she coped well with the situation, Paulus eventually found her presence intoxicating. She, in turn, admired his tireless enthusiasm for their work.

One evening, as Greta was about to leave the office, Paulus, unable to resist his feelings, called over from his desk: "Greta, will you come to see me tonight? I'll cook, we can relax and have a drink, and . . ."

She stopped in her tracks and stood transfixed. Catching her breath, she spun around to face him. As she did, he got up from his chair and walked over to her. They spontaneously embraced and kissed passionately. Both hearts pumped fiercely as they backed into the door, still joined in their passionate embrace. He fumbled for the key in the lock and turned it while their mouths were still engaged in a passionate kiss.

Paulus frantically unbuttoned her coat. Greta shuffled her body, allowing the coat to fall to the ground. She couldn't wait and pulled up her skirt like a woman possessed, wriggling her hips and panting heavily. Trembling in anticipation, Paulus rubbed her crotch, which was already moist with anticipation. She gasped, unclasped her garter and pulled her silk panties down to her thighs. She wriggled some more and the panties slid down her legs and dropped to the floor. All the while they were still locked together, kissing and gasping for air.

She fumbled to undo his trousers and they dropped to the floor. He wasted no time and took her against the door. She stretched back to grasp the hat-and-coat hook for balance. It was exciting, satisfying – a surprising explosion of bliss. He kissed her neck passionately and performed the act like a man who hadn't had sex for several years.

Greta finally responded to his original question in between gasps: "No . . . I'd rather be . . . by myself tonight . . . but thanks for the offer. Ohhhh, but don't stop now . . . we've plenty of time."

The tornado ran its course, leaving both breathing heavily, completely but joyously exhausted. Finally coming to their senses, they dressed and tidied up. Greta travelled home wrapped in a warm glow.

Things were wild and steamy over the next few days, but they kept the sex to the office, after hours. It was delicious, salacious – so good. But both sensed it would have to end soon. They were right. One night Paulus was almost caught with his pants down, so to speak, when a guard walking his round heard a noise from inside and grew suspicious. They barely got away with it, but rumours were soon floating around the office. The lovesick pair realised they were on thin ice and decided they should stop.

Soon after, Greta agreed to apply for another position advertised within the department. Her application was successful and she transferred on the grounds that the position called for her French-speaking expertise. In her new role she became personal secretary to another Hauptsturmführer, Heinz Netzer, who had the same clout as Paulus, and was also answerable to Walther Schellenberg, deputy leader of the secret service.

Finally, in March 1939, Greta was offered the chance to try out her skills in international espionage. Her first mission would take her down into Southern Europe to the Iberian Peninsula and the Portuguese capital of Lisbon. The task involved picking up and exchanging information from agents operating in the area.

Greta and another girl, Vally, operated undercover, working out of a small tourist agency. Identifying agents involved exchanges of coded conversations. Once contact was confirmed, information would be exchanged; the agent would provide intelligence reports in return for details of the next assignment.

Additionally, Greta took full advantage of the excellent climate the Mediterranean offered, catching the train on her days off to savour the niceties of the Algarve, south of Lisbon.

It was routine work, requiring little exertion; but just as she was settling in, Berlin called for her return. Her Iberian adventure was cut short because of the impending action that would embroil Europe in yet another monumental conflict.

Her next assignment elevated her to a higher level of importance and responsibility, and with it came promotion to Obersturmführer. She was headed for Switzerland, where her expertise in the French language and administrative skills would be put to full use; here she was to work at a branch of the Swiss National Bank in Geneva.

Germany's gold and foreign-exchange reserves were being drained, and this would inhibit the acquisition of war material. Germany could not afford to lose the ability to pay for foreign machinery and parts.

By 1937 the party had discovered that by transferring gold to overseas banks in return for currency it would be able to sustain its forthcoming war effort. As well as its original assets, additional gold was acquired by looting its victims, collecting the looted assets into central depositories, and then transferring it to foreign banks. The looting commenced in 1938, shortly after the occupation of Austria and continued during the occupation of Czechoslovakia. By the time Greta started the job, Poland had become the third source. This process continued throughout the war years, and the loot included the personal effects of inmates held in concentration camps.

The Swiss National Bank in Geneva and the Bank for International Settlements in Basel were the main players in the channelling process. They openly carried out gold transactions between neutral central banks and the Reichsbank, and these transactions were known as triangular deals. The Swiss National Bank was the largest gold-distribution institution in Continental Europe, even before the war, and it provided Germany with the most efficient means of disposing of its gold.

Looted gold was re-smelted to disguise the original source, then exported (channelled) through Switzerland to the neutral central banks of Sweden, Portugal, Spain, Turkey and Argentina in exchange for hard currency to finance the war.

Greta was a vital second string to Hans Droler. He was a senior officer in the Allgemeine-SS, and he had been a former executive of the Munich branch of the Reichsbank back in 1937. Together they monitored and kept meticulous records of all gold transfers being channelled through the Swiss National Bank branch in Geneva and out to the various neutral central banks.

Disappointingly, Greta was recalled to Berlin in early December 1939 after spending only five months in Geneva. She discovered the posting had not been a permanent one. Evidently Droler wanted to reunite with his girlfriend, Heidi, who'd worked at the Munich branch.

Despite the disappointment, Greta was soon given her third mission. The following month during the so-called phoney war in Western Europe, when both sides decided to sit it out for a while, she was informed she would need to undergo further training.

Of the three assignments, this would be by far the most dangerous. The operating area would be Prague, Czechoslovakia. Basic training involved instruction in firing handguns. Greta had a choice of five weapons: Luger, Walther P38, Walther PPK, Sauer 38H and Mauser HSc.

The Luger pistol fired eight rounds from a detachable box magazine. It was extremely accurate because of its precision engineering, ergonomic grip angle and shape. From 1938 the Luger was gradually replaced by the Walther P38. The Walther was cheaper to manufacture and a more practical military alternative to the Luger. Walther PPK pistols were reliable and easy to conceal. They were almost half the weight of the Luger and the Walther P38. The Sauer 38H rivaled the PPK; it was heavier than the PPK and a favourite with the German police agencies.

The Mauser HSc was first produced in 1937 and was the most favoured handgun of the German Navy and Air Force.

At the end of the instruction course, Greta chose the Walther PPK because it was the lighter and easier to conceal. Her mission was a dangerous one as it would bring her into contact with enemy agents. Little did she know how crucial her expertise in handling firearms would be during this particular mission.

The assignment in Prague involved locating British agents working there and monitoring their day-to-day activities with the aim of discovering who their Czech counterparts were.

As a result of the capture of two British agents in Holland earlier in November 1939 (the Venlo Incident), the Gestapo had managed to secure a list of British agents working in occupied territories, including Czechoslovakia.

Greta was to be assigned to one of the British agents, codenamed Danube Two. Danube Two worked out of Prague under the guise of a salesman, named Petr Novak, representing the Czech brewery Svijany. A hotel called The Iron Gate, located in the Old Town district of Prague at Michalska 19, served as the place for meeting existing and new 'clients'.

Individuals from the beer industry were invited to regular functions at the hotel. Danube Two would go through his sales talk in three languages – French, German and Czech – addressing a group of both genuine and pseudo customers. Free drinks, sandwiches and cakes were served as part of the promotion drive. One or more of those attending would be members of the Czech underground, and as the evening wore on an exchange of information would take place.

Greta posed as a French-speaking representative of a string of Swiss hotels. She used the alias of Sophie. Her job was to identify the Czech agent or agents. After the presentation, while the guests were enjoying drinks and nibbles, she struck up a conversation with the British agent, who introduced himself as Petr Novak. She also opened up casual exchanges with those whom she suspected might be his Czech counterparts. They talked on trade matters and exchanged business cards.

As people started to leave, Novak walked across to her and, speaking in French, invited her for a nightcap in the hotel's cocktail lounge. He had become suspicious and wanted to check her out.

Greta, a little taken aback, accepted the invitation to avoid fuelling his suspicion. Novak chose to sit up at the bar. He pulled his stool close so that he could study every movement on Greta's very attractive face.

"What's your fancy?" he said, eyeing the cocktail menu: "champagne cocktail, Buck's Fizz, Bijou, Between the Sheets?" With the last, he jokingly flicked his eyebrows.

She smiled. "I'll have a Cuba libre, thanks."

Novak chose a Brandy Alexander.

"So, how do like Prague, Sophie?" He studied her expression closely.

"It's a fascinating city. I like it very much."

"Have you been to Prague before?"

"No, it's my first visit," she replied. "I work for the Swiss Historic Hotels Foundation. The hotels don't sell Czech beer, which has a fine reputation throughout Europe, so they sent me across to look into the most prominent breweries in Prague and report back on the choices." She tried to keep the conversation centred on her work brief.

They exchanged small talk, but every now and then Novak would ask a leading question in an effort to extract a reaction that might expose Greta for what he suspected she was.

"You look so German, my dear?"

"No, I'm not German – I am Swiss, from Geneva," she replied, flashing her eyelids down coyly in an amusing way.

He smiled, admiring her skilled reaction.

Novak had been to Zurich and several other Swiss resorts, including Zermatt, St Moritz and Interlaken, in peacetime and could speak German well. He thought he might catch her out. Assuming she knew Geneva, he thought he might test her for knowledge of the rest of her country.

"Do you like to ski, Sophie?"

"No. I can ski, but I prefer hiking to keep me fit."

"Ah! Yes, you look very fit," he replied, eyeing up her perfectly formed body. "What's your favourite resort back home?"

Greta realised he was checking her out. She'd been to French-speaking Geneva on her previous mission, and in her free time there she had familiarised herself with the nearest resort town of Zermatt, which was German-speaking. It was one of the towns Novak had visited as a tourist.

"I prefer the lake towns myself, but my winter resort is Zermatt."

"Ah, my favourite, but you must speak German, then?"

"Yes, of course I speak German too," she replied.

Novak proceeded to speak to her in German, and Greta provided a suitable response.

"Your German is very good."

"Yes, of course." Greta began to get a little hot under the collar.

Novak was gently working himself into a position to pop the question that might expose her cover.

"I stayed at the Badrutt's Palace Hotel in Zermatt. It's a magnificent hotel. Are you familiar with it?" he asked, eagerly awaiting her response.

Greta was grabbing at straws – she assumed the hotel was five-star.

"Yes, I know that one. But you must be very rich, Petr. I've only stayed at the smaller hotels there." She managed to recollect the name of a smaller hotel and quoted a name.

"Pity," said Novak, looking at Greta rather quizzically.

He'd offered her a red herring: the hotel he'd mentioned wasn't in Zermatt; it was in the other resort town, St Moritz. He felt his suspicions had been confirmed.

To avoid making Greta feel too uncomfortable, Novak remarked, "Let's have one more for the road, then I must go – I've a busy day tomorrow."

"Yes, that's fine by me," said Greta, making sure she didn't show any sense of relief, although his simple small talk was beginning to unnerve her.

The conversation changed back to the job. She knew her stuff, and Novak was hard-pressed to catch her out in this area of expertise, although he tried hard enough.

They finished up and he escorted her through to the hotel foyer. Here he stopped short of the golden swing doors, kissed her hand and bade her farewell.

"You are indeed a beautiful woman, Sophie. I hope to see you again, very soon."

Greta beamed a smile, thanked him for the drinks and walked into the street. Gasping with relief, she hoped she hadn't given the game away but reflected on his comment about seeing her again, very soon; it made her feel uncomfortable.

She stepped into a waiting taxicab and spoke to the driver: "Krakovska Apartments, Wenceslas Square – opposite museum."

The cab drove off and Greta glanced back over her shoulder to check she wasn't being followed. An old Skoda Popular had turned into the street behind her, but it was too soon to jump to conclusions.

As her cab weaved its way out of the Old Town district towards Wenceslas Square she looked out of the back window to check whether the Skoda had gone on its way. Unfortunately, it hadn't – it was still following the cab. Greta started to feel uneasy.

'What is my opposition?' she thought. She could make out the silhouettes of at least two men wearing fedoras.

Her final task that evening should have been to check back with and debrief other members of her team. Thinking on her feet, she decided to place the meeting on hold and concentrate on losing the men tailing her.

She leant across the front seat and asked the driver to stop short of her destination, near Wenceslas Square. She needed somewhere that was busy – a public place to reduce the risk of a dangerous confrontation with what might be Czech agents.

The cab stopped. Greta paid her fare and stepped out on to the wide pavement to mingle with those night owls outside the nightclubs and cocktail lounges of the famous square. As she hurried along she glanced back over her shoulder. The Skoda had stopped and one of the 'agents' was following her on foot.

Despite being gripped with fear, she kept focused, avoiding panic. The experience was a first for Greta. Her heart was in her mouth as she made her way towards a cocktail lounge she had visited earlier in the week.

She pushed open the entrance door and walked through the lounge towards the bar. The interior was moderately filled and several men looked up as she glided over to the empty stools at the far end of a long bar. She hadn't been there at this time of night, and it soon became apparent that the lounge bar was a place where men met up with ladies of the night.

She slipped her coat off her shoulders, folded it neatly, placed it over the stool next to her, then laid her handbag on top of it. She pulled a high stool towards her and delicately perched on the leather seat. Getting comfortable, she crossed her legs, causing the split in her long evening dress to part, revealing a remarkable pair of shapely legs.

Every action she'd made was observed by every male in the lounge, including those who were already accompanied.

She glanced into the large mirror behind the bar and saw that most of the men were still checking her out.

'Christ,' she thought, 'this is just what I need!'

She ordered a coffee, then glanced over to the entrance door just in time to notice the Czech agent slip inside. He took a table near the door and ordered a lager.

What to do? She sipped her coffee, contemplating the situation. Suddenly the image of the exit door beyond the washroom area came to mind. She wondered whether the agent had been there before and if he was familiar with the layout of the premises. Was he aware of the rear exit?

Several minutes passed by and she made her move. She stood up, hung the coat over her arm, and grabbed her bag as if making her way to the washroom. Unfortunately all eyes were on her, including the agent's. The exit door was out of sight from the lounge, and she hoped she would get away before the agent realised she wasn't going to reappear.

To her relief the door opened into the cold night air. Greta pulled on her coat and made ready to lose her tail once and for all.

Instead of taking the alleyway back out to the main street she opted to go in the opposite direction into the second-tier streets that housed seedy bars and brothels.

One comforting thought was that there were plenty of German soldiers stalking the night streets here. If enemy agents confronted her, she might have to appeal to one or several of those boys from home however, that would break her cover.

She walked several blocks, then took a connecting street back to the main street that led into Wenceslas Square.

Once back on the main road, she hailed the first available cab. The short drive back to her apartment took only a few minutes.

The cab stopped short of her apartment. She paid her fare and jumped out quickly, heading across to the entrance of her block.

As she hurried along she unfastened her handbag and took out the Walther PPK, primed it then slid it into her coat pocket for easy access. Breathing heavily, she barged through the entrance doors into a darkened lobby and ran up the six flights of stairs to her apartment. Several bulbs had blown, which meant she had to negotiate a series of alternately lit and darkened landings. Her own landing was unlit.

The short journey up to her apartment unglued her. She fumbled at the lock for several moments, opened the door and slipped inside, panting a sigh of relief.

Having regained her composure, she replayed in her mind her actions that night. She couldn't see how her behaviour could have aroused suspicion. Perhaps they were conducting just a routine check? If so, had she successfully shaken off the agents tailing her?

She locked the door to the apartment then made a phone call to Karl Schroder, her team leader. She apologised for not attending the meeting and then explained what had happened. They rescheduled the debriefing for the next morning.

Before hanging up, Schroder asked Greta if she needed someone to stay at the apartment with her. He could make out she was shaken up by the evening's events. Greta turned down the offer, saying she'd be OK after some rest.

After the conversation she poured herself a stiff drink then made her way towards a wall cupboard in the kitchen. She stretched up and dragged a work bag off the top shelf. Inside the bag was a Mauser MP40 light automatic machine gun. Max had taught her how to use it during a short leave in Berlin just before she had been sent to Prague. It would prove to be more effective than the Walther PPK.

She primed and checked the weapon, then released the safety catch for immediate use and placed it on the bedside table. She undressed, got into bed and lay back, retracing her actions that evening. An hour passed and she drifted off into a light sleep.

She awoke, startled at the sound of someone picking the apartment door lock. She sat bolt upright, gulping in fear. Gently, she lifted away the bed sheets and got to her feet, then she quickly bundled the pillows together and pulled the sheets back over them.

Picking up the light automatic gently, she crept into the shadows, awaiting the intruder.

The suspense was breathtaking. She panted fiercely as the door creaked open. Her heart was pounding and her eyes rounded with fright. Her mind raced.

'How the hell did they discover my whereabouts?'

The moment was upon her. She stared into the darkness and the silhouette of a man appeared at the bedroom door. His arm was raised and he fired a couple of shots at the bundle in the bed; the pistol had a silencer, but Greta heard the bullets thud into the bed.

The intruder moved forward to check his kill. As he went to pull back the sheets, Greta fired a short burst at him. He gasped with surprise and fired off two wild shots in the air as he was thrown against the wall.

To her surprise she heard the sound of a second intruder scuttling back towards the entrance to take swift leave down the stairs. She switched on the table lamp to review the grisly scene. A man in a fedora was slumped against the wall with blood seeping from his mouth.

Moments later she heard gunshots coming from the stairwell outside. It was Schroder. He had decided to personally keep an eye on Greta's apartment as a precaution. Fortunately, he turned up in the nick of time to hear the automatic fire, and he ran headlong into the Czech agent. There was a brief scuffle and gunfight, and he shot the Czech agent. Clambering over the agent's dying body, he ran up to Greta's apartment, fearing she had been killed. Greta recognised him as he bounded along the corridor towards her apartment. She leant against the entrance door, frightened and breathing heavily. He was relieved she wasn't dead.

His attention was drawn to the Mauser dangling from the end of her arm.

"Where did you get that?" he asked, surprised.

"Oh, this?" remarked Greta. "My brother."

"Your brother?" asked an astonished Schroder.

"Yes, my brother taught me how to use it."

He smiled. "Your brother must love you, eh?"

"Yes, he does." She returned the smile.

Schroder contacted Gestapo HQ in Prague and they made arrangements for the clean-up. Greta dressed and the couple talked until daybreak, then connected up with the rest of the team. Greta debriefed them on the situation, saying that she suspected the men were Czech underground agents.

The Gestapo pounced the following day, but Danube Two and other British agents working in Prague had vanished. However, they were captured trying to cross the border into Hungary several days later. They had suspected that their cell had been discovered, and they were on their way back to England via prearranged channels.

Evidently, the role of the British agents was to help the Czechs establish a network of local agents.

Following her daring mission to Prague, Greta announced her temporary retirement from the espionage game. Thoughts of motherhood had once again come to the fore when she chose to have a second Lebensborn child. She chose the father in much the same manner as she had chosen her first.

In December 1940 she gave birth to a baby girl, Kristine. At this point, she made the decision to retire permanently from her espionage activities and settle down with her child. She held a part-time job with the party, but her political career, as she had known it before, had come to an end.

PART TWO

WARRING PLANET

"Life is the testing ground for Soul to discover its true nature, but mature Souls are few and far between; a rare breed indeed. We live on a warring planet. It will always be a warring planet and serves its divine purpose in this way."

Michael Vogel.

17

THE BARON

Paul von Wittenburg was a young officer sent to Spain with Germany's Condor Legion – the Reich's contribution to help General Franco and his Nationalists win the Spanish Civil War.

He was born in Prussia – a large area that forms the northern part of Germany. For generations, Paul's family had served in the Prussian (and later the German) Army following German unification in the 1860s. His great-grandfather had fought with Bismarck in the Franco-Prussian War of 1870–71 and his father and grandfather had served as officers in the Great War. In fact, at the time of Paul's recall to Berlin, his father held the rank of colonel in the army.

German involvement in the Spanish Civil War was minor. The German Government favoured the Nationalists, believing Franco's success would steer Spain away from an alliance with other Western nations.

Paul was among the first Germans to be dispatched; he arrived in Cadiz in November 1936, and his combat experience in Spain soon won him the respect of his seniors at home. At twenty-four years of age, he had proved that courage flourished in his genetic make-up, and he stood out as a popular, well-connected figure. He was a chip off the old block, you might say. After twelve months of action in the field, Paul was selected to handle the training of Spanish cadres and Falangists – members of a political group that formed the leading force on the Nationalist side. His time in Spain ended when orders from Berlin called for his return.

His profile, including his recent battle experience and his

experience in training personnel, provided perfect credentials for him to join a team compiling and conducting training programmes for SS officers at an officer training academy. It was early 1938 when he was assigned to Paul Hausser's Junker School at Bad Tölz.

He was overjoyed at being called back to Germany. In the short repatriation leave granted him before transferring to the Bavarian academy he took every opportunity to maximise his military and social connections and savour the polite society life that was abundant in Berlin at the time.

Because of Paul's aristocratic mannerisms and affectations he would later become known as the Baron. He wore a white scarf and monocle and carried a long cigarette holder; he was a blast from the past. It was easy to imagine his forebears demonstrating the same eccentric behaviour.

He had lofty connections, so he was always on the invitation list when it came to military or high-society gatherings. Despite his junior ranking and, much to the chagrin of some of the senior officers who looked down their noses at him, he'd glide around the room, drawing from his extraordinarily long cigarette holder, getting acquainted with his fellow guests, male and female, knowing they might be influential, even if only in a small way.

In his conversations, he could instinctively discern what his listener wanted to hear, and then his silver tongue would provide what was needed to impress. His keen ear for listening made all the difference. His confidence was astounding, and seniors could only look on in amazement. Senior ranking never appeared to intimidate Paul; if an officer used rank to berate or insult him, he'd instantly bring up the subject of family connections, emphasising his prominent military lineage. This usually silenced any adversaries, bouncing them firmly back into their place.

Such an incident occurred in Berlin just before his departure to the Bad Tölz Junker School when Paul attended a function reserved for senior staff only.

Luminaries from the regular army and the Armed-SS mingled during the reception. Paul arrived as if he owned the place. He plucked an aperitif from a tray offered by one of the waiters, then immediately struck up a conversation with the wife of a high-ranking army officer.

His flying entrance was observed by an army major who was part of the hosting team and aware of the names of all invited guests. Paul's apparent blasé attitude and his junior ranking ruffled the major's feathers.

"Young upstart!" he muttered aloud, to the surprise of the group he was engaged in a conversation with.

He disengaged himself from the group and made his way towards where Paul was chatting. He was determined to teach the junior a lesson in military etiquette.

"I beg your pardon, Frau Liebenau." He bowed and looked up at Paul. "Lieutenant, this function is reserved for senior staff, not juniors. You should leave immediately. The SS may have privileges, but they don't extend to junior ranks attending functions set aside for senior staff. Perhaps you should come back in eight years!" he quipped sarcastically.

Expecting Paul to apologise and leave immediately, the uninformed major was surprised by Paul's swift retort: "Nice joke, Herr Major. I am here by verbal invitation. My father, Colonel Wittenburg, standing over there, invited me." Paul raised his glass and directed it towards where his father was standing, pointing with one of his fingers still holding his aperitif. He looked back across to the Major and flashed a smug smile, then rounded off the conversation with the comment, "Make that four years, Herr Major. Working with the best raises one's game."

The Major gasped and walked off in disbelief, but not before profusely apologising to Frau Liebenau, who apparently knew Paul through mutual connections.

Privately, the Baron was a Casanova. When he wasn't engrossed in military duties his hobby was hunting the fairer sex. Mature women, divorcees, widows or those left lonely because their husbands were away were Paul's preference. In his experience it was this type of woman that usually fancied the younger officers.

Younger women weren't his choice. He recognised that ambition and prestige spurred on the younger women, and their leanings were toward the older officers. He felt he'd be wasting his time on them – besides, most of them weren't well off like the older ones.

Paul had a knack of sensing a woman's vulnerabilities. He sought that giveaway glint in the eye expressing the yearning for a little more excitement in life. He knew the most opportune moment to strike and completed the job with his charm, sharp wit and good looks. He treated the hunt as if it was a military operation: his strategy was to seek, envelop, achieve then reap the benefits of his new conquest.

The hunting season began immediately upon his return to Berlin. He soon happened upon a rich widow whose officer husband had been killed in action in the Spanish Civil War. She was twenty years older than Paul and had two sons who were currently training as officer cadets in the regular army.

Paul and the widow's initial meeting occurred when they were both separately taking lunch at Hotel Bristol located on the famous Unter den Linden. She was taking tea with a scone and relaxing to the sounds of a string quartet playing some of Beethoven's later works. Paul, taking her to be lonely, caught her eye a few times and then walked across to strike up a casual conversation. Within minutes she had practically told him everything about herself – certainly enough for him to interpret her needs and say the right things. Getting her to smile and loosen up was his next objective. The final objective for that afternoon was achieved when he secured acceptance to an invitation for a night out at the Symphony later that week.

The night at the Symphony went well. They shared a love for the music of Beethoven. During the Moonlight Sonata he gently held her hand. The move enabled him to sense her reaction to his touch. Sure enough, he felt a cosy warmth oozing from her body into his, and he instantly knew that Annekathrin's lingerie would be lying on the floor at the foot of her bed sooner rather than later.

Annekathrin hopelessly succumbed to Paul's charm. Any resistance dissolved when their lips met later that evening.

She lived in a town house in Charlottenburg. Because of their age difference she wanted the relationship played down, as did Paul. In public they both insisted the relationship was platonic. Paul claimed her attraction to him was because he reminded her of her sons, who were away attending the officer cadet training school.

Their brief passionate affair in Berlin ended when Paul received his marching orders to report to the Bad Tölz Junker School. His love for and loyalty to the military exceeded his need for the fairer sex. He was the chivalrous type, though, and never left his conquests cold; he'd maintain contact until both parties agreed it was time to move on.

On the journey down into Southern Germany Paul prepared himself for the new appointment at Bad Tölz. Hausser wanted him to align his combat experience gathered in Spain with what was being taught at the academy. He was given the job of writing the programmes, setting up sandpit scenarios in the conference rooms, discussing tactics for the situations displayed, and holding workshops for the trainee cadets. Paul's programmes specifically dealt with battlefield tactics for platoons (up to thirty men) and companies (up to 100 men). In Spain he had led a platoon, and on several occasions he had assisted with taking charge of a company (a company is made up of several platoons).

Paul was eager to excel in his new role, and he was enthusiastically welcomed at the Junker School by the seniors there. He held the rank of second lieutenant (Untersturmführer in SS terms) and carried out his job with skill and thoroughness.

He savoured audiences with his commanding officer, 'Papa' Hausser, and on one occasion, shortly after commencing duties, he met Sepp Dietrich, the commander of Leibstandarte, who had made a flying visit for talks with Hausser. Conversations with seniors never intimidated Paul. He was a natural, so he felt comfortable with both individuals, although he could clearly pick out the differences between Hausser the military professional and the old dog that was Dietrich.

Hausser was part of the traditional military aristocracy, but despite his achievements in moulding his Armed-SS unit, the Verfügungstruppe, otherwise known as SS-VT, into a combat-ready unit, the independence of Sepp Dietrich initially created a rivalry between them. Hausser was frustrated by the fact that, for all his experience, he was outranked in the SS by the former Great War army NCO. Exacerbating the grievance was the fact that Dietrich had easy access to the Führer, and his unit, Leibstandarte, held an exclusive place in Hitler's inner sanctum.

During the Great War, Dietrich had served as a sergeant. He was a hardened, brave soldier who, like Hausser, he had been decorated. Like all good sergeants, he never distanced himself from his men, so he won their respect in every way. As one of Hitler's favourite subordinates, he often spoke his mind to him. In spite of his forthrightness, he maintained this special relationship with the Führer. Sepp was valued for his fearlessness and steadfast loyalty; in Hitler's book, he was as straight as an arrow. As a result Dietrich worked and lived in the Chancellery, close by him.

As time went on, the rocky relationship between Hausser and Dietrich smoothed. Dietrich eventually recognised Hausser's training and organisational skills and acknowledged the great job he was accomplishing.

Paul's conversation with Sepp Dietrich hadn't passed by without notice. In late 1938, Paul, quite unexpectedly, received papers informing him of a forthcoming transfer from Bad Tölz. He had been reassigned to the Leibstandarte-SS Adolf Hitler Regiment. Hitler's personal unit was considered the best of the best, and Paul was delighted with the new posting. He joined Leibstandarte just before Christmas 1938.

As part of the expansion and reshuffling programme for Leibstandarte, Paul's first job was to assess the records of candidates applying for membership of the regiment. The selection process involved reviewing each candidate's Hitler Youth record, proficiency record, training and service record, other experience and honours accrued, then interviewing each one personally.

Interviews for existing members to be reshuffled to new positions also took place.

All new members recommended for the unit, and those reshuffled, were passed on to Dietrich for final approval. Previously, Dietrich had enjoyed welcoming new members into his fold after personally selecting them himself, but as the unit grew in size it became more efficient for him to grant ultimate approval after his most trusted officers had made their choices.

Max, Fritz and Muller were among those Paul assessed as part of the reshuffling programme. Max's old unit was reshuffled in a day's work. His interview with Paul went well.

He entered Paul's office, saluted and stood to attention, eagerly waiting to hear what part he would play in the new reshuffle. His fate was in the hands of someone he'd never met before.

Paul opened up the interview: "You are Max Rieker, twenty years of age and have recently successfully completed the NCO training programme at the Dachau Academy. You currently hold the rank of Oberscharführer."

"That is correct, Untersturmführer."

Max remained bolt upright standing to attention.

Suddenly, Paul lightened up: "You have an impressive record, soldier."

Max instantly warmed to his tone: "Thank you, Untersturmführer."

"As you know, the unit is undergoing upgrading and reshuffling. I am to be assigned to lead a platoon in the anti-tank company, and I will need some good NCOs. What do you think? Would you like to be my platoon sergeant?"

With that comment, Max beamed a big smile. "Yes, I would look forward very much to serving with you, Untersturmführer."

"Can you recommend other suitable NCOs, Max?"

"Yes, Fritz Kohler, Hans Muller and Gerd Reuss. We all attended the same cadet class at Dachau. They're good men, Untersturmführer – all of them."

"Good. I'll sort the paperwork, then. Our company commanding officer will be First Lieutenant [Obersturmführer in SS terms] Kurt Meyer. His nickname is Panzermeyer. Apparently he jumped out of a second-floor classroom window when he was a schoolboy and broke every bone in his arms and legs. From then on he was known as Panzermeyer."

"Should be an interesting journey, then," said Max. "*Ja!* I look forward to it."

All the NCOs recommended by Max were reshuffled into Paul's own unit, 14th Anti-Tank Company, under Panzermeyer's command. Max was promoted to platoon sergeant and Fritz and Muller retained their old roles of senior squad sergeants.

For Max, Paul came across as a friendly, warm type – confident and noble but not arrogant or intimidating. In fact, there was an immediate connection – like long-lost brothers. It was as if they had known each other for years.

Despite the instant bonding, they maintained the protocol of respecting each other's rankings, but during off-duty time the gap was virtually non-existent. Rapport between SS junior officers and their warrant officers became well known during the war years, and it was during this period that Paul and Max forged an unbreakable friendship.

On the surface they were like chalk and cheese, but somehow their personality differences tended to complement each other. Paul loved society life; Max never indulged. Paul was drawn to sophisticated, rich, older women; Max enjoyed the company of 'wilder' women of his own age or younger who would drink beer with him. They both enjoyed their own company. When he had the opportunity Max would spend his free time working out at the gym; Paul, on the other hand, was an avid reader. He was serious about his military career, as was Max, but he went a step further by studying military history and tactics. Max could hold his own in some conversations as a result of his time spent with his old mentor, Vogel. Paul recollected that his father had served with Vogel in the Great War.

Paul admired Max's down-to-earth honesty, physical attributes and unswerving loyalty. Max fought in the boxing ring and Paul in the arenas of the high life.

As time went on, they became almost inseparable. Their ability to bounce ideas off each other was an important ingredient in their friendship, along with their mutual respect. Max gave Paul the nickname 'Baron' and news of this moniker quickly spread through the ranks.

The new Leibstandarte was shaping up, and a perfect opportunity for its members to get acquainted came in January 1939, when the Grand Leibstandarte Ball was held at Berlin Zoo. Sepp Dietrich organised this high-profile gala for his men and invited some famous German performers of the time. The guest of honour was the army commander-in-chief, Walther von Brauchitsch.

The ball was truly a magnificent affair: drinking, eating, dancing, and laughter that echoed throughout the evening into the early hours of the morning. Sepp received wild cheers of appreciation from his men many times through the evening; he was truly a soldier's soldier. The guest of honour, von Brauchitsch, received similar accolades. The cheers could be heard in the Tiergarten, which started its long stretch from the edge of the zoo grounds all the way down to the Reichstag building.

The men were allowed to bring their spouses and girlfriends. The Baron entered the ball with the most gorgeous woman on his arm. She was certainly a head-turner but, surprisingly, a little out of specification for him: she was younger than usual. He'd decided to play safe and cover his true leanings by inviting a close friend of the family, Marlene, who was already spoken for. She was tall, and her evening dress elegantly draped close to her body outlined a firm, shapely figure underneath. She looked like a Greek deity, and she captured the attention of many of the senior officers there.

Max, on the other hand, arrived alone – as did a few of his fellow NCOs. As the decibels increased through the night, the NCOs became the rowdiest bunch there. The toasts kept coming and so did the schnapps, beer and wine.

When the ball finished, most of the NCOs were incapable of walking. Max was incapacitated, but not as much as Fritz or Muller.

The night had been exciting and all in attendance had been fêted well, but the ball was in reality a serious event that would mark the beginning of an eventful year. The speeches had picked up on Leibstandarte's forthcoming role for Germany and its Führer. Most of the men left the hall believing 1939 would be their year of destiny – a year leading to great victories. Back then defeat was unimaginable.

During spring, Leibstandarte became involved with the annexation of Bohemia and Moravia. The occupation marked the final dismemberment of Czechoslovakia and a slap in the face for Great Britain and France, as this was in contravention of the Munich Agreement.

The regiment returned to Berlin in the summer and received several new motorised components, including an armoured-car platoon and a motorbike unit. As a result it was redesignated the Infanterie-Regiment Leibstandarte-SS Adolf Hitler (mot.).

By this time, the men of Leibstandarte were eager to avenge Versailles and all that it stood for. The question was, how would they measure up in their first taste of real combat against an enemy that was known for its fighting spirit and in no mood for giving up its territory without contest: Poland?

BIBLIOGRAPHY

US War Department Handbook on German Military Forces. (Washington, 1945.)

Charles Messenger: *Hitler's Gladiator: The Life and Times of Panzer Army Commander Sepp Dietrich*, pp. 62–3. (Conway, 2005.)

Rupert Butler: *SS-Leibstandarte: The History of the First SS Division, 1933–1945,* pp. 16–39. (MBI Publishing Company, 2001.)

Robert Lewis Koehl: *The Black Corps: The Structure and Power Struggles of the Nazi SS*, pp. 201, 216, 237–9. (Madison, 1983.)

The Third Reich: The SS. (Time Life Books, 1989.)

18

IRON DAWN

On the eve of a battle it is natural for a warrior to summon up his spirit, glance heavenward and pray to God to favour his side. Alas! God looks down on the field disinterestedly, favouring no side. For this is the House of War, the testing ground for the soul.

Those brothers defeated are bound by their bitterness; equally those victorious are bound by their glory. With these binding actions there is no winner; the outcome merely reflects the difference between iron shackles and golden chains.

Such binding actions are initiated by man, not God. Non-binding action is for man to choose, for it is his journey – a personal relationship between him and God. It matters little for which side he fights – seemingly good or bad. God only recognises this personal relationship, not situations or predicaments fashioned by man.

For all Germans lined up that day, the war against Poland was not considered one of aggression but simply the rectification of a shameful injustice perpetrated on the German people by the Treaty of Versailles in June 1919.

The average age for most of the Leibstandarte men that made up the ranks was nineteen years. Max was not much older at twenty years, coming up to his twenty-first birthday. What lay in front of them in the forthcoming campaign would be their testing ground – the most challenging time in their young lives. Some would perish; of those who survived, some would come out of it shaken by the reality of combat and others would emerge courageous and strong after their baptism of fire.

The days leading up to 1 September contained familiarisation meetings between senior NCOs and commissioned officers. For the ranks, rather than remain idle in their bivouacs as they waited for the issue of Directive 1 from the Führer to assume the Conduct of War, most of them helped farmers to gather the local harvest.

One evening Max and Paul found some time to take a walk together. They chatted informally about the coming invasion. Looking up into the inky sky with its millions of shining stars, they marvelled at the peaceful setting around and above them.

Max could not help but ask the rhetorical question that has been uttered throughout Mankind's history: "What's it all about?"

"What do you mean?"

Max's answer was surprising: "Well, surely there has to be more than just this" – questioning the idea of just one single short life. "I believe that we live more than once; in fact, I believe we live countless times."

"What makes you say that?"

"It's something old Vogel once said to me. He considered this planet to be a warring planet by design. He told me Hindus believe life is a series of cycles within what they call the Cosmic Day. The Cosmic Day is around 4 million years in duration. It is made up of four lesser cycles or four ages: the Golden Age, the Silver Age, the Copper Age and the Iron Age. According to Vogel, the Golden Age represented four-tenths of the Cosmic Day, the Silver Age, three-tenths; the Copper Age, two-tenths; and the Iron Age, one-tenth. One might have thought that the Cosmic Day would start with the Iron Age and develop into the Golden Age. No. They believe that the Cosmic Day began with the Golden Age and went into a slow degeneration, down through to the Iron Age, in which the cycle will end in total destruction. What followed is another cycle of equal duration that they call the

Cosmic Night. During this period all is rebuilt, ready to start the cycle again. Apparently, any learned Hindu will tell you that we are now at the front end of the Iron Age. The Iron Age is a period in which darkness and decay overwhelm the world; humanity becomes tormented by thousands of ills, such as poverty, disease, plagues and wars instigated by jealousy. Vogel considered every individual resides in the soul and, by living thousands of lives, the soul goes through the trials and tribulations here in the physical world, eventually becoming a perfected and spiritually mature individual."

Paul couldn't resist a quip: "So you think every star up there represents a free soul? Amazing idea! I'm not sure that I believe in living again, but you're right about this planet being a warring one. There is hardly a time when somebody is not hot of blood and desirous of conquest somewhere in this crazy place. Look at us – we're part of it."

On the eve of the invasion, it was hard to settle down for a restful sleep. To pre-empt this, the men were ordered to force sleep through the early evening until early morning. They awoke in pitch darkness to make the final preparations for the forthcoming invasion.

These preparations included testing all mechanised vehicles and equipment; ensuring all spares, tools, fuel, lubes, foodstuff and other consumables had been checked off and stored in their rightful places; performing munitions and artillery checks; and, finally, carrying out checks on personal attire, weapons, ammunition and rations.

At 4.30 a.m., orders were given to start up engines and all men took up their positions. They were ready as an eerie silence descended. Each man's attention became centred and fully focused. Despite readiness, despite this being the moment they had all been waiting for, a strong sense of anxiety coloured those remaining, compelling moments leading up to the inevitable confrontation.

Suddenly, the silence was shattered as the air became filled with the sounds of whistles, sirens and horns that signalled the advance. They were about to spear their way into Poland.

Leibstandarte joined in the invasion with the 17th Infantry Division, part of the 8th Army. The 8th Army's primary role was to protect the flank of the 10th Army's drive eastwards into Poland.

The villages of Boleslavecz and Wieuroszov were their initial objectives. They were captured, but there was determined resistance and ferocious street fighting.

After crossing the River Warte, the next major objective was the strategic city of Lodz. The Germans became involved in yet another tough battle near the town of Pabianice. Initial attacks pushed the Poles back to the centre of the city, but when the Poles launched their own fierce counter-attack they almost cut off Sepp Dietrich's command post. Finally, in the early evening the impetus of the Poles was broken. As a result, hundreds surrendered, enabling Leibstandarte to return into the township.

The next assignment was to assist with the attack on Warsaw. Their effort involved blocking the main line of the Polish retreat, and for several days they fought against a fierce, stubborn enemy. Hundreds of Polish soldiers died in the fighting, as did hundreds of boxed-in refugees. Dead and crippled horses added to the grisly scene.

The regiment moved on and was involved in the encirclement of Polish forces between Bzura and the Vistula river. Their job was to stop retreating portions of the Polish Army from crossing the river. As before, Polish losses were extensive, and all their attempts to break through were repelled by the German defensive gunfire.

In their final action they assisted in taking the town of Modlin, north of Warsaw. On 27 September, Warsaw finally fell, and two days later Modlin.

Their accomplishments during the campaign did not immediately earn them respect from the army leadership. Walther von Brauchitsch, the commander-in-chief, the guest of honour at Sepp Dietrich's Gala Ball at Berlin Zoo earlier that year, criticised them, saying that Leibstandarte was "untrained for battle, had no knowledge of strategy and had to pay the price for being policemen dressed up in army uniforms".

So began the dogfights between the SS and army personnel.

The fate of Poland was sealed when at least 1 million Soviet troops invaded from the east on 17 September 1939. Any hopes of immediate rescue from the Allies faded away like a forgotten dream. The brave Poles were in a hopeless predicament. By 2 October 1939, action had all but ceased there.

During the battle for Modlin an incident took place that demonstrated the Baron's dedication and his love and respect for the men in his unit.

A radioed message was received from Fritz Kohler; he and his patrol had run into a Polish unit and were pinned down in an abandoned farmhouse two to three kilometres behind enemy lines. Kohler believed the Poles would soon be receiving backup.

Paul, concerned over Kohler's predicament, immediately informed Max of the situation and rushed over to Company HQ to get his commanding officer's permission to take some 'volunteers' on a rescue bid.

Kurt Meyer was perusing a report when Paul entered. He saluted.

"Obersturmführer, my squad sergeant, Kohler, seems to have got himself into a hole. It appears his reconnaissance squad is surrounded by the enemy a couple of kilometres down the road. Can I take some volunteers to get him out?"

"Can't he fight his way out?" growled Meyer.

"No, he's outnumbered and can't make a break for it; they have wounded."

"Well, all right – off you go. Be quick about it."

"Thank you, Obersturmführer." He saluted and turned to leave.

"By the way, Wittenburg, bring back my men all in one piece, will you?"

Without turning, in his impeccable upper-class accent, the Baron responded: "Of course, Obersturmführer."

He quickly arranged two heavy armoured reconnaissance vehicles to support the rescue bid while Max mustered the rest of the platoon.

Just before they moved out, he radioed Fritz: "What's your situation, Fritz? We'll be there in ten to twenty minutes."

"One dead, two wounded, five standing. Can't be long before the Poles' backup arrives."

"Keep centred, Fritz. See you soon."

Outside, the men were clambering into carrier trucks. The two armoured vehicles had moved up into position behind.

Because of the need for speed, the Baron's rescue team risked the dangers of the enemy-occupied main road, which led up to the troublespot. Ten minutes down the road, gunfire was heard coming from a valley. The small convoy wheeled off the main road on to a dirt track leading towards the source of the gunfire. They stopped short of a ridge.

Paul and Max crawled to the edge and focused their binoculars down into the valley. Fritz and his squad were holed up in an abandoned farmhouse approximately 400 metres down the valley. The Poles' backup had just arrived and were about to close in and finish them off.

Absorbing the scene in front of him, the Baron quickly devised his rescue plan. They slid away from the ridge; he picked up a broken twig and addressed his men.

"Right, men, we're about 400 metres from the farmhouse. A dirt track with a gulley along its left-hand side leads down to the farmhouse from our left. On the right a small brook runs parallel with the dirt track and about twenty metres from it. The brook takes a ninety-degree turn to the right, about twenty metres from the farmhouse." He etched a plan in the dirt with the broken twig. "We'll drive a hollow wedge through the Poles surrounding

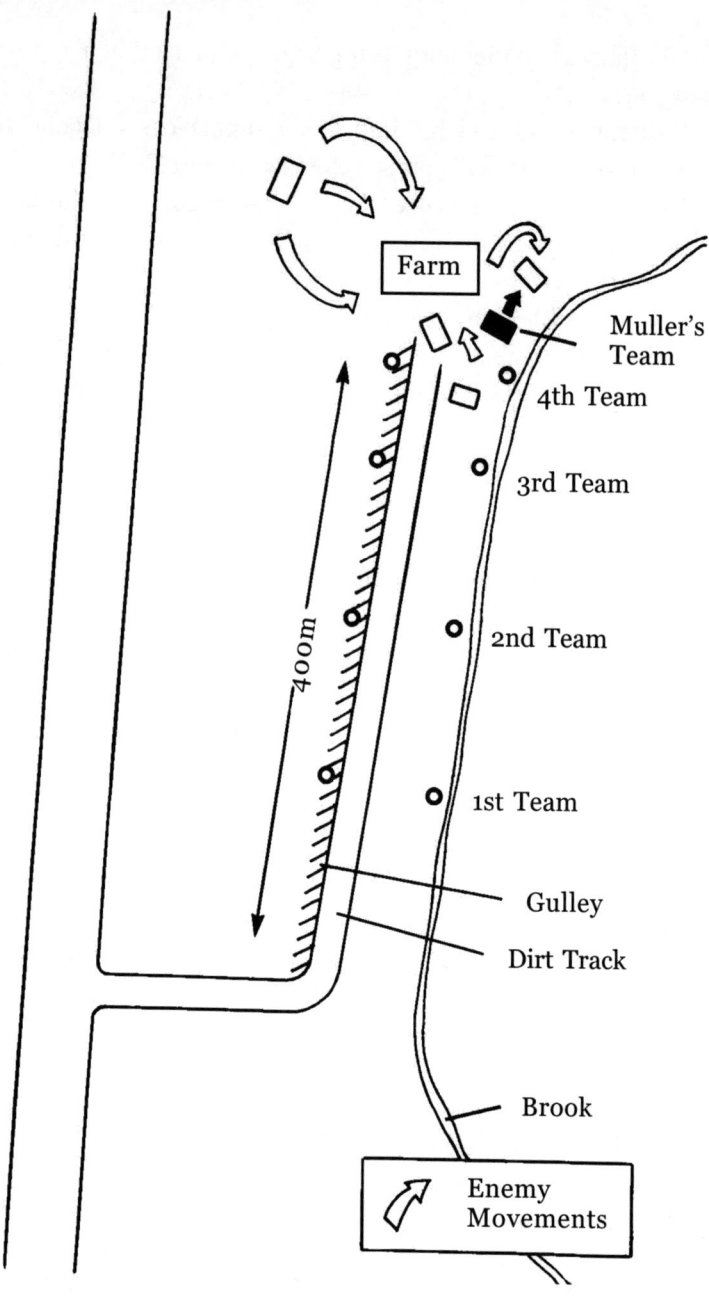

Farm

Muller's Team

4th Team

3rd Team

2nd Team

1st Team

400m

Gulley

Dirt Track

Brook

Enemy Movements

The Fight at the Farm.

224

the farmhouse – creating a 'pipeline', so to speak. The gulley beside the dirt track will act as one side; the banks of the brook, the other. We'll form up into five squads of four, and each foursome will split into two pairs. Our armoured vehicles will lead the attack and all four-man squads will filter down behind using the armoured vehicles as cover. At approximately 100 metres the first four-man squad will split into pairs, one pair setting up on the gulley side and the other pair opposite them along the banks of the brook. The second four-man squad will deploy in the same manner, approximately 200 metres down the vale; the third, 300 metres; and the fourth, 350 metres. Muller will lead the last squad and dig in where the brook makes its ninety-degree turn."

Each pair carried a heavy MG34 machine gun.

The Baron continued: "Muller's team will focus on the enemy on the nearest flank, providing cover fire for Max's rescue bid. Max will lead the rescue squad. They can follow up close behind the armoured vehicles. Once they get to within twenty metres of the farmhouse they'll discharge smoke grenades, break from behind the armour and use the smoke to pull Fritz and his men out. Any wounded can hitch a lift for the journey back up. Our armoured vehicles will act as a rearguard, reversing back up the 'pipeline'. The four-man squads can pull back up the 'pipeline' in front of the trucks, using them as added protection. Right then, pair up and form your squads. Get ready to go!"

Within seconds the unit was lined up, ready to make its descent into the valley.

"Move out!" bellowed the Baron.

The armoured vehicles moved over the ridge just ahead of the men.

Paul was hoping his strategy would deceive the Poles into believing it was a counter-assault rather than just a rescue bid.

They filtered down the valley at top speed. The first four-man squad deployed quickly and began firing at the Poles fanned out around the farmhouse. The sight of the German armoured cars and assault troops totally surprised the Poles, who were focused on Fritz and his boys inside the farmhouse.

The Baron's men followed the armour and deployed as instructed all the way down to where the brook turned away from the farmhouse.

The assault wasn't without its problems, though. Midway through the action the armoured vehicles encountered a unit of dogged Poles entrenched in front of them. The Poles were reluctant to vacate their position; instead they decided to about-face and confront the German armour.

Their Kb ppanc wz 35, 7.92-mm anti-tank rifle (AT rifle) had already destroyed sections of the farmhouse wall, and, without doubt, the Baron's timely intrusion had saved Fritz and his squad from imminent annihilation. Now, from his farmhouse vantage point, Fritz was able to render some payback to the Poles, who, a minute earlier, had been poised to blow him and his boys to bits.

The armoured vehicles pushed on towards the farmhouse, intending to run over the stubborn squad of Poles, but before abandoning their position the Poles managed to fire two rounds from their AT rifle. The shots managed to disable one of the advancing armoured vehicles. The Poles scrambled from their precarious position just in the nick of time and pulled back to a point beside the brook, where they prepared to receive the second armoured truck.

The crew in the smitten vehicle got out and scuttled back up the 'pipeline' to safety while the other half of Max's assault team joined up with him, following the remaining armoured vehicle.

The plan didn't include pursuing the stubborn Poles. Instead, the remaining armoured vehicle kept travelling straight ahead and stopped twenty metres short of the farmhouse. Muller's machine-gun team set up where the brook took a ninety-degree turn and kept the enemy pinned down on the near flank (including the tenacious AT rifle unit, who were frantically digging in to make another stand).

Max and his small squad of men were poised for the rescue bid. They pitched the smoke grenades and raced out from behind the armoured vehicle towards the farmhouse to meet Fritz and his beleaguered squad. With not a minute to spare all the men withdrew just as Polish troops attacking from the rear of the farmhouse climbed through the windows. They received a warm reception: Max had left a number of delayed-action explosives to meet the hapless intruders.

Fritz's wounded were lifted up on to the armoured car. Those still fit sped back up through the 'pipeline' under cover of the four-man teams providing the supporting fire. Muller and his squad were the first to disengage to join them.

Each four-man team then drew back in the same manner as it had deployed. The process was repeated until all the teams had returned to the top of the valley, out of immediate danger.

As Paul's men loaded up into the troop carriers, he glanced back and saw a group of Polish soldiers clambering over the abandoned armoured vehicle. The difficult rescue bid had been a huge success at a cost of three wounded. The Baron's quickly thought-out strategy had paid off.

Celebrations were exuberant that evening. Fritz was enormously grateful for his unit's rescue and would never forget his comrades' courage under fire.

In the days that followed the surrender of Warsaw, Leibstandarte had the opportunity to rest. They were encamped in an area north of Warsaw.

One morning, orders were received to send a 'search and kill' squad into the nearby woods to seek out Polish resistance. Paul advised Max of the orders and Max prepared his squad.

It was a crisp September morn when the squad set off. They soon reached the edge of the woods. To avoid ambush, Max steered the men clear of the paths. After a time they came up to a ridge, where they stopped to scrutinise the terrain below. The ground dipped down towards a running brook, which could be heard in the distance. The countryside north of Warsaw was truly beautiful. On the ridge, Max let his attention slip momentarily as he absorbed the peaceful sounds of nature that the woods had to offer.

Suddenly, what appeared to be a man-made noise penetrated the air, bringing the entire squad's attention sharply back down to earth. Max ordered his men to fan out and advance slowly down towards the brook. On their way down, they startled a deer. The men presumed the animal had been the source of the sound. They continued with caution.

Suddenly Max stopped and raised his arm sharply to halt the advance. He blinked and stared in disbelief at the bank on the far side of the brook. Focusing his binoculars, he confirmed that there were twenty to thirty dead civilians, a mix of men and women, lying neatly side by side. The unit stood there transfixed, overlooking the gruesome scene. Max broke the silence and ordered a search of the bodies for any forms of identity.

It had been a mass execution. All had received a bullet to the back of the head. There had been no attempt to hide the identities of the victims. All carried papers. They were doctors, teachers and students. Max made a record of the details of each victim and instructed the squad to press on through the woods to the road leading back to headquarters. He aborted his mission in order to report the discovery.

Max returned to camp and filed a report concerning the murdered civilians. Later that day a senior administration officer, Karl Bender, from Einsatzgruppe, a section within the Allgemeine-SS, read it and ordered Paul over to headquarters.

Paul stood to attention, awaiting Bender's deliberation.

"Untersturmführer, I understand your master sergeant wrote this report?"

"Correct, Hauptsturmführer."

"This isn't what we want to see, is it?"

Paul looked over in surprise. "Beg your pardon, Hauptsturmführer?"

"Your man overlooked his mission to report this!"

"Yes, Hauptsturmführer. Is there a problem?"

"Yes, there is a problem. Your man disobeyed his orders and should be court-martialled for it," he barked.

Paul was startled at the comment. "He's one of my best men, Hauptsturmführer. Besides, I fully endorsed his actions."

"Then you should be court-martialled too, Untersturmführer!"

There followed a pregnant silence.

Paul spoke: "Let's not get carried away, Hauptsturmführer. I'll discipline my master sergeant, and we'll get on with fighting this war. I'm sure he didn't realise he was out of order; he thought he was just doing his duty, reporting anything out of the ordinary."

"And you think this is out of the ordinary, eh?"

"Well, yes, Hauptsturmführer."

"Well, it isn't, is it? It's a hazard of the war you just mentioned. Make this your last mistake, Untersturmführer – understood?"

"Yes, Hauptsturmführer."

Bender was apparently already aware of the murders, but he had his reasons for wishing to play the incident down. He tore up the report and threw it in the waste bin. Paul walked out. For some reason, he realised, Bender didn't want a report like this on record; he had threatened a court martial in order to justify destroying the report.

Paul had Max report in. Max was expecting to be briefed about his discovery. He was mistaken. Paul rebuffed him for not doing his duty and told him of his meeting with Bender. Max was shocked that the massacre was to be passed over as a normal hazard of war. He said the idea that non-combatants could be rounded up and shot was beyond his understanding. Murder did not fit into his philosophy and, for him, was against the tenets of a master race.

Paul listened and nodded his agreement, but he took it a step further: "In some cases, civilians get involved in the war by aiding and backing the partisan movement. This calls for disciplinary action, but it's knowing where to draw the line, Hauptscharführer.

It's for certain those murdered today were innocents, but you'll need to keep your opinions to yourself. This is war and unpleasant events happen. Dismissed, Hauptscharführer!"

Max walked off, disappointed, but he realised he'd probably said too much. He learnt later that a dedicated German force had carried out the executions. It was Bender's Einsatzkommandos. They did not form part of the Armed-SS but worked independently under the control of a special branch in the Allgemeine-SS.

His introduction to Einsatzgruppe had been a chilling one.

BIBLIOGRAPHY

Paul Twitchell: *The ECK Vidya, The Ancient Science of Prophecy,* p. 163. (IWP Publishing, 1982.)

The Third Reich: The SS. (Time Life Books, 1989.)

Charles Messenger: *Hitler's Gladiator: The Life and Times of Panzer Army Commander Sepp Dietrich*, pp. 71–5. (Conway, 2005.)

Kurt Meyer: *Grenadiers: The Story of Waffen SS General Kurt "Panzer" Meyer*, pp. 1–7. (Stackpole Books, 2005.)

19

EINSATZGRUPPE

Max's grim introduction to Einsatzgruppe did not stop at the discovery in the woods. A second incident was soon to take place that would eclipse the first and affect him personally.

His ticking-off was soon forgotten when, several hours later, the Baron gathered his NCOs to inform them that the platoon had been selected to attend a get-together arranged by the locals. They were to smarten up and dress informally for the function, which would be held at a nearby village later that evening.

In an effort to sweeten their conquerors, the locals had extended a welcome for the men to experience some traditional Polish hospitality. Senior staff decided upon the Baron's platoon, which had pulled off the recent daring rescue. For the men it was a welcome chance to loosen up a little.

It was a chilly evening but the rain held off. Following the traditional dance routines performed by the villagers the men were invited to try out their skills. It gave them a chance to choose one of the many pretty girls available. Max paired up with a young girl named Anna and they danced several times during the evening. She was just eighteen years of age, fair-haired and very pretty with a firm figure under her cotton frock.

Just to hold a woman in his arms after the life-threatening campaign made him feel warm, relaxed and human again. The language barrier didn't stop them from communicating and they managed simple small talk. They spent most of their time on the dance floor, jigging to traditional Polish music and having fun.

The party ended all too soon. They'd formed a warm and friendly relationship in the time spent together that evening, and reluctantly the Baron and his men bade the villagers farewell.

As they sauntered back to camp the conversation reflected on the evening.

Fritz had a dig at Max: "Hey, Max, can't you ever do things by half? Did you see his eyes – they were hanging from their sockets?"

"Wasn't she a dazzler, eh?"

Bader cut in: "Maybe you should have got the village priest to marry you on the spot. Then at least you'd have got a shag out of it. Bet she's a Catholic. Then you would've needed to dip your beef without a condom. Can you imagine Rieker-fathered partisans fighting against us? Not such a good idea, eh?"

"He'll have to go home and take himself in hand now," jibed another.

"Strong possibility that she is Jewish," said Fritz.

"That's even worse – you'll need to have your knob cut first, then," Bader said, bursting out with laughter.

"I'm already circumcised," announced Max.

With that comment the entire platoon came to a halt, looking quizzically at him, awaiting an explanation.

"You're joking," said Bader.

"No, I'm not," replied Max.

The Baron looked on, smiling.

"What do you mean? You can't be Jewish."

Max unbuttoned his trousers and displayed his circumcised penis.

Bader looked over to the Baron in astonishment. "But how?"

"I'm the only Jewish combatant in the Armed-SS – got special permission from Heini himself," said Max.

The silence lingered for a while as the men tried to come to terms with what Max had just said.

Suddenly he burst out laughing. "*Dummkopf!* I was an orphan brought up in a Jewish-run orphanage. To stay at the orphanage we had to be brought up in the Jewish faith. I was less than a year old and didn't have a choice in the matter when they circumcised me."

The laugh was on Bader. The men continued on their way discussing the girls at the party.

"Most of the girls there were sure pretty. Did you see Muller's partner? Wow! What was her name, Muller?" Reuss asked.

"Not sure. Maryla, I think."

Fritz interjected, "You don't know?" He was astounded. "Not too much of a woman's man, are you, Muller? Best looker there and he didn't catch her name! I bet you didn't even ask her."

"All he wanted was to get her on her own for a blow job," jibed Bader.

"Did you get one?" asked Reuss eagerly.

Muller puffed out his chest, smiled, but didn't let on.

The banter continued all the way back to camp.

The following day Panzermeyer's company was broken up into its platoons to undertake patrol duties. It was necessary to secure the area completely before a general withdrawal was undertaken.

A few days later orders were received advising Leibstandarte of its forthcoming return to Germany for a refit and restructuring.

The news compelled Max and Fritz to make hurried arrangements to say their farewells to the girls they'd spent time with at the get-together. The most convenient time would be on their way back from patrol duty. The village wasn't far from the route back to camp. Max and Fritz could drop by, say goodbye, and then catch up with the platoon before reaching camp.

About a kilometre from camp, the Baron gave them leave to take the spur off to the village. They trotted off at the double.

They covered the short distance in no time, then dropped to a normal walking pace as they entered the village. All was very still.

"Bit quiet, eh?" remarked Max. "Maybe they're all gathered somewhere having a powwow or something."

An eerie silence hung over the village – no birdsong, no human sounds, nothing.

"Strange!" said Fritz, looking over at Max.

As they neared the centre, the spot where the villagers had performed their traditional dances, they stopped simultaneously. Their jaws dropped.

"Oh no, not again!" Fritz cried out.

It was a replay of the discovery in the woods several days earlier. Max's mind reeled. The villagers, who'd opened their hearts just a day earlier, were lying on the ground in neat rows, all dead – all murdered.

Max muttered to himself, "Einsatzkommando – the bastards have been at it again."

The stench of death filled their nostrils. They frantically sorted through the bodies, each silently hoping that the pretty girls they'd connected with the evening before were not among those murdered. Alas! they were two of the many that lay dead. All had been executed in the same manner as the civilians in the woods.

Max sought Anna. It wasn't long before he found her. Her eyes were wide open, frozen in fear. Powerful as he was, Max slumped down on to a rock near where her body lay. He held his head in disbelief.

"Why do they have to do this? What is the point of these senseless killings?" His distress quickly turned to anger. "God knows what she must have gone through before they shot her," he said. Then he leant over her body and gently closed her eyes.

Fritz too stood frozen, looking over the dead body of his partner.

After some moments he walked across and touched Max on the shoulder. "We need to get back to the platoon fast. We'll have to keep what we've seen here to ourselves, Max."

Max agreed and they both set off to rejoin the patrol.

They knew that any display of sympathy or any objection would be frowned upon. Reporting the incident would only provoke the same reaction as it had before. Besides, they shouldn't have been there in the first place.

Neither spoke until they were well clear of the village. Fritz was the first to break the grim silence: "What the hell happened back there?"

"Don't know, Fritz, don't know," replied Max, shaking his head. "I sure hope I never receive an order to shoot civilians like this. I didn't join up to murder innocent country folk."

"Me too," said Fritz. "There is only one group that would do this kind of thing–"

"Einsatzgruppe," interjected Max.

Several days earlier a boxing tournament between the two SS regiments, Leibstandarte and Totenkopf, had been announced. The challenge had been thrown out to Leibstandarte from the combined Totenkopf and Einsatzkommando encampment nearby.

Later that afternoon, shortly after their gory discovery, a herald from the Totenkopf camp, Konrad Stief, came across to the Leibstandarte camp to find out if the challenge had been accepted. He announced that his regiment had three fighters standing by to fight anybody Leibstandarte put forward. Max had joined a group of Leibstandarte men assembled to listen to what he had to say.

"I understand you Leibstandarte boys have a number of good boxers who may like to provide an afternoon's entertainment before we leave for home. It's a chance of proving your regiment's worthiness in competition, eh?" Stief added sarcastically.

Max shouted from the back, "I think we can oblige, Untersturmführer. Do you have a heavyweight amongst your group?"

"Two heavies and a cruiserweight, and I don't fancy your chances. Our boys are eager to knock you Asphalt Soldiers off your pedestal. Our heavyweight champion is Kurt Beicher, nicknamed the Fleischer [the Butcher]. He is very hard to beat."

'This is the guy I want to fight,' thought Max.

"We'll see about that in the ring, Untersturmführer. Oh, by the way, are any of your boys from the Einsatzkommando unit?"

"Yes, Beicher is. He leads them. The other two contestants are Totenkopf."

Max's thoughts centred on Beicher. It was he who had been responsible for the killings at the brook and at Anna's village.

"He's certainly living up to his nickname, the son of a bitch!" Max muttered to himself.

With little other response from Leibstandarte, Fritz and 'Fat Man' Breitner volunteered to fill the other two spots. Fat Man had been an amateur boxer, but he had put on some weight since retiring from the ring. He'd joined Leibstandarte in its early days and was one of the older men in the ranks at twenty-five years of age. Despite his excessive waistline, he was still a formidable combatant.

Fritz, too, was eager for payback. Like Max, he felt that the contest would provide him with the opportunity to avenge the dead villagers. Moreover, Eicke's Totenkopf regiment had included some of the individuals who'd tormented Max and himself during their days as youngsters at Dachau concentration camp. It would be satisfying to extract some revenge for those days too.

The following day, Max walked over to where the Totenkopf regiment were encamped to give Stief the names and ranks of the Leibstandarte participants.

Stief looked down the list. "Who's taking on the Fleischer?"

"I am."

"Oh! Don't fancy your chances, Hauptscharführer – he's an animal."

Stief was trying to instil fear and unsettle Max, but his words were only firing a boiler that would explode when the two men met in the ring.

"I've fought plenty of animals before. His type doesn't worry me, Untersturmführer."

Kurt Beicher, the Fleischer, was a good twelve kilos heavier than Max, and he was quite gruesome to behold.

"You want to meet him?" asked Stief, still trying to unnerve Max.

"Yes, let's see your boy, Untersturmführer."

They set off on the short walk to where the Einsatzkommandos were bivouacked. There was a rowdy group gathered in the compound.

A loud curse broke the air. It was aimed at Max. It was obvious the voice behind it belonged to Beicher. He and his chums chuckled over the snide remark. Max looked over the small band of misfits, cut-throats, reprobates and degenerates. The pair stopped short. Max fixed his glare on the bestial figure that had just thrown out the insult – a street-brawling, beer-swilling barbarian from Hamburg.

Not intimidated by the mocking curse, Max had his own agenda. He controlled his anger, glaring directly into the eyes of the evil-looking man in front of him. He was all too familiar with this sort, and he recognised Beicher as a man without conscience who had no respect for life. To make things even meatier, he reminded Max of Berti Braun. When their eyes met, Max's hair stood on end.

The look and the body language stopped Beicher in the middle of a second insult aimed at him. In a pregnant silence, the pair stood staring at each other.

Beicher became uncomfortable and, pretending not to be surprised, shouted across, "Is this all they can send me? It will be over in the first round. Leibstandarte, the Asphalt Boys, should keep to the parade ground and not send their pussies to the slaughter! Heard you boys f***ed up at Pabianice – useless wankers!"

His comments were followed by howls of laughter from the bunch surrounding him. They fell into a stony silence awaiting Max's response.

His eyes never left Beicher's. He responded in a cold, calm manner: "I don't care too much for you and what you stand for, you sausage-eating moron. You'll go down tomorrow like a sack of cow dung."

The Fleischer's face grew reptilian in anger.

"We'll see, pussy," he said, preparing to slaughter Max there and then.

As he stepped forward, Max stepped back and let loose a ferocious right cross into Beicher's face, then backed off and assumed a fighting stance. Fortunately several members of

Beicher's group tried to restrain him, thereby hampering his effort to get a clean shot at Max.

Beicher wiped his bleeding mouth, roared out a mocking laugh and spat the blood on to the floor.

"I can't wait for tomorrow, pansy. I'll take the utmost pleasure in ripping your head off your shoulders. The same goes for the other two pussies on Leibstandarte's list."

Max responded: "You're scum, and I don't care about you or the rabble that support you."

He turned to leave. Beicher called out after him, "I will dissect you tomorrow, soldier. That I promise."

Max walked back to his unit, wondering what he had set himself up for. But images of Anna were still fresh in his mind, fuelling his fury and sweeping away any thoughts of regret.

The following day was chilly, but the sky was clear and blue. Max rose early to salute the sun and go through his stretching and warm-up exercises. By the time he'd finished, Fritz and Fat Man Breitner had arrived. They walked across to the mess area for breakfast. Afterwards they met up with a number of supporters; it was time to leave.

The small group walked across to Totenkopf's camp and were greeted with howls of abuse, boos and mocking gestures. Beicher and the other two boxers waited for them in a makeshift boxing ring, which was elevated on a timber platform to give the onlookers a better view of the spectacle that was about to unfold.

A warrant officer, acting as referee, stood in the centre of the ring. The contestants lined up in their three-man teams on either side of him. The spectators were yelling and baying for blood. The referee motioned the boxers to wheel around and face one another and shake hands as a gesture of goodwill, but instead they just stood there, glaring at one another in utter contempt. Rivalry was blatantly apparent. Aside from Max's personal hunger for revenge, regimental honour was also at stake.

The referee explained the rules. There weren't many. They

amounted to a condensed version of the Queensberry Rules and aggression was encouraged. Each contest was scheduled for three rounds.

Fritz was first off. His long-awaited confrontation with Totenkopf was at hand.

Max and Fat Man Breitner worked Fritz's corner. Fritz sat on his stool eagerly awaiting the start bell.

"Don't give this guy a chance to settle down, Fritz. Keep him off balance, *Kamerad*," advised Max.

Fritz was the street-fighting type, but he had boxed a little during his time in the Hitler Youth. His opponent, Bruno Katzmann, was a little shorter but equal in weight. Katzmann had boxed before, but, because the condensed rules favoured the most aggressive, artistry wouldn't count too much in accruing points. All Fritz had to do was endure and keep his opponent back-footed.

The 'bell' (in the form of a horn) sounded the start of the first round. It opened with both boxers stalking each other around the ring, sizing each other up. It wasn't too long before the punches started. Exchanges grew fiercer as the round progressed and it eventually ended up in a brawl. Fritz was tough, but so was Katzmann. The second and third rounds followed a similar pattern with both boxers slugging it out. Fritz got the decision, though, because he'd bludgeoned Katzmann to the floor once in the second round. He, his corner and the Leibstandarte supporters were elated with the result, much to the disappointment of the majority watching.

Fat Man took up the challenge next. He was surprisingly fit for his bulk, and he had boxed before.

"Use that weight to your advantage, Fat Man. He'll underestimate your speed too," Max advised.

Fat Man's opponent was a sergeant named Willi Fischer. Like Fat Man, Fischer had boxed on the amateur circuit. He was lighter, faster and fitter, and needed to be. Near the end of the first round, Fat Man caught him with a solid combination, almost knocking him out. Only the 'bell' saved him.

Fischer's caution at the start of the second round signified a respect for Fat Man's deceptive physique, but, halfway through the round, Fat Man had to retire because of a cut eye. Max and Fritz shared his disappointment as he slumped on to his bench with long trails of crimson blood running freely down his cheek on to his chest.

Fat Man's defeat left the score even, rendering the third fight even more important. It would decide which regiment – albeit Beicher's Einsatzgruppe weren't connected to Totenkopf – were to be the champions.

Max could see Beicher was raring to get at him, still smarting from the previous day's confrontation; but then, so was he. As they met in the middle of the ring to touch gloves, their stares were ones of pure hatred. It was obvious there would be no mercy shown by either fighter.

Although Max was seething, he was able to contain his icy anger. He was only too aware that a close encounter or a slugging match in the early stages would be disastrous against a much heavier Beicher.

At the sound of the horn Beicher immediately came forward, intending to tear him apart. Max used his footwork to circle around, jabbing furiously and keeping out of his way.

After a few moments, Beicher stopped in the centre of the ring and shouted aloud, "Now they're teaching these asphalt pansies to dance too. What is this war coming to?"

He was hoping his scornful remark would goad Max into losing self-control and doing something stupid. It was apparent that Beicher was confident he would demolish Max in short order. He mocked and taunted and then, as he leant back to let out a faked belly laugh, Max bounced in quickly with an abdomen punch, catching Beicher by surprise. Furious at his own stupidity, Beicher exploded and chased Max around the ring, but he couldn't land an effective punch. His contempt quickly began to turn to respect. He started to take the job more seriously.

He growled like an animal as he threw punches. Surprisingly, just into the second minute, one of his counterpunches caught Max solidly and knocked him back into the ropes. Max used the rebound from the ropes to his advantage, and slipped close by Beicher's body to avoid further blows. But, as Max passed by, Beicher gave him a headbutt and a wild right haymaker hit him in the back of the head. The impact of the combination stunned Max, throwing him across into the centre of the ring. He shook his head to regain composure and looked over at the referee to register the foul. The referee said nothing and motioned him to box on. Max quickly realised that the referee wasn't recognising even the condensed version of the rules.

Max retaliated quickly, coming forward with a series of furious combination punches, but Beicher absorbed the blows and dealt out his own counters. In the fierce exchange, Max came off worse. He reeled away dazed, and Beicher sensed an opportunity for knocking him out; he ran at him and literally clubbed Max to the ground. The referee finally came between the boxers to give Max a count, but Beicher did not want to let Max off the hook. He pushed the referee away, determined to finish Max off whilst he was still kneeling. The referee came back and grabbed hold of Beicher before he could beat Max unconscious. In the heat of the moment, Beicher turned his attention to the referee, whom he proceeded to club out of the way.

The crowd were in uproar.

By focusing on the referee Beicher had unwittingly given Max precious seconds to recover. Up on his feet, he threw a huge punch into the back of Beicher's head. Beicher stumbled forward, regained his balance and spun around. Max, following up close behind, hit Beicher with a low punch, causing him to double over. Max followed up with an explosive uppercut and Beicher staggered back and fell to one knee. This time it was Max who wasn't going to let his opponent off the hook: he followed through with a ferocious combination of punches while Beicher was still kneeling.

The horn sounded the end of the first round. Those watching were beside themselves; both boxers had come out even, but the bout had already degenerated into a street brawl.

Notwithstanding the knocks he'd taken in the first round, Max was by far the fitter of the two. This was just as well, because Beicher could soak up the punishment. From his corner, he signalled to Max that he was keen to get on with it.

As Max sat on his bench, visions of Anna drifted across the screen of his mind. The thought of her reminded him of why he'd taken up the challenge in the first place. It gave him an added incentive.

The horn sounded. Beicher was up and chasing Max around the ring, but his continuous advances were to his detriment: Max simply countered with strong right cross-punches each time Beicher bored forward. The punches aggravated him more than they hurt him.

'This guy's a tough bastard and still very dangerous,' thought Max.

As for Beicher, he'd underestimated Max's fitness and boxing skills. Max was still standing, and it was quite apparent he wasn't intimidated by a much heavier opponent.

He continued pushing Max around the ring like a rag doll with huge uncoordinated haymakers. Max picked up the pace, connecting with several sharp one-twos. Beicher absorbed the blows like a sponge and continued his unceasing advances, relying on aggression to gain points.

The horn sounded for the end of the second round.

The third round started prematurely. Fritz was busily tending grazes on Max's face and had his back to the opposing corner, blocking Max's view. Before the horn sounded the start of the final round, Beicher leapt across the ring, pushed Fritz aside, and clubbed Max from his bench to the floor. Reacting quickly, Fritz threw a furious combination of punches into the back and side of Beicher's head. They were hard enough to hurt Beicher, who spun around intending to demolish him.

From the floor, Max viciously drove his heel into Beicher's ankle and toppled him to the canvas. Max got to his feet and motioned for Fritz to leave the ring. Beicher got up and, crazier than ever, came at Max intending to kill him. As he barrelled forward like a train out of control, Max simply sidestepped and kicked his leading leg away from under him. Beicher crashed to the floor for a second time.

The fight had suddenly become a kick-boxing bout. Beicher went down hard and Max fell on top of him, proceeding to hit him with a barrage of punches. Despite being hit by some of Max's hardest and sharpest shots, Beicher responded with a number of club-like punches that finally knocked Max away. As if reading each other's minds, both boxers got up from the floor and rushed back to their corners, shouting at their seconds to take their boxing gloves off. All the while, the frenzied spectators were cheering for their man to win.

Fritz wasted no time. He drew his knife and used it to cut through the laces. He pulled the gloves from Max's hands, relieving him of the encumbrances. Max literally leapt across the ring and hammered bare-fisted blows into the back of Beicher's head and neck before he could get his gloves off. Beicher fell to his knees hurt. As he struggled to get back on to his feet, Max came in with another fearsome bare-fisted combination. Beicher went down on all fours like an animal, but it didn't stop Max. He gripped his hands together and slammed them as hard as he could on top of Beicher's skull. The big Hamburger rolled over and lay flat on the canvas. Max climbed on top and delivered several more punches to his head.

"This one is for Anna," he said, delivering a vicious right-hander.

Fritz, realising he wasn't about to stop, climbed into the ring to pull him off Beicher.

The horn sounded the end of the final round. Beicher, bloody-faced and battered, stood up; he was swaying. He spat at Max as his corner pulled him away. Max stood his ground and spat back in similar fashion. The contest ended in a draw with Beicher still yelling abuse and promising that he would seek out Max to kill him.

All the while, the warrant officer acting as referee had impotently stood by, watching the two men unleash the full force of their antagonism on to each other.

As the two corners began to settle, Max and Beicher were still eyeing each other, ready to take the contest beyond the three-round challenge. But Max was exhausted and he knew that, although he'd given Beicher his best shots, another close exchange might go against him. Beicher was truly an animal of immense strength.

Beicher continued to throw abuse and hurl death threats. This compelled Max to air his true feelings. He shouted across, "You murdering bastard, Beicher! You're only fit for killing defenceless civilians."

The content of his last remark suddenly silenced Beicher; he mulled over the comments for a few moments. Then, in an uncharacteristically calm voice, he spoke: "So this is why you took up the challenge, eh, Leibstandarte? A man with a conscience, eh? Better get back to your Berlin parade ground, pansy boy, and let the men fight this war."

"We're soldiers, you stupid f**k," bellowed Max, "not cowards who follow up behind the front lines shooting innocent civilians."

"Careful how you choose your next words, soldier; otherwise this issue will go beyond this contest."

Beicher obviously acknowledged Max's fighting skills, but he considered his last comments politically loaded. The contest having ended in a tie, he quickly settled and continued to gloat over Max's 'weakness' – his compassion for others. Max simply spat on the ground, glaring at him.

Fritz finally caught his attention and they eventually left the ring to return to their camp along with the joyous group of Leibstandarte supporters.

This wouldn't be the last time Max and Beicher, the Fleischer, would clash swords. Neither of them knew it that day, but their paths would cross again, and when that happened one of them would die.

BIBLIOGRAPHY

The Third Reich: The SS. (Time Life Books, 1989.)

20

TIME FOR REFLECTION

Recommendation for their first combat decoration, the Iron Cross, Lind class, for the rescue of Fritz and his beleaguered reconnaissance squad had been approved. Paul would receive his for drafting the plan, and Max for pulling out Fritz and his squad under fire.

On hearing the news, Fritz gave Max a good-natured ribbing, claiming his entitlement to a piece of the medal. After all, if he and his men hadn't been trapped in the farmhouse, Max would never have won it.

The shortness of the campaign in Poland was a relief and rumours of following on into Russia were unfounded. The Non-Aggression Pact between Germany and the Soviet Union had only just been signed and it was highly unlikely that either side would breach this arrangement so early in the day. Besides, an entanglement with the Russians in an oncoming winter would be a big mistake. Instead Germany's attention swung around to refocus on Western Europe and their old enemies, France and Great Britain.

During this period, Germany had expected an attack from the Allies, but intelligence reports confirmed they seemed content preparing their defences along the Maginot Line. They were confident they could hold a German offensive, just as they had twenty-six years earlier, in 1914.

Much to the regiment's dismay, instead of returning to Berlin, Leibstandarte was instructed to partake in occupational duties in Czechoslovakia. It was to relieve Der Führer, the remaining SS-VT regiment that missed the action in Poland.

The drive from Poland to Prague took a couple of days. As usual, Max rode up front. He let out a gasp of relief as the convoy of trucks began its move out of Poland. He quickly relaxed into the journey as the vehicle sped south-west back into Germany then south towards Prague, the capital city of Czechoslovakia.

His thoughts meandered from the glorious to the grotesque. The fights (there had been many in the short time) and his role in rescuing his comrades gave him a lift, but thoughts of the massacred villagers made his heart sink – women and children had been cut down as reprisals for their menfolk taking off to form resistance groups. Knowing he'd mauled the Fleischer, one of the foremost perpetrators of the killings, was hardly compensation, but it gave some satisfaction.

The journey back also provided him with the opportunity to review the doctrine he had been brought up with in the Hitler Youth and he thought about how it had represented itself during the Polish campaign. Alas! it hadn't matched his understanding and expectations.

He had to admit that his noble interpretation appeared to be conflicting with the stand adopted by Allgemeine's special units. But the Allgemeine-SS wasn't the Armed-SS – the contrast was clear. The Armed-SS were trained soldiers led by strong and aggressive leadership. In contrast, the Einsatzkommando was a murder squad which simply followed up behind. Its mandate was based upon orders from desk-bound jockeys in Berlin.

He struggled to come to terms with what he'd witnessed, and in the many hours of the trip down to Czechoslovakia he convinced himself that going west would bring back a sense of civility and honour. Maybe the barbarism was connected only with Eastern European nations.

Soon after crossing the German border the convoy connected with one of the new autobahns. It was sheer luxury after having travelled on Polish roads, which were medieval by comparison.

On 4 October Leibstandarte arrived in Prague to relieve Der Führer. Duties were mundane and included guarding public buildings. The routine activities gave the men a chance to relax. Best of all, ethnic Germans living in the area gave the troops a warm welcome.

The stay in Prague proved to be a brief one, but in that space of time Max managed to pick up a flying relationship with an attractive ethnic-German student named Sabina. They met in a library while he was reading a huge encyclopedia on Greek mythology.

He spotted her working keenly at a table buried deep in a pile of reference books. When their eyes met there was an instant attraction.

Max strategically placed himself diametrically opposite her, close enough to strike up a conversation. Surprisingly, it was Sabina who opened up the conversation.

"What's that you're researching?"

She was keen to find out what the contents of the huge tome was.

"Greek mythology. What's your poison?" Max replied.

"Chemical engineering," she said with a proud look on her face.

"Very analytical!" said Max.

"Very dreamy!" was Sabina's riposte, raising her eyebrows and looking down on the book, which was spread across the table.

He smiled and introduced himself: "I'm Max. I'm attached to the Leibstandarte regiment, the Führer's personal unit." It was time for Max to give his own shuffle of pride. "We're garrisoned in Prague to take up guard duties for a while. Just got back from Poland," he added nonchalantly. "Can I have a look at what your project is? It's unusual for a woman to take up chemical engineering, isn't it?"

"No, it's not so unusual for a woman these days. I find it easy.

There are three females in my class of eighteen students. We're just as good as the men."

Max agreed. "*Ja*, my sister qualified in political science, would you believe?" Following a brief pause, Max popped the question hanging on his lips: "Care for a coffee when you finish up for the day?" He nodded towards the books stacked on the table.

"Yes, I'd love to."

So began the brief but sizzling relationship that would stretch Max both intellectually (concerning his belief in the master race) and sexually, with a female whose insatiable appetite for sex included a weird array of fantasies. With Sabina it was maximum sex, the likes of which he'd never experienced before.

When the pair weren't having sex they competed intellectually, trying to establish who was the smarter of the two. Sabina challenged Max on almost all his beliefs. She proved to be strong in character and Max enjoyed the banter they exchanged, even though he took regular intellectual knocks from her. On most occasions, she wiped the floor with him, but every now and again she'd lose herself, and Max, a former student of the dialectical wizard Vogel, would destroy her with her own words. The result would be an hour or two of sulking for her. Their differences dissolved the instant their bodies met in carnal union. Her desires for various kinds of 'isms' kept Max spellbound. He thought he'd seen everything, but Sabina led him into new areas of sexual discovery.

Sabina was strikingly attractive. She had an angular face, and a slender body with small, firm breasts – Max's ideal specification. Her blue eyes sparkled mischievously when she taunted him to prove the validity of his ideas about life. All of her assets, mental and physical, appealed to him, and she knew it. She read him like a daily newspaper, exploiting his needs; she revelled in dominating the relationship in more ways than one.

They made the most out of their few weeks spent together, and when Max received word that Leibstandarte was to ship out and return to Germany they exchanged contact addresses. But, without admitting it, each knew their affair was of the temporary type. Max returned to Germany with wounds worse than he'd received in the field. It left him wondering just how far Sabina would have ventured had they experienced a longer relationship.

'Sexual deviance at its most sordid best,' thought Max, realising such intensity could become an obsession.

Sabina continued her chemical-engineering classes, reflecting on the fun she'd had with her soldier-boy partner.

In mid-November, Leibstandarte returned to Germany to be quartered at Bad Ems-Nassau, near the city of Koblenz. The men were placed under the command of Guderian's XIX Panzer Corps and spent time training and regrouping for the impending attack on the Allies in the west. On 23 December 1939, Hitler joined the unit for its Christmas dinner at the Kurhaus in Bad Ems-Nassau. Here, each Leibstandarte trooper received tobacco, cake and a bottle of wine.

While at Bad Ems, Max made a brief excursion back to Berlin, where he and Paul along with several others were presented with their Iron Crosses by Leibstandarte's commander, Sepp Dietrich.

Max's visit to Berlin coincided with Greta's return from her assignment at the Swiss National Bank in Geneva. It would be coincidental that her third and final assignment would take her to Prague, where Max had recently returned from. For Max, Prague had been a tourist attraction and sexual haven. For Greta, it would be a city of dark secrets, a dangerous place filled with enemy agents working for the downfall of her country.

As soon as he was told of the brief excursion to Berlin, Max telephoned Greta to fill her in on his three-day visit.

"You got a spare bed?" he asked.

She scorned him for even asking the question.

"I only work half-day Saturday. How about we meet up at the Steinplatz for a bite to eat? Lunch is on me."

"That'll be great," replied Max. "Reception at 12.30 p.m., then! See you there."

It was a cold and crisp afternoon when he made his way towards the Steinplatz Hotel, a stone's throw from Berlin Zoo.

The hotel restaurant served traditional-style food and good coffee. Its typical Berlin ambience made it an ideal meeting place. In the reception area, they greeted each other excitedly.

The restaurant was filled with hotel guests and Saturday shoppers eagerly devouring their lunches. In the hubbub Greta managed to find a small table for two. They sat down and Max caught the attention of a portly aproned waiter. He passed them each a menu then bent across to light the candle on the table. The waiter returned with two glasses and a bottle of water and took their orders.

Greta chose bread soup, cold meat cuts with green salad and a dessert of berries in a vanilla sauce, and Max had the potato soup, pork knuckle, potato and sauerkraut main dish with the same dessert.

He took a moment to stretch back and take in the Berlin buzz.

"So what's happening, Sis?" He suddenly bent across the table towards her and, half covering his mouth, jokingly remarked, "Everything top secret, eh? You can tell me now, shoot me later."

She smiled and slapped him on the wrist. "I won't talk here. Walls have ears. Let's go to the zoo after we finish up."

Greta settled for mundane conversation that couldn't be construed as giving away state secrets: "I'm working in the RSHA at Prinz-Albrecht-Strasse 8, not far from here. What's my little brother been up to? How was your time in Poland?"

"Tough bastards!" said Max, referring to the Poles. "But we kept them back-footed until they had nothing left to defend. The Soviets finished off the job when they invaded from the other side. After the campaign, the unit was transferred to Prague."

"Prague?" Greta was aware that this would be the venue of her next assignment.

"Prague is a beautiful city. We got back from there just last week. We're quartered at Bad Ems-Nassau near Koblenz and we'll celebrate Christmas together there."

"Meet any girls there?"

At the question, Max choked on his water and replied sheepishly, "Yes, one or two."

"Was that one or two, Max?" Greta asked interestedly.

"Well, one actually – nice girl, a student named Sabina."

Greta smiled and Max winced as he instantly recalled the brutal batterings he'd received at the hands of his sex-crazed partner.

The conversation moved on to Greta's love life and the more humorous incidents both had experienced. Max's pantomime of the Baron made Greta rock with laughter.

They finished with coffee and left the restaurant, which was heaving with customers busily clamouring for tables and paying bills. They took a brisk walk to the zoo. They entered through the oriental Elephant Gate and began their tour of a place they hadn't visited in years.

Max opened up the conversation in a serious tone: "They didn't tell us we would be killing defenceless civilians in Poland."

"You were ordered to shoot civilians!" she said, surprised.

"No, we weren't, but a special unit called the Einsatzkommando carried out the butchering."

"The Reich's Central Security Office, where I work, houses both SD and Gestapo now. I recollect Einsatzgruppe being a section located in Amt (Office) IV of the building, all headed up by our chief, Reinhard Heydrich," she said. "They were sent to Czechoslovakia to secure government buildings. You must have come into contact with them there too?"

"Yes, I did, but it was a far different group of individuals I met in Poland compared to the administrators assigned to Prague."

"I wasn't aware their duties had been expanded to include murdering civilians."

"Yes – not a nice bunch of individuals these Einsatzkommandos." Shuddering, he snapped his focus back to the present. "So what's been going on with you? You've been getting out of the country too, eh?"

"Yes, I had a great assignment down in Portugal for a short time. It wasn't long enough, though. Life on the Algarve is so easy-going – makes me want to pack up everything and live out the rest of my life sipping cocktails, lazing on a hot, sandy beach watching the sun go down."

"Was it dangerous?" said Max in an anxious tone.

"No. We operated out of a tourist agency. We weren't hunting down enemy agents or anything of that nature, just acting as go-betweens for our own agents, gathering and passing on information. My next assignment took me to Geneva, and the Swiss National Bank branch there. I worked with Hans Droler. We represented Reichsbank, monitoring gold bars going out of Germany and hard cash coming back in from neutral central banks. This assignment wasn't dangerous either. It was a stopgap, though. Droler wanted his girlfriend to join up with him in Switzerland. After an initial personality clash, she became suspicious of my relationship with Droler however, it was purely platonic. I was upset about being replaced but the handover went well. Now here I am back in Berlin, talking to the best young man I know."

Despite the recent lunch, the urge for a thick fried *Bockwurst* sausage in a bread bun was overwhelming when they passed a stand cooking them. Max quickly succumbed to the irresistible smell wafting around his nostrils, and in the coldness of the day Greta accepted his offer to buy her one too.

As Max passed her the bun she backed off, crouched and aimed it at him as if it were a handgun she was holding.

"Pow, pow! They're teaching me to use these things now."

Max was aghast.

"Really?"

"Really," answered Greta.

Her responsibility in international espionage was about to elevate to another level, and Max, realising her training in firearms meant an increase in danger, immediately grew anxious. His thoughts automatically focused on her safety and welfare.

They steadily weaved their way around all the attractions. The temperature outside differed vastly from what most of the animals were accustomed to in their natural habitats.

'But they are hardy enough to survive,' mused Max.

Taking time off to connect up with nature again, the sights and smells transported the pair into another world, for a couple of hours at least.

After seeing all the exhibits, their brief interlude ended. They exited and strolled along to the U-Bahn station and caught a train back to Alexanderplatz. They walked the remainder of the way to Greta's apartment, chatting and laughing.

Max awoke very early next morning with something on his mind. He washed and dressed quickly and told Greta he was making a short visit to the Lichterfelde barracks where Dietrich's 'praetorian guard' battalion was quartered. When he got there he reported to the quartermaster and asked if he could borrow a light automatic carbine until the following day, when he would return it prior to the medal presentation. The quartermaster reluctantly agreed but asked Max to sign for it. Max tucked it into his holdall and made his way back to the apartment, where Greta was preparing breakfast.

After breakfast, he called her away from what she was doing and unfastened the bag. She was surprised to see what he pulled out. Max explained to her that it was a Mauser MP40 light automatic carbine – standard use for German stormtroopers.

He proceeded to strip it down, meticulously separating the parts, arranging them neatly across the table. He cleaned each piece and reassembled the weapon.

It was Greta's turn. After several attempts, under Max's keen supervision, she became adept at stripping and reassembling the weapon. He taught her how to hold it and fire it, but coaching didn't stop there. Later that day he instructed her on how to hop from cover to cover, never staying too long in one position, and a variety of other tricks of soldiery she hadn't been taught at the RSHA.

All afternoon and into the early evening, they talked and practised combat tactics. If she were to be sent off into an area where her life was at risk, Max wanted his sister to know everything she could about surviving a gunfight.

The medal presentation was carried out on the parade ground at Lichterfelde the following morning. Sepp Dietrich presented Iron Crosses to several troopers for their services in Poland.

Greta was allowed to attend the ceremony. She had a deep sense of pride for her little brother. Visions of when she'd raised him at the orphanage crossed the screen of her mind; tears of joy flowed down her face.

After the short ceremony she met up with the Baron. He was exactly as she'd expected, and she found it difficult to suppress a giggle when they met. Paul picked up on it and wondered what Max had been telling his sister about him.

The short stay in Berlin had ended. It was time for Max and the men to rejoin the regiment. He kissed and hugged Greta on the platform and caught the train back to Koblenz to rejoin the unit at Bad Ems.

In March 1940, after an agreement between the army and the SS, the title of the Waffen-SS was officially given to the party's military arm. Thereafter, the party officially recognised the Waffen-SS as the fourth leg of the German Wehrmacht, in line with the army, navy and air force.

The period after the German invasion of Poland up until the invasion of the west seven months later was known as the phoney war. The Germans called it the sitzkrieg ('sitting war', a pun on blitzkrieg). During this period neither side really committed itself to any significant action, despite the fact that the great powers of Europe had declared war on one another.

It was a surreal phase, but it was the lull before the storm, so to speak. It was a time when Paul and Max could relax and spend some evenings conversing. Paul would sip on his Napoleon brandy while Max drank his beer from the bottle. When offering a toast, Paul would hold his glass high in the air, and as the vessels met he would roar his very own ritualistic "*Hoch*", a term picked up from his father and grandfather, commonly used for toasting during the Great War.

One evening they discussed the looming struggle, which was to take place between enemies who'd faced each other just a generation earlier. They wondered if the forthcoming conflict would result in a reversal of fortune or finish up the same as before: a war of attrition.

"What do think of our chances, Paul? Will we win, or will it end up in stalemate and a battle of attrition like before?"

"Surely not! War has become mobile and mechanised now, and it's highly unlikely there will be trenches cut from the English Channel down to the Swiss border for a second time – although, on the surface, it appears the British and French are preparing for a fight similar in strategy to the previous conflict."

Max nodded his agreement.

They went on to discuss the famous Schlieffen Plan. Alfred Graf von Schlieffen drew up an invasion plan in 1905 following the pact signed by Britain and France in 1904, commonly known as the Entente Cordiale, and the Franco-Russian Alliance signed some years earlier in August 1894.

"Remember the old Schlieffen Plan, Paul? It was devised specifically to fight a war on two fronts. The main idea was to defeat the French in the west quickly before the Russian steamroller would be able to mobilise and descend upon East Prussia."

"Yes, the plan foresaw a rapid German mobilisation, a disregard for Luxembourg and Belgian neutrality, and an overwhelming sweep of a powerful right flank through Belgium and Northern France while maintaining only a defensive position in the centre and on the left flank in Lorraine, the Vosges, and the Moselle –

similar to the action of a scythe. The strong right flank would sweep down in a south-westerly direction, bypassing Paris to the west of the city. The plan focused on capturing most of the French Army and so compelling France to surrender. Following the swift defeat of France, the German forces would swing around eastwards and take up the challenge against the Russians."

"But wasn't the original plan modified some years before the 1914 invasion?" asked Max.

"Yes, von Schlieffen retired in 1906 and Helmuth von Moltke became the German chief of staff. He disagreed with some of the plan, believing it to be too risky; so he modified it by substantially weakening the top-heavy right wing and reinforcing the forces on the left wing at Alsace-Lorraine and the forces on the Russian border."

"Do you think it affected the initial invasion?"

"Yes. The decision to weaken the top-heavy right wing probably cost us the early victory we wanted – the aim was to defeat France in forty-two days. Other factors included an underestimation of Belgian resistance and the presence of the British Expeditionary Force. We believed during the time leading up to war that the British Empire would not participate. Then there was the efficiency of the French railway system, which meant that troops were able to be transferred from the Alsace-Lorraine border during the time when the Germans were delayed by the British and Belgians in the north. They agreed that von Moltke had been too cautious. By substantially weakening the right wing, he had denied Germany the early victory it desired. Too much caution can be dangerous and can deny a side a clear victory. The key to any battle is to adopt an aggressive, almost cavalier approach by optimising the use of the available manpower and equipment. But stretching one's resources in an offensive situation requires a robust fallback. It is critical in the event the original strategy fails and there is a need to regroup to take up the defensive. A fine balance is required. Such aggression in the first instance is worth the risk, but the ability to recover and implement a strong defence is vital."

"Several factors favour a victory for us this time. Firstly, we are not considering a two-front conflict, albeit Poland has just been defeated in the east and, yes, if France had actually invaded during this period we would have been hard-pressed to launch any decent counteroffensive owing to our heavy commitments in Poland. However, our gamble on the French not acting immediately paid off. Second, in 1914 the French and British had actually spoiled for a fight. In contrast, current actions indicate that there isn't the same enthusiasm and aggressive spirit as before. And third, Italy, an ally in World War I, has reversed its position. It is participating on our side this time."

The Baron agreed: "All these factors favour a German success."

As confident as they were, neither comrade could have imagined the magnitude and speed of the German success in the days to come.

BIBLIOGRAPHY

The Third Reich: The SS. (Time Life Books, 1989.)

Charles Messenger: *Hitler's Gladiator: The Life and Times of Panzer Army Commander Sepp Dietrich*, pp. 77–8, (Conway, 2005.)

21

BLITZKRIEG

Early in the morning on 10 May 1940, German attack forces roared into Holland and France.

For the initial invasion, Leibstandarte would be attached to the 227th Infantry Division. Their task, by means of surprise assaults, was to penetrate deep into the heart of the Dutch defences and seize and secure all roads and river and canal bridges up to and including the River IJssel.

With objectives met, fresh orders reassigned Leibstandarte to the 9th Panzer Division to support their push through Holland towards Rotterdam. Its task was to relieve elements of Kurt Student's 7th Air Division, which was dropped there on 10 May.

Following a bombing raid, Leibstandarte crossed the River Maas into central Rotterdam, but, unaware of the Dutch surrender, some forward units opened fire on what appeared to be armed Dutch troops close to the Dutch Command HQ building where Kurt Student was supervising their surrender. Student rushed to a window to see what was happening and received a wound in the head from a glancing bullet.

Leibstandarte's excellent performance was seriously marred by the accidental shooting of Student. Despite the upset, they pushed on to The Hague.

Fresh orders reassigned Leibstandarte to Guderian's XIX Panzer Corps. The breakthrough into France had been successful, and the German advance had squeezed the Allies into an ever diminishing pocket around the French seaport of Dunkirk. By 24

May the Germans stood at the Aa Canal, facing the Allied lines of defence near Watten, fifteen miles south-west of Dunkirk. At nightfall on the 24th, the German High Command issued Hitler's controversial order that, for the time being, the German advance should halt. The next morning Sepp Dietrich, his men dangerously exposed to Allied artillery fire directed from the opposite heights, defied the Führer's order and crossed the canal to seize the high ground beyond. Amazingly, for that act of disobedience, which might have cost another officer at least his rank, Sepp was awarded the Knight's Cross of the Iron Cross.

For the Western Campaign, Panzermeyer's command was reassigned to the Motorcycle Reconnaissance Company. He was also promoted to captain.

As in Poland, Meyer's company comprised several platoons, and 3rd Platoon was led by Paul, who'd been recently promoted to first lieutenant; Max was its platoon sergeant. Fritz and Muller acted as two of four squad sergeants in the same platoon.

On 24 May, Leibstandarte had been on the go for fifteen days. It was early evening when it arrived in the Watten area, on the western side of the Aa Canal; on that same day Hitler called a temporary halt to the advance.

An hour or so after settling in, all reconnaissance officers and sergeants were ordered over to Regimental HQ. There to receive them was their company commander, Kurt Meyer, and the old dog himself, regimental commander Sepp Dietrich.

Sepp opened up the briefing: "Good evening, gentlemen. I've been talking to Kurt and we've come up with a plan that will involve the use of Kurt's inflatable assault rafts. Our 3rd Battalion will cross the canal at dawn tomorrow, but before this happens we need Kurt's unit to establish a bridgehead on the other side."

Paul was surprised as he had been notified earlier of the Führer's order to stop the advance.

Dietrich continued: "Reason is, our men will be exposed to enemy artillery should they deploy up on Watten Hill on the other side, here." He pointed to the relevant spot on the operations map. "I need reconnaissance to secure a bridgehead for 3rd Battalion. I don't want the enemy getting entrenched and picking us off from the heights." As if sensing Paul's surprise he added: "Despite our Führer's order to halt, it is important 3rd Battalion takes the hill."

Meyer took over the briefing: "All the bridges have been blown. French and British troops are deployed along the eastern banks of the canal. Using our inflatable assault rafts, we'll cross the canal at two points under the cover of darkness, one north and the other south of the enemy's main concentration." Panzermeyer pointed to the chosen locations. "Paul, you will take 3rd Platoon and make the south crossing." Addressing 2nd Platoon leader Max Wunsche, he said, "Max, you and your platoon will cross at the northerly point. We'll soften up the enemy with a preparatory barrage. Myself and Hugo (referring to 1st Platoon leader Hugo Krass) will conduct a frontal attack utilising salvaged canal barges for our crossing with the intention of deceiving the enemy into believing there is just one direct assault. Hopefully our initial bombardment will be enough to stop them regrouping quickly. It will be too late for them once we open up from both flanks on their side. Our objective, gentlemen, is to clear away the enemy concentrated on the banks of the canal and form a bridgehead of our own. We will hold the bridgehead until the early hours of the morning for 3rd Battalion to make the crossing, follow through and clear the observation post set up on the high ground beyond. Intelligence tells me the Watten area is reasonably defended but there's not a heavy concentration of troops. In order to minimise casualties, we have opted for this three-pronged assault. Your presence on the other side of the canal, attacking from both flanks, should surprise the hell out of them. Just ensure that your crossings go without mishap. Oh, and be sure to bring back my inflatables when the job is over."

"*Jawohl, Hauptsturmführer,*" responded all three platoon leaders.

"Our initial artillery barrage and frontal assault will commence at 0230 hours. Your crossings should commence at 0200 hours, giving you time to regroup on the other side, make your way up to the objective point and dig in within striking distance of the enemy. Brief your men and prepare your inflatables for the crossings."

"Good luck, gentlemen. We'll see you back here in the morning, then," added Dietrich.

Paul and Max left Regimental HQ at the double. At Platoon HQ they briefed the men on the dangerous mission to be undertaken. Four eight-man inflatables would accommodate each platoon for the canal crossings. It was hoped the cover of darkness for the short journey would get them across the narrow stretch of water without mishap.

Having prepared the inflatables, blacked up and donned full battle gear, at precisely 0200 hours the platoons slipped into the dark strip of water, leaving the safety of occupied territory to encroach on enemy-held terrain.

During the short but hazardous trip, Max could hear the gentle sounds of the paddles pulling through the water. The silence of the night worked against them.

'Will the enemy hear us?' he thought.

He strained his eyes for signs of movement on the opposite side. The blackness gave away nothing.

The journey across had been short but nerve-wracking, but to their relief both units reached the other side without being challenged. They regrouped quickly and prepared to press on towards their objective.

The north and south crossings had been distanced in order to minimise the possibility of detection from the flanks of the main concentration of troops. It would be a race against time to meet the thirty-minute schedule.

Success meant making the distance without being discovered, setting up good vantage points within striking distance of the enemy and synchronising with the opening barrage and the frontal assault.

At 0230 hours the barrage began. It surprised the defenders and threw them into disarray. Panzermeyer, leading Krass's platoon, carried out the assault using a canal barge. They maximised firepower during the crossing in an attempt to fool the defenders into believing a major frontal assault was under way.

Orders received from the French headquarters were 'Hold and repel the assault.'

By the time the enemy, a mix of French soldiers and British engineers, had regrouped to receive Panzermeyer's canal barge, they were surprised for a second time when Wunsche's platoon opened up from their own side of the canal. Several minutes later Paul's platoon opened up from the opposite flank.

Having achieved the element of surprise, the Germans set about their task: clear the area of its defenders, link up and dig in to form a bridgehead ready to repulse any enemy counterattack, then wait for 3rd Battalion's crossing later, at dawn.

The French had no immediate reserve to call upon and were now being attacked from three sides. Worse, they had no idea of German strength. Some panicked and fell back, intending to dig into safer positions and form a strongpoint there. Others remained at the edge of the canal to take up the fight on all three fronts in the hope that backup would arrive soon.

Paul radioed across to Wunsche: "Max, I'll target those who have dug in at the rear. You concentrate on those deployed at the edge of the canal."

In no time, Meyer's frontal assault had overrun the British engineers and French positions and prisoners were being taken. Soon after, Wunsche's platoon joined up with Meyer.

Still under fire from the French units dug in some distance behind, Paul's platoon fanned out to form the periphery of an extended bridgehead in readiness to receive a counterattack, should the remaining units be reinforced by any other British or French contingent garrisoned close by.

The speed and surprise of the operation had caught the enemy off guard, but now it would be their turn to surprise. Soon after, enemy reinforcements met up with the units holding their ground east of the German bridgehead. From there, they launched a fierce counterattack. Meyer's company was not expecting such a ferocious response.

The fresh fight broke out soon after the bridgehead had been established. The Germans were now defending the position they had just won and found themselves struggling to repulse the enemy counterattack. Meyer radioed back to the main force on the west side requesting urgent support as his newly won ground was now under threat of being retaken.

Enemy aggression appeared to be strengthening by the minute. The Baron held one half of the perimeter and Max (Rieker) the other. The platoon was thinly spread and at the sharp end, receiving enemy mortar and automatic gunfire. Casualties were mounting as a result. Thankfully, it appeared that the enemy had no armoured support, as yet.

"Fritz, it's time we fell back to a better strongpoint," the Baron instructed. "We're too exposed in our present positions and they're starting to pick us off. Get a messenger around to Max to do the same on his side. Once that's done, stay here with a squad to cover my withdrawal, then get yourself out and join up at our strongpoint."

The Baron began his withdrawal to better cover joining up with 1st and 2nd Platoons, leaving Fritz and a small unit to disengage from the enemy.

Meantime, Max had received the instruction to withdraw, but his situation was even more hazardous. Before he could perform an orderly withdrawal his men had to repulse an enemy bayonet attack.

Just after receiving the instruction, the area in front of him suddenly filled with smoke.

"Christ, they're going to attack us! They're coming at us, men!" he bellowed to his unit. "Prepare for a bayonet attack! Grenades! Shoot into the smoke!"

The following hand-to-hand skirmish was frightening. Most of the Germans were armed with light automatics; others fixed bayonets to prepare for the onslaught. The darkness and smoke turned the situation into a waking nightmare. Combatants clashed in lethal wrestling matches in brutal fights for survival.

Max was in the thick of this desperate exchange. He picked off several as they came forward out of the smoke and managed to change his magazine before a second wave fell upon them. Once he'd emptied the magazine he picked up a bayoneted rifle from a dead soldier and joined in the deadly hand-to-hand contest. It was a hair-raising experience. Just how many more would appear out of the shadows was anybody's guess.

Much to their relief, after several anxious minutes the smoke cleared and all was silent in Max's sector. Most of his men had survived the bayonet attack, but some had fallen. They picked up the wounded and fell back to stronger cover, leaving Gerd Reuss and a squad to act as cover for the withdrawal.

They all managed to settle into their new positions in a now diminishing pocket. The battle became desperate and casualties were continuing to accrue despite the withdrawal to better cover.

From the other side of the canal, artillery shells were whistling over the German-held bridgehead and ripping into the enemy's emplacements. Then, much to Meyer's relief, a company from 3rd Battalion joined in the fight, pouring off a canal barge in support.

The impetus of the French counterattack finally evaporated in the wake of the artillery barrage and the added manpower. Without artillery or armour, the French hadn't a hope of achieving a reversal. The battle swung back in favour of the Germans and, soon after, the French withdrew.

At dawn, the main contingent of 3rd Battalion made its crossing. They would, at a cost of two killed and twenty wounded, follow through to Watten Heights and clear the observation post there.

Meyer's reconnaissance had succeeded, but he had suffered casualties. At one stage, they'd been within minutes of being completely overrun by the enemy.

As 3rd Battalion moved up towards the heights, Meyer was congratulated on a fine job. The company returned to the west side for breakfast and a well-earned rest.

Meyer reported back to Sepp Dietrich and took breakfast with him. The catering unit had been ordered to serve up huge servings for the men. Additionally, each trooper was issued with a bottle of beer.

Some of the men never returned and those wounded were shipped off to hospital. But all of the Baron's NCOs had survived with only a few minor wounds between them. Max had been among the luckiest, having endured the French bayonet attack.

The platoon sat around a long table. They raised their beer bottles and clashed them together followed by a very loud "*Hoch!*" – the Baron's very own rendition, toasting their success.

The Baron stood for a second toast to pay tribute to the two squads that had covered the withdrawals back to the strongpoints during a very critical time.

"Here's to Fritz and Gerd for their fine rearguards under such pressure. Well done, *Kameraden*."

Fritz and Gerd acknowledged the appreciation.

"I heard it was a close call for you, Maxy boy," said Fritz, referring to the French bayonet charge.

"It was. I thought my time was up."

"There was a time when I thought we'd all had it," said Muller.

"Thank goodness for 3rd Battalion!" replied Fritz. "We were a bit luckier than Steiner's Deutschland Boys; they forced a bridgehead but were attacked by British tanks and took a hammering."

"Were they all killed?" quizzed Reuss.

"No. A relief force finally got there to save them from annihilation."

"Poor bastards!" said Max, referring to Steiner's unit. "Some of our boys got killed out there last night too. Let's give them a toast."

They paid tribute to the dead and wounded comrades of their own company, and finished breakfast in silence.

The exhausted crew climbed out of their wooden chairs and went their different ways to grab some well-earned rest.

A few days after the Aa Canal crossing, Max was involved in a second undertaking. This time his services called for the performance of a duty that went against his personal values.

The German advance had resumed on 26 May. The period that followed saw German forces pushing the British Expeditionary Force back to the coast. The British were preparing to evacuate troops back to the safety of England. A number of British and French units were fighting a desperate rearguard action to slow down the German advance and buy those on the beach some precious time to pull off their evacuation.

In the sector where Leibstandarte and a number of regular army units were involved, dogged British resistance was holding up the advance. The stubborn resistance had surprised and angered the Germans; heavy casualties had dented their pride, and they were looking to even the score. In this instance, evening the score meant the harshest response: that of taking no prisoners. Max was selected as one of six NCOs to perform the unpleasant task of shooting any surrendering soldier of the stubborn enclave. He received his orders with a heavy heart.

The order had been relayed to Paul earlier, and he realised that the British unit had been cut off and would soon have to fight to the death, or surrender.

Soon enough, with just seven troopers remaining, the British officer commanding his unit gave the order to throw down weapons and surrender. The white flag was raised and the British remnant climbed out from their defensive positions. At the double, with hands clasped behind their heads, they headed towards the German lines, anticipating spending the rest of the war in a prisoner-of-war camp.

The death squad sent to meet them had been ordered to remove their helmets and jackets and tuck up their trousers in an effort to conceal the identity of the unit involved. The now anonymous unit split up in two halves ready to receive the surrendering British. Armed with a Schmeisser MP28 sub-machine gun, Max was third in a line of three approaching from one side.

It felt unreal that he should be a member of a death squad. His mind raced at the thought of the unwelcome task at hand. Unable to come to terms with the situation, he focused on the trivia of the moment, noting how hot the day was and how strange the NCOs looked: their outer field wear had been removed, revealing black shirts with rolled-up sleeves; their trousers, also rolled up, were held up with wide cream braces.

They strode towards the British in a casual manner, with their automatics hanging down loosely. As the British came closer, they raised their weapons in preparation to fire.

The British officer leading his unit realised that he and his men were in immediate peril, and he frantically protested in an attempt to save their lives. He shouted violently and hysterically, quoting the relevant sections of the Geneva Convention and the rules of engagement. The emotion, anger and desperation in his voice almost knocked Max off his feet, but while he was making his useless appeal the lead NCOs fired several rounds into him and the trooper behind him. The remaining troopers panicked and turned tail, dashing back from where they came. Their move was futile: they ran straight into a hail of bullets fired from the other half of the squad, who were closing in from the other side.

The pleading officer had managed to stumble some metres ahead, and he dropped to the ground close to Max. He stood over the dying man's body.

Gasping for air, the officer looked up at Max and asked, "Why?" searching for the answer before taking his last breath.

Max couldn't respond, but, looking down at him with compassion in his eyes, fired two rounds into him to put the dying man out of his misery.

Max was deeply disappointed that the tough skirmish should end this way, and, in his mind, he silently saluted the officer. He had by now come to understand that the rules of engagement did not apply in the heat of battle. Comrades falling on either side of a man, French, British or German, would, more often than not, fill him with a desire for immediate revenge. In many cases, getting even took precedence over the protocol and rules of war.

Those soldiers who'd enlisted into the Waffen-SS during the 1930s had been convinced that to die for Führer and Fatherland was their loyal duty. For the true diehards, this was still how they felt. In similar circumstances they would have expected no different treatment from the enemy.

Despite Max's loyalty and ability to follow orders, conscience was an integral part of his make-up. Executing defenceless soldiers upset him. News got around later that the execution order hadn't come from the top. Max was relieved, and he hung on to the belief that his seniors would agree with him that such killings were not in line with any code of honour.

'Blitzkrieg' had proved to be a resounding success against a numerically superior adversary. The Allies had been short-sighted in their preparations. They had prepared to fight a static war, similar to the last conflict; Germany hadn't. It had optimised its resources and utilised modern strategies and techniques.

Ironically, in the 1920s it had been the British who were the first to talk about the mechanisation of armies. Unfortunately, the innovations and ideas of J. F. C. Fuller and B. H. Liddell Hart were turned down by the British War Office. Fuller's ideas, however, hadn't passed unnoticed by the Germans – notably Heinz Guderian. It was Guderian who picked up on Fuller's ideas and pioneered the development of armoured warfare.

In June 1940, the British must have been regretting not following up on Fuller's insight.

BIBLIOGRAPHY

The Third Reich: The SS, pp. 151–6. (Time Life Books, 1989.)

Larry Collins and Dominique Lapierre: *Is Paris Burning*. (Warner Books Inc., 1991.)

Kurt Meyer: *Grenadiers: The Story of Waffen SS General Kurt "Panzer" Meyer*, pp. 17–18. (Stackpole Books, 2005.)

Charles Messenger: *Hitler's Gladiator: The Life and Times of Panzer Army Commander Sepp Dietrich*, pp. 78–87. (Conway, 2005.)

22

PARIS GIRLS

The French surrender set off a wave of elation throughout Germany. Its military believed its fighting machine was invincible, and morale throughout the nation was never higher than during the period from June 1940 to the early days of the invasion of Russia in the autumn of 1941. The surrender was signed in the very same railcar as the one in which the German High Command had signed the unconditional armistice back in 1918.

During the German occupation the city of Paris was used as a rest-and-rehabilitation centre for their troops, and postings there were highly prized. Ranks and NCOs, either in transit or on leave, had at their disposal a soldiers' home called the Soldatenheim. For officers, there was an Offiziersheim. Even Hitler visited the city as a tourist shortly after it was occupied.

Now that mainland Europe was under control, all attention became focused on the island on the other side of a thirty-six-kilometre-wide strip of water. Hitler boasted that he would be dining in London by Christmas 1940.

Paul and Max loved Paris. It matched their feelings about what a city should be: wide boulevards, grandiose buildings and charming pavement cafés helped to create an ambience that was unique. Paris had everything: tourist attractions, history (both ancient and modern), fabulous cuisine, great wine and, most important of all, very attractive women.

In their conversations the pair discussed the differences

between French and German girls. While Germans were sexy and attractive, their down-to-earth practicality made them more at ease with their male counterparts; Frenchwomen, on the other hand, had an air of elegance and exuded a femininity that flattered the male ego, evoking a desire to protect these precious creatures.

Amazingly, when it came to a question of what role women should play as part of a master race, both Paul and Max managed to sidestep the thought of a woman working in the kitchen and ploughing a field. In their book racial superiority didn't apply to women. All had paid their tutors lip service in the political-educational section of the doctrine.

Chauvinistic and shallow as it appears, they used women to balance the dangerous lives they led in the field. Women were their source of pleasure and relaxation. Neither of them desired a permanent relationship, nor could they have one. During these times the army was virtually a full-time affair.

Paris was teeming with German soldiers celebrating their victory. All junior officers and NCOs in the Paris area and coastal regions were free-issued bicycles. With rifles strapped across their shoulders, they rode them all over Paris. Daily excursions took them around all the famous sights, where they would take snaps of each other with a famous landmark forming the backdrop.

Max loved the history and Paul, contrastingly, delved into the city's social scene. He took pleasure in visiting art galleries and music houses and in eating good French food in the many fine restaurants that lined the streets of Paris. He spoke French extremely well and was glad to have the opportunity to practise the language with the locals.

No more than a day had passed when he struck up a relationship with a woman of substance. His requirements were met exquisitely; she was an attractive forty-year-old wealthy Parisian, into the social scene and generous with her affection.

He caught sight of her at a theatre during the interval. She had a radiance that stood out like a beacon in a sea of bodies – and this was at a distance. He weaved through the theatregoers to get a better view. He wasn't disappointed. She was outstanding, quite alone, and seemingly in a pensive mood.

Taking in every detail, the Baron stood there goggle-eyed; she looked like Loretta Young. Her shiny neck-length brunette coiffure bounced as she turned to meet his eyes in a subconscious reaction to the depth of his gaze. He acknowledged her with a smile, but she quickly turned away, realising he was a German officer. She wore an elegant beige, full-length, crêpe evening gown. It was softly draped over her shapely hips. The moulded bodice had the slightest fishtail train and there was a split in the front of her skirt. A strapless top was pulled tight around her ample breasts and she also wore a stylish bolero jacket. The whole package came with a pair of full-length gloves and a purse to match. A gold chain adorned her delicate neck. She was absolutely stunning, and it struck the Baron that she presented a challenge even he might fail to achieve. He had only minutes in which to come away with some sort of result. A frontal attack was required.

Without wasting a moment he stepped in close and spoke in French: *"Bonsoir, Madame*, I couldn't help but notice that you were alone."

His fluency in the French language surprised her. She looked at him and under any other circumstance would have ignored him, but his bold approach and command of her mother tongue momentarily threw her off balance. She felt compelled to think of a response.

"My friend couldn't make it tonight. She had to make alternative arrangements. As this is the last night, I didn't want to miss the show."

"Yes, it's a great presentation, isn't it? I didn't want to miss it either."

There followed a brief period of silence.

"Look, forgive me, but you're German and I cannot be seen talking with our enemy. I'm sorry, but—"

The Baron interrupted her: "Soldiers must do what they do, Madame. Fortunes swing from one side to the other. One day victory; one day defeat. But that's out there." He gestured with his hands. "In here, tonight, we are spending a most pleasant time in one of the world's most famous cities. We should leave our differences outside, forget our prejudices, sit back and enjoy the sheer delight of the theatre. I am sorry for embarrassing you."

He bowed and turned to walk away, thinking his goal was unachievable.

"My husband . . ."

The Baron swung around.

"Yes, Madame."

"My husband is a major in the French Army. I have heard no news about his welfare or whereabouts. Can you help?"

The Baron silently felt a surge of hope.

Keeping his cool, he replied, "Can you give me a little more information, Madame? Regiment? Battalion? I will be able to help you."

"I cannot talk here," she said, looking around rather nervously. "Perhaps we can meet somewhere later this week?"

"The Louvre, entrance to Egyptian Antiquities, 10 a.m. tomorrow? We can have some morning tea. My name is Paul."

"All right, I'll see you there, then, tomorrow. My name is Celine." She gave a nervous smile.

"*Enchanté*," said the Baron, as he bowed and turned to walk back to his seat for the second half of the play.

Over the following days the Baron consolidated his relationship with Celine by providing her with information concerning her husband, who had been taken prisoner during Operation Red – the second phase in the battle for France. Paul found out where he was being held and was able to provide her with updates about his welfare. Celine greatly appreciated his help, and she was glad to reciprocate, making sure his needs were met. The Baron had used his lofty connections to glean the information about Celine's husband.

Max was always amazed by the Baron's ability to zone in on

the perfect woman – beautiful, rich and with status. It was a skill he could not match, so he stuck to his own ways of seeking out feminine company. During his stay in Paris, his social activities included, among other things, soaking up the ambience of the pavement cafés and French bars. Although he enjoyed being alone, he equally looked forward to nights out with his fellow NCOs, where his personality would switch from that of a dreamer to that of a clown.

While in Paris, he reserved his interest for two women. Both were bar girls. Unlike Paul, Max did not speak French, but he picked up bits of the language relatively quickly and got by on the few sentences he managed to master.

Roxana worked at a bar named Le Chat Noir, and Michelle at a bar called Le Trefle. He could never make up his mind which girl he liked best, so he settled for meandering between the two. Likewise, the girls shared their time with other German suitors.

His first serious brush with the army came one evening when he was deep in jovial conversation with Roxana at Le Chat Noir. Her other partner turned up quite unexpectedly. He was Erich Lange, an army officer with a chip on his shoulder, and he harboured a serious dislike for the Waffen-SS.

Lange entered the bar and stood there for a moment seeking out his favourite hostess. She was seated at the end of the bar with Max, who was clowning around. Roxana was roaring with laughter. Lange immediately grew jealous. As he neared them, he disdainfully ordered Max to move along.

Caught by surprise, and embarrassed by the comment, a wave of anger shot through Max. His eyes met Lange's glare, but Lange, knowing rank meant everything, kept his composure and waited a moment, strumming his fingers on the bar. Without taking his eyes off Lange, Max stood up slowly and slid the stool towards him. Lange picked up the aggression. Then, recognising his SS unit as Leibstandarte, he jumped in with a criticism: "You SS types are useless – no discipline. Even your commander, Dietrich, blatantly disregarded our Führer's order to halt the advance before the Aa

Canal. He should have been sacked for insubordination."

Max, as sharp as a razor, retorted, "Thank heavens I'm not part of the class-ridden, intellectual-bound hypocrisy that you represent, Herr Major. Take your seat. Oh yes, and our commanding officer [referring to Sepp Dietrich] did get all he deserved for his action – a Knight's Cross."

Satisfied that he had saved the honour of the Waffen-SS, he maintained fierce eye contact with Lange, snapped out a smart Nazi-style salute in defiance of the traditional military salute and excused himself, but not before winking at Roxana as he turned to walk away.

Drilling his eyes into Max's retreating back, Lange spat out the words "Non-commissioned animal!" but he did nothing further to reprimand Max for his quick verbal retort, which in itself was an act of insubordination. Regaining his composure, he pulled up the bar stool and sat down, feeling smug that he had won the prize of the evening – sexy, leggy Roxana.

Max left the bar, fighting down the urge to punch the living daylights out of Lange. But the thought of a court martial tied a knot in any action of that kind. He grudgingly forgot the incident and caught up with Fritz, Muller, Reuss and Bader and some other NCOs at one of the city's famed music halls.

A typical NCOs' night out soon developed. They decided to walk a few blocks along to the Crazy Horse revue bar and watch the sizzling dancing-girl show. It was one of their favourite spots. The night buzzed with all the delights that wine, women and song could offer.

During the carefree days in Paris the rivalry between the army and Waffen-SS units remained intense. Waffen units hadn't yet had a real chance to prove themselves in the field, and they continued to be on the receiving end of insults, jibes and abuse from the regulars. Because of the incident in Rotterdam, when they'd come close to killing Kurt Student by accident, Leibstandarte was one of the main targets for the army's disparaging treatment.

As the young men headed off into the night, they weren't to

know this rivalry was about to rear its head yet again.

While Max and the others were absorbing the raunchy atmosphere at the Crazy Horse, a group of junior army officers arrived. Quickly surveying the scene, they thought they'd muscle in on the prime positions where the Waffen NCOs were seated.

"Move along to the back, boys. You've had your turn," said one officer.

Fritz immediately took umbrage and threw back the reference to 'boys'.

"We're off duty, boys. Rank doesn't matter in here. Get to the back yourselves," he said.

In an effort to mitigate the incident, Max added, "Wait your turn, boys. We're nearly through – this session is almost over. You can have the seats when we're finished."

But Fritz's riposte – particularly the 'boys' remark – had raised some hackles. A hot-headed officer wanted to take it further.

"Take yourselves to the rear immediately. That's an order." He emphasised, lifting his hand with his thumb pointing towards the back, and he fixed his eyes on Fritz.

Fritz was in no mood for yielding. He smiled and looked back at his buddies then shot his head around quickly to glare back at the hothead.

"F**k off!"

"You what!" retorted the angry officer. "I'll have you up for insubordination."

His threat only aggravated the NCOs.

"Do we look frightened, army boy?" said Fritz, preparing to defend himself.

The NCOs' stubborn refusal to yield their seats stunned the officers. Assuming command, the hothead repeated his threat of disciplinary action, directing it at Max because of his senior ranking of platoon sergeant.

Already rattled by his earlier experience that night, Max looked the officer in the eyes and raised his voice: "First, we're off duty; second, protocol aside, there are no rules in the book that state ranks should stand down in an entertainment club, and in this case we choose to ignore protocol because we don't like you or your attitude; third, I suggest that you boys return to the Moulin Rouge, where you usually go, and enjoy the evening together with other boys of similar rank instead of upsetting us non-commissioned boys."

All the officers present were stunned to silence as they watched the NCOs preparing themselves to take it further. They realised the sense in Max's words, turned and walked out without watching the show. Max and his cohorts eyed them as they left the music hall. They enjoyed the rest of the programme that night and left with pride intact.

They agreed to round off the night at a small bar away from the glitz of the Parisian night scene. Borodino's, named after the famous battle between Napoleon's Grande Armée and the Russian Empire, was the venue.

They pushed some tables together and pulled up some chairs, got comfortable and ordered drinks.

Fritz opened up the conversation: "The army boys are a pain in the arse, if you ask me. I wonder why they loathe us so much?"

"The army has always been wary of our Führer's SS," said Max. "The discontent goes way back to '34. At that time, the army was under the charge of von Blomberg, the minister of defence, and General von Fritsch, its commander-in-chief. SA leader Ernst Röhm wanted the army to become part of his SA and at a meeting told von Blomberg of his plan to relieve the army of its responsibility. Evidently, von Blomberg immediately contacted our Führer, Chancellor at that time, about his concern. Contrary to Röhm's comment, Hitler confirmed that the expanded army he wanted would be modelled on the existing Reichswehr, not the SA paramilitary. At the time, von Hindenburg was president. He was also wary of the SA and announced that unless something was done he would declare martial law and bring in the army to sort out Röhm's cohorts. Von Hindenburg's threat forced Hitler to choose between the two. It wasn't a difficult choice. The army was to be the main means of furthering his foreign-policy goals in the future; the SA was merely the tool of the party."

"But the army never got involved, did they?" said Muller. "They made it clear that they would not become actively involved in a purge."

"Yes, our Führer's only fallback was the SS and Leibstandarte, and this subsequently resulted in the Night of the Long Knives. I recollect that night clearly. We were there – remember, Fritz?"

Fritz nodded with enthusiasm.

"After the purge of Röhm's boys, Hitler won respect and support from the army and von Hindenburg, but his action hadn't come without a price. Von Hindenburg died soon after the Night of the Long Knives. Hitler grabbed the opportunity to combine the presidency with the chancellorship and assumed the role of Führer. Having gained total power, he directed von Blomberg and von Fritsch to swear an oath of loyalty to him. Evidently, when von Blomberg had written his concerns to Hitler about the SA earlier, he'd agreed that the army would support a military wing of the SS. In September 1934, Verfügungstruppe (SS-VT) was created. The agreement, however, didn't prevent the army from renewing suspicions following the decision to build a military wing of the party. Our regiment wasn't part of SS-VT. Leibstandarte retained its independent status as the first SS unit, acting as Hitler's personal unit. Nevertheless, it still came under the umbrella of the Armed-SS."

Muller took up the conversation: "In March 1935, Hitler fuelled the army's suspicions when he chose Leibstandarte to enter the Saarland instead of the army. Realising the action had offended them, in an effort to make amends he reinstated military conscription, which had been banned in Germany by the Treaty of Versailles. As a consequence, Germany built an army several times the size the treaty allowed."

"Build-up of the Armed-SS and the regular army was worked very much in parallel. It was a year later in March 1936 that Hitler ordered both the army and our Leibstandarte to reoccupy the Rhineland – a much smarter move," added Reuss. Heini [referring to Heinrich Himmler, the leader of the SS] wanted SS-VT and Leibstandarte to be elite fighting units, not objects for army mockery. That's when he appointed Paul Hausser to establish the two officer training schools, the first at Bad Tölz and the second in Braunschweig. There are major differences between Waffen officer training programmes and the Imperial Army training regime. While promotion in Waffen depends upon personal commitment and merit, promotion in the army is still influenced by class and education. Waffen-SS cadet training schools offered something that those of the army never could – an officer's career for men without the prerequisite of a higher middle- or upper-class background."

Fritz spoke up again: "Thank heavens our training techniques are directed towards closing the gap and breaking down the barriers between commissioned and non-commissioned ranks! The camaraderie between us as NCOs and our officers is exceptional. The army's class divide between officers and men doesn't help to bond the ranks to its leaders. Yes, in Waffen, our pursuit of excellence focuses on talent rather than birthright. Waffen encourages self-discipline and mutual respect rather than a brutally enforced discipline. Its general working atmosphere is more relaxed than that of the army because the relationship between officers and men is less formal."

Reuss stood for a toast: "A toast to our leadership and our company."

They all stood and bellowed a resounding "*Hoch!*" in tribute to their commanding officers – the Baron and Panzermeyer.

Fritz spoke up as if in response to his original question: "I guess we do get up the army's nose somewhat, then. Even rankings differ insofar as all Waffen ranks bear the title of our Führer."

"But again, it's been done to avoid the class distinction of the army's hierarchy," Max added. "On duty, the old military rank prefix 'Herr' implies superiority and dominance. On the other hand, in Waffen even the lowest SS rank can address Heini simply as Reichsführer, not Herr Reichsführer. Better still, off duty we can refer to our seniors as '*Kamerad*'."

Reuss chipped in: "The recruiting process for Waffen differs from that of the army too, eh? For example, candidates for Waffen need certain prerequisites before ever setting foot on the academy grounds. Height restricts membership. To make things worse, recruits rejected by Waffen are sent to the army. Considering army traditions, this alone must be a hard pill to swallow."

"Even our uniforms clearly separate the two groups," remarked Bader. "In 1932 Heini introduced the midnight-black uniform."

"Didn't fashion designer Hugo Boss design the SS uniforms?" asked Reuss.

"Yes," replied Bader, "they were designed to impart authority and they never fail to stand out in a group. We are the boys, eh?"

"Yes, but our overgarments are much more closely matched in the field now. We've adopted army-style uniforms and we only retain our distinctive identity by wearing the rank and unit markings from our peacetime dress."

"Ah! But what about our camouflage attire – smocks and helmets?" interjected Fritz. "Heini's own free issue, eh?"

In 1940 camouflage smocks and helmets became general issue for the Waffen-SS elite units.

"All this doesn't help to bond us together, does it?" said Fritz. "I can see why we have a problem with the bastards now."

They all relaxed back in their seats, ordered another round of drinks and spent the remainder of the night discussing their sexual achievements in Paris.

It wasn't hard to understand how these differential factors had created adversity between the two branches. While Waffen men considered themselves to be closer to the top, the army saw them as upstarts who were new to the military game and couldn't boast of any accomplishments. The army lived on its traditions and its achievements and hated the idea that the Waffen-SS could threaten Germany's fine military heritage.

Himmler's ultimate aim was to achieve complete autonomy for Waffen-SS forces in the field, but it never happened. Hitler, reluctant to change this arrangement, remained unconvinced about complete SS independence in the field. Consequently, he announced that Waffen-SS units would remain attached to regular army groups.

However, it was still blatantly apparent that even being under army command did not end the rivalry between the two groups. The joys of Paris did not stop the acrimonious exchanges between the army and Waffen. Because the army was always looking for a way to cast Waffen in a poor light, it arranged a boxing match. The match would involve the army's finest against the best Waffen could put up.

Max jumped at the chance to get back at them.

BIBLIOGRAPHY

David Pryce Jones: *Paris in the Third Reich: A History of the German Occupation, 1940–44*, pp. 19–43, 78–81, 94–111, 118–28, 157–64. (London, 1981.)

David Pryce Jones: *Paris during the German Occupation: Collaboration in France, Politics and Culture during the Nazi Occupation, 1940–44, pp. 15–31. (Oxford, 1989.)*

Larry Collins and Dominique Lapierre: *Is Paris Burning*. (Warner Books Inc., 1991.)

Charles Messenger: *Hitler's Gladiator: The Life and Times of Panzer Army Commander Sepp Dietrich*, pp. 56–67. (Conway, 2005.)

23

ARMY VERSUS WAFFEN

Playing with Parisian girls and getting to know a little more about French culture didn't stop the military way of life prevailing.

As part of the victory celebrations, a boxing match was organised between the two rival branches of the Wehrmacht. Tensions between them ran at boiling point during this period. Despite Waffen's improvement in the field, it had not yet proved its elite status. The army certainly did not consider the Waffen-SS as elite as the party boasted and maintained the view that its men were reckless and arrogant. The boxing match would be a way to dent Waffen's puffed-up pride, and the army was more than eager to get on with it.

The match was to cover four weights: welter, middle, light-heavy and heavy. Max would be the obvious choice for heavyweight. He was now twenty-one years of age and weighed in at eighty-eight kilos. He stopped growing exactly on the 1.8-metre requirement for Hitler's 'praetorian guard', but he still had to wait another four years before he could join this prestigious unit. However, it mattered little in the present circumstances. Besides, he doubted whether the camaraderie could get any better than it was in his present unit.

He'd never been a heavy drinker and understood the advantages of a fit, healthy body. He always set aside time for regular training sessions. Although nowhere near to the standards of earlier years, his training regime was simple and ranged from shadow-boxing, punchbag training and sparring (when he could get a partner to oblige) to lifting weights, skipping and road-running. He was still able to eat anything put on a plate in front of him without putting on weight, so dietary control never represented a problem.

The army had more boxers by far to pick a team from so it seemed to be a foregone conclusion that it would win the contest. Waffen, however, was pinning its hopes on the heavyweight bout, which attracted the most interest, with Max as its champion. As his reputation was known in some of the older army circles, this particular match began to generate its own atmosphere of rivalry and excitement. Max actually stood a genuine chance of winning.

Choosing the strongest four-man SS team turned out to be a difficult job. Units taking their break in Paris didn't include all Waffen's best boxers, so special privileges had to be granted for the balance of its team to be shipped in from units stationed in the French coastal areas.

Weinmann (the welterweight) and Ruhle (the middleweight) arrived from the coast by train. The Paris-based light heavyweight, Merz, made up the quorum. Max met the two imports at the train station and took them back to the Soldatenheim. A gym was situated nearby, giving the four boxers the opportunity to train together up to the eve of the match. Max, being the most experienced, agreed to take them through a short but intense training programme.

The following day they met up and walked over to the gym. After the warming-up session, Max led them into an adjoining hall, and what happened next was quite remarkable.

"OK, lads, let's glove up and get our head guards on."

"What's going on?" asked Ruhle.

"You'll see," said Max. "Close up, lads. Merz, you cover my back; Ruhle, right side; and Weinmann, left."

The four formed a closely knit square. Max looked across to a pair of entrance doors.

"We're ready!" he shouted.

The other boxers looked on quizzically.

The doors swung open and out walked eight men; they had volunteered to act as sparring partners. To maximise effect, all their vests were standard army issue, bearing the name 'HEER' in huge letters stitched on to the chest. They played their parts well, throwing jibes and digs at the foursome as they circled around them in an intimidating manner. On the command, they launched themselves at the human square. The scene was amazing as they came forward, throwing everything they had at them. Max and his team gave as much as they received. They stopped to catch their breaths every now and again. The process was repeated several times.

As the final session came to a close, the rowdy bunch walked back out of the doors as suddenly as they had appeared. This procedure was repeated on a daily basis up to the eve of the fight. It was Max's way of bonding the four boxers and maximising their passion. Each day they'd run through the ordeal, shower off and walk across to a 'converted' French restaurant for breakfast. On their final training day the boys who had formed the group of antagonists lightened up and joined them for breakfast.

On the day of the contest, they were fired up and prepared to provide the army with a decent challenge. The match took place in an entertainment hall that formed the basement of a huge office building in the centre of Paris. Before the war, it had been a well-known venue for amateur boxing nights. Entrances were located on the ground floor at either end of the building. Hundreds of supporters weaved their way down the metal spiral stairways to a huge pair of heavy wooden doors that led into the basement. Inside, the auditorium was big enough to house the boxing ring and host a capacity crowd of about 600 spectators. A row of high-level windows along one side borrowed light from the pavement above during daylight hours. They looked out on to heavy glass-block grilles that formed part of the pavement where the pedestrians walked by. A mezzanine gallery took up the length of the opposite side of the hall and provided accommodation for about 150 seats. Immediately surrounding the ring were two rows of seats reserved for officers. Ranks and others had to stand behind the seats.

Waffen supporters represented about twenty per cent of the total audience. They settled for gathering in an area to one side of the ring. Remaining officers took up some of the seats around the ringside. As the army made up the majority of spectators they took up all the seats in the mezzanine gallery and filled most other areas. Every now and again a sneering remark directed at the Waffen group could be heard over the din. By the time everybody had weaved their way downstairs, tension between the rival factions had built up to a high pitch.

The capacity crowd consisted mostly of Germans, but there was also a handful of Frenchmen and an assortment of Frenchwomen from all levels of Parisian society.

Celine, a changed woman in such a small space of time, accompanied the Baron, who had brought two bottles of champagne in the hope that they would be toasting Max's victory later that evening. He led the way to a row of seats that had been reserved earlier for the Waffen-SS officers.

The Baron's guests were several other lieutenants, a captain and a lone senior officer eager to see how Max would fare against one of the army's best. They were all dressed in full regalia with immaculately pressed black shirts and trousers. The Baron looked like a film star; his white scarf set off his black attire. All the while he drew on his flamboyantly long cigarette holder, showing himself to be a true representative of his aristocratic breed – much to the disgust of the army, who thought that kind of status belonged only to them.

Gambling was heavy. Paul ensured that his money went on Max to win the heavyweight bout. But if he had seen Max's opponent first, he might have decided to switch his bet.

Max was told he'd be competing against a sergeant, older and heavier than he was, not in the best of condition. This sergeant, it was said, had been close to the top in army boxing echelons before the war. He hailed from Leipzig, and his name was Karl Hoffman. He was out to prove that the army ruled supreme in the boxing world as well as on the battlefield, and that Waffen could never compare. Max was out to prove otherwise, and he was looking forward to getting one over on the army boys.

In no time the basement was full of smoke and the first bout was soon to begin. The challenge opened with the welterweight bout. The spectators cheered their man on as both boxers climbed into the ring. The taller, Waffen, contestant, Fritz Weinmann, put up a gallant show against a stockier, more experienced army boxer. When it came to slugging it out, the army had a distinct advantage and eventually won the bout on points.

The middleweight bout turned out to be equally exciting. The second Waffen import, Heinrich Ruhle, proved to be an outstanding scrapper who wouldn't stop coming forward despite his opponent's distinct superiority in boxing skills. The Waffen supporters went wild, shouting loudly and encouraging their man each time a furious combination of punches sent the army boxer sprawling back into the ropes. Inevitably, the Waffen man took one too many unnecessary chances, and, in round three, dropping his guard he exposed his jaw. The more experienced boxer knocked him out with a well-delivered left hook, ending any hope of levelling the match at the halfway mark.

Erwin Merz, the light heavyweight, was next up. His bout proved just as eventful, with both opponents slugging it out toe to toe. The result went in favour of the army, but not without dispute. The SS contingent there thought Merz had done enough to take the bout and were angry at the judges, who were all army staff. SS onlookers were wound up and started to call the judges cheats. Despite contesting the decision, the result held, giving the army a third win and the match. It was now on Max's shoulders to retrieve some Waffen pride.

The SS contingent in the smoky basement let out a huge roar as Max entered the ring. Hoffman soon followed, and the basement exploded as army supporters bellowed out their greeting. As they outnumbered Waffen four to one, this had to be expected.

'Good odds!' thought Paul. 'That would make it about even, then, *Heer Schwuler* [army poofters].'

Hoffman was about the same height but a good three and a half kilos heavier than Max. Sizing Hoffman up, Max reminded himself that his opponent was sure to be substantially past his best. Max's edge would be in fitness and speed – albeit not as finely tuned as it had been in his heyday.

The referee, a lieutenant, recited the usual Queensberry Rules.

Hoffman, confident he would prevail against Max, growled out some ugly comment about the Waffen-SS: "I'm going to teach you a lesson in boxing, you undisciplined Nazi upstart!"

Max was unshaken; he'd heard it all before. He responded with a fixed stare that was as cold as marble. As they touched gloves, Max thanked his opponent. Hoffman looked at him quizzically, then shrugged and returned to his corner to await the bell to signal the start.

Max thanked Hoffman for the scoff because it had immediately brought his blood up: in that moment, the chemicals cascading through his body had pitched him into full hate mode.

The bell rang and Max came in like a street fighter. Hoffman was totally unprepared, but after a few moments he caught his balance and retaliated in similar style. The spectators were amazed at the initial melee. From the onset Max had deliberately set about upsetting Hoffman, but, as fast as he'd got stuck in, he quickly calmed down and relaxed into neat footwork and sharp jabs. Max's arrogant behaviour upset Hoffman, and as a response he spat on the floor glaring in anger and disdain, signalling him with his arms to try it again. Max ignored the gesture, thinking it to be a common habit for his kind of animal, reflecting back on Beicher's antics in Poland.

Max was aware that this particular contest was being fought for more than personal pride: it involved the honour of the entire

Waffen-SS. A seven-year-old vendetta was being played out in the ring. Hoffman too realised that his opponent was looking for more than a personal win.

Surprisingly fast on his feet, Hoffman countered one of Max's jabs with a strong swinging left hook that caught him. The force of the blow pushed Max across the ring into the ropes to the roar of the crowd, but Max bounced out of danger to avoid the risk of being caught there. Hoffman looked a man who wouldn't be hurt easily – much like Beicher, the Einsatzkommando. At least in this contest the Queensberry Rules applied, enabling Max to use his skills and build a points advantage. He resumed his swift jabs and one-twos while avoiding most of Hoffman's punches.

Halfway through the first round, Max decided it was time to quicken the pace and take some risks. He came in with a barrage of combinations. This prompted Hoffman to raise his own game. Hoffman was indeed a smart boxer. Now sensitive to Max's tactics, he chose the right opportunities to counterpunch effectively. It was a sharp right cross that knocked Max down to one knee to take a count of seven. The cheers from the army supporters were deafening. Paul and his row of SS supporters sat quietly. Max used the count to recover. He switched back to jabs for the remainder of the round, dancing around the ring, still accruing points – but nothing too adventurous. He was buying some time to recover fully. Round one ended with Max ahead on points, but he knew the knock-down would have registered more strongly with the judges.

Round two started at the same pace as the previous round had ended. Hoffman turned out to be fitter than expected, and he was still showing no visible signs of fatigue. He came forward more often in this round – an aggressive style that the judges favoured. But Hoffman soon discovered that his aggressive tactic didn't come without a price: Max simply picked him off with his own fierce right-cross counterpunches. He continued to build a points advantage and, moreover, he was starting to hurt Hoffman too. Just before the end of the round, Hoffman caught him with another swinging left hook that he should have avoided. He fell back dazed into the ropes. Just then, the bell sounded the end of the second round, offering Max a temporary reprieve. But Hoffman threw a punch after the bell – an action that earned him a warning from the referee. The spectators were in uproar in anticipation of a knockout win for Hoffman in the final round.

Despite a substantial points advantage, Max's supporters knew that Hoffman's aggression was not going to help Max's case with the judges – particularly in view of the previous bout when Merz should have taken the decision. Fritz was running the corner bench. He realised that only a good knock-down could win the bout and restore the pride of the Waffen-SS.

"You haven't thrown your best shot yet, Max."

"I know, Fritz. You're right – I need to be a bit sharper," he replied as he stood up for the start of the final round.

Hoffman was enduring and sensing victory. As they touched gloves for the final round Hoffman again scoffed at Max: "Had enough, *Arschloche*? I'm going to finish you off now – but don't cry too much, we haven't a baby's dummy here for you."

With that comment, Max exploded. Casting all caution to the wind, he came in with several savage combinations. As Hoffman came back with his counters, Max was ready to retaliate swiftly with his own. His energy had been suddenly refuelled by the sudden infusion of adrenalin, and Hoffman realised he'd made a mistake in mocking him.

Hoffman attacked, but Max countered ferociously; there was no stopping him. He came in with a deliberate low body punch, which earned him his first warning from the referee. The low punch had hurt and maddened Hoffman. He couldn't utilise his anger half as well as Max could.

The crowd picked up on the emotion in the ring, with both sides bellowing for their man to win.

Hoffman came forward in a belligerent manner, throwing

haymakers, but he dropped his guard. Max saw the opening, sprang forward and delivered a huge left hook that rocked Hoffman to the core.

Hoffman stumbled back against the ropes in a daze. Max leapt up in the air and threw a thunderous right cross into his head; then he followed up with another snappy combination, including several more dangerously low shots, which, for some reason, never attracted a second warning from the referee. The referee's failure to pick up the low blows infuriated Hoffman. As Hoffman turned to appeal to the referee, Max came in with a vicious left hook that ripped across Hoffman's jaw, almost knocking him down. The sudden change of fortune excited his corner and the SS contingent in the auditorium, who began yelling words of encouragement for him to finish Hoffman off.

Max came in again, and in the heat of the moment aimed several punches at Hoffman's neck. The referee gave him a second and final warning. Hoffman, still standing, retaliated with a sweeping hook that knocked Max off balance, into the ropes.

Hoffman shouted across, "Cheating Nazi bastard!"

The referee stepped between them to temper their fury. Hoffman had not yet gone down, and time was running out for Max. Hoffman's punches were still powerful but uncoordinated. He was slowing up and Max was managing to avoid them now.

He was determined to knock Hoffman down before the final bell, and he chose a half-chance, coming in with another fierce left hook. The punch connected and finally put the big man on the canvas.

Paul and his group of officers leapt up in a wild frenzy, but only to see Hoffman get up at the count of seven. Although Max had done enough to salvage the honour of Waffen, he wanted an outright win, leaving no doubt as to the decision.

As soon as Hoffman was up, Max launched into the air with another flying right cross then withdrew to recoup from his efforts. Both boxers were tiring, and the drop in energy levels transformed the fight into a close-quarters slugging match. Max's last punch before he backed off was a desperate uppercut which connected well. Hoffman staggered away.

Based on the premise that he was all but spent, Max followed up with a desperate melee of punches; Hoffman could now only swing huge single punches. One connected and swept Max into the ropes. Disorientated, he glanced across the ring to see Hoffman sink to one knee in exhaustion.

With the final seconds ticking away, Hoffman got up, preparing to initiate his final effort. Max, pre-empting his intentions, threw a swinging right hook, causing Hoffman to fall over with Max on top.

As they lay there, utterly exhausted, Max spat out his mouth guard and hissed his own insult into the big man's ear: "Thanks for the boxing lesson, wanker!"

Then he unceremoniously used his opponent's head to support himself in order to stand up.

As he stood, he deliberately bounced Hoffman's head off the canvas, straddled and glared at him for several moments before walking back to his corner, punching the air with both his arms.

Hoffman remained in a heap on the canvas and couldn't get up.

Before Max could reach his bench, the referee raised his hand to signify victory.

The basement erupted in cheers from the SS and boos from the army. Dazed and only half conscious, Max was chaired out of the ring on the shoulders of several of his supporters. Having won the match, it occurred to him that surely his personal battle with the army was now over.

The next morning Paul was recovering from a severe hangover and Max from a severe battering. Late that afternoon they took to their bikes, strapped their rifles across their shoulders and cycled through the Paris suburbs towards the countryside. Paul's camera hung from his neck. Every so often they'd stop and take turns to take a snap. Skylarking, Paul took close-up shots of the disfigurations, nicks and bruises on Max's face. He was aching all over and moving around like an old-age pensioner.

Paul had won a tidy sum of French francs because of Max's win. He gladly showed his appreciation by arranging a night out for Max with a gorgeous French escort girl. They spent the night in one of Paris's finest hotels, all expenses paid.

The Baron's relationship with Celine had become deliciously intimate. He was genuinely concerned about her husband, and he continued to provide her with regular updates regarding his welfare, but, for Celine, the thrill of the exquisite experience with her young, handsome German officer suitor outweighed all risk. Besides, with the exception of the fight night, he hadn't made it obvious he was a Wehrmacht officer or even a German. Barring the fight night, whenever they met he was dressed in plain clothes and always spoke in the French language.

Despite the allure of Paris nightlife and its wonderful women, such escapades could never eclipse their sense of duty to Leibstandarte. The military was their true passion – the rush of adventure and the challenges and hazards of battle.

Conscience would be the only constraint to their loyalty on the battlefield. For example, how would they react to an order to take the life of a non-combatant? Max had already been personally involved in the unsavoury killings of surrendering enemy soldiers. Could they become unconscionable like some of their 'political' counterparts? If they did, how would it affect them mentally and emotionally? Neither wanted to think about the possibility.

Following their rest period in Paris, Leibstandarte was assigned to makeshift barracks in the Dunkirk area. Here they began intensive training for the combined sea and air invasion of Southern England, code-named Operation Sea Lion.

One of the prerequisites for the invasion of the southern coast of England was to eliminate the Royal Air Force. The war in the skies that became known as the Battle of Britain began on 10 July and finished on 17 September 1940. The outcome was that Reichsmarshal Goering's Luftwaffe failed to destroy the RAF and break the will of the British people.

One evening, shortly after receiving news of the cancellation of the invasion, Paul and Max struck up a conversation debating whether or not Operation Sea Lion could have been a success.

"Do you think we could have pulled off a successful amphibious landing, Paul?"

"I'm not sure. I think we would have been hard-pressed to pull it off. Even if the RAF had been successfully taken out, our makeshift invasion force would have had to contend with a British Home Fleet that fielded a huge advantage in numbers. Our navy cannot match the British. We lost most of our modern surface flotilla in the Norwegian Campaign and our U-boats are unsuitable in the comparatively shallow and restricted English Channel. Additionally, our transport vessels to carry troops and equipment were never the best either. The Rhine river barges weren't built for crossing the Channel. They're not specialised craft and could only achieve a successful landing in ideal conditions. Moreover, the quantity of artillery and tanks that could be transported on them is limited. I admit the thought of inclement weather frightened the life out of me too. I prefer to fight with my feet on terra firma. Remember the Spanish Armada of the 1500s – its attempt to invade England went horribly wrong."

Max nodded his agreement.

Following the cancellation of Operation Sea Lion, Leibstandarte was transferred to the Metz area, where it was to commence upsizing to brigade strength. The men were granted home leave for Christmas. On 26 December 1940 all attended the unit's Christmas celebration. As in the previous year, they were honoured by a visit from the Führer.

In his speech, Hitler reminded the men that they had the honour of bearing his name on their cuffs, and therefore they would have the honour of being at the cutting edge of the battle. It would not be long before they would again be engaged in this 'honour'.

Their thoughts ran rampant: where would the next battle arena be? Turning east, to Russia, appeared to be the only remaining option. Surprisingly it wasn't yet to be. Before this, Leibstandarte was to face another challenge – one that would finally establish it as an elite fighting force.

BIBLIOGRAPHY

The Third Reich: The SS, pp. 143–51. (Time Life Books, 1989.)

Charles Messenger: *Hitler's Gladiator: The Life and Times of Panzer Army Commander Sepp Dietrich,* pp. 88–9. (Conway, 2005.)

24

LEIBSTANDARTE

Where do today's public figures pluck the courage to call these
faithful and self-sacrificing young men party soldiers? These young
men fought for Germany and certainly did not die for a party.

Kurt Meyer, from his book Grenadiers, 2005.

Events during the Balkan and Russian campaigns eventually healed
the fracture between the Waffen-SS and the army. Always at the
sharp end in the field, Leibstandarte and other Waffen-SS units
finally demonstrated their elite fighting capabilities in the face of
countless odds.

In October 1940, Benito Mussolini's Italy invaded Albania and
Greece. By Christmas that year, the Italians had been driven
back out of Greece and were on the defensive. Hitler became
concerned that a Balkan front might affect his plans for invading
the Soviet Union in the summer of 1941. To exacerbate matters,
Britain offered Greece assistance. This enabled the RAF to strike
at the Ploetsi oilfields in Romania. In March 1941, the first British
troops touched down on Greek soil.

The German High Command was forced to draw up plans to
secure the Balkan Front, and this resulted in the invasion of
Yugoslavia and Greece in April 1941. The objective was simply
to drive the British Expeditionary Force from the Greek mainland.

The German invasion force was the 12th Army under the
command of Field Marshal List.

Leibstandarte were to play a major role in this campaign. They transferred to Romania as a full brigade. Meyer's unit had been part of the enlargement process and, instead of the single company he'd led in France, he now commanded a full reconnaissance battalion made up of four companies. Along with the additional responsibility came promotion to the senior ranks as major (Sturmbannführer in SS terms). The Baron now led a full company (4th Company) with Max as its company sergeant. Fritz and Muller were promoted from squad sergeants to platoon sergeants. Max led the 3rd Platoon in addition to his role as company sergeant.

The action in Greece had given Leibstandarte the opportunity to test their skills in mountain warfare. The men from the original regiment had received some experience and training earlier in Sudetenland during the occupation of Czechoslovakia in 1938–9. Since then, replacements and new recruits had had their chance through a brief period in 1940 during their stay in Metz, around the Moselle area. They would confirm that such warfare required supreme fitness, strength, endurance and a sharp mind. Taking part in frontal assaults up steep hills also called for a lion's heart.

The Balkan Campaign would be the real challenge: waging mountain warfare against stubborn opposition. In Greece, much of the terrain was mountainous and high-ground enemy defensive emplacements could only be approached from one way (one way up and one way back down on the other side). At first glance a standard two-flanked approach seemed impossible.

Meyer's reconnaissance battalion would put this to the test at the Klissura Pass, where, despite the fact that there seemed to be only one way forward, he still managed to adopt two lines of attack.

Here he would utilise three battlegroups. Meyer commanded one battlegroup, taking the conventional approach, following the main road. Two motorbike companies formed the second battlegroup under Hugo-Gottfried Krass. They would set off up the side of the mountain. Their task would be to climb the rocky terrain and attack enemy gun emplacements. They would meet up with Meyer at the top, hopefully having flushed out the enemy from its defensive strongpoints along the way up. A third battlegroup, in the form of a small artillery unit, would provide supporting fire and follow up close behind Meyer's unit.

Meyer was anxious to get his battalion to the Kastoria area on the other side of the Klissura Pass in time to cut off and capture the enemy pulling back from Albania.

The road wound upwards in a series of tight curves. To the left the terrain dipped away sharply to form sheer, inaccessible ravines. To the right, vertical rock faces towered up. The mountain village of Werjes was situated near the top, and Greek gun emplacements were set up on the ridges above the village.

In the evening, Meyer gathered his officers to talk tactics for the assault that would commence at dawn the following day.

"Gentlemen, we'll form two battlegroups with our limited artillery providing supportive fire. I'll take 2nd and 3rd Companies and we'll advance along the main road. Neumann's artillery will follow us close behind and concentrate on the gun emplacements up on the ridges. The second battlegroup, Hugo's 1st and Paul's 4th, will spur off the road, scale the rock face, engage and flush out the gun emplacements and strongpoints situated above the village. They will move up the heights tonight, under cover of darkness, hopefully getting the chance to be within striking distance of the enemy's flank at first light. The enemy have the advantage of the high ground, and they will be able to see every move we make from their observation posts. The terrain rules out any possibility of our bypassing them or outflanking them; there is just one way in and one way out, flushing out the enemy from one strongpoint to the next. I remind you, gentlemen, that you will need to be tenacious, but I emphasise that, in order to minimise our casualties, your advances should be as close to non-stop as possible. Success for this mission will rely on your robust leadership and the fitness and bravery of your men. Our assault will begin at 0600 hours tomorrow morning. Hugo, your battlegroup will need to negotiate 800 metres overnight to get a flying start in the morning. Good luck, gentlemen."

The company commanders returned to their units to brief their men on the forthcoming assault.

"This'll be a good tester for the boys," said the Baron as they left Battalion HQ.

"Never tried anything as steep as this – dicey terrain," remarked Max.

"Limited plan of attack, eh! Literally a step at a time all the way to the top!" responded the Baron.

"Mustering for the final storm at the top will be the most hazardous manoeuvre if the Greeks decide to hold their ground."

"Terrain's rough, but there are plenty of rock spurs for cover, Max. Let's brief the men and wait for dark to start our ascent."

Dawn broke. Meyer set off with Neumann following close behind with his limited artillery, an 88-mm Flak and light armour. The small battery opened up, signalling the start of the attack.

The enemy position was well defended and manpower held in reserve in the village was ready to support those along the ridges if the situation called for it. The enemy objective was to delay the Germans as long as possible in order to buy time for the retreating Greek, British and Anzac troops.

Meyer's approach along the road was hazardous. His battlegroup was under continuous fire from the Greek forces entrenched high above. They threw everything they could at him – artillery, machine-gun, rifle and mortar fire. While the battle raged below, Krass's battlegroup moved closer to enemy emplacements hundreds of metres above.

First contact came when they ran into the flank of the Greek defences. In compliance with Meyer's instructions, non-stop advances were implemented to create a continuous and harassing presence.

By late morning Krass's battlegroup had advanced far enough for the enemy troops garrisoned in the village to withdraw and join up with those defending the eastern side of the village.

It was clear that the Greeks were not going to concede their ground quickly. They dug in along the ridges further back, in support of those forces focused on Meyer and his battlegroup running the gauntlet below.

Krass and the Baron's battlegroup was edging towards the fortified gun emplacements, but they were in danger of being hit by their own supporting fire, provided by Neumann's battery down below. Their predicament was as precarious as Meyer's down on the road. Progress for both battlegroups was slow and hazardous.

The men were continually encouraged to maintain their non-stop advances. Fighting proved dogged, and ferocious exchanges ensued. The officers knew that to be pinned down for any length of time would encourage hesitation and caution, and that would put them in more danger than the rapid advances exposed them to. The men forged on with the tenacity, bravery and focus that were required. But the challenge of non-stop progress up the steep inclines was proving physically exhausting.

At one point, down where Meyer's battlegroup was struggling, several of his men stalled in front of a huge crater that had blown the road apart. Tired and out of breath, they had become reluctant to make the next advance beyond the crater to the other side of the road. As a result, Meyer rolled an egg grenade at the last soldier in their line. He shouted for them to make their advance or be blown up. They gasped and all broke away in different directions, all managing to negotiate the hazard the open crater presented.

As brash and as arrogant as he was, Meyer cared for his men. He knew remaining in one place for too long would be more hazardous than continuing the cavalier-type advances he demanded. His action, seemingly reckless, was calculated to minimise the casualty list. He didn't want his men to become sitting ducks.

Meantime, on the heights above, Krass's units kept going, hopping from one rock spur to the next, despite the bullets and shells raining down on them from the enemy emplacements.

Just after midday, they were faced with two enemy strongpoints deployed on twin ridges. The situation compelled Krass to split his battlegroup into its original companies to tackle both heights simultaneously.

The Baron's 4th Company was given the task of storming one of the strongpoints.

Paul addressed his platoon sergeants: "OK, men, our objective is to take that high point up ahead." He pointed to an area where they could clearly make out a concentration of activity. "Trouble is, as you can see, we have to go back down before we can get back up at them. This will test our mettle even more, lads. Our proximity to the enemy will mean that Neumann's artillery and the howitzer battery below will have to cease fire. Muller will remain here with his platoon and concentrate fire across the way, keeping the enemy pinned down as much as possible. Fritz will take his platoon down and back up, approaching from the left, over there. Max and I will approach from the right. Once we're down, we'll need to spur off to the right for a bit before turning back up and actually flanking the enemy, there!"

He pointed to an area to the right of the enemy's strongpoint.

"Take heed of the training techniques taught us for this type of fight, lads. With each movement forward, focus your attention on the next cover point up ahead. At the same time pinpoint where enemy fire is coming from. Don't get comfortable in one position too long. Keep mobile." He repeated what Meyer had said in the earlier briefing: "I cannot emphasise enough the importance of keeping up the momentum. This will reduce our casualties."

Training techniques had taught them to think one or two steps ahead, just as in a game of snooker or tennis a good player thinks one or two shots ahead of the game. Thinking ahead can involve taking split-second decisions, but not at the risk of taking one's eye off what is happening up ahead. Success depends on rapid mobility, securing the next cover point, and catching one's breath ready for advancing to the next safe place. Intuition comes into play during the most dangerous situations under fire. An assault such as this, on two flanks, is all about 'parry, riposte, parry, riposte' – perfectly balanced manoeuvres that require courage in the face of fire. It is raw courage and positive thinking that takes the attackers through to their objective.

The Baron continued: "Muller will work at pinning the enemy down so that they don't get a chance to take some free shots at our boys making the assault. However, he won't be able to cover all situations, and those making the assault will have to provide their own support and cover fire. As soon as we are within storming distance of the enemy positions, we'll deploy smoke grenades and make our final charge. Synchronise watches, gentlemen, and position your men. It's 1220 hours now. Muller will open up in twenty minutes and then we move out."

They all responded with a powerful cheer.

Fritz mustered his platoon in readiness for the see-saw assault, descending into the dip and climbing back up towards their objective, to flush out the enemy at the top. The Baron's approach was about fifty metres off to the right.

"This is going to be one hell of a roller-coaster ride," said Max.

"Sure is! Listen up, Max: I'll create the pace; you can use my cover points. Alternatively, choose one yourself if you think it gives you better cover. This will give our boys following up a choice. Just keep close behind me. We'll start our descent over there," he said, pointing along the ridge to a jagged rock nearby. "Once we've descended into the dip we'll regroup at that cover point, down there." He pointed to a group of rock spurs down below. "We'll spur off to the right and begin our way back towards the flank of the enemy, there." He pointed to another cluster of rocks about twenty metres to the right of the lower-level regrouping point. "This will be the riskiest manoeuvre, and it will expose us to enemy fire. Here we'll be banking on Muller and his boys to keep the enemy pinned down. If we make our ascent over there, we'll get a chance to outflank them." All the while he was pointing out the various vantage points.

At 1240 Muller opened up with a barrage of automatic and mortar fire.

"In the event they nail me, finish the job for me, will you, Max?"

"Little chance they'll get to do that," replied Max as the Baron leapt from his position, heading towards a pre-chosen rock cover below.

The Baron's first cover point was large enough to conceal several men, so Max followed directly behind him.

"The sooner we're on our way back up the better," he said as he raced out to another point further below.

Muller performed a superb job of keeping the enemy pinned down. He tenaciously ran the length of his platoon, one way and then the other, picking out an enemy position now and again that appeared to be getting a shot at Fritz or Max's men. Both platoons made their descents into the dip without casualty.

Having weathered the first part of the assault, climbing back up proved more conventional but equally hazardous. They kept rigidly to their training techniques, and they would be repaid with just a few casualties.

By the time 4th Company had accomplished its objective and cleared the enemy from the ridges, Krass had cleared resistance from the other ridge. They linked up and focused attention on the next enemy strongpoint further up ahead.

As the attack groups neared their final objectives on the heights, Neumann's artillery below refocused on the reserve troops concentrated at the rear of the enemy defence.

At this point, the situation became critical for both sides. Neither side was in the mood to quit; the battle became a clash of mindsets. The Greeks were inspired by the fact that they were fighting to defend their homeland. Leibstandarte, on the other hand, had a reputation to create, and the battle provided a golden opportunity to write its first page. The combination of physical fitness, intensive training, aggressive leadership and enthusiasm gave the men the edge they needed to swing the advantage.

As the assault up the heights was nearing its climax, the Greeks sensed that it was only a matter of time before they would be overcome. Sure enough, after several minutes of hand-to-hand combat they collapsed. The leading group of exhausted Greeks threw down their weapons and raised their hands in surrender.

The surrender at the front edge relayed its way back down the line and, to the surprise of the lead German attackers, more than 600 Greek reserves also surrendered. They all appeared happy to give themselves up.

The village of Werjes proved to be the last stumbling block in the process of securing of the Klissura Pass. For these actions Kurt Meyer was awarded the Knight's Cross.

Success in the Balkan Campaign finally won Leibstandarte accolades from the army. In his speech, General Kurt Daluege said Leibstandarte's critics "must change their opinions once and for all". General Georg Stumme commended the SS troops for their "unshakeable offensive spirit" and he said, "This present victory signifies for Leibstandarte a new and imperishable page of honour in its history."

To rid all threats of Allied presence in the Eastern Mediterranean region of Europe, in May Germany launched an airborne invasion of Crete; and on 31 May, the British garrison there surrendered. This final action enabled Germany to turn its attention east without the risk of fighting a war on two fronts. What it didn't realise at the time was the impact this 'side issue' would have in the east by postponing the invasion of Russia until 22 June that year.

BIBLIOGRAPHY

The Third Reich: The SS, pp. 162–6. (Time Life Books, 1989.)

Charles Messenger: *Hitler's Gladiator: The Life and Times of Panzer Army Commander Sepp Dietrich*, pp. 89–95. (Conway, 2005.)

Kurt Meyer: *Grenadiers: The Story of Waffen SS General Kurt "Panzer" Meyer*, pp. 34, 47–52. (Stackpole Books, 2005.)

25

ALEXANDER

Shortly after a parade in Athens, Leibstandarte was granted a few days to rest up and sight-see around the capital. For a brief time they would indulge in the delights of Greek cooking, wine and women. Acknowledging he hadn't sufficient time to pick up a meaningful relationship with a Greek woman of substance, the Baron contented himself with learning a little more about the local culture, spending his time sampling a variety of Greek drinks and food and having a stab at the language.

For Max, Greece presented a fresh opportunity to reflect on the classical discourses he'd had with his old mentor, Michael Vogel. Greece was a magnificent country with a mythology, ancient history and architecture second to none. The influence of its culture had spread across the globe.

The rugged landscape created stunning scenery and formed a bizarre contrast to the recent fighting. But it shouldn't have, for many a warrior had trodden the land before this: Macedonians, Spartans, Persians and Ottoman Turks had all gazed out upon the same beautiful scenery. Greece's wonderful Mediterranean climate rounded off this brief, unforgettable excursion.

One evening Paul invited Max to his tent for a drink and chat. Spring evenings in Greece formed a perfect setting for drinking and engaging in deep and meaningful conversations.

"Looks like we finally managed to pull off a campaign without mishap," said Max, opening up the conversation.

"The army boys are starting to appreciate our value now, eh?

The Reichsführer intends to use his Waffen-SS units as the sharp end of the wedge in all future campaigns."

"Talking of wedges, and while we're in his country, didn't Alexander the Great adopt the wedge approach in some of his greatest battles?"

"He did. He was adept at exposing the weaknesses in an enemy line-up. Despite being heavily outnumbered in most instances, he never lost a battle. Ensuring his flanks were robust enough to prevent the enemy from breaking through and enveloping his phalanx in the centre, he'd lead the charge and drive his wedge formation of cavalry followed by infantry into the enemy's weakest point and break them up. His bold and risky undertakings always paid off."

"Do you think he was the greatest military leader of all time? I see him as an ideal mix of soldier and philosopher – a positive thinker and a man that led by example back in those ancient, hoary days."

"Surely he was one of them. But all good leaders need to be surrounded by good supporting generals who share the same battle awareness, albeit it's healthy to have a strategy challenged in case something has been overlooked. However, great battle strategies are rarely subject to democratic vote. The great generals always appear to come up with something that is triggered from within – such generals as Alexander and Napoleon, for example. A weaker general, incapable of thinking for himself, might be swayed by fear or overcaution expressed by senior staff. Additionally, the men need to be disciplined fighters – stubborn, capable of defending under extreme pressure and willing to attack despite being severely outnumbered."

Max agreed: "Coupled with surprise, the bold approach by a few can often fool a numerically superior enemy into thinking its strength is actually greater than it is."

They continued their discourse deep into the night, sipping Greek wine and going over the stories of Alexander's adventures. They agreed that Alexander was an innovator in the use of aggressive fighting strategies. He also utilised the envelopment technique: encircling the enemy by breaking through its flanks. This and the wedge technique for frontal assaults both achieve the same result: defeat for the enemy.

In early June, Leibstandarte moved by road back up through Greece and Yugoslavia to Brno in Czechoslovakia. Hitler's way of rewarding Leibstandarte's outstanding performance in the Balkan Campaign was to order them to be upgraded to division strength for the forthcoming effort in the Soviet Union. The ensuing period up to the invasion date of 22 June was one of furious activity.

Division strength for Leibstandarte amounted to almost 11,000 troops. Extra manning was restricted somewhat as Leibstandarte was allowed to retain its stringent entry standards. Unlike the other branches of the German Wehrmacht, which built their numbers by way of conscription, recruits for Waffen were composed entirely of volunteers. At this point the racial-purity factor was still being implemented to maintain Leibstandarte's elite status.

During the short turbulent period of refit, some NCOs and officers were enrolled in Russian language classes. The official reason given was that, in the event that Russia staged an attack on Germany, a basic knowledge of the language would be indispensable – for example, in the interrogation of prisoners.

Paul and his NCOs were shortlisted for the course. They took to the task keenly at first, as it didn't seem too difficult.

Starting with the alphabet, they soon learnt the sounds of and how to write all of its thirty-three letters. Most of the sounds were familiar, but a handful weren't. Then they were introduced to simple phrases and a list of basic verbs they were to learn parrot-fashion. Knowledge of about 200 of the most commonly used verbs was sufficient for basic communication.

The next stage of the course included complicated phrases and adjectives. By this time, the intensity was severe, and all 'volunteers' were beginning to wilt under pressure. It seemed that all Russian adjectives have masculine, feminine and neuter forms. Worse, they change when the noun referred to is plural.

The course turned into a living nightmare. Each session would end up with the men leaving the classroom totally flummoxed and mentally exhausted. Despite this, they persevered, primarily because they were ordered to. In the end, they gained a basic understanding of the Russian language. Their tenacity met with the approval of their merciless Ukrainian language tutors.

Casualties were having a serious effect on German manpower even before the attack on Russia. Manpower available for the invasion was limited because large numbers of men were needed elsewhere to protect and defend Germany's newly won territories in Europe. Were Intelligence and the generals correct in their assessments of the giant task in hand? History would verify whether Germany's decision to invade Russia was the right one.

In June 1941 the Führer's 'Sword of Destiny' was about to be wielded at a giant.

BIBLIOGRAPHY

The Third Reich: The SS. (Time Life Books, 1989.)

Charles Messenger: *Hitler's Gladiator: The Life and Times of Panzer Army Commander Sepp Dietrich,* p. 96. (Conway, 2005.)

PART THREE

ACT OF LOVE

'You have to be the master of your mind. And what part of you is the master of your mind? It has to be the heart.'

Harold Klemp, from his book *Love: The Keystone of Life*.

26

BARBAROSSA

Somebody who did not participate in the Russian Campaign cannot know nor have any concept of what it meant. It was not just the physical conditions, but the sheer intensity of the fighting between the representatives of two ideologies diametrically opposed to one another.

Max Wunsche, Sepp Dietrich's adjutant.

Despite the Nazi–Soviet Non-Aggression Pact signed in August 1939, Hitler had always intended to invade the Soviet Union. Plans were drawn up in June 1940 scheduling an invasion for around 15 May 1941.

The invasion strategy would differ from that employed on the Western Front. Blitzkrieg tactics could not be implemented to their full extent on the Eastern Front because of the sheer size of the territory, the primitive conditions of the Russian road systems and non-standard-gauge railway tracks. Instead, the main focus would be on encircling and capturing defending Soviet troops early on in the invasion to destroy morale. The strategy included seizing Moscow before the Russian winter set in.

At dawn on 22 June 1941, 4 million troops commenced Germany's invasion of the Soviet Union in a three-pronged assault on a 3,100 kilometre front stretching from the Baltic Sea down to the Black Sea.

The three prongs were Army Group North, Army Group Centre and Army Group South. The objective of Army Group North, under Marshal von Leeb, was to strike through the Baltic States to Leningrad, linking up with Finnish forces allied with Germany. Army Group Centre was deployed north of the Pripet Marshes under Marshal von Bock. They would strike through Central Poland and Belorussia all the way to Moscow. Army Group South was deployed south of the Pripet Marshes, under Marshal von Rundstedt. Their objective was to strike into the Ukraine, taking Odessa and Kiev, sweeping down to the Crimea and onward through the heavily industrialised Donets Basin, moving south to the Caucasus to take the rich oil fields of Groznyy and Baku.

Leibstandarte joined von Rundstedt's Army Group South and was assigned to Panzergruppe 1 under the command of von Kleist as one of three motorised units. Its initial task was to protect the flank of the advancing armour and repulse all infantry counterattacks attempting to cut through the German salient.

The drive on Kiev was full of bitter and desperate fighting. Leibstandarte faced numerous air attacks and repulsed frequent infantry attacks. By mid-July, the Germans were at the gates of Kiev.

By early August, Leibstandarte had been fighting without adequate sleep for weeks and were exhausted. To exacerbate the situation, the Russians were the best fighters they had met in international conflict.

There was no time for rest, and their next assignment after the battles around Kiev was to advance south-east towards the city of Kherson.

Kherson was a major port situated at the estuary of the River Dnieper, on the Black Sea. They entered cautiously as intelligence had reported that the Russians had prepared heavy defences there. Their job was simply to flush out the Soviet marine defenders.

Soviet resistance proved stubborn. The Germans slowly and painfully squeezed out the enemy from strongpoints and pockets of resistance street by street. Hand-to-hand fighting caused heavy casualties and signalled a first for many of the new Waffen-SS recruits and replacements that made up the division.

Paul's 4th Company was in the thick of the street fighting in Kherson. For the Russian Campaign, the Baron had been promoted to the rank of captain. This had coincided with Leibstandarte's upgrade to full divisional strength.

Near to the end of the operation, 4th Company was assigned to take a steel factory situated in the heavy industrial and shipbuilding area of Kherson. The Germans wanted it taken intact, but at the time it wasn't known whether the steel facility was heavily defended or abandoned.

"If it is defended, what is the nature and strength of the defence?" Paul wondered.

He was operating blind, and he opted for a cautious approach in lieu of his usual aggressive style.

He called his NCOs to a briefing. They assembled at the company's makeshift headquarters – a room set aside in a former government building. Most of the building had been destroyed by artillery and tank fire earlier.

He unfolded an operations plan of the city, spreading it flat across a small wooden table.

Neatly pressing out the folds, he addressed his men: "Our objective is a steel factory – this area here – quite a big facility made up of two huge workshops separated by a wall. The steel factory is orientated on a north-south axis. An external yard is located at the northern end and its length stretches the combined width of the two workshops. We are situated closest to the west workshop with the east workshop on the far side. The southern walls of both workshops finish hard up against the banks of the estuary. The north end of the far workshop is completely open, with a gantry crane overlooking the yard. Ivan still holds the area beyond the factory to the north-east. Enemy snipers could pick us off should we attempt an assault from the yard. I much prefer the option of accessing the building through a door in the west wall of the west workshop. It is the side of the factory

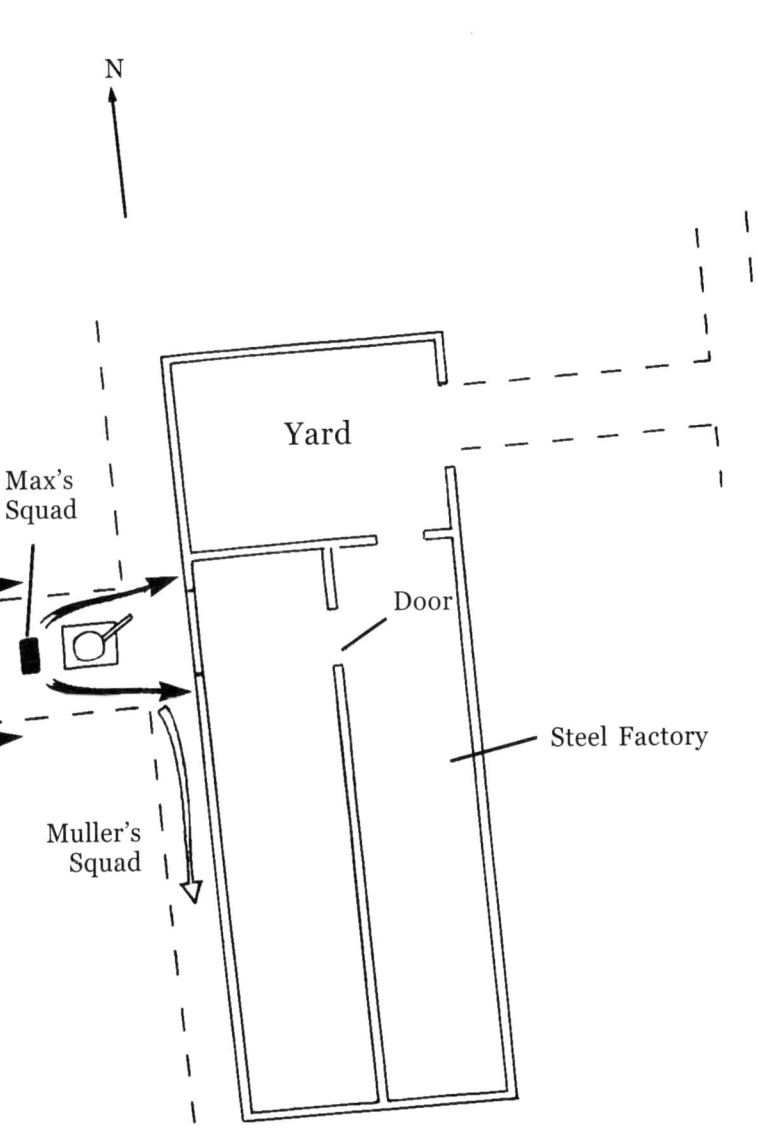

The Fight at the Steel Factory.

nearest to us, and it is out of sight of the yard. We should be safe from enemy snipers, though we may need to flush out any Soviets dug in on either side of the road leading up to the steel doors of the factory. Gentlemen, a Pz.Kpfw IV medium tank will support our assault. It will use the approach road leading straight up to the west-wall entrance. Max and his squad will follow up close behind, facilitate an entry and hold a position inside to test the strength of the enemy – if any. We'll be close behind and will provide added support on Max's instructions. Buildings on the right of the approach road finish two metres or so short of the factory's perimeter wall. We may be able to filter a squad down the gap in between and open up a second battle face at the rear of the factory if need be, but we'll think about the prospects of this later, in the field. Before we commence our assault, the Luftwaffe will carry out an air strike on the warehouses and other buildings on either side of the road leading up to the steel factory. The purpose is twofold: first, to assist in flushing out any enemy gun emplacements positioned there; and second, so that we can use the demolished buildings for our own cover during our approach, in the event the factory is heavily defended. Gentlemen, brief your platoons. We'll move up straight after the air strike scheduled for 0730 hours tomorrow morning. Good luck!"

The following morning, as the dust settled from the air strike, 4th Company commenced its advance from the west. They used both sides of the road and approached cautiously. The panzer screeched down the road, spearheading the advance, with Max and his squad following up close behind. Max and his men would be the first to enter the factory. His task was filled with danger.

The panzer stopped twenty metres short of the huge steel sliding entrance doors. It adjusted its turret and fired a shell into the block wall on one side of the metal doors. Boom! The turret swivelled and fired a second round into the wall on the other side. Boom! Max had expected some sort of reaction after that, but all was silent.

The area was strewn with debris and, as the dust settled, Max scrutinised the newly formed voids for signs of movement and listened for noises from within. The only sound was the creaking of one of the huge sliding doors, which had broken loose of its housing and hung there precariously.

The panzer moved forward, intending to smash through the damaged door, but just short of making contact an explosion from a roadside mine ripped into its underside, blowing the track off, rendering the panzer immobile. The explosion at the front end of the tank startled Max and his squad; they crouched instinctively, preparing for an enemy response, but their fears were unfounded. Nothing else happened. All remained still.

The squad regained composure and prepared to enter through the openings blown into the walls.

Max gave his instructions: "Reuss, take Hesse and Gotz over to the right side, and I'll take Wiebens and Schmidt over to the left. Before we make our entry, we'll lob in grenades and fire a short burst to prompt a reaction. If there is still no response, we'll deploy smoke grenades, enter and set up behind the nearest cover. On entry, you filter to the near side; I'll take Wiebens and Schmidt across to the far side."

"*Jawohl, Sturmscharführer*," replied Reuss.

"Ready – let's go!" shouted Max.

The squad swiftly broke away from their cover and filed hard up against the wall at their designated access points.

Max gestured for Reuss to toss his egg grenade inside, then he followed suit. After the explosions they followed up with short bursts from their light automatics and ducked back quickly, expecting a response from within. Still nothing – just an eerie silence as the dust settled! It appeared that the factory might be abandoned after all. They tossed in their smoke grenades.

"We're going in, lads!" shouted Max.

They scrambled over the rubble and rushed inside to take up

positions behind the first available cover. Reuss's men found some heavy steel containers and a stack of large-bore steel piping several metres beyond the entrance. Max and his men raced across to the far side to settle behind a stack of steel plating.

Max scanned the interior. The workshop was a vast area filled with pipes, steel plates, lifting appliances, gantry cranes and all sorts of other materials and equipment. Behind him an entrance to the adjoining workshop was built into the wall separating the two massive workshops.

"Wiebens, cover the access way to the adjoining shop back here. We don't want to be hit from behind!"

"*Jawohl, Sturmscharführer.*"

Wiebens fell back to settle behind a huge steel column.

Max shouted across to Gotz: "Gotz, go support Wiebens!"

Gotz shuffled out of his cover and then raced across to join Wiebens on the other side of the opening. He tucked himself behind another steel column.

As the smoke cleared, the men were alert for noises or signs of movement up ahead. After several moments, Reuss tossed a smoke grenade towards the entrance they had just come through; it was a signal for the Baron to provide additional support. Two squads from either side of the road moved across to the entrance and began clambering over the rubble through the breaches.

Suddenly it began – all hell let loose. The air was filled with the sounds of gunfire from the far end of the factory. Several men fell at the entrance. A few managed to join up with Max's squad inside, but the others pulled back. Max and his small unit immediately returned the gunfire. Enemy strength was difficult to assess.

"They're all concentrated further down the factory!" shouted Max. "Didn't see the bastards!"

The Russian mariners remained well hidden behind an assortment of machinery and steel structures. Bullets were ricocheting off the steel everywhere.

"Keep your heads down!" bellowed Max.

Having survived the initial barrage, Max lay back to catch his breath and search his mind for leads that would indicate the strength of the enemy force.

The strategy outside called for the Baron to send Muller and a squad towards the rear of the factory, and attempt to open up another battle face there. Muller's unit was armed with a portable *Panzerfaust*, an anti-tank weapon. His objective was to keep the enemy occupied there and then force an entry, if possible. But it wouldn't be easy. Before Muller's boys could make their mark, the Russian mariners opened up from their own vantage points, pinning his unit down. The dogfight reopened when a couple of rounds fired from his *Panzerfaust* team breached the wall near the single-door rear entrance.

Hearing the battle raging at the rear, Max decided it was time to apply some pressure from his position and launch an assault. His strategy was to deploy smoke grenades, advance to the next cover point and close in on the mariners concentrated at the rear.

"Gerd, smoke grenade!" he shouted.

They lobbed the grenades up ahead and, as the smoke began to fill the workshop, Max gave the order to advance to the next cover point. Just then, the workshop became filled with gunfire again and wild cries signalling an impending onslaught from the other end of the factory. The Soviet mariners were using the smoke to mount their own attack. But their yelling served as a warning for Max and his squad.

Max and his men stopped in their tracks.

"Christ, they're coming at us! Grenades, *Kameraden*!" Max bellowed.

They lobbed hand grenades into the smoke and returned to their original cover positions preparing to meet an enemy of unknown strength.

As the grenades exploded Max's unit followed up with bursts of automatic gunfire. The strategy had taken its toll of the attackers, but it hadn't stopped a number of mariners reaching the thin German line. They were like a crazed mob, coming from everywhere, it seemed at the time.

The attack, evidently, was a last-ditch effort by the factory's defenders. They'd little ammunition and had used it up in preparation for their final assault. They stormed the Germans with bayonets, knives and shovels – anything that could maim or kill their opposition. Max and his men managed to pick off a number of the attackers as they appeared through the smoke, but a few had got through and a desperate hand-to-hand contest ensued.

The situation looked grim as the small German squad engaged with the Russian mariners in deadly tussles. Just as it appeared Max and his men were in serious danger of annihilation, Fritz and his squad came to the rescue. The Baron had ordered Fritz and his platoon to storm the entrance in the hope that the added muscle would be adequate to finish the job.

Within seconds the situation was reversed, but Max's unit (the original squad and three that had joined them earlier) was down to just three standing. Muller's fight at the rear of the workshop continued for only a few moments more before all enemy resistance was laid to rest.

Max had survived by the skin of his teeth. Fritz's timely entrance had saved the squad from certain annihilation and repaid the favour for Max's rescue almost two years earlier, during the Polish Campaign.

Nursing a wound to his arm where he had deflected a knife thrust, he surveyed the aftermath of the skirmish. Three of his six stricken comrades had received serious wounds but would live. The other three, including his loyal sergeant, Reuss, lay dead. Max looked down on his dead body grief-stricken.

Muller's unit emerged from the smoke to meet them. The factory had been seized intact except for minor damage to some of the machinery and a piece or two of equipment.

The hand-to-hand clash had lasted only minutes, but for Max

it had felt like a lifetime. He thanked the gods as he left the workshop. Outside, the Baron congratulated him for his efforts and told him to get along to first aid to get his wound stitched up.

As he left the area, Max turned around to take one last look. He was saddened, and he stood in silence contemplating the men from his platoon who had died that day.

Reuss had attended the same NCO cadet class back in '38. The old guard who had fought with him since Poland had been reduced by another three. He saluted his dead comrades and, looking up at the Soviet hammer-and-sickle emblem welded above the factory's huge entrance, saluted that too to honour a brave enemy that fought to the last man with just shovels and knives. Gloomy-faced, he turned away to report to the medics.

The loss of a fellow comrade always disturbed Max. Barely two months into the Russian Campaign, the old guard was crumbling around him far too quickly.

'Will any of us come out of this hellhole?' he wondered.

By mid-1941 Leibstandarte was already witnessing a rapid depletion of the men that had formed the original regiment two years earlier. To make it up to divisional strength, manpower had been substantially increased, but the new recruits had not been trained and indoctrinated like those who had made up the old guard. Further, casualties were always heavier wherever Leibstandarte conducted its business. Since the Balkan Campaign, they had always been deployed at the cutting edge of the fighting and were paying the price accordingly.

Hitler's comment regarding the role of Waffen-SS troops ("Troops like the SS have to pay the butcher's bill more heavily than anyone else . . .") was coming home to roost.

Leibstandarte was finally relieved following the fall of Kherson on 19 August. Now, for the first time in the campaign, it was given the opportunity to rest up.

Enemy capabilities had been severely underestimated at the onset of Operation Barbarossa, and German losses were never expected to be this extensive in the initial loss-ratio assessments. It was at this point that Paul, his NCOs and many others of the old guard were brought back down to earth.

Despite the huge territorial gains, resistance appeared to be stiffening. The enemy seemed to be everywhere, and, on top of this, Leibstandarte and Army Group South would soon be facing a vicious full-blown Russian winter.

As Max made his way across to the medical centre he wasn't to know that he had just reached another major milestone in his life. An incident was soon to occur that would reawaken his subconscious demons yet again. For the perpetrators in the forthcoming incident it would just be another day-to-day affair, but for Max it would mean everything. His worst nightmare was about to manifest, compelling him to make choices that he would most certainly regret.

BIBLIOGRAPHY

Charles Messenger: *Hitler's Gladiator: The Life and Times of Panzer Army Commander Sepp Dietrich*, pp. 96–101. (Conway, 2005.)

Kurt Meyer: *Grenadiers: The Story of Waffen SS General Kurt "Panzer" Meyer,* pp. 71–96. (Stackpole Books, 2005.)

27

THE DAMNED

The unconscionable mind of a brute is not unlike the mind of a man filled with guilt. Brutes hate and destroy others; a man filled with guilt hates and destroys himself. Those who indulge in this behaviour are bound by their actions.

The brute chooses to ignore accountability for his actions and compassion towards others; the guilt-ridden man chooses to ignore his obligation of compassion towards himself.

Max's emotional salutations to his dead comrades and the Soviet symbol welded above the workshop entrance would prove to be a grave error of judgement on his part. The cloak of protection that providence had always offered him was about to be rudely torn away. The reality of war was soon to become terrifyingly transparent, revealing all its grisly agendas and stark horrors.

Unknown to Max, his behaviour outside the workshop had been witnessed by a certain senior SS officer of Einsatzgruppe, Sturmbannführer Philip Wolfe. Wolfe headed up the regional Einsatzgruppe D, whose headquarters were about to be set up in the Kherson area. He had promptly ordered his adjutant, Felix Bauer, to discover the identity of the sentimental Sturmscharführer saluting his dead comrades and the Soviet emblem.

Wolfe's adjutant made enquiries to ascertain the identity of the emotive NCO. Later that day, he made his way to the tent where Max was bivouacked. Max was boiling some water to make a cup of coffee when Bauer pulled back the entrance flap.

"Sturmscharführer Rieker?"

Max immediately picked up on the tone and looked up at him quizzically.

"Yes, what can I do for you, Obersturmführer?"

"Wound from yesterday's fight at the steel workshop, Sturmscharführer?" asked Bauer, focusing his eyes on Max's heavily bandaged arm.

"Yes, how did you know I was there, Obersturmführer?" Max glared at him.

"We saw you outside the factory saluting your dead comrades and you also appeared to be saluting the Soviet emblem above the entrance there."

"We?" asked Max.

"Yes, myself and my commanding officer, Sturmbannführer Wolfe. Wolfe heads up Einsatzgruppe D in this region. He'd like to have a chat with you."

"What for?" snapped Max.

"I wouldn't know, Sturmscharführer. Tomorrow morning 0630 hours sharp, then?"

"Einsatzgruppe, eh? That's fine by me," replied Max.

They saluted each other and Bauer left the tent.

As Bauer left, Max muttered, "Einsatzgruppe – murdering bastards!"

Next morning, he made his way along to their headquarters, wondering what Wolfe wanted to talk about. He felt a little uneasy as dark thoughts began to cloud his mind, bringing back memories of his brush with this sinister group back in 1939 during the Polish Campaign.

He was aware that the rules of engagement adopted by this group in the Soviet Union was a notch worse than what took place in Poland: a brutal policy of genocide had been carried out on the civilian population. Why they had done this was beyond his comprehension. The Einsatzkommandos had been ruthless, and all they'd achieved was to incite hatred and vengeance among the Red Army and the Russian populace.

It would be the Russian Campaign that would introduce to Max a new kind of enemy – an intangible one. But as intangible as it was, it would prove to be one of the major determining factors that tipped the balance of the conflict on the Eastern Front. What kind of intangible force could play such a major part in driving the marauding German forces back to where they came? It was hate – simply hate.

Here, on the Eastern Front, the darker side of war was unleashed in its full ferocity when party policy called for the enforcement of its genocide ruling. The strain of cruelty was to grow like a malignant cancer in this campaign – particularly in the Ukraine, where the common folk were dealt with even more savagely than elsewhere.

Thoughts raced through Max's mind as the Einsatzgruppe D headquarters came into sight.

"Arrogant bastards – I wonder what they want," he thought.

As he walked into the reception area, Bauer was waiting there to meet him.

"Ah, there you are, Sturmscharführer. Please be seated. I'll see if the Sturmbannführer is ready for you."

Max sat and waited for only a few moments.

"Yes, he'll see you now. Step inside, will you?"

Bauer held the door ajar for him to enter. He entered the office and snapped out a crisp Nazi-style salute.

"Heil Hitler!"

Wolfe received Max in a mild manner. They fixed eyes on each other momentarily as if weighing each other up. Max diverted his attention to the front swiftly so as not to appear ruffled or antagonistic, but Wolfe remained silent with his eyes fixed on him.

He finally spoke, coming straight to the point: "Why did you salute the Soviet emblem welded above the factory entrance yesterday?"

"We'd had a fight with Russian mariners defending the steel workshop. They put up a gallant show, considering they had very little ammunition left. When their ammo ran out they came at us armed with anything they could lay their hands on: shovels, lengths of tubing, knives, hammers and spanners. They didn't stand a chance. Still they kept coming – to the death. Several of the boys in my platoon died in the skirmish – old friends. I am upset because of the steady pace my boys are dying over here. I saluted my dead comrades and a brave enemy who had died to the last man."

"A brave enemy, eh? Such a demonstration of emotion and sympathy for Soviet scum is outrageous, Sturmscharführer. What if the younger recruits and replacements under your command had seen you babbling there? What would they think of you – eh? – their very own platoon and, indeed, company sergeant?"

"I do my job well, Sturmbannführer. I wasn't babbling – just showing some respect."

"I say that you are a snivelling idiot, Sturmscharführer. You're supposed to build the confidence of the men of your company by example; you're supposed to keep them inspired and eager to fight."

"I do keep my men inspired, Sturmbannführer. I made the salutes in the privacy of my own space; no one was there to pass judgement. It wasn't a dispiriting act – just a gesture of respect in honour of my comrades and a fierce enemy, that's all."

"Oh! Bauer and I saw your antics, along with a score of other soldiers milling around the area. You gabble on about honour – romantic drivel, man! Loyalty! Loyalty must be upheld if the SS is to maintain its reputation."

"I am loyal, Sturmbannführer," said Max.

Then, like an exploding volcano, Wolfe, falling into an unparalleled fit of anger, shouted, "No, you're not, Sturmscharführer; you're weak. You're not fit to lead an SS squad let alone a full company! You must never display this type of sympathetic behaviour in front of your men again, or I'll have you court-martialled!"

By the time he'd finished his face had turned purple.

Max was staggered by Wolfe's anger and pettiness. Despite his inner alarm, he maintained an outer calmness, ensuring that Wolfe would not detect any facial expression he could construe as one of fear or anger.

Max had learnt to cover his true feelings from an early age, during his term served at the Dachau concentration camp. He considered Wolfe's behaviour the norm for the majority of 'political-type' senior staff – particularly those from Einsatzgruppe. These men were elements of the Allgemeine-SS assigned purely to carry out the party's political agenda. Wolfe served as an archetype for men with this brutal and amoral state of mind.

"Your comments are understood, Sturmbannführer."

Max snapped out a smart party salute and awaited dismissal. He felt relieved that he had got away with just a ticking-off, but he still remained amazed at the ferocity of Wolfe's verbal dressing-down.

Unfortunately, his relief was short-lived.

Instead of dismissing him, Wolfe continued: "I would like you to meet Obersturmführer Bauer," he said, gesturing with his eyes to his adjutant, who was standing behind Max.

Max glanced over his right shoulder towards Wolfe's adjutant, Bauer, who was standing there. Bauer's presence instantly angered Max as he must have snuck in during the admonishment. He was clearly gloating and Max was clearly upset. Despite the blow to his ego he managed to hold his anger in check. He looked back to the front, awaiting Wolfe's comments.

"Obersturmführer Bauer has a special task for you, Rieker."

Max realised he had been set up. He felt another wave of anger followed by a pang of fear. What on earth could Wolfe want from him?

"Completing this task will be a way of rectifying your erroneous ways and confirming your loyalty to our Führer. After all, you are privileged to wear an insignia on your cuff with the Führer's name inscribed on it, aren't you?" said Wolfe.

Max understood his words. His heart sank. Seldom had fear ripped into him so savagely. His thoughts raced, but his face remained composed. Any expression of fear would provide Wolfe with an excuse to hand out an even more vindictive punishment. He now knew that Wolfe was a crazed individual, full of himself.

"Step this way, Sturmscharführer. We're going for a short drive into the country," said Bauer.

As he was about to leave the office, Max fixed his eyes back on Wolfe. Wolfe was gloating with delight and he had a wry smile. Max turned stony; his eyes drilled into Wolfe's. Wolfe was beginning to feel uncomfortable; but just as he was about to react, Max snapped out another smart salute and wheeled around to join Bauer.

On his way to the truck, Max's thoughts ran wild. He was on the edge of losing control. He wanted to throttle the life out of Bauer there and then, but, only just managing to pull himself together, he settled for focusing on his racing thoughts.

'What makes these people like they are?' he asked himself. 'What makes them behave like this?'

An absolute ruthless streak ran through their nature. They appeared void of any conscience, unforgiving, without the capacity for compassion, vain and completely selfish. They were simply lost in a little universe of their own – a universe they could control because they had the power and clout to do so.

Max debated in his mind whether they were aware of their own ignorance. He decided they were.

For some malevolent reason they chose to ignore their failings.

He saw their attitudes and behaviours as ignorance at its barbaric worst, for it involved taking the freedom and lives of others in a cold, callous, brutal manner.

Then he questioned: "Could it be that they are just unaware?"

He pondered the difference between ignorance and unawareness. He remembered what Vogel had once said to him:

"Ignorance is the first step to enlightenment. Unawareness is, as it states, being unaware, oblivious to the outcome of one's actions. But ignorance differs insofar as one consciously chooses to ignore, turns a blind eye so to speak, cocks a deaf ear. One makes a conscious choice to ignore, but then a self-protective mechanism takes over once that choice is made. The body turns off; it desensitises itself; it goes into denial. It removes itself from feeling, using a distorted rationale to support its decision. The further removed a man is from feeling, the more conscienceless and insensitive he becomes. In men of this ilk, certain self-indulgent behaviour traits are apparent. Anger comes first to mind; then there is an absence of a sense of humour, unless it is in the form of sick mockery. Life takes on a sombre, grave outlook. What are the offshoots of anger: malice, evil gossip, profanity, jealousy, impatience, intolerance, resentment, ill will and prejudice. Angry people don't listen to others, because they don't want to hear what others have to say; it might rock and upset their comfortable and cocooned personal universe – a universe they control. They often have a silver tongue. In their raging deliberations they use this gift negatively to obscure genuine reason. Their rationale is superficial and petty; they make mountains out of molehills and, when called for, molehills out of mountains. They belittle, mock and destroy any opinion that is a threat to their survival – their way of thinking.

Vanity comes next to mind; driven by ambition, a person of this ilk will ruthlessly tread on anybody who gets in his way. He makes his way up the promotion ladder by exercising pettiness for the benefit of his superiors. He appears to keep them well informed, but tells them only what they want to hear. Such a man is full of himself, arrogant, untrustworthy even amongst his peers, and always bears a grudge."

In Max's own case, campaigning had knocked the arrogance out of him. His side were still winning, but they had bitten off more than they could chew by going east with inadequate numbers of men and limited resources against a formidable, numerically superior foe.

He remembered what old Vogel had said about arrogance: "The arrogance of a prevailing aggressor can give him a false sense of security. Being on the receiving end of a serious defeat or two in the field soon dulls its lustre. Confidence slips away like a thief in the night and the gloss of arrogance, shallow and brittle as it is, quickly turns to caution and fear."

After anger and vanity the third indulgence was lust. Of lust, Vogel said, "The lust to punish comes from having power over others. Power to punish gives a sickly sense of self-satisfaction. Individuals riddled with the deadly combination of anger, vanity and lust play God, so to speak. They act like demigods, knowing they have the power to control the events and circumstances immediately around them."

"Why do they do this?" Max had asked.

The answer drifted back into his mind: "Because they can."

This was power. It was not a new state of consciousness, but one as old as the mountains and valleys of Central Europe – simply a state of prejudice and jealousy. It hadn't changed.

"Why don't people ever learn from the past?"

Again the answer drifted into his mind: "An individual only stands up and listens when he is or has been on the receiving end of life; but, even then, he must go a step further and replace bitterness with forgiveness. The two cannot exist side by side."

Max realised the likes of Wolfe were bitter and chose the way of ignorance. It's the bitterness that turns a man into a brute, void of the capacity to tolerate or to show compassion.

Max sensed that his forthcoming task would mark the beginning of the end for him – a thorny road that he might never be able to turn back from. Tragically, his fears were close to the truth.

The truck left Einsatzgruppe HQ and headed north for about a mile. It came to a halt near a remote cottage on the outskirts of a small village. Two guards were standing to attention outside the cottage, apparently awaiting Bauer's arrival. It didn't take

Max long to realise that a number of civilians were locked inside the cottage. Piles of brushwood were stacked along the front of the cottage. His undertaking wasn't difficult to guess. The whole ghastly scene seemed to have been set up just for him.

Bauer got out of the truck and walked to the rear. He leant over the tailgate and pulled out an oil-filled torch.

Handing it to Max, he said, "Here, Sturmscharführer, take this, will you? All you have to do is to pop along to the cottage over there and fire the stack of brushwood."

Max's heart slumped as he tried to come to terms with the horrible consequences of the order. This was the first time he had been ordered to murder civilians. He snatched the torch from Bauer's hand and glared at him. Their eyes fixed on to each other for an extended period of time.

Bauer smirked and gestured with his eyes. "Get on with it, man."

Max wheeled around and walked across to the cottage. He knew that he would need to carry out the order or be arrested for insubordination – even shot.

As he neared the cottage he lit the torch with his cigarette lighter. He could see several sets of eyes peering from the gaps in the broken-down shutters. With a heavy heart he stepped on to the ramshackle veranda and walked up to the front door. Gasps of fear could be heard from what appeared to be a group of women within the cottage. He stopped, turned around and looked back over to the truck. Bauer had instructed the troopers to aim their rifles at Max and shoot him if he did not carry out the order.

"Get on with it, Sturmscharführer!" he shouted.

Anger and pain ran through Max's body. His saddened eyes sent compassionate messages to those poor souls inside the cottage who were about to meet a horrible fate. He fired the brushwood with the burning torch and walked away from the cottage, off to the side. He could hear the cries of the women. He estimated there must have been five or six of them locked inside. He crouched as the heat grew in intensity and the flames took control. He stared into the flames and wanted to be engulfed in the inferno himself, but he couldn't find the courage. The salamanders of evil chuckled in delight as the huge flames licked around the frail timber structure. Max finally backed away from the intense heat.

He made his way back to the truck and saluted Bauer, but he didn't look him in the eye. Bauer gloated and returned the salute, then gestured Max to get back into the vehicle.

"There, that wasn't so bad, Sturmscharführer, was it?" said Bauer.

Max bit his lip. He wanted to strangle him. His mind swayed in the balance as he struggled to resist the urge to kill.

The stark horror of the scene that had just taken place sent a series of shock waves through his body. Any credibility in the master-race theory was wiped away for ever with this one act of hate orchestrated by Wolfe simply because he had the power to do it.

Max's own hate for Einsatzgruppe was branded into his mind by the heat of the cottage. He would never completely recover from this experience; the incident marked the beginning of the end of his love for his Führer.

Max and Bauer reported back to Wolfe, who greeted them formally but appeared satisfied and mellow. The volcano in him had abated with knowledge of Max's act of loyalty. He was pleased Max had carried out his orders without resistance of any kind.

As Max saluted and wheeled around to leave the office, Wolfe commented: "Welcome back to the—"

"The damned!" interjected Max, glancing back around and getting the words in before Wolfe could finish his sentence.

Instead of getting angry, Wolfe picked up on Max's anger and gave out a mocking laugh.

"We'll get the worst out of you yet, Rieker!" he said.

Max ignored the comment and left the office raging with

thoughts of how he would like to end Wolfe's life. He glared at Bauer on his way out, but all Bauer did was smirk.

As he walked away, Max reflected. It wasn't surprising that his problems had always been caused by men attached to the Allgemeine-SS. Further, they had all occurred during the periods between active duties, and this was another reason why he was more comfortable in the field under fire, where 'political types' were virtually non-existent.

He returned to where the company was bivouacked, and there to meet him was Paul. The Baron couldn't fail to notice the desperate look on Max's face and he asked where he had been so early in the morning. All Max could do was to say that he had been ordered over to Einsatzgruppe HQ to take a stiff admonishment from Wolfe for his display of emotion outside the steel factory. He never mentioned the sickening task Wolfe had set him up for, and he quickly went on his way. He spent the remainder of the day locked inside his own thoughts.

All through the rest-and-recreation period Max mulled over the ever deepening predicament he appeared to be getting himself into. Instinct told him that his dealings with Wolfe wouldn't stop with this one incident.

His deed at Kherson would give rise to a new subjective enemy within: guilt. Max would need all the inner resources he could muster to overcome the guilt caused by what he had done. Guilt would open the door for other demons, such as fear. Another one would be depravity – it was waiting for him in the dark corners of his mind.

BIBLIOGRAPHY

Paul Twitchell: *Eckankar: The Key to Secret Worlds.* (1988.)

28

ROSTOV: THE FIRST SETBACK

Fighting in a vast, inhospitable foreign land against a merciless enemy that hated with a vengeance was never marked down as a courage test in the proficiency records of the Hitler Youth.

As well moulded as they were – the long route marches, the war games and sand-box scenarios, the proficiency in crossing rivers and mountain warfare, shock strategy and mobility – the Waffen-SS elite were never trained for the ferocity of a full-blown Russian winter.

In 1941 it came early.

After enjoying a welcome but brief rest-and-recreation period (albeit Max was the exception), on 3 September Leibstandarte was on the move again. It was reassigned to von Schobert's 11th Army, which had been given the task of spearheading Army Group South's drive down into the Crimea, then onwards, east, towards the Donets Basin.

By mid-October 1941, Leibstandarte had seized the famous city of Taganrog.

Weather-wise, it was about this time that things took an ominous turn for the worse. Fierce winds and heavy rain marked the prelude to the Russian winter.

For Army Group South, the war so far had been gratifying, with substantial gains but at a cost of manpower and equipment. The question arose, 'What were the chances of defeating an enemy with seemingly unlimited access to manpower in such a vast inhospitable place?" Millions of casualties and prisoners didn't appear to be breaking the Soviet morale – the prime objective of the Germans in their conquest of the Soviet Union. Now, on top of this, was an oncoming Russian winter.

In November, the Germans were knocking at the gates of the city of Rostov-on-Don. The severe winter conditions had struck early, and with particular harshness, around the city, and frostbite took its toll on lives. Dysentery was also rife. Von Kleist was reluctant to take Rostov as the weather was deteriorating and slowing down his advance. Nevertheless, on 21 November, his 1st Armoured Army rolled into Rostov. Leibstandarte's participation involved launching an attack from the Aral Sea coastline.

The Russians were determined not to let Rostov fall into the hands of the enemy that winter, and they launched a series of counterattacks. They finally pushed out the German garrison established there, and, despite specific instruction from Hitler not to abandon the city, von Rundstedt, overall commander of Army Group South, ordered the retreat. As a result, Hitler sacked him.

The battle for Rostov lasted eight days amid the bitter cold in the harshest of conditions. The Soviets attacked north-east of Rostov from across the ice-covered River Don. They battered the German thinly spread defences relentlessly, hoping to achieve the breakthrough they desired. The Germans were hopelessly outnumbered, fighting against three divisions supported by heavy armour.

This battle would stretch the hardened soldiers to the limits of their capabilities. They used explosive charges to form shallow dips in the frozen-solid earth. They had no winter clothing, so clothing was taken from dead soldiers – even dead Russians. Many could only lie in the trenches, their heads covered with tarpaulins thick with ice.

Panzermeyer's severely depleted reconnaissance battalion of

barely 300 men was assigned to hold an eight-kilometre strip along the Donets River where it separated from the Don, north of Rostov.

With just sixty-six men 4th Company defended 1,500 metres of the stretch. Muller's platoon took the right flank, Max the centre and Fritz the left flank.

It was the early hours of the morning. The wind howled across the vast, desolate plains. Icy gusts rattled the rigid tarpaulin covering Max's weary body. Dawn was about to break as Max opened one eye. He listened to the fierce wind for a few moments before opening the other. He stretched, then spent some awkward moments freeing up the tarpaulin frozen to the ground and weighed down with newly fallen snow. He forced an opening and finally managed to squeeze his body through it, only to be greeted by one of the most inhospitable environments on the planet.

He fumbled for his lighter and lit up his last cigarette; then he took a long drag and gazed back down the German line of defence. It was indeed a thin grey line. The thought of defending their position in the face of countless odds made him wince.

"*Guten Morgen*," announced Fritz.

"*Morgen, Fritz*. Sorry I can't offer you a cigarette – this is my last one."

"You can have one of mine later. I have ten sticks left," replied Fritz.

They both listened to the wind howling across the River Don.

Fritz broke the silence: "If Ivan doesn't get us, this goddam weather will."

"Cuts you in half, doesn't it?" responded Max.

"I could do with a warm and cosy sheepskin overgarment right now, Maxy boy," mused Fritz. "We could all run around like cavemen."

The pun prompted a comment from Max: "You know, Fritz, Jason's Golden Fleece wasn't too far from the very place we are standing now."

"Really?" remarked a surprised Fritz.

"Yes, according to the Ancient Greeks, if we were to follow the coast around to the south we would reach the end of the world – Colchis."

"Little wonder they thought that place to be the end of the world, Max! Not wrong, eh? Trust you to talk about the Ancient Greeks now! You are truly crazy, Max."

Fritz flashed a wide grin, and Max responded in similar fashion. The Baron joined the happy pair.

"*Morgen, Kameraden.* What will the day bring us?"

"Certainly not sunshine, Hauptsturmführer. It doesn't exist in this land. According to Max we are very close to the end of the world. It's just down the coastline over there."

The Baron smiled. He trained his binoculars southward, scrutinising the foreground and back across to the banks of the ice-covered River Don. It was here that the Russians would launch their counterattacks.

Just then a barrage of artillery fire opened up from beyond the Don. Fritz immediately scuttled back to his position. The thin grey line suddenly came to life, albeit all they could do was to return to their potholes and pray to God a Soviet shell didn't score a direct hit.

After fifteen minutes the bombardment ceased. German losses were nil: they were spread too thinly and there was nowhere the enemy could train its guns.

As the dust cleared, all of a sudden hundreds of Russians streamed over the high banks of the Don, preparing to assault the fragile German defences.

"Here they come!" bellowed Max. "Prepare to engage, men!"

Muller and Fritz spat out similar orders along their sectors.

Out of the greyness appeared a continuous row of Russian infantry, singing and shouting. It was an incredible sight. The front row had linked arms and the Russians were pressing forward in a tight line. Their powerful song echoed in the early morning light of dawn. The Germans looked on awestruck.

As the Russians walked across the ice, their front lines were ripped apart by landmines. The explosions slowed the advance, but didn't stop them from coming forward.

"Fire!" shouted Max.

The heavy machine guns opened up and mowed down the remainder of the first wave. It was all over in minutes. Just as Max breathed a sigh of relief, a second wave emerged on the banks of the Don, coming forward in similar fashion.

"Hold!" he yelled. His command echoed down the line.

The Soviets crossed the frozen river, singing and shouting just as they had before. Max couldn't believe what was happening in front of him. As the solid brown line negotiated the shallow ridge on the nearside bank they came within range.

"Fire!" Max bellowed.

Immediately mortar and machine-gun fire opened up, and within minutes the fate of the second wave was sealed.

By the time the sun had come up, the snow-covered landscape in front of them was strewn with the black spots of Russian dead and wounded; there were hundreds of them.

After the amazing episode was over, Max managed to catch up with Fritz.

"I've never seen anything like that before. Truly remarkable!"

Fritz shook his head. "I'll take that memory to my grave," he replied.

Despite similar massacres, the Soviets relentlessly pounded, day and night, and eventually breached the German defences. After the eighth day of fighting under the same horrific conditions, Leibstandarte was finally instructed to vacate its positions. The withdrawal from Rostov constituted its first setback.

Despite the setback, a letter from General Eberhardt von Mackensen to Himmler at that time commended Leibstandarte for 'its discipline . . . cheerfulness, energy and unshakeable steadfastness in time of crisis . . . a real elite unit'. Never had gallows humour been so appropriate amongst the men than during this period, under these appalling conditions.

Leibstandarte pulled back from Rostov-on-Don to a position behind the River Muis. By Christmas it was occupying a defensive line with its right flank on the Sea of Azov, just east of Taganrog. It spent the entire winter of 1941/2 fighting ferocious defensive battles in temperatures down to -30°C, with insufficient winter clothing and only 150 grams of rations per day, per man. Incredibly, against these odds, the division held.

Encounters were fought with vicious ferocity, and it was during this particular campaign that the combat reputation of Leibstandarte probably reached its peak.

But their achievement had taken its toll of lives. By the end of November 1941, manpower figures showed that the Division had 157 officers and 4,556 men against an original count of just under 11,000 men.

By December 1941, Russian resistance had managed to check all three major Army Group offensives launched earlier in June in Operation Barbarossa.

Leningrad, the strategic objective for Army Group North, had refused to capitulate. The Germans had not linked up with their allies from Finland.

Army Group Centre's push to Moscow was placed on hold by Hitler on 19 July 1941. He stripped them of their two panzer groups and didn't return them until ten weeks later. This delay plus the initial five-week postponement due to the Balkan Campaign now totalled at least fifteen weeks. The stoppage, overextended supply lines, and the first eruption of partisan resistance by civilians proved to be the stumbling block for the German occupation of Moscow before the onset of the Russian winter proper.

The Germans came within fifteen miles of Moscow, but on 6 December the Soviets launched their counterattack. Supported by 800,000 troops they put an end to Hitler's hopes of taking Moscow in 1941. By the end of the year one in every four German soldiers on the Eastern Front was dead or had been wounded.

As for Army Group South, their huge tactical victories around Kiev in July 1941 did not enhance the overall strategic position on the Eastern Front. The main objective – achieving a decisive victory that would conclude the war – was not achieved.

The myth of the invincibility of the German Army was broken.

BIBLIOGRAPHY

Rupert Butler: *SS-Leibstandarte: The History of the First SS Division, 1933–1945*, pp. 83–9. (MBI Publishing Company, 2001.)

Charles Messenger: *Hitler's Gladiator: The Life and Times of Panzer Army Commander Sepp Dietrich*, pp. 102–5. (Conway, 2005.)

Kurt Meyer: *Grenadiers: The Story of Waffen SS General Kurt "Panzer" Meyer*, pp 148–52. (Stackpole Books, 2005.)

29

A WOMAN'S LOVE

The main objective of the new German summer offensive of 1942 was to capture the Grozny and Baku oilfields. First, however, Hitler needed to secure the city of Stalingrad in case the Red Army decided to launch its own offensive and cut off the German drive down into the Caucasus.

Leibstandarte initially partook in the fighting to retake Rostov-on-Don but, severely under strength and completely exhausted, their situation compelled Hitler to pull them out early in the campaign. They were ordered back to France for remanning and upgrading as a full Panzergrenadier division. Refitting would include the most modern materials and equipment as well as the new sixty-tonne Tiger tanks. Leibstandarte was to be stronger and bigger than ever.

Max had never uttered a word about his experience at Kherson. Guilt and all the negative emotions that came with it filled him with shame. Paul knew there was something seriously wrong, but he gave Max space to get through whatever was troubling him at his own pace. Besides, it never appeared to affect his performance in the field. Fighting the Soviets kept him focused on his duties and obligations to the men under his command. During these times he was able to push the incident back into his subconscious. Much in the same manner he'd dealt with the atrocities he'd witnessed in Poland and had undertaken in France, albeit the Kherson incident had been far more personal and difficult to deal with. But during the quiet, non-action periods Max struggled to suppress the thoughts tormenting his mind.

The trouble was that his subconscious was quickly cluttering up. All this and now having to cope with the added burdens of guilt and fear – qualities he'd rarely experienced in his pre-war days – were beginning to take their toll on his emotional and mental welfare.

His inner torment came to the surface in horrible nightmares. One night he dreamt he was struggling to keep his head above water. He felt as though he was being dragged under. A horrible stench filled the air. All around him were floating dead – decomposed and bloated bodies.

He awoke in a sweat and attempted to interpret the symbolical meaning of his bad dream. He believed the body of water represented his subconscious – it appeared as though he was about to be swallowed up by it. The dead bodies represented the thoughts he'd been trying to suppress. They were resurfacing. His subconscious was in overload and his demons were spilling over, causing the dreadful nightmares.

Would he crack up mentally under these new inner developments?

The sudden news of the recall to France came like a breath of fresh air. The men of Leibstandarte were more than ready for the break; they had fought almost continuously on the Eastern Front for more than a year.

The Baron and his three platoon sergeants had survived two major campaigns in the east, the invasion of Western Europe and a campaign in the Balkans. But many of their comrades hadn't been so lucky and had fallen; they were being whittled away at a steady pace. Casualty statistics suggested their own days would be numbered if they were to return to the Eastern Front.

Max began to wonder who was the luckier: him, acting out a living nightmare, or his dead comrades, free from all the hazards in the field and the ugliness of the system.

Crossing the border into France was exhilarating. On the evening of their arrival the remnants of 4th Company (down to fifty per cent of their original strength) gathered together and celebrated their return to France and normalcy. The Baron shared some of his best red wine and brandy with them. Stocks would be easily replenished now he was back in the west engaged in a 'civilised' war.

The following morning the division awoke to the sounds of a skylark hovering above. The Baron stretched, took in the fresh air and saluted the day with a lemon tea – a nicety he had picked up in the Ukraine. The tea tasted fresh on his lips. He leant back and basked in the warmth of the morning sun. A few minutes later Max walked across, greeted the Baron and pulled up a wobbly old fold-up wooden chair. They sat back, exchanging small talk, soaking up the front end of a fine day. There was a light breeze, but the sky was cobalt blue and visibility stretched as far as the horizon.

Enduring the challenges of the Russian Front had been a milestone in their young lives. They sat and chatted like two old war veterans. The defensive actions in the Muis and Donets area during the harsh winter had given them priceless combat experience and had transformed them into matured warriors. They discussed the Russian Campaign.

Max opened the conversation: "Fighting in Russia was savage and bitter. The enemy fought fanatically, desperate for vengeance."

"Yes, it looks like we've picked on someone our own size, if not bigger," agreed Paul. "The Eastern Front is witnessing a kind of 'Match of the Century', our Führer's National Socialism versus Stalin's communism."

"A clash of ideals, eh!" Max remarked. "Can we learn from our mistakes?"

"We gambled on being in Moscow before winter set in," said Paul. "Capturing Moscow was strategic, insofar as all lines of communication led into and were dependent on Moscow. Cutting these lines of communication might have been the deciding factor for an early Russian surrender, but success didn't materialise. Now we are trying for a second year, albeit our strike is primarily in the south. Intelligence reported that the Red Army's strength was 4.7 million at the time of the invasion, but, despite the crippling losses they suffered in the first six months (almost all that number), they still had the capacity to recover and replace such losses twice over – an incredible advantage. What's more, contrary to what was reported, the Russians had good tanks – some better than ours – and more of them."

"Their access to unlimited manpower will be a key factor in determining the outcome of this war if we cannot succeed this year. The vastness of the territory doesn't help either. Have we made the same mistake as Napoleon did back in 1812?"

"Maybe, eh? Back then, campaigning in Western Europe was fought traditionally, by direct confrontation. One army simply faced off against the other. More often than not, the outcome would be decided in just one or two major battles. Western European countries, however, aren't expansive like Russia and don't have the advantage of endless manpower and vastness of space. In Western Europe, a retreating army is confined within its own borders. Without fresh replacements or alliances with neighbouring nations, having committed most of its manpower to the one or two battles, the only alternative is to capitulate. Napoleon's mistake was that he took this strategy into Russia with him. He hadn't figured how Russia's scorched-earth strategy would affect his Grande Armée. Besides, the Russians could lose several major battles and still put up a fresh army in the field in another part of the country. So, why should it surrender when, first, the battlefield is literally millions of square miles in area and, second, its manpower still outnumbers the enemy tenfold?

"Having entered Moscow following the non-decisive Battle of Borodino in 1812, Napoleon expected the Tsar to sue for peace and present him with the keys to the city. From the Russian standpoint, this simply didn't make sense. They put Moscow to the torch, sat back and watched the Grande Armée run out of supplies, forcing Napoleon to retreat in midwinter conditions. The weather, Russian snipers, and continuous harassment carved chunks of manpower off the retreating Grande Armée. It returned to Western Europe with only one-tenth the manpower with which it had begun.

"Our own Operation Barbarossa was a cut above the traditional approach. Our strategy called for encircling and capturing or destroying pockets of Soviet forces. The idea was to break down morale and capture Moscow before the winter set in. According to intelligence, more than 5 million Soviet troops were killed or captured in 1941, but their morale hasn't been broken. Losses appear not to have dented the surface. Vastness of territory and superior numbers are still the key factors."

In December 1941, America entered the war on the Allied side. Its industrial strength gave Great Britain a new lease of life; 'the Bulldog' appeared far from having a beaten empire. So far, America's involvement had not influenced the European war arena: they were busy avenging Japan's sneak Pearl Harbor attack. Truly, almost the entire world was at war in the summer of 1942.

Paul loved France and enjoyed the easy access to Paris. As soon as he settled in he set out to catch up with his beautiful Celine. Alas! she had moved into Vichy France to live with her retired husband.

Despite the break from fighting on the Eastern Front, Max still wasn't his old self. In fact he was fast deteriorating. He spent most evenings in seedy bars, stewing over his past actions. His time spent in France wasn't helping him recover, and his former warm-hearted, fun-loving self was fast sliding away from him. His nightmares continued to haunt him. To alleviate his mental burdens he was now drinking heavily and spending most evenings with prostitutes. In his mind, he connected the women of the night with the women burnt to death in the cottage.

In September 1942, some of Leibstandarte's old guard were granted three weeks' leave to visit families and friends. All looked forward to the break and a chance to see their hometowns.

The train journey back to Germany gave the privileged group time to relax and indulge in some light-hearted banter. The train pulled into Berlin Lehrter Hauptbahnhof in the early hours of the morning. Max's heart raced as he stepped down from the train and took in a deep breath of Berlin air. He was eager to catch up with Greta.

Before catching the tram he stopped off at a *Bockwurst* stall to savour his favourite sausage in a bread roll. It had been over two years since he had enjoyed the comfort of his hometown. There was a full three-week rest-and-recreation in front of him, and he wasn't going to waste a second of it.

Likewise, Paul would be engrossed in the prospect of reviving a relationship with a lawyer friend, Frau Litten. Her husband was an army officer currently fighting with Friedrich Paulus's 6th Army on the Eastern Front at Stalingrad.

The tram ride through the city proved enlightening. It took a roundabout route that gave Max a chance to see some of the new sights of Berlin. He noticed that for Berlin it was business as usual. The current focus of Allied bombing was on industrial targets. It wouldn't be until September of 1943 that the bombs would start to fall on Berliners.

The tram even passed by Max's old barracks at Lichterfelde, and it was a sight to behold. Lichterfelde had been given a facelift between 1940 and 1941 to alter its previous sombre image. The entrance was now accessed from a pleasant tree-lined street, and the main gate was dominated by two heroic-sized statues of overcoated soldiers who wore coal-scuttle helmets.

As the tram trundled along its way memories of happier days lined up in a procession of images filing across the inner screen of his mind.

'Those were the days!' he thought.

A number of new buildings had been constructed since his last visit, and he remembered that the Führer was deeply interested in architecture.

In 1935, Hitler had commissioned Albert Speer, his favourite architect, to build a new Reich Chancellery, and after three years of construction the building was inaugurated in January 1939. Hitler chose hand-hewn natural stone for his buildings. More expensive in the short term, their durability meant they were economical in the long term. The Reich Chancellery is a fine example.

Max eventually reached his destination in East Berlin and, soon after, met up with Greta at her apartment. Both had tears in their eyes as they hugged each other tightly. The new addition to the family looked on excitedly.

"Say hello to Kristine," said Greta.

Max looked across the room, and there, standing in front of him, was a beautiful little girl with huge green eyes. Kristine knew he must be someone very special and looked on excitedly and with awe at her Uncle Max.

He walked over, picked her up and softly whispered, "You're beautiful, just like your mama."

In that instant, love overflowed; Kristine took an instant liking to him.

Max parked his kitbag in the bedroom she had prepared for him. The sheets were fresh and the furniture newly polished.

He sat back and relaxed: the stench of war and death was far away. Greta brought him a coffee. They used up the remainder of the day and evening catching up on each other's adventures since they last met. Greta described her last mission to Prague and explained her decision to have a second baby, and Max enlightened Greta on his campaigns in Greece and Russia. The strength of their bond hadn't changed. It was as though they were picking up from where they left off – seemingly just a day or two before, not a period of two years.

But, despite the loving rapport, Greta soon picked up on the changes in Max. His mannerisms were different; new lines of anxiety were etched on his face; he looked worried and had become more serious and sometimes distant, lost in a world of his own. His clowning antics had disappeared, replaced by a heavier, moodier presence.

She was soon to discover that the Russian Campaign had been the catalyst for the transformation. It took a couple of days, but eventually he opened up and talked about the savagery of the war in the east – most of all the mindless killings of the civilians there, carried out by the Einsatzkommando units of the Allgemeine-SS.

Using Greta as a sounding board, Max managed to get a lot off his chest, but he still found himself unable to fully disclose the incident at Kherson. Instead he talked around it. One evening they finished a deep and meaningful conversation with a cuddle, and, as they embraced, Max whispered that he could not get the death of the young women behind him. He heard their screams regularly in his mind. He stood there totally disillusioned. She stroked his face as they remained there in silence. The guilt had drained the colour from his face and the light from his eyes. Greta empathised with his plight, and she gently shifted the conversation away from the topic.

In France, he had suppressed much of his anxieties by getting drunk. Unfortunately, his nightly visits to the seedy bars had only exacerbated his problem. He had indulged in perverted sex orgies with cheap, sorry-looking whores. As time passed, his activities plummeted into depravity. The situation reached a climax when one night his session included the services of a young boy. The combination of drink and sex was beginning to undo him. His bizarre nightlife helped him forget the war and the atrocities that had come with it. It was a weird solace, but it worked for him, helping him endure from one day to the next. Nevertheless he didn't like the control it had over him.

It was during his stay with Greta that he realised his indulgences had reduced him to an animal. It was then that it occurred to him that he was no better than Berti Braun, his ignorant, perverted boss from the old SA days. It had been a revelation.

He'd become incapable of living a normal balanced life during the times he was at home and away from the battlefield. The imbalance in his mind had overflowed into his physical life, forcing him to adopt the weird nightlife. Clearly, his outer world was a mirror image of his inner world.

He felt like a fish dangling on a hook: the harder he tried to break free, the deeper the hook embedded itself and the more helpless he felt. He found he had something in common with those who had no self-esteem or self-respect. He hated himself and the system, feeling that it had horribly deceived him along with millions of other youths.

When he realised he was no better than Berti Braun, it got to him. In an effort to rationalise his position he considered his sexuality. Many bisexuals and homosexuals are genuinely capable of falling in love with others of their own gender, but others simply choose to enjoy raw sexual activity where gender doesn't matter. It is pure lust: an insatiable appetite for sex to satisfy the pleasure principle. For Max, the pleasure appeared to offset his pain.

When intoxicated, he was capable of doing anything to gratify his uncontrollable urge for sex. The day after, he'd always curse his lack of discipline and inability to control the habit.

It was during his stay in Berlin that he decided to do something about it, but gathering the strength and discipline to reverse the situation was the challenge.

He began by analysing his actions, and he noted that it comprised three steps: first, the urge to enter a bar; second, the urge for alcohol to intoxicate the mind and weaken his resistance; and third, the overwhelming urge for sex to satisfy his desires. All three steps were preceded by strong urges, but he realised he had a choice. This brought him a step closer to the solution. He now knew that he had the power to change the situation merely by controlling his choices.

To accelerate his recovery, an unexpected incident occurred one night. It was Friday, the end of his first week of leave. He'd found himself a comfortable bar in the Alexanderplatz area. There were many bars in this part of Berlin to accommodate combatants on their rest-and-recreation leaves. Max had become so drunk he could hardly talk. He ended up slouched over the bar while a fun-loving bar girl placed dandelions in his hair. He was virtually unconscious. The manager of the bar saw an opportunity and had a word with his head bouncer, Oskar. Oskar and an assistant dragged Max through the bar to the rear entrance, threw him on to the pavement outside, relieved him of his wallet and then proceeded to bludgeon him unconscious just for the thrill of it.

Max came around shortly after. Inebriated as he was, he made a mental note of the bar then staggered home, knowing that he was hardly in any shape to get even with the thugs now. As he made his way back across to Greta's apartment he searched his mind, trying to recollect who his assailants had been. Suddenly he remembered that he'd shaken hands with the head bouncer just after settling in – his name was Oskar.

He lurched and stumbled his way back to the apartment and collapsed in a heap on to his bed. The following morning he awoke with a mission. Stripped of his wallet and his entire leave allowance, he climbed out of bed determined to recover his pride and money. He didn't shave, as he wanted to look as ugly and aggressive as he could. He kissed Greta and Kristine good morning then prepared himself to leave almost immediately. His aim was to get even, one way or another. Greta instantly recognised this behaviour from when he was a youngster.

"I'm going out for a walk."

"Be careful," she said as he left the apartment.

He walked out of the apartment block, greeted the day with several deep breaths of fresh air and set off to find the bar. It was a breezy early morning and a gust of wind whipped up some litter in the gutter as he jumped on a tram that took him westwards back to Alexanderplatz. After some difficulty in locating the bar he finally happened upon it, recognising the name, 'Gaslight Club', and an ornate china vase that adorned one of the windows.

'Very inappropriate!' he thought, but it served its purpose in helping him find the source of his misfortune the previous evening.

He walked through the bar, completely oblivious of the early morning cleaners. His objective was a room at the back, where he expected to find Oskar. He was right: Oskar lay spreadeagled on a makeshift bed with his woman much in the same position. Both were out cold.

Oskar was a huge man. He stood a good ten centimetres taller than Max. As he lay on the bed he looked half dead – not unlike Max the night before. He was ugly, and mean as hell. An opened bottle of schnapps stood on the bedside table. Max couldn't wait to even the score. He poured the schnapps that remained in the bottle over Oskar's face and stood there in anticipation. Oskar, still drunk and wearing only his underpants, awoke, startled and choking on the schnapps. He rolled over gasping for breath. As he rolled back around to see what was happening, Max hammered the bottle over his head. Oskar slumped back into the bed, dazed. Realising he was under attack, he shook his head in anger and growled. Just as he was about to get to his feet, Max came in with a powerful right cross to the jaw. Oskar bounced off the edge of the bed and fell to his knees. Max threw a second ferocious punch into the side of his head. The punch rocked him and he sunk to all fours. He looked up at Max scornfully and prepared to get to his feet.

His purple face raged. Max stepped forward and lashed a kick into his head. Oskar groaned and fell back down to the floor in agony.

Max gave no quarter. He knelt across his victim, pinning him to the floor, and threw a powerful one-two into his head. Then he pulled out his SS dagger and pressed it into Oskar's neck. The skin oozed blood. By this time Oskar had regained his sobriety. He lay quiet, gingerly eyeing the blade and Max's raging face. He recognised that the knife was no ordinary blade – it was an SS dagger. At the sight of it, he quickly realised his error of the evening before.

Without even being questioned, he muttered that he had given the wallet to his manager. Max pushed the dagger nearer to the centre of his throat and Oskar knew he would need to satisfy Max very quickly or suffer the consequences. He gestured to a safe housed in the wall and said he knew the code number to open it. Max lifted the dagger, got up and backed off. Oskar, disadvantaged in just his underpants, made his way slowly towards the safe. After fumbling for several minutes he opened the door. As he did, he turned around and let out a monstrous roar. Despite the threat of the dagger, he intended to tear Max's head from his shoulders. But Max had anticipated this and had already drawn his Luger as a safeguard. Oskar's rage quickly turned to fear as his eyes locked on to the barrel of the pistol aimed at his head. He raised his hands, looked over his shoulder and, with his thumb in the air, pointed towards the safe.

"It's there," he muttered sheepishly.

Max motioned Oskar to stand aside and walked up to the safe. The wallet was inside, complete with its contents.

"Get on to your knees!" he barked.

Oskar knelt on the floor and Max followed through with another kick. Oskar keeled over. Max offered no mercy. He bent across to hit him again, finally knocking him unconscious. All the while, Oskar's woman friend was lying on the bed, frozen at the sight of what was happening in front of her.

Moments before, the guy who'd helped work over Max the previous evening had entered the bar. Hearing the commotion in the back office, he'd come in armed with a short piece of timber. Max glared at the intruder, snarled like a dog and pointed his Luger at him, inducing the frightened man to toss away his weapon. He motioned for Max to pass safely.

Max kept his eyes fixed on him as he backed out through the door then quickly strutted through the bar across to the entrance. Before leaving for the safety of the main street outside, he picked up the china vase that adorned the front window and threw it at the bar. The cleaners gaped at him dumbstruck. He walked out into the street and jumped on a tram, heading back to the safety of Greta's apartment.

Back home, Greta noticed Max appeared satisfied with himself.

"Nice walk?" she asked.

"Nice walk." He nodded.

"Had breakfast?"

"No. I'd love some."

She smiled.

Greta had recognised the disillusionment written all over Max's face. She reflected back to happier days: 1936, when, as an eighteen-year-old, the world had been his to take. She had felt the same. The future had held promise for them, but now their destinies were changing; life wasn't the rose garden they had expected.

She spoke openly: "The party, it appears, has used the nation to carry out its own personal agenda. For the few up there – those that hold the power – a whole nation has become expendable. They've led us down a path just to satisfy their ambitions and prejudices. It appears that there is nothing we can do to stop them. As a nation, we never endorsed such a policy of barbarism, but we find ourselves in it up to our necks. We were deceived, seduced." Greta was clearly overwrought.

"I've been thinking hard about this, Sis, and I'm not so sure we were deceived. Ask yourself why we voted for the party. It's because it offered hope; we believed our ambitions and dreams could be achieved. Rose-coloured as they may have been, they were still our heart-set desires. None of them included supporting a policy of genocide. It was the same for every German: the party gave the nation a sense of reawakening. We believed it was a chance to rediscover our national heritage after flying through the first thirty years of this century by the seat of our pants. That's what we wanted to embrace: a kind of German renaissance. Take a look at the events that shaped our national character during those thirty years. We lost the biggest war in history, although at one time it was unimaginable that we would lose. Then the humiliating Treaty of Versailles stripped us of our overseas colonies as well as vast areas of our homeland. Imagine if Great Britain had lost the war and had been stripped of all its colonies in Africa. Unthinkable? Well, the same applied to Germany when it signed the Versailles Treaty. It was truly unthinkable. Imagine also that a part of the British Isles – for instance, the country of Wales – was given to Austria; don't tell me the English wouldn't make every effort to get it back. So it was with Saarland, the Rhineland and Danzig (the Polish Corridor). Czechoslovakia never existed before the Great War; it was part of Germany and Austro-Hungary. The Weimar government was accused of being weak for signing the treaty, but, to be honest, it had little choice. With the exception of right-wing extremists, the nation knew this. Remember what happened in 1920? Berliners actively supported Ebert's appeal for a general strike to restrict the movements of participants in the Ludendorff, Kapp, and Lüttwitz National Association's attempted putsch. Versailles crucified us. Our nation was made to sit out in disgrace for fourteen years and pay back huge war reparations with borrowed funds before being accepted back into the European community again.

"Then there were the revolutionary years when the Marxists

attempted umpteen takeover bids. Soviet policy in the twenties and thirties was to turn the world red. Soviet Russia always presented a threat to Germany and, indeed, the rest of the world. A tussle between two contrasting ideologies was inevitable.

"To cap it off, the Great Depression of 1929 prompted America to call in its loans. As a result, unemployment figures exceeded 6 million. The Weimar government was helpless and couldn't find a solution. Little wonder these events steered our people into believing the promises outlined by National Socialism! Its pure-race theory gave Germany an identity, restored national pride and promised a glorious future. This is why the people voted for it. But this discussion cannot avoid the party's vehement policies of prejudice against others. Anti-Semitism and ill feeling towards selected minority groups is running rampant. It appears our leadership has taken its master race policy and ill feeling too far. They have created a monster and undone all the good they initially achieved for our country.

The problem is that leadership appears to be entirely made up of extremists, with the Allgemeine-SS supporting them. They control the whole system, so it's assumed by the rest of the world that they speak for every German citizen. This is wrong! The German people shouldn't have to suffer for a minority that has abused its power. We didn't vote for the party for these reasons."

Greta nodded her agreement. "It appears the party has adopted the master-race doctrine to justify its actions against others."

"Yes, but this focus is taking precedence over the war effort. We have taken our eye off the ball and it's a recipe for disaster. The entire world has turned on us. Every German is a target of hate because of the actions of a misguided few."

With that, the conversation drew to a close. They sat looking at each other in silence. It wasn't hard to imagine what was going through their minds. Both could clearly see the errors of their choices.

Greta had made her mind up to work on Max's mental and emotional issues. The first job was to get him to cease his nightly visits to Alexanderplatz. She broke the habit by arranging a date for him with one of her girlfriends. He was receptive to the idea of change, particularly after the incident at the Gaslight Club. He'd always enjoyed the company of Greta's girlfriends anyway. Some he knew from the past; others were more recent.

So began the journey: his escape from Avernus.

Greta had given him her love from the time he'd first arrived. The combination of good healthy food cooked with love, relaxing and listening to his favourite classical music, playing and clowning with Kristine and holding meaningful conversations in the evenings in good company had started to take effect.

Midway through his break, Max returned to the gym to participate in a light training programme. They weren't heavy-duty workouts, but they were effective enough to improve his physical fitness and mental welfare.

Needless to say, his health had deteriorated during his time spent in France, and for the first time in his life he'd developed love handles around his waist. In the field he hadn't a weight problem. Combat on the Eastern Front had kept him trim, lithe and sharp. Besides, field rations hadn't been enough to feed a young boy, let alone a soldier. The sudden appearance of love handles wasn't part of life's deal, according to Max, but his new lease of life in Berlin helped him set about putting things right.

One evening, near to the end of his stay, Greta suggested to Max that he should meet up with Katherine, a girlfriend she'd recently met. Greta's invitation brought the two together, and her persistent nudges through the evening persuaded them to agree to spend the following day together.

Katherine had reminded Max of the American film actress Carole Lombard: stunningly attractive with soft, wavy, mid-length blond hair, slim and small-breasted with pencilled features that housed a pair of soul-piercing eyes. Full cherry lips rounded off one hell of an alluring woman.

The date went well; the conversation had been refreshing, uplifting and enlightening. Katherine talked about the Berlin scene and her business and personal ventures.

"Wow, you certainly lead an exciting life, Katherine!"

"Not half as exciting as yours!"

"Well, it's not exciting, as such – scary, yes. The adrenalin is always flowing, and there is never a dull moment, except sometimes when there's a lull between campaigns. I've been involved with the military, one way or another, since I was thirteen years of age when I became an aide to Michael Vogel of the SA back in 1931. I must admit, at twenty-four years of age I feel as though I am an old war veteran. So many battles! It's in my blood, and that's basically all I've had to offer this world."

"But surely you have ambitions?"

"Not too many – only to survive this war, I think. But I do have personal beliefs that have been seriously challenged throughout this conflict." He pondered a while then continued: "I thought they were compatible with the path I chose, but I was wrong. My choices have steered me in the wrong direction – into a situation that couldn't be worse, unfortunately. I should have heeded an old axiom: be careful what you wish for. I've ended up a warrior who's drawn his sword and thrown his scabbard away. So many campaigns, yet still more to fight! Unfortunately, unlike the ancient code of the Japanese samurai, some of the party do not recognise honour, just loyalty. In my book there is no comparison. If an oath of loyalty calls for the slaughter of innocents, then, if I had to do it all again, I would make different choices and leave the slaughter to the conscienceless. Don't get me wrong – all of our leaders in the Waffen-SS are exemplary soldiers; it's the desk boys behind the front lines and the goons that carry out their wishes in the field that bring dishonour to our efforts.

"Having gone this far, no amount of miracles can turn the clock back. I am left having to live with the outcome of my choices and deeds. I am not an evil man, yet I frighten common folk. I am not a cruel man, yet I have become one – live by the sword and you surely die by the sword – but I've only myself to blame, not God. In my situation, it's useless to whip myself, but I do. All I hope for is that things will eventually come right, now that I understand that a person creates his own path simply by the choices he makes in life. Even honour is misplaced if it is in any way connected with power. One cannot be honourable and be involved in the use of power to control others at the same time; it's all an illusion. If I had to do it all again, I would choose to be a loving person, strong but not cruel, firm but not violent. That would be my ambition."

When Max had finished, Katherine looked at him in a new light. She had picked up on his honesty and depth and his passion about life. There followed a short period of silence. They gazed into each other's eyes and pondered whether or not in other circumstances they could have formed a successful relationship together.

It had been one of those magical evenings. Max escorted Katherine back to her apartment and finished the evening with a long, warm and tender kiss.

It was during the final days of his leave that old signs of Max's sense of humour returned, thanks to the help of young Kristine. Remaining days included sightseeing in and around the city with Katherine. Early morning walks through the city were increasing his health and fitness. Katherine worked downtown, and they would meet for coffee at one of the many cafés on Unter den Linden. He looked forward to these pleasant midday sessions, chatting and sipping coffee; they helped slow his forever racing mind. Greta had done a great job of helping her brother achieve balance in such a short space of time. The seedy bars of Alexanderplatz, and their Paris equivalents, no longer represented a threat to his well-being. He'd virtually kicked the habit overnight; his recovery had been quite remarkable.

The day before he was due to return to France the small group visited Berlin Zoo. When they'd finished their tour of the zoo they agreed to go for a walk through the famous Tiergarten. Tiergarten, which is situated next to the zoo near the centre of Berlin, is the oldest and largest park in the city. Max had often walked along the promenades, and indeed had run along them during his training sessions years earlier.

Max thought it would be a good idea to take a drink at the *Bierhaus* located at the junction of Charlottenburg Chausee and Altonaer Strasse, overlooking the Victory Column. It was his way of saluting a city that he loved with a passion.

The Victory Column had been erected back in 1873. At that time the monument had three segments commemorating Prussian victories over Denmark, Austria and France. On Hitler's explicit orders, a fourth segment was added – for a war still to be won. In 1938 Albert Speer had moved it from its traditional position in front of the old Reichstag to its present position.

The day finished off well, but as it drew to a close Greta became nervous. She was aware that the time for Max to leave was at hand. Her love had almost transformed him back into his former self, but she feared that his return to France would steer him back into habits that had previously taken grip of him. Max felt otherwise. His immediate future looked more promising; his rehabilitation had been a great success.

The following day the small group bade their farewells at the train station. They hugged and kissed one another and parted in a sea of emotion. The train slipped away from the platform and another chapter in Max and Greta's life had concluded.

While Max had enjoyed the tenderness of feminine company, the Baron's short excursion had also been memorable. He'd managed to rendezvous with Frau Litten. She looked as lovely as ever. It seemed the war had not constrained her in any way, despite recently being informed by German High Command of her husband's death. He had been killed in action on the Eastern Front. She didn't appear to be too upset about it – maybe because she had inherited everything he owned. She'd greeted

Paul with enthusiasm, open arms and a yielding body.

Max joined up with Paul, Fritz and Muller in the train and exchanged stories of what they'd got up to in Berlin. Fritz had spent his time with his de facto wife, Zelda, and their child, young Josef. They had celebrated his son's second birthday during his stay.

Muller, on the other hand, had shacked up with several other NCOs and spent the time roaming the Berlin bars. By the time he'd finished satisfying his warped sexual appetite he was ready for the journey back to France. Muller and Max's sexual habits weren't dissimilar; but whereas Max was trying to clean up his act, Muller unashamedly bathed in it.

From October through to the end of 1942 Leibstandarte was given 'occupation duty' and transferred to Vichy France. It also spent some time in Normandy and was put on alert during the Canadian landings at Dieppe.

Active duty in France was soft compared to what it took to survive the defensive actions fought along the Donets and Muis rivers in Southern Russia. On the Eastern Front, the men's lives were on the line every day, every hour, every minute. In France, only occasional active operations heightened the risk of wounding or death. Leibstandarte's duties while stationed in Vichy France involved seeking out local enclaves of the French Resistance.

Despite Greta's rehabilitation programme, Max wasn't able to completely shake off the guilt connected with the cottage atrocity at Kherson, but by the end of the year his anger for the 'political types' had subsided – probably because of their absence. His loyalty to his beloved Führer had waned and crumbled in the wake of his experiences. Only his sense of duty to Leibstandarte, its 'warrior' leaders and his men still held fast.

With dwindling manpower Germany faced an ever strengthening enemy in the east. All hopes of a reversal in 1942 would be destroyed at the Battle of Stalingrad. The Allies had been reinforced by the industrial and military support of America, and Germany would be hard-pressed to achieve any kind of reversal in 1943.

Despite the writing on the wall, the Führer was about to deploy his own personal phalanx, Leibstandarte, back into the field to fight its fiercest action yet.

BIBLIOGRAPHY

Klaus von Krosgk: *Der Berliner Tiergarten*. (Berlin Edition, 2001.)

Andreas Kaldar: *Masterpieces of Architecture*. (Woodbridge, 2002.)

The Third Reich: The SS. (Time Life Books, 1989.)

Charles Messenger: *Hitler's Gladiator: The Life and Times of Panzer Army Commander Sepp Dietrich*, pp. 107–9.(Conway, 2005.)

30

KHARKOV

Author's note: This chapter takes up from chapter one after Leibstandartes initial engagements east fo Kharkov.

Despite fighting a brave defensive action against vastly greater numbers, the Germans were unable to cut off the flow of Soviet troops attempting to encircle Kharkov. The Soviet southern pincer achieved its objective and met up with the Soviets that had battered their way through the German units deployed in the area north of Kharkov.

On 12 February 1943, Hitler gave Paul Hausser explicit orders not to abandon the city of Kharkov. They were to stand and fight to the last man.

Drawing from lessons learnt at Stalingrad, Hausser defied Hitler's order, and on 14 February he withdrew to safety. He joined up with von Manstein's Army Group South, and they regrouped west of Kharkov on 16 February. By this time 3rd SS-Panzergrenadier Division Totenkopf, under the command of Theodor Eicke, had arrived to link up with Hausser and join Army Group South. Having regrouped, they took up the offensive against the two Soviet armies streaming towards them. By the end of February German forces had encircled and completely destroyed the two Soviet armies.

The plan drawn up by von Manstein and Hausser proved a masterstroke in military tactics and provided some redemption for the bitter defeat suffered several weeks earlier at Stalingrad.

The one remaining task was to retake Kharkov. With other German forces, Leibstandarte moved around to a concentration area north-west of the city, from where the assault would be launched.

At 2100 hours on 8 March 1943 at Leibstandarte Divisional HQ Leibstandarte commander Sepp Dietrich addressed his senior officers:

"Gentlemen, it is my pleasure to inform you that Leibstandarte has been given the privilege of retaking this city, along with others." He pointed to a huge operations map hung on the wall. "Our objective is simply to flush out and destroy or capture all enemy troops garrisoned there. We are concentrated here, to the north. Tomorrow at 0800 hours we'll advance due south into the city, utilising the main north–south Belgorod–Kharkov highway, here. Our objective is the city centre. Once that is secured, we'll mop up remaining pockets of resistance. Joining us will be units from Eicke's SS-Totenkopf, entering from the north-west, and units from SS-Das Reich and Grossdeutschland, entering from the west. As for our part in this operation, we'll implement a three-pronged approach, forming three separate battlegroups. Fritz [Standartenführer Fritz Witt], you will take the center with SS-Panzergrenadier Regiment I. Teddi [Standartenführer Theodor Wisch] will form the right flank with SS-Panzergrenadier Regiment II and Kurt [Sturmbannführer Kurt Meyer] will form the left with Reconnaissance."

Dietrich took down the huge map from the wall and spread it across a wide, rickety wooden table. Making meticulous references to the city map, the officers discussed in more detail each battlegroup's role in the assault and the routes they might take. The wrap-up was followed by a period of small talk, coffee and biscuits. Dietrich wished them luck and all officers left the headquarters to cascade details of the task down to their junior officers and master sergeants.

The advance into the city commenced the following morning at 0800 hours. Initially, Leibstandarte's entire siege force utilised the main Belgorod–Kharkov highway. There was little resistance as they made their way through the northern outskirts.

An hour or so into the advance Panzermeyer stopped his column to review his role. Officers assembled around him as he made reference to the operations map spread across the front of a half-track.

"We'll take the next turn off to the left, over there," he said, pointing to a narrow spur road. "We'll use the cover of the forested area and cut off the road going to Liptsy, here. Any questions?"

Nobody wanted to challenge Panzermeyer's plan.

"That's it, then. What are we waiting for? Move out!" he barked.

As adventurous as the idea was, the route chosen soon revealed its constraints. The heavier vehicles (armour and half-tracks) were not making the progress he'd envisaged, and he was fast falling behind schedule; they weren't keeping pace with the other battlegroups.

In an attempt to regain the lost time, he sent a small unit up ahead to simulate the progress he had originally intended to make.

The snow-filled tracks they were travelling along became narrower, forcing the column to stop regularly to manhandle bogged and ice-bound vehicles. During this period the Baron's 4th Company men spent more time out of their half-tracks than in them.

Failure to maintain schedule was frustrating and forced Meyer to break away from the main force. Leaving his subordinates to deal with the donkey work, he picked a unit, split from the main force and hurried on to catch up with the lead section. The unit he chose was Max's half-strength platoon from 4th Company, and its company commander, the Baron, went with them. Fritz and Muller's platoons remained with the main force.

To their relief, the track they were following to catch up with the leading group led through a large clearing, and here they spotted the men of the advance unit taking cover at the far end.

As they approached, the officer heading up the squad pointed down the slope to the main road, where a long winding column of hundreds of Soviet soldiers could be seen, together with artillery and tanks.

At this point, the Germans had only light armour and little more than a score of soldiers to attack the Soviet column. It would have been madness, even by Panzermeyer's standards, to launch themselves against such overwhelming odds. All they could do was sit back and wait until their main force arrived.

Unfortunately, the progress of the main force had not improved, and it continued to struggle its way along the narrow snowy track. It would be some time yet before the entire force would be together again.

In the meantime, all the advance unit could do was to look on at the long column of enemy troopers passing by.

"I hate to think what would happen if any of that lot down there caught sight of us just now."

"I couldn't imagine it," said the Baron.

"It would be like Custer's Last Stand."

Suddenly, an ominous drone filled the air above. Every man – German and Russian – looked up. The noise overhead turned out to be two squadrons of German Stuka dive-bombers.

The small group of Germans watched in amazement as cannon fire and bombs descended from the Stukas, smashing into the Soviet column.

About the same time, the first of the heavier tanks made their appearance in the clearing behind them. It wasn't long before Meyer gave the order to attack the confused and panicking soldiers below.

"We're just about to attack the redskins," the Baron quipped.

"He's mad," said Max, referring to Panzermeyer.

"Just like the old man! Good odds, eh?" replied the Baron.

The sudden appearance of the Germans from out of their hiding place fooled many of the Soviets into believing they had walked into an ambush. Max couldn't believe his luck as they began to raise their hands in surrender.

Pleased with the result, Meyer became happier. But he wanted to press on.

Seeking to maximise the advantage of surprise, and leaving only a handful of grenadiers to guard literally hundreds of prisoners, many of whom had been wounded in the airborne attack, he set off towards the centre of Kharkov. They made good progress through the northern outskirts of the city until they were forced to halt at a ruined brickworks on the edge of the city. Here they came upon a concentration of enemy armoured vehicles.

The small German unit found itself in the same position as it was in prior to the Stuka attack: they were undermanned and under-resourced, so they knew that confrontation would be unsuccessful. They had no option but to return to the site of the earlier engagement.

An incredible sight greeted their return. There were now thousands of Soviet prisoners guarded by just a few grenadiers.

After a few uneasy hours the leading contingent of the main force finally caught up. Earlier, Meyer had radioed base and arranged for the Russian captives to be marched off to a marshalling area for prisoners set up north of the city.

By dawn the next day, the entire battalion had regrouped and was ready to resume its advance towards Central Kharkov. Its advance included engaging the enemy concentrated near the brickworks.

Unfortunately, further progress proved impossible when they ran out of fuel. Accordingly the battalion was ordered to dig in where they were. No sooner had they dug in than they were confronted by hordes of Soviets fleeing out of the city centre. Meyer had his men dug in to form two rectangular strongpoints on either side of the road, staggered to ensure their own would not be caught in crossfire. Paul's 4th Company formed two sides of the front rectangle. The short side looked back down the road, and the long side faced away from the road in case the Soviets decided to attack from that direction. Max was positioned in the corner where the short side met the long.

"Carriers approaching – two, four, five in total. They're not stopping! Let's give them a warm reception, *Kameraden!*" he bellowed.

The convoy of trucks ran into a hail of machine-gun fire and *Panzerfaust* shells. Infantry units following up were initially fooled into believing the Germans were stronger than they actually were. They settled for an exchange of gunfire until the main force caught up. Max assessed the situation.

"Hauptsturmführer, it looks as though they are preparing to outflank us!" he remarked.

The Soviets fanned out to form a wide front then launched their attack. It was frightening to see thousands of Russians coming straight at them. Those on the outer edge easily outflanked the German block of men and wheeled around to attack from that side. German firepower was intense and took its toll on the frenzied attackers.

Halfway through the battle, Max shouted across to the Baron, "They keep on coming. There are thousands of them."

"Do you know why, Max?"

"Haven't a clue, Paul! Just our luck, eh?"

"No, it's the main escape route from the city centre."

"Trust the old man! We always end up in deep water."

"Look over there, Max. The Soviets have changed tactics. They're keeping going."

"Thank heavens for that. Looks like the enemy is more concerned with escaping than actually finishing us off."

"Let's hope the panic continues, eh?" quipped the Baron.

Through the raging gun battles, a fuel truck finally reached them, bringing with it a mix of good and bad news.

The bad news was that the road had been cut off further north, thereby denying Meyer's men the opportunity of withdrawing in the event the Soviets decided to refocus their attention on annihilating them instead of avoiding capture. The good news was that the central battlegroup under Fritz Witt had actually entered the city centre and seized Kharkov's Red Square.

Reluctant to dig in, Meyer had intended to continue southwards towards the city centre to join up with Fritz Witt's regiment. But in the face of even more fanatical opposition, Reconnaissance was stuck where it was. Meyer and his men were incredibly lucky not to be massacred on the spot. The focus on avoiding capture outweighed the desire to launch a concentrated attack against Reconnaissance.

Reconnaissance hung on all that day (12 March) and was eventually relieved by Sturmbannführer (Major) Jochem Pieper and his SS-Das Reich Panzergrenadier Battalion penetrating Kharkov from the west. Joining forces, they battled their way into the eastern and south-eastern sectors to flush out the remaining Soviet defenders.

Much to Hitler's delight, Kharkov had been successfully retaken, and it was Leibstandarte's Fritz Witt who took the credit for entering the city centre first.

At 1130 hours on 13 March 1943 a column of Leibstandarte Panzergrenadiers headed for the city centre, making their way on foot behind one of the new Tiger tanks. A long procession of Russian captives filed by in the opposite direction, weaving their way out of the city bound for a prisoner-of-war camp somewhere in Poland or Germany.

Max glanced over his shoulder at the dejected Russians, and several of them returned his eye contact. He looked pensive as he refocused his attention to the front. He was carrying one of the new-issue 7.92-mm MG42 heavy machine guns on his shoulder. The unit was on its way towards the centre to commemorate the victory.

Unknown to the Germans at the time, despite achieving all their objectives in the Kharkov campaigns so far, they had just won their last strategic battle on the Eastern Front.

With Kharkov safely in German hands again, and the Russians falling back to a more secure defensive position, the scene was now set for an even greater battle – the mighty Battle of Kursk, which marked the turning point of Germany's fortunes on the Eastern Front.

For the time being, German forces were to be reinforced and a camp set up on the outskirts of Kharkov in preparation for the forthcoming Kursk offensive. Paul and Max shared accommodation: one of the very small square houses built on the periphery of Kharkov. They nicknamed their dwelling 'the Bunker'. It was here they spent evenings discussing the ills of the world and how they would go about remedying them. One evening they discussed the benefits of an effective follow-up and the constraints of manpower shortage. Paul opened the conversation.

"In the majority of cases, the follow-up is critical in achieving an overall decisive victory. An enemy can get off the hook in the absence of a successful follow-up. The Brits got off the hook at Dunkirk back in 1940 – we should have followed up sooner. Why on earth the Führer called a halt to our advance beats me. It bought them precious time to set up the evacuation.

"The Battle of Gettysburg in 1863, during the American Civil War, is another example of not following up. The Confederates under the command of General Robert E. Lee had been unsuccessful in outflanking or penetrating the Union defences deployed on the high ground. Their final attack, on the third day of the battle, also failed to break the Union's defences. The Confederates were basically a beaten army suffering from total exhaustion and hardly in a position to regroup in order to prepare for what they thought would be an imminent counterattack. It never came. The Union side just stood by. Failing to follow through with a strong counterattack lost them the opportunity of pulling off a decisive victory. As a result the Commander, General George G. Meade, was sacked by President Lincoln. The mistake of not following up gave the Confederates a chance to withdraw their main force and live to fight another day, thereby prolonging the

American Civil War by another two agonising years.

"Regarding manpower shortage, a lesson can be learnt from the same war. After Gettysburg, Ulysses S. Grant, the new Union commander, realised that the Confederates lacked manpower, just as we do on the Eastern Front here, and so he set off to fight a war of attrition. Simple statistics revealed the Confederate disadvantage. Grant knew that if he constantly harassed and chipped away at his enemy's manpower, they would eventually lose. On the Eastern Front here, the Soviets are aware of this too. We just cannot afford to lose manpower at the present rate. Despite our recent win here at Kharkov, it will be difficult to achieve an overall victory against the Red Army now."

"So how can we reverse the situation?"

"Don't know. There's no easy way out, unless we negotiate a peace with the Russians, fall back to a consolidated line in Eastern Europe and wait for the Allies in the west. Unfortunately, I doubt whether Stalin would ever agree to such a peace treaty, considering the Führer broke the last one."

"Well, what about our own supposed allies, the Empire of Japan? They haven't lifted a finger to assist Germany. Had they lined up in the Russian far east during Operation Barbarossa in 1941, Marshal Zhukov would have had 500,000 fewer troops than the 800,000 he had for the counteroffensive he launched at the gates of Moscow. The Japanese still haven't declared war on Soviet Russia. Fine allies they've turned out to be!"

Paul felt the Japanese had a different agenda.

"It's a little perplexing for me," he said. "Had they assisted in invading Russia from the east they would have access to all the raw materials and resources they need. Instead, they declared war on the strongest nation on the planet. It doesn't make sense. Anyhow, it's too late now. The Americans have got them tied up; they need all the equipment and manpower they can muster to beat the Yankies.

"You know, I've heard rumours we are working on some new weapons that can cause widespread destruction. These could make the difference. I haven't a clue how near we are to producing such weapons for use in the field. The course of the war may depend upon how long we can hold out."

"Not a warm and cosy predicament, then, eh?"

Kharkov was a beautiful city, the old capital of Ukraine. Although half blown away by the ravages of war, it was still possible to pick out the wide boulevards, park areas and squares near the centre of the city. The onset of springtime enhanced its captivating charm.

For the Germans concentrated in the Kharkov area, the period between the springtime build-up and the forthcoming summer offensive at Kursk proved interesting.

A German soldier wrote the following eyewitness report:

"Along with other replacement units a new Leibstandarte replacement battalion arrived at the front fresh from Berlin-Lichterfelde in April 1943. Further support that jestingly was called 'Herman Goering's Donation' came from soldiers of the Luftwaffe. Among them were trained recruits and NCOs of all ranks. Most of the Luftwaffe soldiers were without any combat experience.

"After the arrival of the replacement units they were trained intensively in their respective weapons to bring them up to speed as fully-fledged frontline soldiers. Repairs to the German tanks and the captured T34s were carried out at the tractor fabrication shop. Repairs of vehicles were carried out in the ground floor of the new opera house. Tank driving teachers of tank companies conducted tank driving schools. The course lasted one week and examinations were taken at the end. Despite passing the examination, none had practice or experience on the battlefield.

"Accommodation for the soldiers, with just a few exceptions, was at the periphery of Kharkov. Accommodation comprised of very small, square houses, almost like bunkers, at ground level. The walls were built of bricks of mixed clay and dung and the roofs were covered in straw. The 'cellar' and the 'toilet' were always situated a few metres away from the 'bunker'. The 'bunkers' were very often situated just alongside the roads that could not be driven on during times of hard rain.

"The troops slept on anything that was available mostly,

however, one alongside the other on the loamy soil. During the night we had very often unpleasant visitors; small 'animals' that fell down from the ceiling, the damned bugs were everywhere, including lice. We killed them with lead gasoline and we preferred to wash our laundry with the same.

"Relationships with the inhabitants of Kharkov were relatively good.

"The long combat break, which had already lasted for weeks and months, affected the morale of the troops. However, sport and physical training were not missed out. There were sports competitions arranged based upon the motto 'in a healthy body there lies a healthy spirit'.

"On the 20th of April soldiers were decorated for their engagement and bravery in the recapture of Kharkov the previous month. Afterwards they were photographed, by whom we did not ask at that time. In the following weeks several fighting exercises with limited use of gasoline and ammunition took place.

"Leaders, too, underwent intensive training and refresher courses. They arranged sandbox games and map exercises."

It was during this period that Providence was about to write yet another turbulent chapter in Max's very chequered life. Indeed, new chapters were about to be written for Paul, Fritz and Muller too.

BIBLIOGRAPHY

Gordon Williamson: *The Blood-Soaked Soil: The Battles of the Waffen-SS, 'The Battles for Kharkov'*. (Osceola Press, 1995.)

Kurt Meyer: *Grenadiers: The Story of Waffen SS General Kurt "Panzer" Meyer*, pp. 189–96. (Stackpole Books, 2005.)

Charles Messenger: *Hitler's Gladiator: The Life and Times of Panzer Army Commander Sepp Dietrich*, pp. 113–14. (Conway, 2005.)

31

MY IRINA

Notwithstanding his loving blood relationship with Greta, Irina was the only true love in Max's life. He met her in the same way as he'd met Anna several years earlier during the Polish Campaign: at a village get-together, this time arranged by Ukrainian village folk.

For Max, it was love at first sight. She was chatting with a small group of friends when he first noticed her. She had a wonderful smile, but when it was directed towards him the ground opened up and simply swallowed him whole. He waited for the gathering to warm up before venturing over to open up a conversation with her. As he walked across he tried to guess her age: early twenties, twenty-one, twenty-two maybe.

He introduced himself in Russian: "*Zdra-stvooy-tye. Mye-nya za-voot Max. Kak vas za-voot?*" (Hello. My name is Max. What is your name?)

"*Mye-nya za-voot Irina,*" (My name is Irina) she replied, smiling.

His eyes met with a sparkling pair of emerald jewels. Her face was captivating. There was something about her that he couldn't quite fathom. His Russian wasn't the best, but he could get by on the few sentences he had mastered under the keen tutelage of his Ukrainian linguists back in the summer of '41 and the words and sentences he'd picked up since.

She accepted an invitation to dance and seemed genuinely impressed by his attempt at the Russian language. As her hand rested in his, he felt a warmth run through his entire body; he wondered whether she'd felt it too.

'Surely it takes two to generate such a strong reaction!' he thought.

Her remarkable green eyes glittered like two twinkling stars. She wore a blue cotton floral dress, and he could make out the contours of her slender figure beneath it.

As they danced, he repeated her name over in his mind – "Irina, Irina" – all the while gazing deeply into her mysterious, alluring eyes. She was bewitching and he was besotted by her. He soaked up the femininity that exuded from her, flowing into him.

She glanced up now and again but generally avoided meeting his eyes direct. Then, suddenly, as if reading his thoughts, she met his gaze full on and beamed that unforgettable smile. He'd erred regarding her age: she was just twenty years old. She was pretty, but when she smiled her face transformed into one of glowing beauty. Never before had his heart melted like soft butter in a woman's presence. The warm and cosy sensation continued as they glided around the floor in a dreamlike state as though nobody else was around. The war, his guilt and his anxiety all disappeared in these brief, exquisite moments.

When the music stopped he snapped out of his trance and accompanied her back to her giggling girlfriends. He thanked her for the dance and clowningly wiped his brow, suggesting it had been something incredibly special – which, of course, it had been.

He walked back to rejoin his comrades, but kept a watchful eye on her for the remainder of the evening. When it was time to leave he made sure that he was strategically positioned to be able to snatch a parting conversation.

"Can I see you again?" he asked in Russian.

"*Da,*" she said.

"How about tomorrow evening, then?" he asked.

"*Da, da!*" she replied enthusiastically.

Max walked away a very happy man. He jogged the distance to catch up with his buddies.

"Nice girl!" said Muller. "When are you going to marry her?"

"Never seen anything like that! Love at first sight, eh, Maxy boy?" remarked Fritz.

"Hell of a girl, eh?" replied Max.

"What you going to use as a wedding ring, Max – an egg-grenade clip?" jibed Muller.

They poked fun at him all the way back to the encampment.

That night Max couldn't sleep. All he could think of was Irina. Every time he closed his eyes, there she was. In his mind's eye he replayed their dance over and over again.

They met as often as they could in the days that followed, spending the nights together chatting, getting to know each other better. Irina was quick to pick up some German. Max took the cultural risk of kissing her fully on the lips soon after their first meeting; she didn't seem to mind.

The kisses became longer and more passionate, leaving them breathless and eager to try again, over and over. He'd never before experienced feelings like those that now swept through his body. She had full ruby-red lips that, to Max, tasted like sweet red wine. When they embraced they would gaze into each other's eyes for long periods of time. The gaze was hypnotic for both; they'd drift away then reawaken when the experience had passed. He scrutinised every fold, nook and curve in her face, then his scrutiny would always finish with another long, lingering kiss.

Thoughts of returning to the field with Leibstandarte became the furthest thing from his mind. Max had finally discovered something that even eclipsed his verve for the military – it was love.

One evening they gazed up into the star-filled canopy of space and focused their attention on some fluffy clouds racing across the sky. Borrowed light was radiating from a crescent-shaped moon suspended in the blackness.

"What would you wish for now, Irina?" asked Max.

"I'd wish we weren't part of this godforsaken war," said Irina. "I wish I was far away, somewhere hot and tropical, soaking up the sun."

"Wouldn't you want children?" said Max. "Most of your womenfolk like to have children."

"Yes, a girl, and I would call her Kristina. She would be my best friend and companion."

"My sister, Greta, has a daughter. The child's name is Kristine," said Max.

"Oh yes," said Irina, a little surprised at the coincidence.

They looked up to see a shooting star blaze its way across the vast dome of night. Its arc took it through at least four constellations before disappearing into the other side of eternity.

'Love has no boundaries,' he thought.

He was truly smitten.

She held him close and he feathered his fingers through her long mahogany hair, then settled for tenderly fondling her neck. His hands were eager to discover other parts of her body. They ran softly down her back and found her firm, shapely derriere. He squeezed her lightly and she opened her mouth to meet his lips again.

The following evenings saw the passion take new turns. Desire for more stirred within both. Kisses were deeper and feelings were stronger. His wandering hands discovered the sweet contours of her firm, rounded breasts. Her nipples hardened to his touch, revealing her feelings. It wasn't long before they made love, bringing with it happiness and contentment.

Max realised Irina was Jewish. This didn't bother him; any trace of prejudice that had been instilled into him had been swept away with the disillusionment caused by the party's harsh political stand towards the peasantry, including old and young folk.

Despite being besotted with each other, both knew that they were on borrowed time. Living in such turbulent times meant that it would only be a matter of weeks before their dreamy interlude would have to end and they would be obliged to part.

Irina, despite being younger, was more of a realist than Max. Fears for her future were always close to her thoughts, and she knew that the dangers would be even greater if it was discovered she was Jewish. But it didn't stop her from falling hopelessly in love with Max. She literally melted in his kindness, care and attention.

She'd eagerly look forward to his nightly visits. He'd tell stories from his Hitler Youth years and of the escapades he and his comrades shared before the war. They found lots of time to laugh, play and enjoy sex before he returned to his 'bunker'.

It was during this period that Max began to grasp the meaning of unconditional love. For him unconditional love meant acts of giving without the thought of wanting anything in return. It was natural and spontaneous.

"If two people truly love each other unconditionally, such love will be imbued with a trust that bounces freely from one to the other without the thought of placing conditions on the relationship." This is how he initially imagined it: two lovebirds singing sweetly to each other's musical serenades.

It was as though all the wholesome love he'd grown up with had finally come together with his love for Irina. He was amazed how easy it had become to say "I love you." A whole new world had opened up for him in a very short period of time; his heart had opened.

Alas! the feeling was to be short-lived. It soon became apparent that unconditional love was too lofty a target, and soon both were laying down stipulations, sparked by the deep emotional attachments each had for the other. Max wondered if his new relationship was truly one of love or just a wild infatuation.

They began to quarrel, and he entered a phase of mixed feelings; it was all too fast. Anxieties returned as his attachment to Irina aroused old inner conflicts.

Paul made light of his concerns, reminding Max that it was

only a temporary arrangement. Once they got back into action, he said, the confusion would subside and lose its impact and Irina would soon be forgotten. Max wasn't convinced that he could return to his former self. For some reason, meeting Irina had steered him in a new direction, but he was unable to ascertain where this new direction would lead.

His attachment to Irina aroused jealousy in him. He was aware that some of the blue-eyed, blond-haired junior commissioned officers were showing an interest in her, and, as a result, he'd become suspicious and resentful of them. His desire had suddenly become a two-edged sword. Jealousy finally got the better of him when he accused Irina of meeting up with one of the officers.

She argued that she'd known him before she and Max began their relationship, but this didn't help Max. When she'd stop to talk to him out of courtesy, the thought of losing her wrenched his stomach.

He realised Irina had a certain magnetism about her. She hadn't been as shy as Max had initially supposed she would be. She knew how to play a man with just a short single glance. He couldn't quite put his finger on what she had, but it made her a very desirable woman. Was it her smile? No, it was more than that: she knew the secret of capturing men's hearts with a glance or gesture. She had a vibrancy about her that was irresistible to men, and she knew it.

Max finally convinced himself that Irina was having sex with one of the officers. The relationship, only three weeks old, began to deteriorate fast. He would continuously question Irina on her whereabouts and what she had been up to. Both had fiery characters, and before long arguments would break out. Irina would respond by accusing Max of seeing other women in the village.

Despite the heated arguments and brief periods of discontent, the infatuation and desire remained for them both. Temporary break-ups regularly occurred, but the relationship was quick to be restored in a hot, passionate evening of sex.

The on-off relationship continued to slide. Finally both lost their sense of humour through distrust and suspicion. Max finally cracked and, in a fit of anger, walked out on her.

He volunteered for a two-week search-and-kill operation involving sifting out local partisans threatening the German forces in the Kharkov area. Stubborn as he was, he immediately felt sorry and deeply regretted his decision, but it was too late; he couldn't back out. Irina was shocked by his decision.

Days turned into weeks and Irina received no news of his welfare. She became sad and vulnerable.

Martin Barris, one of the blue-eyed, blond officers, got to know of Max's absence, and he thought this would be a great opportunity to take advantage of her. He orchestrated a 'chance' meeting, and then with his silk tongue and keen sense of humour quickly got her smiling again. He fabricated stories about other girls Max had been seeing. Irina grew angry and scornful. In her vulnerability, she believed his deceitful whispers and it wasn't long before she gave up her body to him too.

Unlike Max, Barris wasn't in love with Irina. He just wanted to satisfy his need for sex. Forming a meaningful relationship wasn't part of his plan. Within the week, after a few nights of sex, he dropped her like a hot brick. His sudden rejection shocked Irina and she wept with shame, wishing she were back with Max, but Max was still away fighting partisans.

He finally returned from his mission, which had been extended for another week. On his return, his desire to meet up with Irina was intense, but his pride got the better of him and stopped him from contacting her immediately.

Then the unthinkable happened: two weeks after Max's return, Irina discovered that she was pregnant. Knowing that the father could be Barris, she became anxious and depressed. Max was the man she really loved. Now, in a matter of weeks, her whole life had been turned upside down by the thought that she might be pregnant with someone else's baby.

Max was desperate to catch up with her. During his time away, he'd thought a lot about his behaviour and he wanted to start anew. He eventually got a note to her through one of her friends, Elena. Irina read his words of love, but the note left her bitter and angry. She refused to meet up with him and returned a brief note through Elena informing him of her decision.

Max knew she was strong-willed and stubborn, but he was disturbed by one of her comments: "It's too late now." Unable to understand why it was 'too late', he grew anxious. He felt that she still loved him.

After several pleas through Elena, Irina made up her mind to tell him the truth. Elena returned bearing the bad news.

Max was mortified. His fears had manifested: she had fallen for one of the officers while he was away. Now she was pregnant, and, in his mind, she had betrayed him. It was agonising, but his agony soon turned to rage. He spent the next few days drinking and frequenting army brothels in an attempt to forget the whole affair.

Meanwhile, Irina was now expecting an unplanned child, with no means of support, no future to look forward to, and without Max's love. Her depression took a turn for the worse: her will to live was quickly declining.

For Irina the writing was already on the wall shortly after the arrival of Philip Wolfe. It was Wolfe who'd headed up Einsatzgruppe D at Kherson back in 1941. In April 1943 he took command of the area around Kharkov, replacing the previous chief, who'd been assassinated by local partisans. Wolfe was the same obnoxious individual who'd given Max his special mission of torching the cottage outside Kherson.

Wolfe was an intimidating bastard. He had a long scar down the left-hand side of his face, caused by a sabre slash while duelling in a Munich beer hall back in the thirties. He had also developed a nervous twitch that worsened when he became angry. Originally transferred from the Gestapo to Einsatzgruppe, his nickname was the Hangman. It isn't difficult to understand how he got this name as hanging was his favourite way of executing partisans and Jewish civilians. He loved to see them dangle from the end of a rope. He appeared to have devoted his entire career to hunting down 'enemies of the state'.

Once settled, Wolfe was eager to make an impression. His administrative structure covered all Ukraine. His hunt for Jews systematically covered every city, town and village in his vast area of jurisdiction. All Soviet citizens were ordered to produce their identification papers. The city of Kharkov and the villages in and around where Irina lived were the first to be scrutinised. Irina was one of the luckless individuals who were interned. Most were women and children, as the menfolk had either been executed or were away fighting as partisans.

During the interrogations at the detention centre, Wolfe's attention was drawn to Irina because she looked particularly sorrowful and frightened.

"Why are you trembling, girl?" he remarked impatiently.

Irina wept and said that she was pregnant with nobody to support her.

Her sobbing made Wolfe feel uncomfortable, and consequently he fell into one of his uncontrollable rages.

"Stop whimpering, woman!" he shouted.

She wouldn't stop.

"Bauer, shut this woman up, will you?" Wolfe barked at his adjutant to do something about her.

His adjutant, Bauer, quickly ordered two guards to take her outside and lock her up in the timber latrine near the detention centre and keep her there overnight. They frogmarched her outside, threw her into the latrine and locked the door.

"A dose of solitary confinement will stop you bawling," Bauer muttered through the wooden door.

Irina had worn her blue dress that day – the dress in which she'd first met Max.

Max had got to know about the Jews being rounded up for questioning at the detention centre. When he got to hear about the incident involving Irina he grew frantic, knowing Wolfe's capabilities. The next morning, throwing all caution to the wind, he made his way toward the rear of the detention centre, where Irina was locked away. A guard stood outside the latrine. Max acknowledged him and knocked on the door, asking if she were OK. There was no response. The silence sent a shock wave through Max. The guard realised something was wrong and fumbled for the key to open the latrine. Inside, Irina's body lay lifeless, huddled in the corner, her eyes wide open. She was dead. She had asphyxiated from a panic attack.

Max was horrified at the sight of Irina's limp body huddled in the corner. He whispered to her sweetly as if she could hear him, then he bent down and gently lifted her out of the latrine. He held her in his arms and kissed her forehead, whispering how much he loved her. He carried her to a nearby tree and placed her softly on the ground, then he sank to his knees beside her and wept, holding her head, pressing it to his chest and running his fingers through her mahogany hair. His beloved Irina was dead. He laid her down and lurched away, looking into the sky with hands spread as if he wanted God to talk to him. No solace came. He staggered on for a distance, spun around and walked back to stand over her fragile body. He buried his head in his hands.

"What is this place?" he muttered. "Where am I? Is this hell?"

Filled with remorse, he thought that if he hadn't been so stupid and proud maybe Irina would still have been alive.

Fritz had not been far behind. He'd seen Max's reaction when he'd heard Irina was being held at the detention centre. He eventually caught up with him at the tree and leant across to place a kind hand on his shoulder. As Max settled they talked for a time. Just about then two soldiers from Einsaztgruppe walked up to collect and dispose of Irina's body. Fritz helped Max to his feet and together they walked back to camp.

All seemed lost in the thick pall of emotion. Waves of despair and anxiety rolled through Max's body. He raged inside at his own stupidity, and in the days that followed he became his own worst enemy – far more dangerous to himself than any Russian partisan or Red Army combatant was.

His hatred for Wolfe welled up every time he passed Einsatzgruppe HQ. Soon enough a situation would arise where one of the adversaries would end up suffering the same fate as Irina.

32

MASTER RACE

One night, Max suddenly woke from one of his nightmares, violently choking and gasping for breath. Panicking, he staggered around trying to catch a breath of life-giving air. Bile had blocked his windpipe, and he fell to his knees literally choking to death. After some very anxious moments his struggle subsided as he managed a small intake of breath between the violent cycles of heaving. After a while he was finally able to breathe naturally again. He relaxed and lay stretched out on the floor, remaining there for several minutes. He closed his eyes and melted into a void of nothingness, gradually regaining a balanced state of mind.

As he relaxed, thoughts of where he stood in life now filled his mind. It had become a life of double standards. On the one hand he was an elite soldier fighting for his country, and on the other he was a witness to the senseless slaughter of civilians. Conflicting emotions threw him into a quandary, reminding him of one of old Vogel's discourses concerning emotional dishonesty. Emotional dishonesty simply meant not being true to oneself – living a lie.

Mixed feelings were causing havoc to his inner balance. Guilt and fear were the last things a soldier needed for enduring the cold-blooded exchanges on the Eastern Front. Max needed heart, courage and will power to endure the new challenges now, just as he'd needed them in the old days, back in the ring, when he'd fought tough opposition. But these virtues weren't as easy to come by as they had been in his youth. In his boxing days Max had known no fear; now it was overwhelming his well-being and affecting his mental and, indeed, his physical health.

Despite the shift in fortune in favour of the Allies and the Soviet Union, the party never wavered in its policy of genocide against the civilian populace; murderous rampages carried out by the Allgemeine-SS special units remained the norm.

'They haven't learnt a thing,' thought Max.

Belief in the alluring ideal of a master race had steered Max to his present situation. He reflected on what part of the ideology had caught his imagination.

He recalled that his early interests had developed during his time spent at the orphanage, long before old mentor Vogel had taken him under his wing. He'd read the classics – in particular, two books written by the Roman author Tacitus (AD 56–118). In his books, *Annals* and *Histories*, he talks of the Germans, their character, culture and origins. Of their origin, Tacitus wrote:

> The Germans derive their origin from no other people and are nowise mixed with different nations arriving amongst them since, in ancient times, those who went seeking other climes, travelled not by land, but were carried in ships. They avoided settling in Africa, Asia Minor or Italy but opted for the land where the climate must have been like its native country.
>
> In their old ballads they celebrate Tuisto, a God, sprung from the earth and Mannus, his son, as the fathers and founders of the nation. To Mannus they assigned three sons, after whose names so many people are called. Some say that God had more sons, that hence came more denominations of people and that these names are truly genuine and original.
>
> Germany appears to be a recent word, where the name of the tribe prevailed, not that of the nation. But occasioned by terror and conquest they chose to be distinguished and assuming a name lately invented, were universally called Germans.

Of the German race Tacitus wrote:

For myself, I concur in opinion with such as suppose the people of Germany never to have mingled by intermarriages with other nations, but to have remained a people pure, and independent, and resembling none but themselves. Hence amongst such a multitude of men, the same make and form is found in all, eyes stern and blue, yellow hair, huge bodies, but vigorous only in the first onset. Of pains and labour they are not equally patient, nor can they enjoy thrift and heat. To bear hunger and cold they are hardened by their climate and soil.

The belief that the German race was directly descended from the gods fitted in well with Max's dreamy, romantic images. At that time, he genuinely believed he was part of a superior race – part of a direct lineage to the ancient gods.

In aligning his personal beliefs with party ideology it appeared that he had gone a long way into fooling himself. Party ideology chose to settle upon the Aryan race as their point of origin. The term 'Aryan' derives from the ancient peoples who lived in Persia – modern-day Iran and the Indus Valley. But Nazi theorist Alfred Rosenberg claimed these were dynamic people who originated from northern climates in the forests of Southern Germany. From there they migrated south, eventually reaching India. They were supposed to be ancestors of the ancient Germanic tribes, who shared their warrior values.

Max's original research plus the spellbinding experiences of the thirties made it easy for him to fully commit to party doctrine, but for the policy of genocide that developed later during the war years.

For Max, it wasn't clear whether the party actually intended to use its master-race doctrine as a justification for genocide from the outset, or whether it developed during the war years out of desperation. Whatever the truth is, by 1943 Max's toleration of party policies was beginning to wear thin, and enlightenment came at about the same time for many of the old guard that made up the ranks of Leibstandarte and other units. Despite the recent victory in the Third Battle of Kharkov, many were beginning to feel disillusionment.

Old fanaticism was crumbling in the wake of the ravages of war. The fanatic, once ready to die for his Führer, had changed into a seasoned soldier. The allegiances of those that had survived were shifting towards their comrades and officers. It was a joint effort to overcome the enemy and prevail.

This realignment arose out of hardship. Strategic victories finished with the Kharkov campaigns, and, from that point, the Führer would go on to blame his generals for failing to achieve reversals. As a result, discontent grew within the military.

The Eastern Front was stretching Max to his emotional and mental limits. Battler that he was, one day he set out to analyse his problem to see if he could discover ways of overcoming his demons within – guilt and fear.

'What is guilt?' he thought.

He knew that when it came it welled up in his body as if he had been injected with some intoxicating serum; the symptoms were feelings of unworthiness, depression, mental fatigue and a fear of retribution. His sense of humour vanished as life descended into one of grim memories. The ghastly clutter stored in his subconscious burst its banks, and his torment manifested in awful nightmares. Most nightmares were symbolic and invariably included rats – sometimes in their hundreds, at other times just one on its own. Max interpreted the rats as depicting uncleanliness, feeling that his very soul had been tainted. Guilt, he realised, was a key to open the door to fear.

He figured that a person riddled with guilt wore it on his shirt sleeve, unconsciously wanting everybody to know about it: "Look – see what a bad person I am!" It was a sort of self-inflicted punishment. He wanted to punish himself, and he subconsciously invited others to join in the punishing process. Guilt created low self-worth which others picked up on; and, unhesitatingly, they joined in the punishing process. People riddled with guilt become victims – they simply assume that role.

It is a sad affair and a lonely road to self-destruction, if maintained.

'But what are its mechanics?' he wondered. 'Guilt is all about recalling the incident and experiencing the deed over and over in the mind. The mind never differentiates between what is real and what is imaginary. Hence with each recollection comes the agony and pain that was wrapped around the original incident.'

Max's initial attempts at controlling guilt included trying to rationalise his actions; he attempted to talk himself out of his problem. He reflected on why he'd set fire to the cottage. Was it a sense of duty? He realised the orders given him were purely vindictive and a form of punishment; they weren't of strategic importance. Further, Wolfe hadn't tested Max for his loyalty or his ability to obey an order; that was a cover. He was simply an angry individual who wielded the power to punish. Max had infuriated him with his simple honest comments and Wolfe took it upon himself to punish the upstart for being honest – a quality he never had. The records showed that Max was one of the finest NCOs in Leibstandarte, but Wolfe's feeling that he had been slighted outweighed reason and all he wanted to do was to make Max suffer for it, because he could.

Despite initial success with the rationale technique, respite was only temporary and fell flat in a few days; the positive energy ran dry and Max slipped back into his old state. His rationale hadn't been convincing enough.

During this time Max realised that although Wolfe punished so too did he. But, unlike Wolfe, who punished others, Max chose to punish himself. This discovery allowed him to revisit his problem from a loftier position.

A victim of guilt, he realised, locks himself into the past. The incident creates a fear of impending doom – a fear of retribution.

Fear, he realised, compels an individual to focus on negative postulates for himself. Having established this, Max suddenly realised he was back to his old law of reversed effort – a principle he'd been well acquainted with since he was a young lad; it had sneaked in from another direction. He recognised his behaviour as part of the same principle. He was now able to summarise his findings.

Fear of what the future might hold for him had been based on actions that had taken place in the past.

He'd discovered that the common thread linking guilt and fear was time. Guilt is generated by recollecting a memory from the past and fear sowed a seed for the future. Moreover, both guilt and fear rely on the imagination that forms part of the emotional fabric of man. Establishing how the deadly combination interacted helped Max devise a way of combating them.

The key to breaking the time-based problem was by viewing his life in the present moment. Living in the moment was easy to achieve when Max was fighting in the field; there he survived on a moment-to-moment basis. It was during those periods away from active soldiering that his thoughts and imagination got the better of him.

Focusing on the present moment – the here and now – eliminated the concepts of time and space. It allowed him to stop reducing himself to an emotional cripple. He became mentally alert, and when he felt his thoughts and imagination falling back into previous negative patterns he would simply pull them back into the now.

As he developed his technique he took it a step further. If he was to focus on the past he would use his inner tools of memory and imagination in a positive manner: by recalling the days when he was confident and strong. Further, he focused on the people he loved, such as Greta. He recollected one of old Vogel's axioms about love: "Where Love knocks on the door of Fear nobody answers." The two qualities cannot live together. It's either one or the other, love or fear.

His inner tools became the weapons used to fight these subjective ills. By picking up the challenge every day, regular practice helped Max steadily regain strength. He learnt that living in the present moment, focusing on his daily tasks and duties, did indeed mitigate the fatigue and anguish caused by dwelling on the mistakes of the past. Day by day, three steps forward, two back, he began to build a resistance to the deadly vices of guilt and fear.

The road to recovery was tough, but he persevered. Gradually replacing the hate he had for himself, his self-worth and confidence began to return, and with it his health improved.

Only time could tell whether Max would return to a normal balanced life, but fighting on the Eastern Front was hardly a guarantee for long life expectancy – and, truly, if Max had been a cat, his nine lives would have already been used up.

The Baron and Max were quartered together in one of the bunkers built along the roadside. Candles for light, two bunks, a table and two chairs, a cupboard, a bookshelf, a mirror and a small wood-burning stove made up the contents of their small dwelling. The bookshelf acted as a bottle shelf, housing Paul's favourite drinks. No matter to which front he had been assigned, he'd always managed to secure a bottle or two of his favourite Napoleon brandy. His lofty connections carried to the remotest of battlefields.

Every Saturday evening would involve a weekly ritual. They'd return to the bunker, relax, place their chipped cups on the table, pour a shot of Paul's brandy and toast the end of the week, bellowing a hearty "*Hoch!*" as they chinked vessels. Then they would settle down for their nightly discussion. They'd already resigned themselves to losing the war. In fact, they knew that if they came away from the Eastern Front unscathed, it would be nothing short of a miracle.

One particular evening, Paul opened the conversation: "Here at Kharkov, Germany is regrouping for its third major summer offensive in an all-out effort to destroy a large Russian concentration of manpower and equipment. The outcome will decide the course of this war."

Max agreed. "We've been pushed out of North Africa, and Sicily has just been invaded by a combined force of Americans and British. Everything is taking on a different flavour now. Sweetness is rapidly turning to hardship and bitterness. Fortitude and enthusiasm are slipping away as the Red Army increases in strength by the day. There is no way this new generation of combatants could see the world in the same light as we did, Paul."

"An outright victory is needed this summer to increase morale," said Paul. "The recent Kharkov Campaign has been a good one, and has served to stabilise the front lines, but it is hardly a turning point, eh!"

The two men sat in silence for a few moments.

In April that year, Paul had been awarded the coveted Knight's Cross and Max his second Iron Cross for their actions in the Third Battle of Kharkov.

The Baron picked up the small casket housing the decoration and pulled back the top, revealing the black-and-silver cross. He eyed it pensively.

"Was it worth it?" he quizzed.

Max opened his, staring at it in the same manner.

"Yes, I think so," he said.

"Guess we should wear them, then, eh?" said the Baron.

They held them to their chests, stood to attention, puffed out their chests and burst out laughing in scorn of their trophies, in the light of their current situation.

They celebrated with a second toast. The china cups clashed to yet another resounding "*Hoch!*" As their laughter died away they grew serious and looked each other in the eye; both seemed to read each other's thoughts. The master-race theory had brought them here, to this ungodly spot, unkempt, unshaven and battle-weary. They smiled at each other, knowing their days were surely numbered. They were surviving by the tip of an angel's wing, so to speak. The fear of death in combat didn't bother them, for they had been part of the old guard, where to die for

Germany and its Führer was considered a privilege. They spontaneously hugged each other and sat in silence for several minutes, both contemplating their inevitable short futures.

Paul broke the silence: "Fancy a cup of tea, Max?"

"Yes, please," he replied.

The Baron boiled some water on the hotplate over the crude wood-burning stove and poured out two cups of tea in the same cups as they had just used for the brandy. As lemons were hard to come by, he added some sugar to complete the small domestic ritual.

The nightly debate continued, but the topic changed and focused on the master-race theory and what it meant to them now. Max wanted a shot at expressing his own recently gained enlightenment on master race, and he started off by quoting the old Christian axiom 'Man is born in God's image.'

"Perhaps man being born in God's image doesn't mean man in a physical body," said Max. "After all, God doesn't have a body."

Paul added, "Maybe the axiom has a more subtle meaning, then. Instead of a body it may mean the mind or soul. Some of the Greek philosophers spoke of a higher self – Socrates, Plato and Pythagoras, to name a few. They say that written over the entrance to Pythagoras's school were the words 'Worship the Gods if you must but above all, Know Thyself.' Pythagoras believed that a man's soul was spiritually free, unfettered by the passions of mind and the ills of the body. Maybe this is God's image."

Max nodded his agreement. This fitted in with his recent enlightenment concerning the master-race theory. He never doubted that a superior race existed, but not a singled-out race of earthly beings in material form – i.e. Aryans. His belief was for every individual to realise himself as a soul, just as Pythagoras had taught. Max believed that those individuals who had come to this lofty realisation were the real members of a master race; they'd become *master* of their own destiny, so to speak. This being so, a pure race was of spiritual essence, not physical. The designers of party doctrine had not gone far enough in recognising the spiritual significance and, instead, they had adopted a material version that served their purpose.

The evening was summed up: it was agreed that the soul was the 'greater self' and the mind was the 'little self'. It was the soul, not the physical body, that reflected God's image – the spiritual part of every human being, no matter what their race, religion, creed, colour or belief. Distinction between races disintegrated in the wake of this realisation.

They toasted the Greek philosophers and settled down for some sleep.

Max slept well that night, but the morning greeted him abruptly when an NCO banged on the door of the bunker instructing him to report for special duties. The rain fell in torrents that morning. Reinforcements, including new mobilised artillery and fresh troops were due to arrive, and Max's duty was to take delivery of trucks laden with small arms, materials and ammunition destined for the front.

He stood in the rain contemplating his recent experience and what it might mean for his immediate future.

BIBLIOGRAPHY

Paul Twitchell: *The Far Country*. (1987.)

Paul Twitchell: *Eckankar: The Key to Secret Worlds*. (1988.)

33

ILYANA

It was June 1943. The summer morning was overcast and a downpour was imminent. Max was due for his third brush with Einsatzgruppe. He wore a full-length oilskin in case the heavens decided to open up. They didn't disappoint. Within minutes he found himself up to his ankles in a river of water. Trucks, armour, mobile artillery and manpower decided to converge into the receiving area all at the same time. It was hectic as Max busied himself relaying instructions, checking off arrivals and helping manoeuvre some of the heavier deliveries into final position.

Just before the deluge stopped, a grey L3000S Mercedes-Benz cargo truck came through the barrier with a shipment of old men, women and children. Max raised his hand to stop the truck to verify the truck's payload with the officer accompanying the driver. The rain came down in sheets, lashing into the windscreen. The wipers were ineffective in washing off the water. Reluctant to get wet, the officer pulled his window down partially. Max peered in, but in the confusion of the day failed to recognise the officer in the cabin. He'd been rushed off his feet all morning, and he brashly asked what the truck was doing in the receiving area that day. The officer, referring to the civilians as 'vermin', replied that they were there to be locked up in the detention centre.

"What for?" asked Max jokingly. "Did they blow up Army Group HQ?"

The officer didn't see the funny side of the comment.

"It's none of your business," he retorted.

Max still hadn't recognised the officer as Felix Bauer, Wolfe's adjutant and right-hand snitch.

Not wishing to get into an argument with the arrogant bastard, he snapped out a salute and shouted, "Move on, then."

He turned his back on Bauer in a condescending way and carried on with his duties.

Despite the turnaround in his outlook toward himself, it didn't shift his hatred for Philip Wolfe. He'd realised that if Irina hadn't died in the latrine, she would have been hanged by Wolfe for being a Jew.

Wolfe was a meticulous, clever administrator, but he lacked a soldiering mind. Max concluded that he didn't need one, considering the job he did. The Final Solution – the policy of killing all European Jews – had been in effect for over a year now and Wolfe seemed to thrive on carrying out its mandate in whatever locale he was assigned to.

Those serving under him feared his tantrums, and, as a result, though they didn't express it openly, they had little respect for him. He had a knack of disrupting anything that came within his sphere of influence; he was a catalyst for destruction and discontent. His tongue was two-sided: one side was smooth as silk when it came to providing his superiors with the words they wanted to hear; the other was destructive and brutal when it came to handling his subordinates.

Seniors got the impression that he was carrying out his duties in the most appropriate way, but his subordinates knew otherwise. His face would twitch and contort with rage as he spat out threats of severe disciplinary action if he sensed that compassion or sympathy was being shown towards the local civilian populace.

Wolfe was utterly ruthless, but Max's hate for him equalled his ruthlessness.

Failing to recognise the officer in the cargo truck was a serious mistake. Unlike Max, Bauer hadn't made the same mistake. He was infuriated by Max's comment. As a result, he reported the incident to Wolfe. Scarface instructed Bauer to go back and bring the insolent master sergeant to his office.

Bauer returned to where Max was busily carrying out his duties.

"Sturmscharführer," he called out.

Max looked up.

"Sturmbannführer Wolfe wants to have a word with you in his office immediately."

Just then, recognition dawned upon Max. It had been Bauer. 'Oh, f**k – it's that wanker!' he thought, and he cursed himself for being a *Dummkopf* and not recognising him earlier.

"I can't right now, Obersturmführer. I'll need to secure a replacement here before I can report to Wolfe. As you can see, it's busy here today," he replied.

"OK, but make it snappy, Sturmscharführer. Wolfe doesn't like to be kept waiting."

Max's heart dropped. He knew he might be up for some kind of disciplinary action for his joking remark. He was due for replacement anyway, and when he was relieved made his way to Wolfe's office soon after. The door was open and Max stepped inside.

He snapped out his initial salute, "*Heil Hitler!*" and was met with a sneer.

"Well, well, if it's not our little compassionate NCO from Kherson," Wolfe muttered. He got straight to the point: "Well, here we are again, soldier. Why were you so concerned about the civilians in the truck?"

Max didn't hesitate. He had decided to give an 'authoritative' response – besides, he was getting to the point where he didn't care much about what Wolfe thought anyway.

"My orders were to check off and direct all arrivals and deliveries to their assignation points, but I had not been briefed about any truck carrying civilians. Your truck wasn't on my

392

checklist and I didn't know what to do with the civilians until your Oberst urmführer explained that they were to be locked in the detention centre."

"And why did you cast your disparaging remarks? You believe Einsatzgruppe are a good-for-nothing bunch of murdering bastards, do you?" Wolfe's question filled the air with scorn and signalled oncoming rage.

'Such pettiness!' Max thought, but he stayed centred, ensuring that he would not show any fear or anger.

"I cannot say why I made the comment, Sturmbannführer. I got carried away with my duties. It's very busy out there today and after the incident I was aware that I had acted beyond my jurisdiction. Besides, my comment was a joke, rather than a serious jibe."

Wolfe scoffed and eyed Max suspiciously. "You think light of our work here, Sturmscharführer. Still your little compassionate self, eh? To answer your query as to the reason why they have been brought here, Sturmscharführer: they have been brought here to be hanged. Did you think they had been brought here to party with us?"

Wolfe exploded in anger. He slammed his fist on the table and his face grew reptilian and reddened with rage as he glared at Max. But Max's explanation had been satisfactory.

"I tell you, Sturmscharführer: any more jokes like this," he repeated, "any more and I will have you court-martialled. Now get out!" he bellowed.

Max's authoritative response had saved the day, but he'd heard enough. Filled with anger, his eyes met Wolfe's squarely; they were full of hate and scorn. He reeled around to leave the office, but he'd taken a second or two too long. Wolfe called him back and he reeled around again. His eyes were set fast on Wolfe's, apparently unconcerned as to the consequences that might arise out of the obvious confrontation.

Wolfe's face was now purple with anger and twitching furiously. He surveyed Max's face and was itching for a reason to punish him. In turn, Max stared at Wolfe and thought how he wouldn't hesitate to kill him if he had the chance.

Suddenly, for no apparent reason, Wolfe calmed.

"What is your full name, soldier?" he demanded.

"Maximillian Rieker," was the reply.

Wolfe ran his finger down a list he had in front of him and recognised Max as one of the soldiers who had received a second Iron Cross.

"I commend you for your bravery in the field, Rieker," he said.

"Thank you," replied Max, wondering what was happening.

Then, as nonchalantly as he could, Wolfe added, "I trust that supervising the hanging of these hostages will be OK with you, then, Rieker?"

Max glared at Wolfe and said nothing.

After a few moments of silence, Wolfe shouted, "Good! We'll be hanging these traitorous scum in three days, unless someone steps forward and hands over those responsible for assassinating Standartenführer Blass. Dismissed, Sturmscharführer!"

Blass had been the officer Wolfe had replaced, and one of Wolfe's jobs was to investigate and root out the enclave that had assassinated him.

'Weird f**k!' thought Max as he walked away from the building.

A number of the menfolk had recently left their village to join up with the partisans operating nearby. Their families had stayed in the village and, as a result, had been rounded up and locked up in the detention centre for summary execution.

That night Max spoke to Paul, asking if he might put him on special duties to avoid supervising the execution of the villagers. Paul arranged for Max to lead up a squad to sift out an enclave of local partisans suspected of operating from an area nearby. The attempt to get Max off the hook failed. Wolfe held a higher rank than Paul's, and he denied the request with a condescending smirk on his face. Their short exchange even unhinged Paul.

Max became anxious about the gloomy task ahead. He wondered how he would ever be able to live with himself in the event he actually survived the war. That evening he talked to Paul about it. Surprisingly, Paul too was fed up with the casual murders of innocent women and children. They both slated Wolfe for being the crazed psychopath he was.

The night ended with an agreement to rescue the youngest child of the group and smuggle her away to safety. The civilians were locked away in the detention centre – a former administrative block recently converted to perform its special function for Einsatzgruppe.

Paul was familiar with the building, and he drew up a sketch on a piece of paper. It had a reception area and several rooms used for interrogation. A converted canteen acted as a communal lock-up. A kitchen was next to the canteen area, and a serving hatch had been built into the wall separating the two areas.

The plan was for Paul to access the detention centre in the very early hours of the morning, when there would be only one sleepy guard on duty in the reception area. His reason given for the visit would be to question the hostages. Once inside the lock-up he would need to convince the mother of the child quickly that he was the child's only chance of survival. Much risk was involved. Paul would need to lift the tiny child through the serving hatch into the kitchen, walk back around to the kitchen, giving the impression he was going to make some tea, then lower her through the rubbish chute, where Max would be waiting outside to take up the next stage of the rescue. Under cover of the thickets and bushes, he was to carry her to a motorbike parked close by and then transport her to the safety of a village several kilometres away.

To pull the rescue off, Paul had to consider ways of concealing his identity. He currently sported a moustache – an addition he'd grown during the preparation period for the forthcoming summer offensive; he would shave it off once the deed was done. He chose to wear one of his former uniforms, to conceal his true rank, then, to enhance the deception, he sewed the Totenkopf insignia over the familiar 'shield and key' motif of Leibstandarte. Finally, he would wear sunglasses. In the event the midsummer morning was wet or fresh, he'd throw an oilskin over his shoulder.

They awoke very early the next morning to an overcast day. Paul hoped the guard at reception would still be drowsy and would fail to take in what was going on. He strode into the building and explained to the guard that he was there to question the civilians confined in the canteen area. The guard passed him the key.

Having achieved his first objective without arousing suspicion, he walked along the corridor, unlocked the door and entered the holding area. Most of those confined were still in slumber; those awake eyed Paul fearfully. He closed the door and searched for the young child. He walked across to a young mother cuddling her child and gestured for her to be quiet. He took her by the hand and spoke to her in Russian, explaining that he was there to take her child to a safe place. He told her she should trust him, but there was no time for further explanation. She could either agree to his offer or let her child remain and be hanged along with the rest of the party. She looked into his eyes for a few moments and instinctively knew Paul was a man of his word. She sensed his compassion as he gently held her hand in his.

She whispered to the young child that Paul was a good man, and she should go with him; he would take her to a place of safety. Ilyana listened to her mother intently and nodded her agreement.

"*Da, Mama,*" she replied.

The mother looked back at Paul. "Her name is Ilyana and she is just six years old."

Ilyana took Paul's hand. He gently picked her up and carried her over to the serving hatch, but the hatch had recently had a new padlock affixed.

He thought about the glitch in his plan, put her down and placed his finger to his lips as a sign for her to keep quiet.

Then he quietly opened the door and checked out the passage. The guard was out of sight, so he quickly picked up Ilyana and carried her around into the kitchen. He lowered her through the rubbish chute, telling her that Max would be on the outside waiting for her.

Outside, Max had pushed away the rubbish container and was waiting to receive young Ilyana. He lowered her gently to the ground and pushed the bin back into place. Then he wrapped her in an oilskin coat and swiftly carried her through the bushes to the dirt road where his motorbike was parked. On their way through the bushes Ilyana couldn't keep her eyes off him. Max looked at her with his big bear eyes and smiled. She smiled back.

The rescue operation was going well. Back inside the detention centre, the Baron had made himself a cup of tea, returned to the canteen area and spent several more minutes chatting before leaving. He locked up, handed the keys back to the reception guard and left the building. The dank early morning gave him the excuse to don the oilskin. Lady Luck had played her part, and for the anxious journey back he buttoned up his oilskin to conceal the deceptive rank and regiment in the event he bumped into someone that knew him.

Meanwhile, Max had concealed Ilyana in the sidecar, covering her with the oilskin. He wore his summer overgarment. He started the motorbike, adjusted his goggles and proceeded in a southerly direction to a village several kilometres down the road.

He arrived at the village and met up with and spoke to the villagers there. Max's command of the Russian language didn't match the standard of Paul's, but it was enough to get by. He asked them to look after little Ilyana as one of their own, and they agreed.

Max plucked little Ilyana out of the sidecar and, with outstretched arms, held her high in the air and smiled up at her. He gently lowered her to the ground and knelt down so that he could tenderly kiss her on the cheek. She looked up at him, put her little arms around his neck, then affectionately pressed her cheek against his. Max melted to her soft gentle touch. A villager touched his head kindly as if she knew his pain. After a few moments he regained his composure, saluted the villagers and walked back to the motorbike.

Ilyana smiled and waved goodbye as he reeled the bike around and sped off down the road. He too returned to the bunker safely without incident.

The following day Max was due to supervise the executions, but relief came in the form of an emergency. Partisans had blown up a rail depot just five miles from the encampment. Panzermeyer ordered Paul's 4th Company to conduct a search-and-kill operation. The order, given by a Leibstandarte senior officer, overrode Wolfe's. Max was delighted and Wolfe was furious.

During the operation, the company eventually caught up with the partisan group, who were skirmishing with regulars not far from the rail depot. Those that hadn't been killed in the skirmish were rounded up and summarily executed.

Meanwhile, the hangings were carried out by Wolfe's own officers.

The route back to their bunkers took the company along the road that passed the detention centre. The scene outside was grim. As they passed by, most of the troopers fell silent at the sight of the final batch of women and children still hanging there. It was a dark and sombre scene. There was one compensation: little Ilyana hadn't been one of them.

When the pair reached their bunker they congratulated each other for the rescue of the child. They toasted to their success in the usual fashion with a slug of the Baron's Napoleon brandy.

The bunker with its straw roof had become their sanctuary – their retreat from a bitter world outside. Within it, they shared their feelings and thoughts and expressed their opinions. Truth, or at least their truth, charged the bunker with a special light. Dark and damp as it was, it was an oasis bringing forth solace to a bleak, hopeless situation.

34

GRASS AND SAND

Saving young Ilyana from the gallows set the destinies for the Baron and Max. Wolfe had received a report that the number of villagers executed was one fewer than the number of prisoners on the original list. This had been passed over as an error in the paperwork, but Wolfe, forever suspicious, wouldn't let it drop. He instructed his men to dig a little deeper and recheck the documentation. The senior administration officer came back later that day to confirm that the youngest of the group, a six-year-old girl named Ilyana, had gone missing.

That evening Wolfe sat brooding over the missing child. His suspicions ran wild and for no apparent reason kept coming up with an image of Max. That evening he called Bauer into his office.

"Obersturmführer, find out where that irritant Rieker is quartered, can you?"

"That's easy, Sturmbannführer, he's sharing a bunker with Hauptsturmführer Paul von Wittenburg along the main road not too far from here," Bauer told him.

"Thank you, Obersturmführer. Wittenburg, eh?" He rubbed his chin in deep thought.

Wolfe recollected that he'd met Paul in the officers' mess on several occasions and hadn't liked him much. His suspicions were fuelled when he recollected that Paul had visited him earlier in an attempt to get Max off the hook for supervising the hangings.

He decided to pay them a visit. His plan was to turn up at

their bunker very early in the morning to test their reactions. To create a greater air of authenticity he arranged for a massive Totenkopf guard to accompany him.

Early next morning Wolfe walked along to the bunker accompanied by the guard and rapped on the door. Paul opened the door. Wolfe's ploy had worked. The Baron, caught off guard, was visibly startled as Wolfe glared at him with the huge guard standing behind him. They stared at each other for a few moments too many. It was a giveaway.

Paul came to his senses and broke the silence. "Morning, Sturmbannführer. Can I do something for you?" he asked casually, but far too late.

Wolfe silently gloated. Paul's initial surprise had said it all.

"No, I just dropped by to congratulate you and Rieker on receiving your awards for bravery," he said, lying through his teeth.

"Thank you, Sturmbannführer," said Paul, acting surprised.

Wolfe continued: "Yes, we need you honourable, brave types, don't we?"

"Not sure what you mean, Sturmbannführer," said Paul.

"Well, it wouldn't be right if all SS officers were murdering bastards, eh?"

"We leave the murdering to your Einsatzkommandos, Sturmbannführer," replied Paul. "The Waffen-SS gets on with the job of winning this war for Germany."

Wolfe was a little surprised at Paul's directness. Paul realised he'd been back-footed and, thinking on his feet, had opted for an aggressive riposte.

Just then Max came to the door. Having overheard the conversation, he casually wished Wolfe good morning. Wolfe ignored the greeting. His face began to contort and twitch with repressed anger and suspicion.

"One of my hostages went missing from the detention centre last week; she appears to have been spirited away before she got to the gallows – the youngest one, a small child named Ilyana.

Know anything about that, do you?" He left the question hovering in the air, waiting for a reaction.

Paul spoke: "Sounds odd, Sturmbannführer, but surely there must have been an administrative error?"

Max added: "Can't say I remember the small child in the wagon during the conversation with your lieutenant that morning, Sturmbannführer."

Wolfe responded to Paul's comment: "There was no mistake, Hauptsturmführer. We believe she was smuggled out of the detention centre." His eyes flicked from one to the other.

Both settled for quizzical looks, trying to cover up any signs that might suggest they had knowledge of the matter.

Wolfe broke the pregnant silence: "I'm conducting an investigation into the matter. If I catch the guilty party, or *parties*," he emphasised, looking up at Max, "and I surely will, I will have him, or them, shot for treason. I won't stop until I have got to the bottom of it."

"I'll make a few enquiries myself, then, Sturmbannführer," said Paul.

Wolfe snarled and said, "Treacherous scum! I believe it to be one or two of our own. Mark my words, they will be shot for their actions; it is an affront to the Reich."

He looked at them with a malicious grin. His smirk suggested that it was just a matter of time before he gathered the evidence to charge them.

As he left, they closed the door and looked at each other in horror. They knew Wolfe would be determined to compile evidence to prove their guilt. Paul's mind raced as he backtracked over his movements that morning. The guard at reception hadn't actually taken much notice of him at the time, but interrogation by Wolfe, under pressure, would most certainly smarten up his memory. Besides, Paul's visit, so early in the morning, was out of the ordinary, and, despite the guard's sleepiness, the incident wouldn't escape his recollection.

They were anxious all day. That evening they sat in the dim

candlelit bunker just looking at each other wondering what to do.

"How the hell are we going to get out of this one?" said Max.

Paul, the more vulnerable of the two, replied, "We simply have to eliminate Wolfe; his perseverence might uncover something we've overlooked, alternatively he might fabricate some evidence and pin it on us anyway."

Max stared back, his face ashen through the stress of the situation. Unlike the bravery they both demonstrated in the field, the adrenalin in this situation was working in reverse: fear not fight. The silence lingered as they both got lost in their thoughts.

Paul spoke again: "We have to do this, Max, or they will shoot us. Look at it this way: Wolfe is a despicable bastard. Nobody likes his attitude and arrogance and all his subordinates hate him."

Wolfe's obnoxious behaviour made him unpopular, even within the SS. This was an advantage, insofar as the majority would probably not be too unhappy about his demise. However, his seniors in Allgemeine tolerated him because he was thorough in his work and kept them amused off duty with his inexhaustible supply of sick jokes about Poles, Russians and Jews.

Despite the grave repercussions if they were caught, they could hardly be in a worse predicament than they were already in. They agreed to kill Wolfe rather than waiting until he had them shot. They quickly came up with a plan to carry out the deed.

They discussed his weaknesses. Two things he loved about the Russian Ukraine were its vodka, which he drank by the bottle in a single session, and its women. Bauer routinely arranged for one, two or even three women at a time to meet up with Wolfe at a city apartment set aside for senior staff (major and above) in order for him to satisfy his rampant sexual appetite.

Unlike Max, Paul was privy to officer gossip. He recollected a conversation with Bauer several weeks back. It was Bauer who'd told Paul about Wolfe's sexual deviances and his use of the apartment in town. Bauer said his job was to drop Wolfe off at the apartment and pick him up later the same evening.

Despite his junior ranking, through his connections Paul had managed to obtain the address of the downtown apartment. It was here they hoped to find an opportunity to eliminate Wolfe and Bauer together. The killings would be made to look like assassinations carried out by local partisans.

"All we need do is to verify when Wolfe will be making his next visit, wait for Bauer's return to the apartment to collect him and, under cover of darkness, nail the pair while Bauer is accompanying Wolfe down the stairwell," said Paul.

The plan was to perform silent kills using knives or a heavy instrument for bludgeoning purposes. Gunfire would arouse the attention of people living nearby or, indeed, Germans patrolling the area. Paul was hoping the killings would divert attention from any investigation set up connected with missing Ilyana.

Their final step would be to create an alibi. Max had a good chance of persuading fellow NCOs to support a false alibi; Paul, on the other hand, would be unable to count on his fellow officers. It would be difficult for him to provide a watertight alibi, particularly if the consequential investigation widened to link the murder with the rescue of young Ilyana from the detention centre.

The following morning Paul sought out Bauer, intending to strike up a casual conversation with him in an effort to ascertain Wolfe's next night out in town.

"When is the town apartment next available?" asked Paul in an effort to deceive Bauer into thinking that he wanted to use it himself.

Bauer reminded Paul that the apartment was for the use of senior staff only.

"I have connections," replied Paul.

"OK," said Bauer, "but you won't be able to use it tonight. Wolfe has it booked, unless you want to use it after midnight. That's my pickup time."

Paul declined the midnight offer. By the end of the short exchange he'd gleaned all he needed to know.

Meanwhile, Max set about creating his alibi. He was due to lead up a squad for patrol duties that night. The idea was that Fritz would take his patrol in lieu. Fritz would persuade the most loyal men in the squad to swear it was Max who led that night, not him. It wouldn't be difficult to do this as the leading NCOs were loved by their subordinates.

As it was proving difficult to provide a sound alibi for the Baron, they decided to claim that he too was out on patrol that night with Max's squad. Unfortunately for the Baron, it wasn't necessary for commissioned officers to participate in patrol duties. But, as thin as it was, it was at least a fallback; the men in the squad would support his presence there. Max outlined the situation to Fritz, who willingly agreed to arrange the deception.

All was set.

Evening came around painfully slowly that day. They made their way over to the Kharkov apartment on Max's motorbike. Like owls of the night they waited in silence for their prey. Just before 2100 hours Bauer's truck arrived. The street was a short one and they could observe him from their cover in an alleyway close by.

The truck turned into the street and came to a halt just a block away. Bauer didn't leave his driver's seat. Wolfe got out and nimbly slipped across the road into the entrance of a five-storey apartment block. Bauer drove away almost immediately.

Several minutes later they witnessed the arrival of three very young local girls; then they waited for full darkness before setting out. By this time Wolfe was drinking heavily while enjoying the first part of his orgy. They made their way over to the apartment block and slipped inside without being noticed.

They climbed several flights of stairs and settled for the half-landing overlooking the apartment door. There, they would wait in the dark until Bauer's return.

At around 2300 hours, one of the girls left the apartment, apparently in a huff. Wolfe had upset her. As the door opened they could hear Wolfe shouting some drunken obscenities at her.

She slammed the door shut, but it bounced back open and remained ajar. They couldn't believe their luck. It was an ideal opportunity to act immediately. They would forfeit the killing of Bauer. Pulling black balaclavas over their heads they rushed down the short flight of steps and passed through the door towards the source of the commotion.

As they entered the room where Wolfe lay, he looked up and gasped in surprise. He swung around and stretched for the Luger lying on the table beside the bed. The two girls, who had just resumed their lesbian act in front of him, screamed with shock. As Wolfe lunged for his pistol, Paul pounced and cracked him over the head with a piece of lead tubing. Wolfe collapsed short of his target, stunned and bleeding from his head wound. The Baron hit him again, knocking him unconscious.

Meanwhile, Max was busy hushing the paranoid youngsters. Speaking to them in Russian, he quietened them down. Then he pulled his knife out, refocused his attention and finished off Wolfe with a thrust into his throat. The deed had been achieved in seconds. In an attempt to make the incident seem more authentic the Baron, assuming the role of a partisan, cursed Wolfe, calling him 'German scum'. As they left the apartment the Baron commanded the women to leave and keep silent about the incident. He and Max hoped their deception had fooled the two girls into thinking the assailants had been Russian partisans who had got wind of Wolfe's regular sex parties and were hiding in wait to kill him.

They quickly left the apartment, slipped into the cover of darkness outside, and made their way over to the alleyway where the motorbike was parked. They sped away back to the safety of their bunker.

Despite Wolfe's merciless nature, his murder was unbecoming and distasteful for a pair who took pride in the notion of loyalty and honour. They were totally unprepared for the impression it would leave on their minds. They were unable to control their racing thoughts on the drive back to camp.

It soon became apparent that murdering someone was a

personal act and did not equate with the impersonal act of killing an enemy in the field.

They settled in and Paul poured out two shots of brandy.

He was the first to break the silence: "It's done," he said with a sigh of relief.

"Oh, how I wish we were going to the front line tomorrow," Max responded.

Max recapped his alibi; it was robust. His squad had been out on patrol that evening and Fritz had stood in for him. Fritz ensured that all the men in his platoon would verify that Max took the patrol, not him, thereby ruling him out as a suspect.

On the other hand, Paul didn't have a strong alibi. Commissioned officers weren't needed to lead patrols. Volunteering to go out with Max that night was weak and suspicious; nevertheless they couldn't think of any alternative. The risk had been worth it. They were in a better position now than before Wolfe's death. Wolfe would undoubtedly have had them shot as soon as he had gathered enough evidence to prove they had spirited young Ilyana away.

The actual killing had been pulled off cleanly, without complications. On the surface it looked as though it had been perpetrated by Russian partisans. Further, they had made it back to camp without being noticed or arousing suspicions. All appeared well.

One question remained: was it a mistake not killing Bauer? Their decision to take advantage of the open entrance door had resulted in one less killing – one less murderous deed to sit on their consciences. They hoped their fluency in Russian had been enough to convince the young girls they were two Russian partisans.

A week passed and a replacement for Wolfe was flown in from Berlin. His first assignment would be to lead the inquiry into Wolfe's assassination.

Standartenführer Kurt Schumann was a tall, gangling, big-boned individual, one of the original SS old guard. The contrast between Wolfe and Schumann was vast. Wolfe was ex-Gestapo, seconded into Einsatzgruppe because of his administrative expertise. Schumann was one of the original 'praetorian guard' personally picked by Sepp Dietrich in the early thirties. Schumann hadn't been earmarked to take over Wolfe's job; he would remain on the Eastern Front and perform duties in a military capacity following closure of the inquiry.

Wolfe had been shorter and a little rotund, bald and ugly. Schumann sported an ebony mane of hair and was extremely handsome – a woman's man, but not the perverted type, like Wolfe. Wolfe had been paranoid about Jews, forever searching for victims for the gallows. Schumann took the moderate line, as did Sepp Dietrich, focusing attention on military objectives on the Eastern Front, not the incarceration of Jews.

All the way down to humour, the men differed. Wolfe was malicious with a macabre fascination for sick jokes, whereas Schumann had a fine sense of humour and a rare easy-going attitude that was extraordinary among senior ranks. His relaxed manner didn't affect his deep loyalty or his sense of duty, though. For this reason, Max and Paul knew he'd be zealous in the inquiry he was about to conduct in an effort to catch the killers of Wolfe. In happier times, they would have been very comfortable serving under someone like Schumann in the field.

Schumann was thirty-eight years of age and had obviously kept fit in his younger days. He had been a lover of winter sports – a keen skier in peacetime. Evidently this assignment was his first on the Eastern Front. Whether the harshness would colour his attitude remained to be seen. Upon closure of the inquiry, his main duty would be to coordinate all logistical issues connected with the forthcoming summer offensive aimed at the Kursk Salient.

Through Bauer's efforts, the three young girls were located and questioned. At the interrogation, one girl mentioned that the assassins spoke in the Russian language, but she felt they weren't

Russian. Schumann leant back in his chair and felt uncomfortable with this comment. Something wasn't adding up and he remained unconvinced that partisans were responsible.

Suspicion made him focus attention on the murder victim, Wolfe. The inquiry revealed that Wolfe was a very unpopular leader. His violent tantrums and vicious admonishments had gained him the disrespect of his subordinates, while his seniors tolerated him. After several days, Schumann built up a profile that gave him an insight into Wolfe's character and reputation. Because of Wolfe's unpopularity Schumann had to consider the possibility that someone from the same side had performed the deed.

Wolfe did have a few loyal followers, though, such as Bauer (his adjutant), his chief administration officer and a handful of others. It was here Schumann would start his questioning in an effort to compile a shortlist of suspects in the unlikely event that the murder had not been committed by partisans.

Schumann got his breakthrough following the routine questioning of Bauer. During a relaxed questioning session, Schumann asked Bauer if Wolfe had mentioned anyone who'd upset him recently. Bauer recollected Wolfe's irritation when he'd discovered a child, Ilyana, had gone missing from the detention centre. Bauer recalled Wolfe airing his suspicions following his visit to Hauptsturmführer Paul von Wittenburg and his NCO Rieker. Bauer recalled Wolfe saying that, despite both having received medals for bravery in combat, they were, in his mind, traitors to the Fatherland and deserved to be shot if he could prove they had spirited the child away.

Schumann had stumbled upon a motive and two suspects. The next step would be to gather evidence that implicated them. Further evidence came, circumstantial as it was, when Schumann asked whether they were aware of Wolfe's schedule at the Kharkov apartment. Sure enough, Wittenburg's name came up again. Suddenly the Baron became the prime suspect.

Schumann's final question for Bauer, as he was leaving the

interview room, was "Oh, by the way, Bauer, does Wittenburg speak Russian?"

"Yes, evidently he's quite fluent at it," replied Bauer.

All that was left was to bring Paul in for questioning, and, if his alibi wasn't sound, to get him to confess under pressure.

The outcome was inevitable. Attaining a confession from Paul wasn't difficult; he'd already become tired and nervous during the inquiry, and he was on the verge of giving himself up. Murder had not been a part of his ambitions for the military. Only minutes into the interrogation the Baron duly admitted to his crime. Schumann was relieved he had caught the murderer, but he was deeply disappointed that the perpetrator had turned out to be such a fine German officer with a historical lineage and that he was a recent winner of the coveted Knight's Cross.

Schumann had no alternative other than to summarily sentence Paul to be executed. He was to be shot by a firing squad the following morning. As to his accomplice, Paul revealed that his assistant was an NCO recently killed in partisan action. Schumann knew he was lying, but he could not prove that the Baron's statement was false. Further, under questioning, Max's alibi held strong and saved him from a similar fate.

Paul was marched away under guard and locked up in the detention centre from which he had rescued young Ilyana.

Schumann's last attempt to force Max into admitting his guilt as the accomplice was to order him to head the execution squad to carry out the sentence; he was to prepare a six-man firing squad.

Max broke the news to one of his subordinates and instructed him to arrange for the entire company to meet at headquarters and bring their tin field mugs with them.

He walked back to the bunker in a trance and slumped into his bunk in disbelief. That he would never see his beloved comrade again was beyond belief. After all the campaigning, hazards and adventures they'd been through together over the years, Paul was to be executed by his own men for ridding the world of a piece of excreta.

After several hours he collected his thoughts and sorted out an old cardboard box. He took the last bottle of the Baron's brandy and two bottles of French wine from the bookshelf and placed them in the box, then set off for 4th Company HQ. The men had gathered to hear what Paul's fate was.

He entered the headquarters solemnly, placed the box on a table, sat down on the table in front of the men and stayed silent for some moments to centre himself. After the pause he stood up, as if he had come to a decision. The men moved in closer to hear what he had to say.

"Well, it's not good news, men. Earlier today I was instructed by Standartenführer Schumann to lead a firing squad to end the life of our comrade, our brother, our very own commander." He spoke in a monotone, holding his emotions back. "The Baron is accused of killing Wolfe, the commander of Einsatzgruppe, a malicious, obnoxious animal who spent most of his time hanging woman, old men and children. In my book the world is better off with Wolfe out of the way. He thoroughly deserved what he got. Wolfe wasn't a soldier; he was a psycho – a maniac who got carried away with his own indulgences and delusions of self-importance. He had civilians slaughtered because he could. He wielded his authority and power like a crazed demigod, because he could." Suddenly his emotions came to the surface: "I tell you now, I cannot, and will not, give the order to shoot our commanding officer. Whoever lines up with me in the squad tomorrow morning will not shoot our captain, no matter who gives the order, regardless of rank. For the benefit of those new replacements who don't know too much about the Baron, I'll elaborate. Paul is from a renowned military family. His grandfather's father fought in the Franco-Prussian Campaign of 1870. His military lineage goes back to the Napoleonic Wars and beyond. I've personally known him since 1938. Some of you have also known him since then, right, Fritz? Muller? It was the Baron who assigned us to his platoon as part of the original Berlin regiment before the war. The old guard has been through

410

many campaigns with him. He is a great, inspirational leader in the field, and he always leads by example. He needs no orders; his insight in battlefield situations is second to none. This man cares for the men under his command. He saved you, eh, Fritz?"

Fritz nodded his agreement.

"I and six of you will march out there tomorrow morning and will be expected to shoot a man we love – shoot down one of the Reich's finest warriors like a dog; he is to die in dishonour and shame, all because of the stupidity and ignorance of a worthless madman." His emotions came to a head: "We cannot, we will not, carry out this order. One thing they taught us in the Hitler Youth . . ." He was unable to conclude the sentence. He cleared his throat, regained composure and continued: "One thing they taught us was never to leave a comrade to die. You all know the penalty for insubordination. We should prepare for the worst tomorrow. I, for one, know in whose company I would prefer to die. We were deceived, *Kameraden*. Those behind desks, far from the killing plains of this godforsaken country, have given us and the entire nation a bad reputation, eh? Over the years we have become seasoned fighters. I, like you, have long realised that those up top are removed from what actually goes on here in the field. Loyalties change when the bullets and the stench of death are as close as your heartbeat. Our loyalties stand with one another now. We should maintain this loyalty for the Baron – not for those 'up there'. We were arrogant and foolish enough to believe that we could take on half the world and win, eh? We've punished the Russians and our Einsatzkommandos have killed their women and children; now the entire world hates us for it. A Russian partisan, not even a soldier, will hide and wait in 30° of frost all day if he thinks he has the remotest chance of shooting one German soldier. This is the intensity of hate we have aroused in Ivan. By our acts, we have made our enemy stronger. We've turned Ivan into a better fighting machine than we are. I personally don't have a capacity to hate innocent women and children."

411

He paused for a few seconds, to let his words sink in.

"All old guard who wish to form part of the squad step forward, but keep in mind the possible consequences, as I will not give the order to fire."

Fully aware of the consequences, Fritz, Muller and four remaining old guard stepped forward.

Max spoke: "Hans, step back, can you? You'll be all that's left to lead the company should we all meet our fate tomorrow. Step back, my friend."

Max asked if any of the replacements would make up the sixth slot. To his amazement they all stepped forward. He chose a new NCO from his own platoon.

He smiled: "We are in good, brave company, then. I have the last bottle of the Baron's finest Napoleon brandy and two bottles of his best red wine here. He once told me that, in the event he was killed on the battlefield, I should pass around the bottles to the men of his company and toast him."

They'd all brought their tin field mugs for the tribute. Max opened the bottles and passed one each to Muller and Fritz. He went around each man of his platoon charging the mugs with shots of brandy. Muller and Fritz followed suit with the wine bottles. Once the mugs were charged every man there raised his mug and bellowed the Baron's very own "*Hoch!*" Then they all stood there in silence.

Max broke the long silence: "Tomorrow morning at 0500 hours, then." He dismissed the men and walked back to his bunker.

The bunker was silent and melancholy that night; its light had been extinguished. No more light-hearted banter and deep and meaningful discussions would take place within its fragile walls. Staring into the darkness, Max begged for someone to free him from his nightmare. After several hours he managed to fall into an uneasy slumber.

He climbed out of his bunk before sunrise, washed, dressed himself in his battle smock and pinned on his medals. He made his way across to Company HQ, where Fritz had assembled the squad and was awaiting Max's arrival. Max smiled at his men, battle-hardened from the years of campaigning. They were ready. They began their march, and Max opened up with a well-known song they'd sung in the Hitler Youth. The thin line marched towards the sand-and-grass area next to the detention centre, where the hangings of the villagers had taken place earlier. Their song lit up the morning.

Max halted the squad. They stopped singing and stood in silence for several moments. He looked across at the Baron, now a bedraggled figure wearing a long grey coat.

"For . . . ward!" he snapped.

He led the unit across the path of Paul.

"Halt!"

They stopped about eight yards in front of him. Schumann stood off to the side with a full platoon of men. The platoon was there as a deterrent in the event Max had second thoughts about his task that morning.

Max looked across to where the Baron stood. Disbelief was etched into his face as he took in the madness of the scene. The Baron had his hands tied behind him, and he was leaning to one side with his head bowed. He looked up to acknowledge Max with his eyes.

Max saluted Paul, as did all the members of the firing squad. Paul acknowledged the salutes by shuffling his body and standing to attention; he'd refused to be blindfolded.

The sky was clear that morning and there was a slight breeze. A falcon soaring above caught Max's attention; it glided gracefully on the updraught.

Max pondered: 'A tribute to my friend,' he thought.

Schumann eyed Max suspiciously. Max looked across to Schumann, who waved his hand in casual 'let's get it over' style.

Max turned and stood motionless.

After several moments Schumann looked up, straightened his back, and gave a more determined order to carry out the execution.

413

"Carry on, Sturmscharführer!" he shouted.

Max remained motionless.

Realising Max had no intention of carrying out the order to shoot, Schumann bellowed a final warning: "Sturmscharführer, this is my final order. You will carry out the execution immediately or you and your entire squad will face charges of insubordination and the harshest penalties that go with it."

He instructed his platoon to raise their weapons ready to fire at Max and his firing squad.

Surprising Schumann, Max bellowed an order equally loud for his squad to face half right towards Schumann and his platoon. His six-man squad reeled around forty-five degrees; every second trooper fell to one knee. All aimed their rifles directly at Schumann.

Max called off his name: "Max Rieker, 4th Company, Reconnaissance Battalion, Leibstandarte-SS Adolf Hitler."

Fritz followed: "Fritz Kohler, 4th Company, Reconnaissance Battalion, Leibstandarte-SS Adolf Hitler."

All the other troopers in the squad followed suit.

Schumann's platoon was faced with a stand-off.

He shouted, "Are you ready, platoon? Aim!"

Just then, a firm voice pierced the air from the rear of where Schumann and his platoon were standing; it was Muller with volunteers from his platoon. In similar fashion to Max's squad, they were lined up with every second trooper down on one knee, sounding off their names, with rifles trained on Schumann's unit.

Astounded by 4th Company's reckless behaviour, Schumann reeled around aghast and stood there completely confounded as to what to do. The position had become an impasse.

All the while, Paul took in the scene before him. His face creased up as he smiled widely.

"That's my boys!" He spoke softly to himself.

He saluted Max and the others with a nod of his head; a semblance of dignity reappeared on his face.

Schumann stood there enraged at the insolence of the three

platoon NCOs. He took out his Luger, stomped across the ground to where Paul stood, lifted the Luger and shot him in the head.

The shot echoed into the early dawn, and then everything became silent. Max could hear the breeze in the trees on the far side of the sand-and-grass area. The falcon reappeared in the sky. It hovered over the dead body of Paul for a moment, and then took flight in a westerly direction.

Max's glance followed the flight of the falcon. The spirit of the Baron was being carried off.

'He's going home,' Max thought.

Schumann exasperated retorted: "There! It's all over now." Then he barked out an order for Max's arrest: "Hauptscharführer [Fritz], arrest this man for insubordination?"

Fritz never moved.

Max realised Fritz was waiting to take things a step further, as he always did. He was apparently not intimidated by the senior-ranking officer.

Max spoke to Fritz: "It's all over, Fritz. Go ahead with the Standartenführer's order."

Fritz stood motionless, ignoring Max's command.

Max walked across to Fritz and in a soft voice said, "Fritz, we did our job, comrade. It's all over now. Carry out the order."

Fritz slowly came to his senses and ordered an armed guard from the firing squad to escort Max to the detention centre.

The wind came up as they left the sand-and-grass area.

Max glanced back across to where the body of Paul was lying and whispered a final farewell: "I'll see you soon, my friend."

Schumann had arranged for Max to lead the firing squad in order to induce a reaction. He had strongly suspected he was the second man involved in the murder of Wolfe, not the NCO killed in action as Paul had alleged during his interrogation. But Max's alibi had been strong, and he could not find any evidence against him. Despite this, Schumann had fulfilled his objective indirectly by compelling Max to commit an act of insubordination. However, he was aware of Max and Paul's exemplary records and was extremely upset at the thought of losing two of his finest men at a time when they were needed the most.

Max was held in the detention centre until late that afternoon, when he was taken to Schumann's office for summary sentencing. Thoughts that he might be executed the following morning filled his mind.

As he entered the office, to his surprise, Schumann ordered the armed guards to leave. Schumann instinctively knew Max would not cause any problems now that the episode was over. Max snapped out a smart salute and stood to attention.

"The end of an era, Rieker!" said Schumann. "I have just read your personal file: 'Max Rieker, connections with Leibstandarte since 1934.' That's almost longer than me. 'Boxing Gold Medal winner for the Hitler Youth, 1936; contender for the Olympic boxing team, 1936' – and a winner of two Iron Crosses."

Schumann then proceeded to slam his fist on the desk in anger

"This is a waste!" he exclaimed. "Such a waste! Two fine careers blown away in a day, not even at the hands of the enemy! We could have used your field experience in this forthcoming offensive, but instead you chose to foul up and waste it. Such a pity, such a pity!"

Schumann regained his composure.

"I have strong reason to believe that you assisted Wittenburg in the murder of Sturmbannführer Wolfe. However, I cannot prove it – I have no evidence. The men of your squad say that you were leading them on a patrol on the evening of the murder. As for your insubordination this morning, you should be shot; but because of your past loyalty and fine military record I cannot do this. I have decided to send you to Majdanek concentration camp in occupied Poland for punishment duties. There you will be stripped of your rank and taught to obey orders again. Six months will give you time to contemplate your mistakes, and maybe by then you can return to the front and help us finish off this godforsaken conflict. You will be sent to the camp at Majdanek to carry out day-to-day duties alongside SS and Ukrainian guards. Believe me, you will wish that you had never been sent there. You'll soon want to return to active duty. But first you must relearn to obey orders."

Max asked Schumann if he could speak his mind. Schumann agreed that he could go ahead.

"Wolfe was a murderer of non-combatants, Standartenführer," Max said in a soft voice. "This isn't what we were taught in the Hitler Youth or at the NCO academy. There is no honour in the senseless slaughter of innocent women and children."

Schumann interjected: "We must obey orders, Rieker. Loyalty and discipline will win this war."

"I beg to differ, Standartenführer," said Max. "Discipline and loyalty isn't enough. In a closely fought contest like this one it will be the side with the strongest passion and willpower that will win. Agreed, Germany hates communism, but Ivan hates us more. We've taken our eye off the ball, so to speak. We have wasted our energies by killing old men, women and children. Our actions have created a strong, common hatred throughout the entire populace of all our enemies. The Soviets are centred in their fight against us. The Red Army grows stronger every day; they have countless tanks and partisans are everywhere. The party used us. It will go on to use others until there are no reserves to draw upon. It is hardly a regime that one would want to die for. Don't get me wrong: I would die for my country. I want so much for Germany to win this war, but my loyalties have changed. I prefer to be loyal to my comrades and field commanders who look death in the face every day at the sharp end of the wedge. Those murderers of the ilk of Wolfe have destroyed the concept of honour, nobility and loyalty – and, indeed, the dream of a superior, pure race. I realise that, as part of the juggernaut I have signed up for, I am now compelled to share its downhill journey to inevitable ruin.

417

Having made my bed, I will have to lie in it."

"You are a philosopher too, Rieker?" Schumann responded quizzically.

"I have my beliefs, Standartenführer – beliefs that do not align with our doctrine any more, although at one time I thought they did. Two years of campaigning here, two years of butchery and senseless slaughter, have taught me different. You should shoot me right now, Standartenführer. My enthusiasm for fighting for the Fatherland has waned now that my comrade and commanding officer, Paul von Wittenburg, lies dead."

Schumann interrupted, saying that he had made his decision and would not alter his mind on the matter. He dismissed Max.

As Max reeled around to leave, Schumann confirmed that platoon sergeants Kohler and Muller would be joining him. Max's heart sank – Fritz and Muller would meet the same fate as he would. Schumann had been right in his opening address: this really was the end of an era.

The summary verdict was quick and clinical. A small team of senior officers deliberated on the firing-squad incident and the three NCOs were stripped of their ranks and sentenced to the Majdanek concentration camp for six months. There they would learn to take orders again. Once their sentence had been served they would be returned to the Russian Front and reinstated with their original rankings.

Max knew that working under the Allgemeine-SS units at the Majdanek camp would be horrific. The thought of escape had already entered his head. He hated with a vengeance the special squads that ran the detention centres and concentration camps. Thoughts of his previous experience at Dachau filled his head and no doubt filled Fritz's head too.

On his way from the summary court hearing he stole a chance to try to persuade the other two to make a break once they got to the camp, but his plea fell on deaf ears. Both Muller and Fritz were in favour of serving the time and getting back to the front. He gave a sigh of frustration. If he were to make an escape, it would need to be performed alone.

They spent the night in Wolfe's makeshift detention centre. In the morning they were ordered to pack and prepare themselves for the journey to Majdanek, Poland.

They were ushered into a covered truck. All three were denied requests to say farewell to their platoons. Their disappointment turned into joy as they left the compound. About 100 metres from the entrance the entire 4th Company lined the road, saluting their final farewells. It was an honourable farewell and the last feeling of comradeship the NCOs would ever experience again, save their own priceless bond.

The truck took them to an airstrip north-west of Kharkov. They stepped up into a Junkers JU 34 aeroplane destined for the Polish camp.

The plane journey was long, and every now and again the plane would stop off for refuelling. They sat through the entire journey in complete silence. Each was lost in his own thoughts; the romance that the military had provided them with during all these years was gone for ever.

Max focused on what they might be up for at the concentration camp. They could be involved with trivial labour duties assigned to the SS work gangs, or more despicable duties such as torturing and beating inmates.

After many hours in the air, the Junkers lurched to the side, signifying that it was about to land. It cut through the heavy cloud cover, revealing countryside and a township up ahead.

Majdanek concentration camp had been established in October 1941 as an Allgemeine-SS-run prisoner-of-war camp, under the command of Karl Otto Koch. A little later, Koch was arrested for forgery, embezzlement and exploitation of camp workers. He was sent to Buchenwald to serve his sentence and was executed in April 1945.

The current commander was Hermann Florstedt, who had taken over in October 1942. The camp also provided forced labour for munitions works and the Steyr-Daimler-Puch weapons factory. Also, in October 1942, several female SS troopers arrived at Majdanek from Ravensbruck camp in Germany, where they had been trained. These women included Elsa Erich, Hermine Braunsteiner, Hildegard Lachert and Rosy Suess. All these female overseers were infamous for their sadistic treatment of inmates.

In the early years many Jews had been sent to concentration camps in Germany, from 1942, most Jews were deported to the six new concentration/labour camps in Poland: Auschwitz-Birkenhau, Belzec, Chelmno, Majdanek, Sobibor and Treblinka..

In all his wildest imaginings, Max could never have believed that he would end up working at one of them.

35

GOD'S COMPASSION

Anyone who has convinced himself God doesn't exist is wrong. Anyone who believes God to be vengeful and wrathful is misguided.

God looks over mankind's theatrical stage plays disinterestedly, but paradoxically It knows when Its smallest sparrow falls.

Behind the backdrop of the concentration and labour camps, where prejudice, malice, hate, fear and despair reign supreme, the grace of God awaits those unfortunates; for God in Its simplicity is Love, and death is but God's compassion.

They landed at an airfield several kilometres from the camp. The unit garrisoned there was a unit of the Allgemeine-SS. The camp guards would be similar to those types Max and Fritz had worked with at Dachau in 1936. They weren't nice, and the thought of having to work with these ruthless camp-bound thugs renewed old grievances. As for Muller, he was about to experience a first.

All was quiet in the early hours of the day as they climbed down from the plane. They stretched their legs and bodies to greet a dismal day that reflected their mood. After a few minutes a covered truck wheeled into the airfield and they were ushered into the back.

The truck drove in an easterly direction towards the camp. In just a few minutes it was travelling the road leading up to what was to be their home for the next six months.

Max and Fritz were well acquainted with the goings-on in concentration camps; Muller wasn't. At Dachau they had encountered Eicke's concentration-camp system when Max had considered that evil couldn't possibly get any lower. He was wrong. Majdanek represented the basement level of evil.

'We're right here at rock-bottom,' he thought.

As they approached the camp a pungent stench filled the air.

'So this is the smell of fear and death!'

He coughed to clear the foul air stuck in his throat. The tragic scene unfolding there before him did not come as a shock, though. He entered the camp as if it had been awaiting him. The vile scene in the material world greeted Max's emotional and mental states like it had been waiting there for him. Just like the inmates, he felt sick and fearful, lost in a sea of hopelessness.

As they walked towards the reception area, each was in a world of his own. For Max, pictures of his life drifted across the screen of his mind: happier days spent in the Hitler Youth; Paris; the smiling visage of the Baron; and a multitude of other pleasant images. The situation he was grappling with now wasn't God's fault; in his ambition and verve for life he hadn't stopped to consider the consequences of his choices. Vanity had driven him to make some wild decisions, waiving accountability for the outcome – an outcome that was right here in Majdanek. He snapped back to the moment.

"This truly is hell," he said aloud. The camp was a Hades on earth, as were all the other concentration camps. Max accepted that he'd made the journey there under his own volition, with no one but himself to blame. The camp squads and Ukrainian guards who ran Majdanek were the rulers of this little section of hell; here they prevailed.

As the luckless three neared the administration block they

could see three Allgemeine-SS officials awaiting them: the commandant, Hermann Florstedt, his adjutant and a bulky, savage-looking individual, nervously and impatiently standing to attention alongside them.

The demoted NCOs saluted the officers in Nazi style – "*Heil Hitler!*" – then introduced themselves and handed their papers to Florstedt's adjutant. Florstedt scrutinised each of them.

"Welcome, my naughty little insubordinates. You have been sentenced and will be detained here at Majdanek to serve six months of disciplinary duties. At the end of your sentence you will return to the Eastern Front and be reinstated with your previous ranks. If, during the six months, you are insubordinate, you will be shot. If you attempt to escape, you will be shot. You will work six months without recreation periods and there will be no privileges. I'll hand you over to Sturmscharführer Beicher, who will provide you with a brief induction. You will be under the charge of my Sturmscharführer."

He gestured toward the gross individual standing next to them, and Beicher smirked as his name was mentioned.

Florstedt finished up: "He will keep a sharp eye on you. That's all for now."

Florstedt and his adjutant left Beicher to brief them.

A sullen, depressed and unhealthy Max glanced up at Beicher. As their eyes met he felt a wave of fear shoot through his entire being. The obnoxious NCO looked familiar to him. He scanned his memory banks.

Suddenly an image popped into his mind. Max recognised Beicher as the same vile slob he'd almost bludgeoned to death some four years earlier in Poland. He was the Fleischer. Max couldn't believe his eyes and his bad luck. He silently prayed that Beicher would not recognise him, knowing that if he did, death would be awaiting him not too far down the road.

As the Commandant and his adjutant walked off, Beicher spat out the words "Welcome to hell, you disobedient gutter dogs!"

He keenly scanned all three unfortunates. When it came to Max, his expression changed into a quizzical stare. Max kept his focus to the front, avoiding eye contact. Alas for Max! the comparison with hell hadn't been an exaggeration: the individual standing in front of him was about to recognise him!

Beicher came nearer to Max to scrutinise him more closely. Max could smell his foul breath. His heart sank as their eyes met. Yes, it was indeed the very same Beicher that Max had almost battered to death. This time the boot was well and truly on the other foot.

Beicher, the Fleischer, gazed hard into Max's eyes and calmly said, "Well, well, well! We meet again, soldier." Following a pregnant silence, he said quietly, "You will die here, soldier. You will die like a dog, just like one of the common inmates." Then he scrutinised the other two. His memory came flooding back. "And one of your seconds accompanies you [referring to Fritz]. This is all just too good to be true." He gloated in delight, slapping his hand hard on his thick thigh. "God has indeed been kind to me today. I will personally see that none of you survives your stay here. You will die in this corner of hell, just like the rest of the scum that are sent here. You'll wish you had never been born. The Leibstandarte babies – only good for shiny boots and performing circus stunts on the parade ground! Homos, no doubt! Bet you shag each other every night. We should sew the pink triangle on each of you."

"I believe the division has proved itself to be one of the finest fighting detachments on the Eastern Front," retorted Muller.

Beicher looked over to Muller and shouted, "Shut up, man, or I'll have you shot for insubordination this afternoon. I promise that you will all die before your sentence is served. Now off you go – your quarters are over there." He pointed to a timber block not far from where they stood.

"What about our induction, Sturmscharführer?" Fritz said.

"You can handle it!" retorted Beicher.

As they moved forward into their quarters, Fritz was the first to break the long silence: "I guess we should take up Max's offer now and make the break and die with some honour, at least."

Muller, still stunned by Beicher's comments, agreed.

On hearing this, Max's eyes took on a familiar glow. A glimmer of hope rippled through his body. They all appeared to be on the same wavelength now, just as they always were back on the battlefield.

'Escape – but how?' thought Max.

They would be under constant surveillance, treated like prisoners, so they would have no freedom to access items that would facilitate an escape. All would be their enemy in this place, inmates and overseers alike.

As Beicher had predicted, they were quickly and unceremoniously inducted into the camp-guard way of life. Just as they had at Dachau, camp guards scornfully referred to them as Leibstandarte with no differentiation between the three.

Max soon discovered that the German camp guards and the Ukrainians performed different tasks.

The Ukrainians were assisted by special labour groups made up from the Jewish inmates and were assigned the more grisly tasks, such as picking up prisoners that had died from disease (many inmates died from infectious diseases, mainly typhus) or had been murdered, and transferring them to the mortuary. From the mortuary the bodies were loaded on to wagons and transported to an area close to the crematoria.

Bodies were incinerated by selected Jewish inmates. The crematoria constantly needed to be cleared of ash, which would be shovelled on to tipper trucks and scattered over fields outside the camp.

Coal or coke fuelled the crematoria and was delivered to the camp in coal wagons. On arrival it was unloaded and carted around to brick bunkers behind the crematoria. New arrivals hair would be cut and gold teeth extracted. The hair and gold would be packaged and, together with the clothing and belongings left in the changing rooms, transferred to a sorting block, where it was packed in boxes ready to be transported to Berlin.

German guards performed tasks such as overseeing Jews disembark the trains that had transported them from Western Europe; taking photographs of the hapless arrivals once they were clothed in their free-issue camp garments; summarily executing insubordinate inmates; and carrying out punishment duties, including beating inmates. Germans formed the nucleus of the garrison there. A unit garrisoned at the airport could provide the extra muscle if the camp garrison ever required support.

Recognised civilised duties included accompanying the more fortunate prisoners to and from the local armaments factory, where they worked all day, and occasionally acting as armed guards for senior staff and camp visitors.

Each day the ex-NCOs would never know what they would be up for, but most of the time they would be dispatched to carry out a task normally reserved for a Ukrainian guard or a Jew.

They were provided with camp guard's clothing. Max was issued a set almost twice his size in an effort by Beicher to make a mockery of him. Another action by Beicher was to put them on half-rations. Even half-rations were far in excess of what inmates were issued, so they considered themselves lucky. Yet another order by Beicher was that they should carry out all tasks at the double. By the end of each day they were completely exhausted.

Of the three, Max was always given the more grisly tasks to perform. Within a month he was moving around the camp like a zombie. The ugly ordeal got to him early; he threw up countless times in reaction to the stench that filled the air and the jobs he had to undertake.

The camp guards were callous and cruel. They were made up from lowlifes – despots, criminals and reprobates. Max hated them for what they represented. He should have killed the Fleischer in Poland, he thought.

He reflected back to where he had taken the wrong directions in life. What had been those choices he'd made to bring him to where he was now? By far his most momentous choice was when he accepted the offer to become an aspirant in Leibstandarte back in the summer of '34. But then he'd embraced it; it had been the right thing to do at the time.

Even before the war there had been warning signs. Dachau and Eicke's philosophy of terror hadn't been enough to shake him from his ambitions. There was the dog incident at the NCO academy. It all could have ended there and then. Had he been an NCO in the regular army his life wouldn't have been so influenced by the political edicts laid down by the party. Albeit the Waffen-SS got on with the job of fighting the war for Germany, they had been part of the ugliness, tainted by and smeared with bad blood.

'Such an unrelenting God!' he thought, but somewhere in the back of his mind he knew he couldn't blame God for his lot; he was responsible for his own short-sightedness when making his choices.

Despite his melancholia, he continued to fight his fear and guilt. A pitched battle raged within his mind during this, the most difficult part of his life. It was taking its toll on his body. He developed a stoop – maybe as a result of his ordeals – and was in poor health, a mere shadow of his former self.

One rainy morning a guard picked him out and barked out an order for him to replace another guard on duty on the other side of the camp. On his way over he passed a group of young Jewish boys who were being transferred to another part of the camp. For no apparent reason, one child of about seven or eight years old stared up at Max and cursed him at the top of his voice. Junior as he was, Max caught the full brunt of the small boy's anger and literally reeled back in shock. The youngster's rage almost knocked him off his feet. The guard he'd come to replace witnessed the incident and growled some words of scorn, ordering him to pull himself together. They changed places and the guard walked away, making snide remarks.

Max stood there in the drizzle, his eyes glazed over. He was only half conscious. He felt as if he were the loneliest man in the universe. The soft rain joined the bitter tears running down his face. The once proud boxing Olympian, the shining example of all that was youth, the salt of the earth, could barely stand upright now. He was on the verge of a mental breakdown, utterly exhausted, a pitiful figure in the savage scenery that surrounded him. He was a beaten man, as wretched as the inmates.

Aware that Max was taking the cutting edge of Beicher's vengeance, Fritz and Muller encouraged Max to endure. In the days that followed he fought back from the brink of collapse, as thoughts of escape offered a sense of hope.

One morning, Beicher ordered Max to the punishment block, where two unfortunate inmates were due for punishment. Beicher thought it an ideal opportunity to stretch Max a little more. They assembled in a small yard and Beicher spat out the charges as he had the inmates tied to a crude timber flogging post. He produced a length of soft annealed wire laced with wire barbs and wrapped one end around his hand, which was protected by a piece of cloth. He then took great pleasure in lashing one of the inmates three times with the crude barbed-wire whip. He left the inmate screaming in agony and passed the whip to Max, ordering with his eyes for him to inflict punishment on the other inmate in the same manner.

"Three lashes, Leibstandarte," he said.

Max slowly wrapped the cloth around his hand, looking at Beicher scornfully. He wound the wire around the cloth-wrapped hand, still staring at Beicher. He knew that he would have to wield the wire with at least the same intensity; otherwise Beicher would intercede and make it worse for the luckless victim.

Max administered the three lashes with similar intensity. He stood to attention after the third lash and stared emotionless to the front. The bloodied barbed-wire whip hung limp by his side. Beicher looked Max hard in the face. Max noticed how fat he was now. He'd lost almost his entire black mane of hair in the four-year period since they first met. A slight limp suggested that Beicher had received a major wound along the way. The years since the Polish Campaign had aged him considerably. He was like an animal, gloating, totally void of any compassion.

Beicher mocked as the two victims were dragged away in agony. He glanced up at Max and said that there would be many more punishment duties like this to carry out. Then he began walking away, ordering Max to 'carry on'.

As he strode off, Max called back, "Why do you do this, Sturmscharführer?" It was a genuine question. Max continued: "How can you be so enthusiastic about what you do here?"

Beicher looked a little surprised at Max's bold questions, but he picked up on their sincerity and responded: "It's what we do, soldier. It's what we're here for, eh?"

He turned and went on his way.

That lofty exchange of words would be the one and only conversation Max and Beicher would ever have together without wanting to tear each other's throats out.

Max held back. He stood in the punishment area for a few moments reflecting on his deed and the conversation. He slowly came back to the present and wrapped the length of barbed wire into a ball. He covered it with the cloth and stuffed it into his grey coat pocket as the one and only 'weapon' he now had access to.

The following day saw the three insubordinates shovelling the ashes from the incinerators at the crematoria. Beicher was maintaining his regime of half-rations and 'at the double' disciplines, and by now all three regarded him with an almost fanatical hatred.

Next day, while carrying out his duties at the double, Max almost ran into a woman in German uniform. He recognised her as one of the female officers from Ravensbruck – the leader of the small group of the SS women based at the camp. She smirked at his oversized attire and stopped to question him. Max explained that he was at the camp with two other ex-NCOs who had been sentenced to six months hard labour for insubordination; following completion of their sentence they would be returned to the Eastern Front and reinstated with their former ranks. She looked at him in a weird way, and carried on her way.

That evening he was ordered to report to the administration block, where he received an instruction to report to the woman he'd bumped into earlier that morning. She had specifically requested that he help to transfer some boxes and files from one office to another in an adjacent administration building. The offices were near the women's-labour sector, which was situated at the north end of the camp.

Max reported in and she explained what was required. This was, of course, a front; it was evening and she had arranged it so that they would be on their own. After several minutes had passed, she came into the room where he was working and struck up some small talk. The conversation took a turn here and a turn there, and it wasn't long before the verbal exchange moved to sex. She asked if he would like to have sex with one of the women internees, and she said she could arrange it, despite Max serving out a sentence.

"Every healthy guy likes a woman, *Kamerad*," he said.

"When did you last have sex? I guess you must be desperate for it by now?" she asked.

He smiled.

Her next question was "Do you prefer Ukrainian women to German women – who is better at sex?"

Max gave a diplomatic answer, explaining that it depended on the woman – whether or not she was running hot or cold at the time. She eyed him up and down and nodded her agreement.

Then she asked, "Would you like to have sex with me here, now, soldier?"

Max was aware of her sadistic reputation and he knew he

needed to respond in a way that would amuse her or at least satisfy her game-playing approach. To hesitate or to appear timid in his response would be a mistake in front of a woman of this ilk.

He instantly looked into her eyes and simply said, "If you are up for it, *Kamerad*, then let's go."

On that remark she walked up to him, put one arm around his neck, looked him in the eyes and, with her free hand, grabbed his penis and rubbed it inside his trousers.

"Mmmm," she said as his penis started to harden.

Max sensed that a woman of her nature would be far more interested in receiving pleasure than giving it, so, without hesitation, he took hold of her, slid his fingers through her hair just above the back of her neck, grabbed a clump, pulled back her head and kissed her neck passionately. His other hand pulled up her skirt and groped the bare flesh inside her thighs above her stocking line.

He massaged her warm, accommodating crotch over the silk underwear. They petted heavily for some time. She got excited very quickly.

He hastily pulled off his trousers and dropped his underpants as she unbuttoned her skirt to let it drop to the floor. They resumed their heavy petting and kissed deep and excitedly. She took his penis and pushed it against her moist crotch, moaning in delight. He dropped to his knees, undid her suspender belt and pulled down her panties. She wriggled out of them as Max hurriedly cleared a leather-covered desk. He motioned for her to lie across it. She moaned like an animal as he took her from the front. After a time, he pulled her up, turned her around and came in from behind. It wasn't long before she reached a climax.

It wasn't enough for her. She sat up on the desk, leant back to support herself on her arms, spread her legs and arched them clear of the desk, indicating for Max to take her orally. He fulfilled her needs.

After a while she came to orgasm again and then asked Max

to finish himself off by masturbating in front of her. This he did, and, as if his ejaculation was an alarm bell, the session ended abruptly. She quickly dressed, after which she instructed Max to finish off transferring the files. As if nothing had happened, she bade him farewell and walked back to her office.

He finished the job and reported back to her. She repeated her promise concerning arranging a woman for him, but she added a condition: as long as she could watch.

In the days that followed, Max never heard anything else from her. Evidently her desire for indulging in sadistic treatment of female inmates exceeded her desire for sex, although both actions were governed by the same distorted passion. Lust to inflict pain or lust for sex, it didn't matter. It was still lust, and the rush was practically the same. Max had done the job, but he never uttered a word to anybody. He knew that if word got back to her, she would have him punished.

Weeks soon turned into months. It was early September 1943 and they had already served almost half of their six-month sentences. But Beicher did not intend the Leibstandarte boys to finish their sentences and return to active duties. His thoughts turned to how he could kill them and get away with it. He decided to provide the ex-NCOs with an opportunity to escape, or set up circumstances to make it look as if they were trying to escape. They would be shot on the grounds that they were attempting to escape.

This was the reason for his ill-treatment of them. He knew that by dishing out the grimmest of tasks, keeping them on half-rations and exhausted, he would drive them to the point of wanting to break out.

An opportunity presented itself when a new batch of motorbikes was delivered to the camp. Beicher knew the ex-NCOs were all good motorcyclists and that this might present the perfect opportunity to set up a situation where they could be killed while 'escaping'.

Beicher's plan was wrapped in a formal duty that required the ex-NCOs to form part of a six-motorbike escort squad. Several senior officials were due to visit the camp from Berlin for a couple of days the following week. Max, Fritz and Muller would participate in the initial pickup and final drop-off at the airfield.

Following the drop-off, before returning to camp, Beicher was to order the ex-NCOs to stop off at a local village and load up their empty sidecars with bread, baked and supplied by the villagers. Beicher's men would be hidden just outside the village, ready to ambush them and kill them on the premise that they were attempting to escape. Some shots would be fired from the ex-NCOs' Lugers to convince any subsequent inquiry that the men had decided to fight their way out. Beicher had borne his grudge for a long time and his motivation was pure hatred.

A week before the scheduled arrival of the Berlin VIPs, Beicher briefed them on their forthcoming escort duties. Max hadn't lost his skills in smelling a rat, and he suspected that Beicher might use the occasion to carry out his threat of killing them. Fritz and Muller agreed, and they all settled on arranging an escape plan that would foil the set-up.

In the following days Beicher pretended to have a change of heart. His first concession was to rescind the half-ration and 'at the double' orders. His explanation was that the boys needed to be healthy if they were to be shipped back to the Eastern Front. He also provided Max with clothing to fit. Beicher hoped his apparent change of heart would give the three a false sense of security. They went along with Beicher's act, and even saluted with a smile when their paths crossed during the working day.

They wondered what devious plot Beicher had conjured up. With only a few days' notice, they had to think fast and devise a robust escape plan.

On the morning scheduled for the pickup they were ordered to wash and shave and were kitted out in smart new formal dress. It was the smartest they had looked for months – maybe years. They were even issued with rifles and Lugers for the event.

For the pickup, the ex-NCOs would form the lead section of the escort ahead of the VIPs' limousine. The rear section comprised another three motorcyclists selected from the camp guards. Each sidecar carried a gunner armed with a detachable MG 34 – a heavy machine gun.

The journey for the pickup was filled with trepidation; the three assumed that any attempt to kill them would be after the officials had left the camp rather than on the day of their arrival. They were not entirely certain whether any VIPs would be arriving at all, but the pickup went as scheduled. The officials from Berlin and the staff car were there as Beicher had stated.

Two days later they were due to escort the visitors back to the airport. This time the arrangements called for Max, Fritz and Muller to ride with empty sidecars, whereas the rear motorcyclists were accompanied by gunners. They were, however, still to be issued with rifles and Lugers.

The men forming the rear section had been handpicked by Beicher. After the drop-off at the airfield they were to follow up behind and ensure that nobody in Max's group survived the ambush.

By now, the three ex-NCOs were convinced that the diversion to the village bakery had been orchestrated by Beicher in order to set them up, but they were still struggling to come up with a counter-strategy. It appeared as though they'd have to think on their feet on the day.

The drop-off day arrived. As before, Max was chosen to lead the entourage. In their final verbal exchange Max told Fritz and Muller that they should follow his lead, no matter what; they would be flying by the seat of their pants for this one.

They left the Majdanek camp for the last time – that in itself was a relief. Max's thoughts ran wild as he led the entourage. As they approached the airfield he could see in the distance the armed guard of honour, made up of soldiers from the garrison stationed there. The men were encircling the plane, ready to see off the VIPs from Berlin. The main gate to the airfield was on their right, up ahead. He noticed that the propellers of the plane were already in motion.

As they neared the turn-off, Max made his move: he accelerated past the main gate. As he took off he assumed the first hazard would be to pass the rear entrance, further along the road; it would be manned by garrison sentries. Whether they would be alerted before Max reached them remained to be seen, but the race to freedom had begun.

Fritz and Muller followed Max's lead. Taken completely by surprise, the driver of the Mercedes carrying the VIPs ground to a halt just short of the airfield entrance. The three motorcyclists taking up the rear stopped momentarily to avoid colliding into the limousine. Realising that the Leibstandarte boys had outwitted them, they quickly wheeled around the Mercedes and followed in hot pursuit. The limousine turned into the airfield quickly. The VIPs from Berlin were unaware that they were witnessing the ex-NCOs' bid to escape. They feared for their lives, thinking the whole affair might be part of an assassination plot.

The gunner in the lead motorcycle pursuing Muller swiftly busied himself, priming his machine gun ready to pick him off.

Max reached the rear entrance of the airfield before the alarm was sounded. The sentries posted there were unaware of what was going on. Fritz also made it past the rear entrance without mishap. Muller was desperate to make as much headway as possible before the pursuing motorbikes could lock him into their sights. The soldiers at the rear entrance were surprised when they heard the first automatic gunfire and rushed out into the roadway to see what was happening. Just at that point, Muller sped by, pointing his Luger towards Fritz up front, pretending to fire at him as if in hot pursuit.

All three had safely negotiated the first hazard, but the road was long and straight and Muller was still at immediate risk of being picked off by the gunner in the lead sidecar. The road continued westwards towards the city of Lublin. Max and Fritz maintained the lead and took advantage of a long winding bend, frustrating their pursuers. Muller wasn't so lucky, and before he could take advantage of the bend the lead machine-gunner finally fixed a lock on him and fired a burst.

Muller took a hit before disappearing into the curve. By this time the VIPs had taken flight and the airfield garrison were scrambling into their trucks, preparing to join the pursuit.

Max knew they would need to leave the main road as soon as possible, as road blocks would surely be awaiting them nearer the approaches into Lublin. He also knew that the garrison would only be a few minutes behind the pursing motorcyclists. His next objective was to eliminate their most immediate danger and take out the three motorcyclists following them. Then they'd need to make progress by way of minor roads to maximise their distance from the trucks carrying the airfield garrison.

An opportunity came when a spur road up ahead came into sight. Max made the turn and Fritz followed. Over to the right, about thirty metres along the road, was a small opening between the trees of a thickly forested area running parallel with the road. Max quickly pulled into the opening with Fritz close behind. They signalled Muller to continue on ahead, then quickly backtracked twenty yards, stopping short of the corner. Each settled behind a tree just inside the treeline along the edge of the road and waited.

They hoped the attention of the lead rider would be well and truly focused on Muller. With just seconds to spare the first rider came around the corner followed closely by the second. Fritz and Max took aim and fired simultaneously. Max took a shot at the lead rider and Fritz the second rider. As the men fell off their motorbikes on to the road, the two motorbikes careered into a long ditch running parallel to the road on the other side. The third motorbike followed through quickly in an attempt to avoid the immediate danger. They took aim and fired off a quick round each, then immediately turned their attention to the gunners of the crashed motorbikes.

They drew their pistols and raced out from the cover of the trees, firing while they ran in an attempt to take out the gunners struggling to disconnect their machine guns from their housings.

Fritz's shot found its target and one gunner fell back, grasping his chest. Max fired off his shots but only managed to wound his adversary. Panicking, the wounded gunner fumbled for his rifle, but couldn't line Max up in his sights before he was on him. Max finished it with a shot to the head, then quickly uncoupled the machine gun from the sidecar, gathered up the ammunition and rushed back across to his own motorbike.

In their desperate attempt to silence the men on the first two motorbikes, they'd completely forgotten about the gunner in the third sidecar. The third motorcyclist had slowed down to a halt after receiving a hit in the back; he was mortally wounded and slumped over the handlebars, but the gunner had successfully disconnected his machine gun and had Max and Fritz in his sights. They looked over in horror just as he was about to open fire, but the bullets never came; instead he rolled to the ground dead. Muller had doubled back and picked him off with his rifle.

Max returned to his motorbike, threw the machine gun and ammunition into the sidecar, started the engine, backed out into the road and rode up towards Muller. Fritz chose to throw the dead gunner from the sidecar and manhandled the motorbike back on to the road. Using this in lieu of his own motorbike, he caught up with Max and Muller.

To their dismay, Muller was now slumped over the handlebars gasping for breath. When they reached him he was still alive, but it was obvious his wounds were fatal; he had lost much blood. He whispered that he would be unable to continue. They stood there thinking of what to do next as the garrison in pursuit couldn't be too far behind now.

A ridge lay up ahead. On top of the ridge was an old ruined castle. They thought it could be the place to make a last stand.

Muller whispered that he would be unable to make the journey up the steep incline to the defensive position. He told them to help him over into the cover of the ditch and asked them to leave him a machine gun and an extra Luger.

They carried him over to the ditch and set him down in a comfortable position, then wheeled the motorbike across as additional cover. They set up the machine gun salvaged from the third motorbike and huddled around, bidding him their final emotional farewells.

Clasping the sides of his head, Max looked him in the eyes and said, "I love you, Hansy. Give 'em hell, man."

Fritz, supporting his chin, simply said, "Goodbye, my friend."

Muller stuck his hand out, Max clasped it with one hand and Fritz clasped their hands with both his. They held one another there together for several seconds of silence.

Muller broke the silence: "Go – go now!"

The two began their journey up the hill to the old ruined castle, leaving Muller to host a hot reception for the men in pursuit.

They made their way up the steep incline, each toting their rifles, salvaged MG 34s and ammunition. They were halfway up when the lead carrier screeched to a halt opposite the spur road. It backed up and wheeled around into the spur road with the other carrier following close behind.

They could make out Max and Fritz almost at the top, but they failed to give any attention to the motorbike upturned in the ditch at the foot of the hill. The lead carrier ran into a hail of bullets as Muller opened fire, aiming first at the petrol tank and then into the covered portion holding the troopers. The vehicle exploded into flames and their hopes of picking off Max and Fritz before they got to the top of the hill were dashed. Muller had bought them precious time.

Several troopers managed to clamber out of the burning truck, and they ran into the woods on the other side of the road for cover. The second carrier had also screeched to a halt, having witnessed the fate of the lead truck. Most of the troopers had alighted, but not before Muller managed to fire off some bursts, wounding several of the soldiers scuttling along either side of the road to safety.

Having reached the cover of the castle ruins, Max and Fritz immediately set up their two MG 34s and concentrated their fire on the flanks closing in on Muller. They could see the whole fight scene down below. Muller never stopped firing. He used up all his ammunition, including emptying the Lugers.

From the top of the hill they heard him shout, "See you in hell, boys!"

Several hand grenades were tossed his way to finish him off. His assailants zoned in on his dying body.

The group of men that converged around Muller presented easy targets for Max and Fritz. Combat inexperience led to momentarily taking their eye off the ball, and as a result several more fell.

The toll of dead and wounded for the airfield garrison was increasing by the minute. The remainder of the unit regrouped, furious that they had suffered so many casualties in such a short space of time.

They regrouped, returned fire and began their uphill assault. The siege of Max and Fritz's gun emplacements was on.

Forming two flanks, they commenced their climb up the hill in the face of fierce gunfire from above. A mortar team and heavy-machine-gun crew set up below to provide cover fire. For those assaulting, finding a place for cover proved difficult, and Max and Fritz's defensive action was very effective. Moreover, being aware of the assault tactics, they were able to maximise the casualty ratio. Their experience, gained fighting the defensive actions on the Donets and Muis rivers in the midwinter of 1941, was paying off handsomely now. Their pursuers had radioed back for reinforcements, but, despite this, they chose to continue on, hoping to take credit for the killings: incensed by the dogged resistance they wanted satisfaction.

The mortar and machine-gun fire from below became deadlier, and Max and Fritz's chances of repulsing the attackers grew slimmer by the minute. The fire was constant, in an attempt to pin them down and minimise their chances of picking off the men making their way up the steep incline. Finally, having run out of MG 34 ammunition, Max and Fritz shifted from one position to another, picking off individuals with their rifles.

As the attackers edged closer, Fritz barked out for Max to withdraw down into the valley to the rear. Perhaps he could hold them off for long enough to give Max a chance to fight another day.

"Maybe you can even get back to Berlin to see Greta," he shouted.

Max refused. He said they should make their last stand on the hill, but Fritz wouldn't hear of it.

"Get out of here, Max! You may get an opportunity to kill more of these bastards if you can slip away now."

They clasped hands and looked deep into each other's eyes. The look said it all.

"I'll kill as many of the bastards as I can, then," Max promised.

"Go, go!" demanded Fritz. "Hey, if you get the chance, tell Zelda and the boys I love them very much."

Those were Fritz's last words.

Max disappeared down the other side of the hill armed with a Luger, a knife and the length of barbed wire that he had carried with him since the whipping incident at the concentration camp. At the bottom he disappeared into the cover of another forested area.

Now it was up to Fritz to buy some time for Max. He fought on as his assailants edged forever closer. Inevitably three hand grenades invaded his position; his adversaries were preparing to launch their final storm. He managed to toss two back over the stone wall before they exploded, but the third detonated and blew him against another part of the wall. Barely alive, he fired off the last rounds into the troopers as they clambered over the wall. They finished him off with automatic fire and immediately set about looking for Max.

Max had reached the safety of the forested area below before his pursuers could get a fix on his position. A small stream ran through the forest, so he used this in the event his pursuers engaged the services of German shepherd dogs. His aim was to put the maximum distance between him and his enemy. Eventually, totally exhausted, he crawled into thick undergrowth and awaited nightfall.

He could hear the sounds of those hunting him coming nearer, and at one time voices sounded as if they were only metres away, but his cover proved adequate and he managed to avoid the scrutiny of his infuriated pursuers.

He welcomed the cover of nightfall, and gently crawled his way out of the thick undergrowth into its dark cloak. Following an hour of frustration, he stumbled across a clearing that led on to a dirt track which eventually led down to a tarmacadam road. Moonlight assisted him in ascertaining his position but exposed his silhouette. He followed the road using a roadside ditch for cover. After some time he ventured across the road. From here he could hear the sounds of shunting trains below. He ventured off-road towards the sounds, and, to his surprise, found himself on the top of a railway embankment.

Below the embankment were two rail tracks that formed part of the main Lublin line – Max's passport back to Germany. Up ahead he could see lights and siding workshops. He knew that some trains travelled back to Berlin laden with Jewish loot and clothing, and equipment manufactured by forced labour.

If he could manage to hide away undiscovered in one of the carriages and reach Berlin, he might just get the chance to see Greta before the Gestapo closed in on him.

BIBLIOGRAPHY

Paul Twitchell: *Coins of Gold*. (1973.)

36

LOOT TRAIN

He glanced up at the moon hanging in the sky. Any other night he might have stopped to marvel at the scene, but tonight Max's life was in the balance. He refocused, ready to make the descent down the bank into the shadows.

Once at the bottom, he made his way toward the sounds of trains busily shunting and hooting, preparing to leave for Germany. The two main tracks fanned out into a multitude of lines for maintenance, cleaning, loading and watering.

On the far side of the tracks he could make out an engine pulling two passenger carriages and four coal wagons. He reckoned this would be the train returning to Berlin. If he could cross the tracks and make it to the rear wagon without being discovered, it might offer him the chance of taking the next vital step in his escape. It was indeed one step at a time – one mistake would mean certain death.

Some activity was taking place up ahead near a large workshop, and several flashlight beams were piercing the darkness from a group gathered there. Max assumed they were a search party. More activity could be seen aboard the train engine across the lines. The driver and his assistant appeared to be making preparations to set off.

Max waited for cloud cover, then took his chance to sneak across the tracks towards the last wagon. He reached the wagon without being spotted and scrutinised its payload. The coal wagons had been filled with wooden boxes from camp workshops. He worked his way along the far side to the passenger carriages.

He pulled himself up to a window and peered through to find out what was inside. Sure enough, he recognised the packing cases that were laden with loot from the camp inmates. Activity up at the front indicated that the train had been refuelled and watered; the journey back to Berlin was imminent.

Max assumed the search party would make a final pass through the train before they let it go back to Berlin. He hauled himself up on to the roof of the carriage closest to the engine and crawled on his stomach up behind the scalloped ridge board to get a better view of what his pursuers were up to.

He kept watch on the movements of the search party gathered outside the workshop. Suddenly the group split up and two torch beams headed his way. They separated about fifty metres from the carriage. One diverted to the wagons, while the other continued walking directly towards him.

He checked his weapons: a Luger, a knife and the short length of barbed wire, which he took out of his pocket and unravelled. He lay there, praying that his searchers would not think to look along the roof of the passenger carriage. Remaining as stiff as a board, he carefully listened for sounds of movement. Suddenly, the sound of footsteps on stones came into earshot. He never moved a muscle. The footsteps came closer, then stopped. Someone was almost beneath him.

He remained rigid, trying to regulate his breath. The deathly silence was rudely broken when the man below cursed aloud using Max's name, and to his amazement he recognised the voice – it was Beicher, and he was no more than two metres away.

Max couldn't believe his luck – a prize beyond his imagination! But what about the other man searching the wagons at the rear? Max fumbled for the length of barbed wire. Suddenly, the sounds of the engine up front pierced the air. Using the noise to cover the sound of his movements, he kneeled up into a better position and wrapped one end of the wire around his hand. The whistling stopped as he prepared to make his move. He pulled a coin from his pocket and tossed it in the air over Beicher's head. As the coin spun in the air, Max gripped the other end of the length of wire.

The coin hit the ground and Beicher swivelled around in the direction of the sound. In that same moment Max stood up and leapt from the roof of the carriage. A startled Beicher looked up as Max deftly looped the length of barbed wire around his now exposed neck.

Max landed on both feet, rammed his knee into Beicher's back and fell back, pulling the heavy weight of Beicher on top of him. Beicher could only fire off a shot from his Luger into the air. The barbs cut deep into his throat. Max rolled over, manoeuvring for a position that would enable him to get a better grip. He pulled back on the wire with the tenacity of a bulldog. Beicher gasped and spat blood into the air, and the gory episode was over after a few more seconds. As Max loosened his grip, images of his faithful German shepherd, Winston, came flooding back into his memory.

'That one is for Winston,' he thought.

Hearing the gunshot, Beicher's companion immediately ran towards the source of the sound. He was only yards away by the time Max had done the deed. He lifted his rifle to shoot, but in the blackness he couldn't make out who was who. As he hesitated, Max grabbed Beicher's pistol, rolled over and shot twice at the silhouette. The man slumped to the ground. Max fired another shot into Beicher to eliminate any chance of his survival.

Wondering what to do next, he scrambled back beneath the carriage and managed to hide himself in the steel chassis, hoping that the first to reach the scene would believe he had scuttled away into the blackness of the night.

Soon enough, the remaining members of the search party were zoning in on the dead bodies of Beicher and the other man. Two crawled under the carriage beneath Max, but focused their torches beyond, into the trees and bushes on the other side of the track. One trooper climbed on to the roof and scanned the night for any sign of movement. Nothing! Max lay there silent, suspended in the chassis, fighting to regulate his breath.

The arrival of the engine driver saved the day. He walked up to the group, stating that the train was due to leave shortly; was that still a possibility? The senior officer, speaking for the party, confirmed it could leave, but with six troopers, one allocated to each carriage and wagon. This was a precautionary measure in case Max had hidden himself on the train or was seeking to hitch a ride back to Berlin further down the track, before the train had gathered full speed.

Having overheard the entire conversation, Max now had the advantage of knowing the strength of his opposition. He even caught the names of the two men allocated to the first two carriages. These would be his first ports of call. He would need to eliminate the entire squad if he were to stand a chance of reaching Berlin safely. His desire to kill these men to even the score for Muller and Fritz far outweighed any fear he had for his own life.

After several minutes the train shunted into position and laboured its way to join the main track, which would take it through Poland, over the German border and on to Berlin.

So far Max had remained undetected. He was actually on his way back to Berlin, where, with equally good luck, he might be able to see his beloved Greta before his inevitable capture. He knew the journey back to Berlin would take the best part of nine hours; so he couldn't stay where he was, exposed to the elements that were already beginning to numb him.

He assumed the search party would conduct an initial search together and then split up, remaining vigilant for the first five to ten kilometres of the journey to ensure he hadn't hopped on to the train further down the track. He then assumed each would settle down for the night and enjoy the journey through to Berlin. Edging along the underside of the carriage proved exhausting.

He finally settled for a spot between the engine and the first carriage to gain strength and composure before swinging into action.

After twenty minutes the train had built up speed and was on its way home. He edged to the door of the first carriage, then took in a few deep breaths to prepare for what was about to happen. His fate was in the hands of God. He brazenly opened the door and immediately headed toward the source of movement and light.

"Karl!" he called.

Karl was seated with his back to Max. Remaining seated, he twisted around to see who it was. Max moved in quickly and smashed him across the head with the large flashlight acquired from Beicher. Karl fell forward across the armrest, and Max drove his knife into the back of his neck.

'One down, five to go,' he thought.

Gerd occupied the second carriage. Without hesitating, Max maintained his momentum to minimise thoughts of caution or fear. He left the first carriage and crossed over into the second. Unlike Karl, Gerd was standing when Max entered the carriage.

"It's Karl, Gerd!" he shouted.

For this kill, Max had drawn his Luger. As he closed in on Gerd the two made brief eye contact. Gerd gasped and went for his light automatic, but Max fired two shots into him before he could use his weapon. Max picked up the light automatic, hung it over his shoulder, then swiftly ran the remaining length of the carriage toward the first wagon. Just before reaching the rear door of the carriage he dived off to one side into the shadows, waiting for the next man.

Had the gunshot been heard above the noise of the engine and rattling carriages? Sure enough, it had. In the darkness the third trooper burst through the door, shouting for Gerd. As he came into sight, Max sprayed him with a burst from his automatic.

He stepped over his body and turned towards the back door. The fourth man was already clambering down the ladder on to the steel decking outside. Max fired a burst through the window and saw him fall from the train.

With just two to go, Max felt safer outside. He opened the door and squatted on the steel grille hard up against the first wagon. He had to think fast.

'What to do?'

The two remaining troopers had used their heads. They mustered at the second-last wagon. Crouched on either side, they worked their way across the tops of the wagons using their flashlights to locate Max.

Max was now just one wagon's length away from two well-armed, very alert soldiers. He began to get anxious and frustrated. He had a choice: jump to relative safety from the train and make an attempt to reach Berlin some other way, or finish off the kills and remain on the train. If he jumped now, his chance of seeing Greta would get slimmer by the day; so he reconsidered his position for a final push.

At this point in the journey the train slowed down to negotiate an incline. He figured on using the reduction in speed to his advantage. He hung the automatic over his shoulder with the weapon close to his chest, intending to jump off the train then climb back on to the rear of the last wagon, bypassing his enemy and surprising them from behind. This would be a good strategy, he thought. He lowered himself down and jumped from the wagon. As he hit the ground his body became illuminated in torchlight. With lightning-fast reactions, he raised the automatic and fired a burst at the light as it passed by. Fire was returned but missed its target.

Max wheeled around to catch the buffers of the last wagon. Using every ounce of remaining strength he pulled himself back on to the wagon, knowing there might be just one remaining trooper. The surviving trooper scuttled to the rear of the last wagon, thinking that Max had escaped into the night. He shone his flashlight into the distance, but to no avail. Max caught a glimpse of his arm, but could not get a free shot at his body from the position he was in. The trooper went back to attend to his comrade.

By this time Max was completely exhausted, gasping for breath. He manoeuvred into a more comfortable position in an effort to recover from the immediate exertion. He knew that he would need one more concentrated effort to finish off the last man. He raised himself to the top of the wagon and peered over it. He could make out the trooper's silhouette bent over. Just as he was about to line him up for the kill, the trooper, obviously very edgy, decided to double-check behind him with his flashlight. A surprised Max fired a short burst into the beam in the hope that he would hit him, and then ducked back down. Fire was returned, but Max couldn't determine whether it had been returned by the trooper with the flashlight or the other soldier, who might have been only wounded.

Several minutes passed; there were no signs of movement from up above. Max began to panic. He was unable to assess his position. What remained out there? Two men? A single man? Or had both been eliminated?

His mind whirled. He had fired into both their flashlights; surely he had hit at least one of them. He wondered whether their wounds had been substantial or even fatal.

A distance of about twelve metres separated them. There had been no flashlight beams since Max had fired the short burst.

'Good news!' he thought, but he also thought that his enemy might be hoping to lure him out into the open.

Despite the risk, he climbed up and fired blindly into the night, still keeping out of sight. He awaited a response. Nothing! After several more painful moments he took his helmet and held it above the top of the wagon, anticipating a reaction. Still nothing!

He risked glancing over the top. There in the far right-hand corner he could make out the shape of a body slumped over the wagon. He raised the automatic and sprayed the body.

'Five definite,' thought Max, 'but where is the sixth trooper?'

He climbed back down and gingerly checked either side of

the wagon to make sure he was not about to be outflanked. There were still no signs of the last trooper. He decided to edge his way along the wagon towards the rear of the next wagon. As he came to the end he looked up at the body slumped across the edge on the other side; there was still no sign of the sixth man.

'Did he fall off the train? Is he hiding in wait for me?' thought Max.

After several minutes he resumed his advance and crossed the steel grille between the wagons to the other side. The body of the sixth soldier was dangling from the steel gauge step-up just below deck level.

Max gave a gasp of relief. His objective was achieved: he'd eliminated all six; he was the last man standing. His ordeal was over – at least for the time being.

He regained his composure and kicked away the dangling body; then he made his way back to the first carriage, where he secured some fresh ID and clothing from one of the dead troopers.

Soon after, he made his way towards the engine and calmly struck up a conversation with the engine driver, stating that the fugitive had been discovered hiding on the train and subsequently killed after a lengthy gun battle.

Max settled for a short conversation and asked the driver how much longer it would take to get to Berlin. The driver said that it would arrive at Berlin Ost (East) at around 5 a.m. The first stop in Germany would be the city of Frankfurt, close to the border.

Armed with this information, Max went back to the rear and disposed of the remaining bodies after taking their money and any personal effects that would help to facilitate his escape. He settled down, but he knew he would never be relaxed enough to sleep, despite being completely exhausted after an entire day of hiding and fighting for his life.

He rested in the first carriage. Soon enough the train arrived in Frankfurt. After an anxious stopover the train continued on to its destination. Knowing the approach into Berlin's Guterbahnhof Goods Depot would be a slow one, he hoped to find a good opportunity to jump off several local stops short of the destination, just in case a reception had been arranged to meet his now dead assailants.

This he did: he jumped clear of the train, crossed the tracks and scrambled over a picket fence separating the main line from the local. He crossed the tracks of the local line (S-Bahn) and hopped up on to the platform, where he entered the warmth of a waiting room.

The final leg would be across part of East Berlin on foot to Greta's place. As he set off, fatigue and anxiety were beginning to get the better of him; he was fading quickly under the extreme stress.

Greta's apartment was near Schesischer Bahnhof, a main-line station which was also part of the S-Bahn system. He decided upon a route that would take him past all the remaining local stations leading up to Schesischer Bahnhof. There he would spur off to Greta's place and, God willing, get the chance to say his final farewell.

37

FAREWELL TO GRETA

The relief of having reached Berlin without getting caught didn't help Max's fast-deteriorating condition. Now, so close to Greta, his fear and anxiety intensified. By this time, he was a broken man living on his nerves. All he wanted was to achieve this final goal: to see his beloved Greta before being arrested or killed.

His imagination ran wild. Unable to control it, he reacted to every sound in the street. As he approached each new street corner, bolts of fear shot through his body. He convinced himself that the Gestapo were waiting for him there. He staggered his way across this little section of Berlin, determined to complete his mission at all costs, regardless.

He wasn't sure Greta would be at home. Indeed, he wasn't sure that she even lived at the same address any more. Further, even if she did, there might be a reception party waiting to cut him down before he got there. One bolt of fear after the other ripped through his body as he lurched his way across the now unfriendly city.

Snapshots of memories from his past popped up on the screen of his mind. He tried to focus on happier times to alleviate the stress and mitigate the overwhelming dread, but his fears had made him their puppet. He dangled from their strings, unable to control his thoughts and actions. He pleaded for God to guide him through these final stages as he tottered his way toward Greta's apartment. Anybody walking the streets at that time of the morning could have easily mistaken him for a drunk returning from an all-night session.

Max could still smell the stench that surrounded Majdanek like a black cloud; he'd carried it with him all the way from Poland.

Germany and Berlin, the country and city that were once a part of his very heart, had become his biggest enemies. As if affronted by his incursion, every corner he approached seemed to come alive. In his imagination he could hear it whispering to the forces hunting him down, exposing him as the intruder he was.

The city was different now. It had succumbed to Nazism and had harboured its secrets for ten years. It was as if its heartbeat recognised Max as an enemy of the state and hated him for having the audacity to challenge its authority by simply being there.

Max had the idea that his fear was a magnet, attracting his enemies ever closer to him. It could only be a matter of time before the inevitable would happen, he thought. Barely alive, the only thing keeping him going was the thought of seeing Greta. Pain and panic riddled his body as he stumbled through the city, mouth agape, crippled by intense emotional stress.

As he came closer to Greta's apartment, his thoughts started to clear. His ordeal in getting through the city without being discovered was nearly over. Schesischer Bahnhof was in the distance, and he needed to spur off short of the station. He made the turn with just one more street to negotiate. He turned the final corner, but there was no ugly reception waiting for him. Up ahead he saw the apartment. Greta lived on the second floor with little Kristine, who was now almost three years old.

He pulled the Luger from his pocket and crossed the road, looking around him numerous times for any sign of movement. He reached the entrance doors to the apartment block and slipped inside like a hungry rat seeking food. Once inside, he leant back on the wall next to the door and gave a gasp of relief. Then he prepared to climb the two flights of stairs up to Greta's apartment. He listened intently for any sounds. There were none; the building was silent.

He made his way up the first flight of steps to a half-landing. All in the apartment block were sleeping. There were sounds outside, but it was of a city awakening to a new day. He slowly stepped up the second flight of stairs and stopped outside the door to Greta's apartment.

He prayed to God that she would be there and pressed the buzzer with two short bursts. He turned his ear to the door but could hear no movement from inside. He buzzed twice again, lengthening the buzz time a little more than before. Additionally, he gently rapped on the door with his knuckles.

Joy! He heard someone stirring inside and, moments later, footsteps headed towards the door.

"Who is it?" A woman's voice spoke in trepidation.

Max rejoiced. "Greta, it's Max!" he said. His eyes welled up with tears as he repeated his words: "It's Max!"

"Max!" she cried.

Following a brief silence he heard the sound of a multitude of locks turning. The door opened and Greta gasped in shock as she beheld the wretch that stood before her. He put his finger to his lips, gesturing her to be quiet. The sweetness and familiarity of her face instantly swept away the anguish and fear that had embued him since Poland.

There were no words of greeting. He stepped into the apartment and gently closed the door behind him. They held hands and looked into each other's eyes for long, long moments. Tears ran freely down their faces. Max smiled and they both hugged each other as if neither would ever let go.

Finally, breaking the incredible moment, Greta said, "Let's get you some food and hot coffee."

She took his big hand and led him through to the kitchen. He ripped off his overgarments and made his way to the bathroom to wash away the sweat and blood spatters created in his bitter fights for survival on the train from Poland. He did not flick the light switch. Instead, he made do with borrowed light from the hall outside. Darkness seemed to be his only companion now.

He looked in the mirror above the washbasin, staring at the ghost of a man who had experienced first-hand the evils of mankind. He stood there mesmerised for a while. Then he stripped to the waist, blocked the plughole and filled the basin. The water was refreshing as he splashed it over his face and body. He rinsed off and grabbed the towel that hung over a metal bar set below the washbasin.

Feeling fresher, he leant on the washbasin, gazed into the mirror again and took several deep breaths, letting the air fill his lungs and taking in the loving presence that was Greta and little Kristine.

He became lost in memories dancing across the screen of his mind, flashing pictures of the city in happier times – a city he once loved. His thoughts moved back in time to the Berlin of his birth and his early years. It had survived rebellion, revolution, disease, famine, hyperinflation, the Great Depression and a multitude of other degradations and upheavals. Despite all these disasters it had managed not only to endure, but to produce an intellectual and social scene second to none.

'Every city reflects the character and nature of the people that make up its life force,' thought Max.

Berlin was no exception, and, for sure, the Berliners of the Weimar period had turned it into one of the most exciting cities in the world. Brief as its glory was, it truly shone a golden light. But the thriving metropolis that it had been now stood sombre and suspicious under its new management.

The party had considered intellectualism and music to be the biggest threats to the system they had set up.

The intellectual freedom that was being enjoyed in other parts of Europe and the Western world at the time could unhinge the party's ancient way of maintaining control and manipulating the masses. It had chosen to reawaken a darker force – one of domination through fear.

Max realised that music too had a stunning impact on the way a nation makes its statement. The regime was aware that new melodies, such as jazz, could create their own forces strong enough to break up old patterns. Consequently, the party set about banning such revolutionary melodies, replacing them with staid military-style bands and classics that helped entrench the system and maintain the consciousness that aligned with it.

Even the excitement of cabaret, recognised as an institution in Berlin since the turn of the century, subsided when the party took over. In 1933, cabaret had been one of its first victims. Some writers and performers were arrested and sent to concentration camps. The few who tried to return to cabaret after the war found it had lost the zest, charisma and controversy that had made it such a remarkable form of entertainment during the early part of the century.

Max's thoughts were suddenly broken when Greta announced that coffee and breakfast were ready.

He came back into the kitchen where two boiled eggs, three *Bockwurst* sausages, a hunk of cheese with pickles and two buttered rye buns awaited him. The slits that were his eyes lit up as he beheld the feast laid out before him. He thanked her, sat down and engulfed the food voraciously. The spread was gone in no time, and he thanked Greta for a second time, eased back in his chair and sipped on the hot coffee.

Greta looked Max over. She noticed he had developed a stoop. It was as though he carried the weight of the whole world on his shoulders. She felt his anguish but realised that nothing could be done now; he had reached the end of the line. Every now and again he would break out in a rasping cough. His muscles were lean, but stripped of the vitality they had once had.

He looked up at her and, reading her thoughts, broke into a smile.

"I'm OK," he said.

They hugged again.

"You look beautiful, Greta. Is life being kind to you?" he asked.

What followed was just small talk – nothing in particular, a comfortable exchange with each totally absorbed in the other's presence. He asked if she had found herself a partner, but she said that her pleasure lay in bringing up little Kristine.

"Men have always been too problematic," she said.

She maintained a part-time job at the RSHA, but her ambitions for promotion up through the ranks of the party had died with her decision to raise Kristine. The part-time job she'd settled for involved mundane work and far less confidentiality.

They walked back into the kitchen and their conversation slowly developed into one of nostalgia and the recollection of happier times – after all, there would be no future now, at least not for Max.

He talked briefly about Irina and Ilyana, his part in the killing of Wolfe and the fight on the train coming across from Majdanek.

Max had gone as far as he could to defy the system, and, as usual, had given a good account of himself. His best consolations were the saving of young Ilyana and the slayings of Wolfe and Beicher. He found some comfort in these deeds, although they had been less than a pinprick in the side of a huge juggernaut.

The sun began to bring some warmth to the day. He sensed there would be someone awaiting him when he set foot on the pavement outside. He stood up, brushed himself off, dressed and prepared to kiss Greta for a last farewell. She stopped him and led him into the bedroom, where Kristine lay in sweet slumber. Greta gently awoke her. The eyes in her pink glowing face slowly opened. Greta greeted her with a warm kiss and lifted her from the bed.

She whispered, "Uncle Max wants to say goodbye. Do you remember him – my little brother? He loves you very much. I want you to say goodbye to him as he has to go back to war now."

Max and young Kristine's eyes met, and, in that moment, the love exchanged between them lit up the dimness of the room; their eyes sparkled. He kissed her gently on her cheeks, whispering that he indeed loved her.

"I love you too," she said and sleepily closed her eyes.

Greta gently laid her back down on the bed and tucked her into the blanket.

"Oh, my little brother, I love you too," whispered Greta as they hugged tightly.

They watched the sun climb higher into the sky for some moments as it filled the grey streets with colour.

"I must go now," said Max. "They'll be waiting for me. Can you do something for me?"

"Yes, of course. What is it?"

"Can you look up Zelda for me? Fritz wanted her to know that his last words were that he loved her and the boys very much."

"Surely. I will, Max."

They gave their final hug. Max gazed into Greta's beautiful eyes for the last time.

"What else is there to say, Sis. I love you so much. It's been a great journey, my love. God bless!"

"I love you, Max," responded Greta. "God be with you."

With this, Max opened the door and told her to close it quickly.

He made his way down the stairs, but before he entered the street he took a few deep breaths, preparing to face whatever was outside waiting for him.

38

THE PINES OF BERLIN

Max pushed the doors open and stepped out into the street. His intention was to make his way to the Lichterfelde Barracks and give himself up to his own unit, Leibstandarte. But before he could get five metres down the road a voice from the other side of the road pierced the morning air.

"Good morning, Sturmscharführer. Please do not resist arrest. I am sure that you will accommodate my order. Please put your weapon or weapons on the ground and raise your hands in the air."

Max turned his head and gazed across the road at the major and two huge troopers who had their rifles trained on him. The voice sounded familiar. He scanned the archives of his memory to place the voice. Yes – a name materialised – its familiar tones belonged to SS Sturmbannführer Anthony Riessman. He'd led up the NCO training academy at Dachau back in 1938.

"Sturmbannführer!"

Max raised one hand into the air and gently pulled the Luger from his pocket with the other and placed it on the pavement. He followed the same procedure for his knife. Then, lifting both hands in the air, he walked across the road towards Riessman.

As he crossed the cobblestone carriageway he recalled his days in the training academy at Dachau. Riessman had been a good sort, he thought – tough but fair.

Likewise, watching Max cross the street took Riessman back to that same class of '38. Max had been one of his best cadets.

The entire class had been one of the best that had passed through the academy. There was no way he would have given the order to shoot him there and then unless Max had resisted arrest.

He recollected that Max had an excellent military head. He had earned the respect of his comrades. Since then, his courage in the field and care for his men showed him to be a fine leader. He recollected that Max lacked a vindictive streak but was most loyal and honourable. He'd overlooked his compassionate leanings on the basis that the Waffen-SS needed the best in its middle ranks. Right or wrong, Riessman had made his own mind up about this ruling and circumvented the system in his own way.

Max reached the other side of the road, saluted and returned the 'Good morning' greeting. Riessman looked directly into Max's eyes.

"I remember you well, Rieker. You were a very, very good NCO. Your record since then has been equally impressive: two Iron Crosses, a veteran of the Russian Front, Leibstandarte, now a full Panzergrenadier division, and the best of the best."

"For sure, Sturmbannführer," confirmed Max. "You taught me well."

Just then the remaining assault troops sent to arrest Max revealed themselves from their various places of concealment.

Max hadn't scrutinised the two guards accompanying Riessman. As the others came towards him he recognised them as members of Leibstandarte. They were from the battalion that remained in Berlin charged with the lofty task of protecting the Führer.

Max couldn't believe his eyes – soldiers from his own unit. He managed a smile and one or two acknowledged him. Riessman noticed the wry smile on his face.

"Yes," he said, "I knew you would prefer Leibstandarte, Rieker."

Max beamed a second smile. "Thank you, Sturmbannführer. You knew that I would be here, then?"

Riessman knew that Max had a sister, Greta, who had produced one child for the Reich and was raising another. He also knew her address. It wasn't hard to guess that Max would want to see her if he returned to Berlin.

Unknown to Max, Riessman had always monitored the progress of every one of his cadets that had successfully graduated from his academy. He knew to which unit and battle arena they had been assigned; which of them had been wounded; who was missing in action and who had fallen. So he had heard about the court martial of Max, Fritz and Muller, and he had been following their progress ever since.

After receiving information that Max had escaped from Majdanek, Riessman had made a quick phone call to Leibstandarte HQ in Berlin, offering to bring Max in. For this, he said he would require the services of eight of their troopers. Sure enough, the agent assigned to watch Greta's apartment reported Max entering in the early hours of the morning and immediately contacted Riessman, who quickly mustered the small unit assigned to him and made his way to the apartment.

"I heard that you gave the garrison at Majdanek a bad time," he quipped.

"Sure did! Hans Muller, Fritz Kohler and I whipped their arses for a brief time anyway."

Suddenly, a covered carrier came from around the corner and screeched to a halt where the pair stood. Riessman motioned for him to climb into the back accompanied by eight of Germany's finest.

The journey back through Berlin to Lichterfelde didn't take long. Max would be detained overnight and, the following morning, driven to a place in the countryside just east of Berlin, where he would play out the final act of his very chequered life.

The truck entered the familiar iron gates and came to a halt close to the administration area, not far from where a similar truck had brought a teenage Max in 1934, some nine years earlier – a lifetime in itself.

Max stepped down from the truck and Riessman said, "Let's talk for a while."

He led Max into a building nearby where they walked along a corridor to a nicely furnished office that Riessman had seconded as an interview room for questioning Max. They settled in and Riessman ordered two coffees.

"So what happened to three of my finest NCOs?" asked Riessman.

"Unfortunately, our training at Dachau never catered for every eventuality," stated Max.

"Oh!" exclaimed Riessman.

Max continued: "Sure we covered almost every scenario that involved fighting an enemy, but a number of us weren't ready for the butchery that would be perpetrated on the civilian population – particularly the women and children. Granted, the Waffen-SS weren't the perpetrators of these policies, but they inevitably affected us in the field and, dare I say, helped to derail the entire war effort. The academy taught that loyalty and willingness to obey and carry out orders formed the backbone of discipline, and that, in the words of Standartenführer Schumann, it would be discipline that would win the struggle on the Eastern Front. I can understand this, but the merciless massacre of women and children was never a sandbox scenario acted out at the academy. I can only assume that back in 1938 the academy trainers never envisaged that such murders would take place in the field. If the policy was already planned, then the academy deliberately avoided facing the fact that such butchery would take place. Maybe the academy thought it was too shameful a scenario to cover?"

Riessman replied, "Partisan activity led to our having more contact with the civilian population than expected, Rieker. In Russia, the partisan contribution is indeed effective and needs to be tackled in a rigorous way."

"I disagree, sir. If we had given the civilian populace its freedom when we first invaded – particularly the Ukrainians, who initially greeted us as their saviours – then we would have avoided half the problem. We created the hostility in the first instance, and partisan action may very well be a deciding factor in the final outcome."

Riessman pondered Max's answer, and after a short silence he reopened the conversation.

"Yes, you may be right, Rieker, but you cannot be seen to be going around knocking the system. Party principles form the basis of our system; one cannot be seen to be disgruntled or unaligned with party policy. Insubordination is frowned upon, and in these times the penalty is serious punishment. Your mistake, Max, was that you wore your discontent on your shirtsleeve for all to see. Others may have the same opinion, but they keep it to themselves."

"How can a person live with himself with so much emotional dishonesty raging inside?" asked Max.

"Better held within than making waves against the system, Max. Look at you now – a shadow of the soldier you once were. Has it done you any good to buck the system? No – you'd have been better off keeping it locked up and getting on with the job at hand."

"I couldn't, sir. It just overflowed; the guilt was too much to bear. No matter how you see it, I am accountable for my deeds; no one else, regardless of orders. One cannot use orders as an excuse to hide behind. That goes for both the soldier complying with the order and the officer giving it. When I am the trooper vested with the responsibility of committing murder, then I must take responsibility for that act. I am the one performing the act. The officer giving the order tells himself he is merely following party policy. He might hide behind it, but he cannot overlook the consequences of his order. In my book, ignorance and insensitivity are hardly the qualities of a master race."

"But you miss the point, Rieker. Your emotions got the better of you. One thinks to survive. Other NCOs under the same circumstances thought with their head instead of their heart. They survive, but you must die. I know in which of the two circumstances I would rather be."

"How does such a man live with himself, sir? How can he face himself? Tell me."

"He avoids energising it; he ignores it. He survives. Look where you have ended up, Rieker. One has to ask oneself, was it worth the effort?" said Riessman.

"You would do this, sir?" asked Max.

Riessman smiled wryly. He was a good listener. Unlike some of the horrible ignorant bastards behind desks and an ocean away from the front line, he listened. He relied on feedback, and in some cases he even voiced the opinions of his subordinates.

"I've never fought on the Eastern Front, Max," was his diplomatic answer.

Max pondered Riessman's previous question. "Well, sir, it was worth it; do you know why?"

"No, tell me, Max?"

"It's because the thought of caring about the consequences has given me the ability to discover an inner strength within myself. Tell me, sir: what do you think the inner strength is?"

"I wouldn't know," said Riessman.

"It's a feeling of comfort and satisfaction that I gave life my best shot in accord with my own values. In the end" – he paused to emphasise the point – "in the end, I owe it to myself. Yes, I owe it to myself, sir. I showed respect for myself and was able to love myself. I embrace my mistakes, as they have taught me what not to be. Tomorrow draws my efforts to a close. I am a happy and contented man because I know I was honest to myself."

Riessman nodded and the room grew silent. Riessman wound up the conversation by stating that it had been good to see Max again after so many years, and he said that, despite the sour task he was faced with the following morning, he was proud of Max's record and outstanding achievements since the onset of the war.

Max received the compliment with a beaming smile, and he

thanked Riessman for the opportunity given him to talk from his mind and heart. He left the room escorted by two guards, who led him out of the administration area to a detention building. He didn't sleep until the early hours of the day, when he dropped into a light slumber.

In the morning, as Max left the detention building, the guards he passed acknowledged him with their eyes. He silently bade his beloved Leibstandarte farewell as he squinted in reaction to the rising sun.

Outside, Riessman was there to greet him. To Max's surprise the covered truck had been replaced by a Mercedes-Benz staff car. Riessman sat in the front with the driver. Max, withered and emaciated, sat between two huge Leibstandarte guards in the back.

Riessman had gone out of his way to make Max's execution the most comfortable he could arrange, and he fixed up the trip to look like a Sunday outing.

The Mercedes-Benz set off on its short journey. It cleared the city limits and sped through a long avenue of pine trees. Max looked out of the window. He could see the clear azure sky above as the tops of the pines whisked by. His mind wandered and he thought about his beloved Greta and his beautiful Irina and the adventure they had shared for just a brief moment in eternity.

It had been a long time since he had looked up at the sky in daylight. Just the sight of it had a therapeutic effect on him. The tenseness in his body eased and he relaxed back into the black leather seat. The green pines appeared to brush against some white fluffy clouds that floated above. A feeling of peace came over him, as if preparing him for what was to come.

Thoughts filled his mind as if summing up his whole life. He revisited the deed he performed at the cottage near Kherson. Instrumental as he was, if it hadn't been him, it would have been somebody else. At that stage of the journey he had created for

464

himself, the job had been the perfect vehicle for him as a means for enhancing his own spiritual growth. Those women locked inside the cottage were part of his journey, as he had been part of theirs; an ongoing universal drama of life had been played out by its actors.

His thoughts shifted to the party, the Führer and his henchmen. How on earth could they be forgiven? Could they be forgiven?

To his amazement the answer came back: "Yes, of course."

They had been no different to him, because they too were merely instruments in the grand, man-made scheme of things. Each would need to confront the consequences of his acts and make amends later down the track.

Max had always separated the two forces, good and evil. Now he had a new view. 'There is only one force and it is how one chooses to use it that makes the difference,' he thought. 'Some use it maturely, with love, while others remain unaware that opportunities given them to have power and control are only temporary. It's one's choices that determine the calibre and nobility of the outcome.'

Twenty minutes went by and the car came slowly to a halt. Max got out. His thoughts returned to the present; his heart was beating fast as he envisaged what he had to do that fine morning. He looked back down the avenue he'd travelled along and saluted the journey that had just taken place, for it had been enlightening and had prepared him for this moment.

Two Leibstandarte guards closed in on either side of him and Riessman pointed the way ahead into an adjacent field.

They walked across the field towards an old oak tree. Max noticed that the leaves had begun to fall.

'The Russian winter didn't take me, after all,' thought Max, but the winter of his life was at hand. 'There will be new life in the spring of the following year – new life, once the bitterness of cold winter has passed,' he thought.

All four walked towards the oak tree as if they were on a field trip. The two guards stopped short of the oak tree and remained with weapons at the ready in case Max decided to attempt to save his life in lieu of taking it.

Riessman handed Max the Luger. Max asked if he could have some brief moments with his thoughts before he carried out his duty. Riessman nodded in agreement. Max thanked him.

He walked into the shade of the mighty oak tree, and took a last look at the wonderful blue sky. All the diamonds in his life came together in that very moment. There he was back at the orphanage with cheerful Greta giving him good love; then there was Fritz in his Hitler Youth uniform marching alongside, singing a happy ballad; and Paul, the Baron, drawing from his familiar extra-long cigarette holder, sipping his favourite brandy. The scene changed to Irina – there they were dancing, and she was smiling as only she could smile. He felt the ecstasy of her touch run through his body, even then.

The pictures in his mind finally settled on to little Ilyana, remembering those moments when he lifted her out of the motorbike and kissed her rosy red cheeks. Her smiling face swept away the last dregs of fear in him.

It had been a long time since he had felt so comfortable with himself. The guards grew restless, but he gestured with his free hand that there was no need to worry.

Max then stood to attention and lifted the Luger to his head.

Riessman formally barked out the mandatory address: "For our Führer and the Fatherland!"

His eyes opened and he looked at Riessman. Dipping his head in recognition, Max smiled, and said in a soft but firm voice, "This one won't be for our Führer, Sturmbannführer. For Greta and Kristine, yes; for my *Kameraden*, yes; for Irina," he paused, "for my Irina, my final salute, sir, will be to Love." Just before he pulled the trigger, he raised his voice: "I'll see you in hell, then, Riessman!"

He fired the shot and collapsed in a heap below the mighty oak.

The sun shone bright that morning. The crisp autumn freshness replaced the dark past as if it had been a dream from which Max was about to awaken.

Riessman walked over and looked down at the body of Max in a puzzled way, pondering his comments before he had pulled the trigger.

Suddenly from out of nowhere flew dozens of birds, and they settled in the branches of the oak tree overlooking the body of Max. They spontaneously broke into a chirpy, colourful song, breaking the silence that had followed the gunshot.

Riessman looked up at them as they sang a final farewell. They seemed to be speaking for Max: "I'm free now, I'm free." The birds continued their beautiful song for a period of time then flew off as suddenly as they had appeared.

THE TRIUMPH OF THE SPIRIT

Max's death coincided with a change in the combat fortunes of the German Wehrmacht. After its failed 1943 summer offensive on the Eastern Front at Kursk, all Germany could do was defend. Its last strategic victory in the Second World War had been at Kharkov.

Max had fought his war on four fronts: as a German national he'd fought the Red Army and the Western Allies; as a member of the Waffen-SS he'd fought the taunting of the German regular army; as an NCO he'd fought against the brutality of the Allgemeine-SS (the struggle between the compassion in his heart and the pettiness of the political bureaucrats); and as an individual he'd fought personal battles in his mind against the insidious passions of guilt and fear.

He'd ended by following his heart and had recognised his true goals for what they were: truth, honour and freedom of the spiritual kind. His final statement to Riessman indicated that he hadn't cleared all his guilt, but he'd gone a long way towards understanding it.

So what is love? For Max it had several meanings. With a woman it was unconditional; he gave her loving attention, but offered the space for her to be herself without imposing conditions on the relationship. For himself it was confronting himself and all his weaknesses, being kind and true to himself and honest with others. He had chosen to live by the sword and he had accepted that he would die by it.

He'd discovered that love and truth had been at the bottom of all things, not the top. The knocks of life had been his greatest teacher. They helped clear away the dross to reveal those loftier spiritual qualities latent within.

The forces he'd played with had emerged barbaric and evil; his destiny was a far cry from the adventurous life he enjoyed during his years in the Hitler Youth. But at the eleventh hour he'd fought tough battles with his mind to claw back his self-respect and come to a better understanding of life. He'd summoned up the courage to confront the consequences of his earlier actions, and this, in itself, shows a measure of spiritual maturity – a maturity he discovered at his lowest ebb.

WHAT HAPPENED TO THEM

Second Reich (1871–1918)

The dissolution of the Holy Roman Empire, combined with the growth of German nationalism, led to repeated attempts at unifying the multitude of German territories. Final success was due to the tireless efforts of Otto von Bismarck. Between 1862 and 1871 the great Prussian politician, using a combination of persuasion, strategy, skill and militarism, created a German Empire dominated by Prussia and ruled by the Kaiser.

The Second Reich came into being with the defeat of France in the Franco-Prussian War of 1870–71 and finished with the German Empire's defeat in the Great War.

First Reich (800–1806)

The First Reich is better known as the Holy Roman Empire. It was a medieval state comprising modern-day Germany, Austria, Hungary and Italy, and it came under the rule of German kings from AD 962 to 1806. In 962, Otto I of Germany responded to Pope John XII's pleas to assist him in countering threats from Berengar II, the belligerent King of Italy, who wanted to take over the Papal States. Otto came to the rescue, and, as a reward for his deed, the Pope crowned him 'Emperor of the Romans'. From then on, the German kings claimed the right to rule the Holy Roman Empire.

The aims of the Holy Roman Empire were, first, to unite all

Christians into a single state answering to one holy Catholic Church and, second, to form a hierarchical political organisation with one ultimate head over all existing states. Such ideals were lofty and never realised. Old enemies, primarily France and England, never really acknowledged any obedience to the emperor. Further, the empire's vast size and the disparity of its peoples were serious obstacles to effective rule and good government.

The Holy Roman Empire was considered to be a restoration and continuation of the ancient Roman Empire, despite having little in common with it. Before 962, in 800, the Frankish King Charlemagne, Charles the Great, was crowned emperor of what became the Holy Roman Empire, a territory that covered much of Western and Central Europe; this institution would remain, in one form or another, for more than 1,000 years.

In 1806, the empire was abolished by the then emperor, Francis II, partly as a response to the Napoleonic threat.

The tags 'First Reich' and 'Holy' were attached in the twelfth century, during the reign of Frederick Barbarossa.

The Hitler Youth (1921–45)

In the summer of 1921 a youth named Adolf Lenk tried to join the Nazi Party but was refused on the grounds of age. He was considered too young. He persisted and in 1922 the NSDAP formed a youth section under the leadership of Lenk.

Membership was for German Aryans only. Foreigners and Jewish youths were not permitted entry. Membership was split into two sections, the first for fourteen- and fifteen-year-olds and the second for sixteen- to eighteen-year-olds.

The Sturmabteilung (SA) kept a sharp eye on the youth section to see that they kept in line with party policy and didn't steer an independent course. Lenk was eventually ousted for reasons relating to financial irregularities. Lenk's replacement was Kurt Gruber. The movement under Gruber did not grow significantly, although during his office the youth section was renamed the Hitler Youth. Later, in 1926, leadership was transferred to Franz von Pfeffer of the SA. In 1931, von Pfeffer was dismissed and replaced by Baldur von Schirach, holder of the coveted Blue Max.

By this time, the Hitler Youth had swallowed up most other youth organisations. In June 1934, following the Night of the Long Knives and Röhm's assassination the SA was disbanded. The Hitler Youth remained under the leadership of von Schirach but was now tied to the SS. In 1936, membership of the Hitler Youth reached a staggering 8 million.

In the early days, the Hitler Youth took in volunteers only. Later, the SA put pressure on other groups, stating that if they were to survive, their members would have to be members of the Hitler Youth. Hence groups were forced to amalgamate with the Hitler Youth and the organisation grew steadily.

Recruiters kept an eye out for talented youngsters, and those exceptionally talented were drafted in regardless of age limitations. This included those youngsters with talents for music. The probationary period was six months. Following approval, youths were awarded the brown shirt and leather belt. Each youth kept records of sports achievements and special courage-test achievements such as jumping from a first floor window 'in full pack'. Sports included boxing, jiu-jitsu, cycling, running and swimming. Games included piggyback fighting and chariot racing.

Membership included youths from all walks of life. Rich and poor, aristocrat and orphan – all were equal in the Hitler Youth. If there were any distinctions at all, they were distinctions of ability, reflected in the individual's proficiency records. The Hitler Youth had its own flag, and members were taught that the flag was more important than death itself; to die for the Fatherland in battle was an honour, and death was not to be feared.

Compulsory service in the Hitler Youth came in March 1939, and in 1941 the minimum age was lowered to ten years old.

It is interesting to note that the Hitler Youth was never formally disbanded at the end of the war. It just died with the passing of Adolf Hitler in April 1945.

Josef 'Sepp' Dietrich (1892–1966)

Sepp Dietrich was a butcher by trade. He served in the Imperial Army in 1911. He fought in the Great War as a paymaster sergeant and was decorated for bravery. In the early years of the Weimar Republic, he joined the Freikorps and helped clear Munich of a communist takeover bid. As an early member of the NSDAP he came to Hitler's favourable attention and was made commander of Hitler's bodyguard in 1928. In 1933 he became commander of Hitler's Armed-SS bodyguard regiment, later known as Leibstandarte-SS Adolf Hitler. In 1934 Dietrich played an important part in the Night of the Long Knives, the purge against the SA. That same year he was promoted to the rank of Obergruppenführer, the equivalent to a German Army general.

Dietrich distinguished himself and his unit, Leibstandarte, during the Second World War. Their arenas of conflict included the Polish Campaign, the Western Campaign, the Balkan Campaign and the Eastern Front up to the summer of 1943, when his unit was recalled to fight in Italy. In April 1944 he returned to the Western Front, where he was promoted to SS-Oberstgruppenführer, the equivalent of a German Army Generaloberst. During June 1944, he commanded the SS 1st Panzer Division in the Battle of Normandy.

Hitler never lost faith in Sepp Dietrich, and he entrusted the December 1944 Ardennes Offensive to him. Dietrich's last battle was fought in Vienna, when his outmanned, outgunned and exhausted panzer force failed to stop the Red Army from taking the city. He surrendered his army to US General George S. Patton on 8 May 1945.

Dietrich was found guilty of complicity in the massacre of US soldiers near Malmédy during the Ardennes Offensive, although his responsibility for the deed was never proven. He was sentenced to life for an 'offence against customs and ethics of war', but scores of officers, among them Field Marshal Heinz Guderian and General Hans Speidel, came to his defence and his sentence was commuted to twenty-five years.

He was released in October 1955, but he was later sentenced by a German court to serve an eighteen-month prison term on the charge of being an accomplice to manslaughter in the June 1934 massacre of Röhm and the SA. He was released in February 1958.

In his final years he spent time with his family and former comrades. He stayed well clear of politics and died on 21 April 1966.

Paul Hausser (1880–1972)

Paul Hausser served in the German Imperial Army during the Great War and received two Iron Crosses for action during this conflict. He retired from the army in the interwar years but he was reinstated as a Standartenführer in the SA. In November 1934, Hausser transferred to the Armed-SS unit Verfügungstruppe (SS-VT). In 1935 he became inspector of the new SS officer training academies and was promoted to Brigadeführer a year later.

During the war, Hausser served in Poland as an observer with the mixed army/Panzer-SS division Kempf. In October 1939 SS-VT was formed as a division with Hausser in command. He led the division through the battles in the west and during Operation Barbarossa. During his command of Das Reich in Russia, Hausser was awarded the Knight's Cross (KC) and was severely wounded, losing an eye. After recovering, he commanded 1st SS-Panzer Corps and disobeyed Hitler's orders, withdrawing his troops from Kharkov to avoid encirclement. Later Hausser recaptured the city in March 1943 with his Panzer Corps. He led Das Reich, Leibstandarte and Totenkopf during Kursk. After Kursk, Hausser was stationed on the Western Front until he was promoted to commander of the 7th Army. During the Falaise encirclement Hausser remained with his troops, ensuring that as many men could escape the Allied pincers as possible. Hausser ended the war on Field Marshal Albert Kesselring's staff.

Kurt Meyer (Panzermeyer) (1910–61)

Over the course of his career, Kurt Meyer was awarded the Knight's Cross with oak leaves and swords, the third highest decoration. He was promoted to become the youngest divisional commander on either side during the war.

Kurt Meyer was a commander of exemplary courage, chivalry and accountability. Unfortunately his record as a brave and daring officer was tarnished by his conviction for war crimes committed during the heavy fighting around Caen in 1944. Meyer was sentenced to imprisonment and set free in September 1954, after serving nine years. In 1957 his war biography *Grenadiers* was published. He died in Hagen, Westphalia in December 1961, on his fifty-first birthday.

Max Wunsche (1914–95)

In November 1932 Max joined the Hitlerjugend, and in July 1933 the SS. After a five-month NCO training course he decided to become an officer, and he attended the SS-Junkerschule at Bad Tölz, graduating in the class of 1936. He was assigned to Leibstandarte, also in 1936. In 1938 he was assigned to Hitler's personal escort detachment, where he served as an orderly officer.

In 1940 he was transferred back to Leibstandarte under the command of Kurt Meyer. He remained in this post throughout the invasion of France and the Low Countries but rejoined

Hitler's personal escort detachment only to be dismissed after a complaint tendered by Hitler's butler.

Despite the dismissal, he was reassigned to Leibstandarte and served as Sepp Dietrich's adjutant throughout the Balkan Campaign. It wasn't until Operation Barbarossa that he distinguished himself. In June 1942 he was promoted to the rank of Sturmbannführer. He played an important role in the Third Battle of Kharkov, and his actions there won him the Knight's Cross.

In June 1943 Wunsche was transferred to Panzerdivision Hitlerjugend. On D-Day, 6 June 1944, the Allies ran straight into the Hitlerjugend and, in the ensuing battles, Wunsche and his regiment were credited with destroying 219 enemy tanks. For this he was awarded oak leaves to his Knight's Cross, but a few days later, as the Allied forces encircled the German divisions in what was known as the Falaise Pocket, his successes came to an end. He was captured following an epic attempt to escape through Allied occupied territory.

Wunsche survived the war and became a manager of an industrial plant in Wuppertal, Germany.

Erich von Manstein (1887–1973)

Erich von Manstein was known to some as 'Hitler's greatest general'. After his successful campaign at Kharkov in March 1943 von Manstein proposed a daring action for the summer nicknamed the Backhand Blow. The aim of this proposal was to outflank the Red Army at Rostov, but Hitler instead chose the more conventional Operation Citadel, which aimed at crushing the Soviets on the Kursk salient.

During Operation Citadel, von Manstein led the southern pincer. Despite losses, he managed to achieve most of his initial goals, inflicting far more casualties than he sustained. In his memoirs, Marshal Georgi Zhukov, who led the Soviet defence at Kursk, praised von Manstein. But Hitler called off the offensive because of the almost complete failure of the northern sector's pincer led by Gunter von Kluge and Walther Model, a chronic lack of infantry support and an operational reserve, as well as the Allies' commencement of Operation Husky, the invasion of Italy. Von Manstein protested, asserting that the victory was almost at hand. He felt he had achieved local superiority, and that with a little more effort he could crack the Soviet defences before they could bring up their reserves. After the failure of Operation Citadel, the Soviets launched a massive counterattack against the exhausted German forces.

Were the Germans close to victory when Hitler called off the offensive? A German victory in the sense of annihilating the surrounded Soviet forces required them to complete the encirclement (that is the linking of the northern and southern German pincers) and to hold the encirclement long enough to overcome the encircled Soviet forces. Even if the first of these requirements had been met (which it had not), it does not follow that the second would automatically have followed. After Stalingrad, the German forces were never able to force the Soviets into significant retreats (except for temporary reversals, such as Kharkov). The ability of the Soviets to launch counterattacks indicates that they might have been strong enough to break out of any encirclement.

In September, von Manstein withdrew to the west bank of the Dnieper while inflicting heavy casualties on the Red Army. From October to mid-January of 1944 he 'stabilised' the situation. The Soviets established a salient from Kiev, and they were within reach of the crucial town of Zhitomir, but the Germans staged a successful counteroffensive. SS panzer divisions Leibstandarte and Das Reich, 1st, 7th, 19th, and 25th panzer divisions, and 68th Infantry Division (part of the 4th Panzer Army) wheeled around the flank of the Russians in front of Zhitomir. Several notable victories were won at Brussilov, Radomyshl and Meleni, under the guidance of General Balck. But as a result of the lacklustre judgement of Colonel General Rauss, the new commander of the 4th Panzer Army, the Kiev salient could not be eliminated. In late January, von Manstein was forced by the Soviet offensive to retreat further westwards. In mid-February 1944, he disobeyed Hitler's order and ordered 11th and 42nd Corps (consisting of 56,000 men in six divisions) of Army Group South to break out from the Korsun Pocket. They did so on 16/17 February. Eventually, Hitler accepted this action and ordered the breakout after it had already taken place.

Von Manstein continued to argue with Hitler about overall strategy on the Eastern Front. He advocated an elastic, mobile defence; he was quite ready to cede territory, attempting to make the Soviet forces either stretch out too thinly or advance too fast so that they could be attacked on the flanks and encircled. Hitler, instead, insisted on static, attritional total war. Because of frequent disagreements of this kind, von Manstein publicly advocated that Hitler relinquish control of the German Army and leave the management of the war to professionals. He also suggested that the position of Oberbefehlshaber Ost (Supreme Commander in the East) should be established; Hitler, however, rejected this idea numerous times, fearing it would weaken his hold on power.

After von Manstein was dismissed, he entered an eye clinic in Breslau, recuperated near Dresden and then retired. He did not take part in the attempt to kill Hitler in July 1944. He had been contacted by Henning von Tresckow and others in 1943, but, while he did agree that change was necessary, he refused to join them as he still considered himself bound by duty. (He rejected the approaches with the statement *"Preussische Feldmarschälle meutern nicht"* – Prussian field marshals do not mutiny.) Although he didn't join them, he did not betray the plotters. In late January 1945, he collected his family from their homes in Liegnitz and evacuated them to Western Germany. He surrendered to Field Marshal Montgomery and was arrested by British troops on 23 August 1945.

The Waffen-SS (1940–45)

After 1945 a flood of hatred was poured on the Waffen-SS. The things that were said about this component of the German Armed Forces do not, in the main, stand up to detailed inspection. Not only foreigners, but also many of our own population, lump the soldiers of the Waffen-SS with the members of the SD and those of the Allgemeine (General) SS.

Heinrich Eberbach, General der Panzertruppe a.D.

From their inception, the best Waffen-SS troops fought with incredible courage, constancy, decency and love for their country. They gradually won the respect of the German Wehrmacht as they were given increasingly difficult assignments. Waffen-SS troops expected to be sent to the most dangerous areas and to see the heaviest fighting. But their zeal came with a price – heavy casualties. SS officers and Panzergrenadiers suffered extremely high attrition rates. This loss of highly trained and highly motivated soldiers undoubtedly effected Waffen-SS combat effectiveness, and morale. Time and again, SS troops displayed their willingness to keep on fighting even when their tactical situation was desperate, or (later) when it was clear Germany was losing the war.

The turning point for Waffen-SS combat fortunes was the 1943 Battle of Kursk. Despite their best efforts and their powerful tanks, 1st Panzer Corps, made up from Panzergrenadier divisions Leibstandarte, Das Reich and Totenkopf, could not gain a decisive penetration into the Soviet defences. Their waning strength became even more obvious during the 1944 Battle of the Bulge in the west and the attempt to relieve the siege of Budapest in the east. SS combat capability was in decline and the SS troopers realised it.

In the final months of the war a rift opened up between Hitler and the Waffen-SS. Hitler began to blame them for Germany's plight. The Waffen-SS, disillusioned and facing sure defeat, consequently abandoned their oath of loyalty to him, transferring their loyalty to their units, their comrades and their commanding officers. In the words of a Leibstandarte man from Reconnaissance:

> *Our lack of understanding and inner rejection of everything we heard from 'up there' or 'back home' led us to accept only one final homeland. That was our unit, our 'little heap' of men.*

By 1945, as the Reich began to crumble, the Waffen-SS had given up all adherence to any standards whatsoever for its recruit selection. If they could walk and shoot a rifle, they were good enough for the SS. At this time all German military forces were scraping the bottom of the manpower barrel, and, in January 1945, army and Waffen-SS recruiting centres were combined. Waffen troops were increasingly men transferred from other military branches of the Wehrmacht, from paramilitary and labour formations.

Amazingly, despite the abandonment of previous standards, many Waffen units maintained a high level of combat efficiency and esprit de corps, and they won the admiration of their comrades and their enemies alike. The elite consciousness built earlier on had carried through to the bitter end.